Living in Shadow

Georgia Florey-Evans

In this book, Beau Harding is willing to give up everything to do what he knows is right.

While not to the degree of being placed in life threatening situations, a couple I know very well also doesn't care what they give up in order to follow their Savior's instructions.

Peer pressure, ridicule, temptation…they shake their heads and find strength in their faith to walk away. And, what's more, they are saddened and pray for those who don't realize the path they're on.

So, I'm dedicating this book to my brother-in-law and sister in my heart, Bill & Myrna Evans. The Lord has blessed our family by providing such remarkable individuals to emulate.

I love you both.

ACKNOWLEDGMENTS

Thank you to Nicole Gordon for another amazing cover. You bring my ideas to life

Also…
Another thank you to Detective John Niccum
for answering the gazillion questions I had.
with your help, I was able to keep my
crimes as realistic as possible.

*The Federal Safety Administration is my creation and while loosely modeled after the FBI and CIA, is not meant to symbolize them.

Keep your life free from love of money, and be content with what you have, for he has said, "I will never leave you nor forsake you."
Hebrews 13:5

You'll meet Elliott and Callie Lawrence in *Living in Shadow*. They didn't exactly fall into each other's arms.

Their tale, an award-winning short story, "Gotcha!" is located at the end of this book. Enjoy!

Callie:

"I wouldn't even be at this stupid party if my mom hadn't forced me to come!" Her voice rose as she spoke. "It's not that I don't think it's for a worthy charity; it's just that I hate getting dressed up and hobnobbing with idiots like you!"

The Legend of Shadow

During the early nineteenth century, Virgil Clayton Richmond, always seeking greener grass, decided to travel west. Even though she wanted nothing more than a permanent home and family, Betsy traveled dutifully beside him.

After months of trudging through many unpleasant conditions, Betsy was finished with their adventure. The petite, soft-spoken, devoted wife stood toe-to-toe with her six-and-a-half foot giant of a husband.

"I'm through. This is our home."

Virgil, too stunned by his meek spouse's attitude to argue, instead stammered around until he managed a coherent sentence. "Tomorrow, Betsy, when we get to a place I can't see my shadow, we'll be home. I promise."

Though self-taught, the pioneer woman was highly intelligent. She saw through his ruse, knowing even moonlight produced shadows. If Virgil thought he outsmarted her, he was in for a surprise.

Early the next morning, Betsy asked, "May we go for a short walk before we leave? Just to stretch our legs."

Feeling expansive, Virgil agreed.

As they walked by a large oak tree, lush with green leaves, Betsy doubled over, as though in pain.

"What is it?' Virgil leaned over his wife.

She quickly straightened, and with every ounce of her strength, shoved her husband back about five feet.

He was understandably confused. "Betsy?"

Her smile outdid the sunshine. "You can't see your shadow under that tree, Virgil. We're home."

Thus, the farm which later became a settlement, and then a town, still bears the name Virgil gave it: Shadow.

Chapter 1

Harding Davis was plowing soybeans. After five years pounding the street and nearly five more working undercover for the Chicago Bureau of Organized Crime, this situation seemed preposterous. However, here he was, fifteen miles outside a downstate Illinois town with a population of less than ten-thousand, named Shadow, of all things. There had to be a story behind that name.

Name. The concept had taken on a new meaning for him. He had gone from being plain Hardy Davis to living a second life as Joe Ryman. And now, he was Beau Harding. At least, he'd been able to ask people here to refer to him as Hardy, simply by shortening his new last name. He supposed he was lucky the powers that be hadn't insisted he use a name like Elmer Fudd. After seeing the system from the inside, it wouldn't have surprised him.

Since Hardy wasn't exactly in the official program, he'd been given more freedom than would otherwise be allowed. Thanks to his brother-in-law shamelessly using his Federal Security Agency connections, Hardy had some say in where he would reside. When Hardy's dad set him up to farm for an old friend's son, Elliott made sure their plans were approved. The FSA had given him his turned around name and thirty-two-foot camper. His mother would say God put Hardy where he was supposed to be. Hardy figured it was thanks to his brother-in-law and dad.

It helped that he liked his new boss, though. Luke Walker was out of commission for six months after he stepped into the path of a bullet to save a kidnapped Holly. Hardy was all too aware of the irony, a barely healed gunshot victim working for a newly shot one.

The situations fit together like pieces of a jigsaw puzzle. Luke needed somebody to take care of his farm. Hardy Davis needed to disappear from the face of the earth—or at least Chicago. Thanks to summers spent at his Grandpa Swayzee's place, Hardy was perfectly capable of the job. So, Hardy was introduced to Luke by his dad simply as an old friend's son, needing temporary work. Luke didn't hesitate; he hired him on the spot.

Hardy left everything behind and drove the well-used truck and camper to Shadow. While Luke recuperated at his wife's house in town, Hardy spent the summer supervising and working with three teenage boys Luke hired. When Hardy first found out about the teenagers, he'd almost turned his truck around and headed somewhere else. Anywhere else.

He grudgingly developed an admiration for the boys, though, after seeing how hard they were willing to work for Luke. Their respect for him was apparent, as was their love for Holly Walker who, it turned out, was their school guidance counselor. Hardy managed to get along with them just fine, although he hadn't let any of them cross the line to develop a close relationship.

Now, things were changing. The boys were back in school. Luke and Holly had just moved to the farm, where he would spend the last four weeks of his recuperation. And though Hardy was still working the farm alone, Luke frequently showed up. Not that Hardy begrudged him; Luke 's desire to be on his tractor again was evidenced by the wistful look in his eyes.

Yes. His mom would say it was God's hand in all this. But, Hardy didn't know how he felt about God anymore. If God were such a great Planner and loved people the way the Bible said, why did so many terrible things happen? All the cruelty Hardy observed through his job. Criminals who didn't care what they had to do, or who they had to hurt, as long as they got their money, lived long, cushy lives while innocent people, including children, died for no reason at all. Hardy just couldn't come to terms with a loving God allowing such an atrocity.

And it didn't help anything that this seemed to be the Bible belt. He long ago lost the count of invitations to attend worship. Even his three young co-workers tried to get him involved in youth group activities set up by their church. According to them, Luke's substitute kept planning "little kid" or "lazy" things. They frequently tried to persuade Hardy to volunteer for the task.

Hardy politely, but firmly, turned down every invitation. He wasn't on good terms with God, so he wasn't about to go to church and spend more time with him.

He wouldn't have to worry about residents of Shadow much longer, anyway. His job here would be finished in less than a month when Luke could resume work. Where he would live and work depended on what Hardy and the FSA could agree on.

When Hardy pulled into the machine shed an hour later, a huge dog that looked as though he'd stuck his nose in a light socket came running to the tractor. Clarence. What a name for a pet. Hardy quickly discovered, however, not only was Clarence not thought of as a pet; Holly and Luke treated him like a member of their family. They talked to him like the mutt could understand every word they said. Much to Hardy's chagrin, he found himself conversing with the animal too often for comfort.

"Clarence! Get back here, and leave Hardy alone." Luke's deep voice resonated through the large building.

Hardy scratched behind Clarence's ears. "He's not bothering me."

Luke appeared at the open door. "I'm not going to remember how to drive that thing." He nodded toward the tractor.

"I hadn't driven one for over ten years when I got here," Hardy admitted. "It came right back."

Luke took a few steps farther into the shed, still slightly favoring his right side. "You'd never know you weren't a career farmer, Hardy. What did you do before you came here?"

Hardy had been dodging that question since his arrival. "Nothing much. Just worked odd jobs to keep food on the table."

The look Luke directed at Hardy told him he hadn't fooled the man one bit. But, just as he had so far, Luke let it go. "Any plans after you're finished here?"

"Not really." Hardy managed to produce a smile. "Something will come up, though."

"God takes care of us." Luke smiled amiably.

"I'd better get in the shower. I thought I'd go to the diner for dinner, and I'm covered in dust." Hardy wasn't about to get into the whole religion thing.

Luke's expression told Hardy the other man was once more aware of Hardy's evasion. "You're welcome to eat with Holly and me anytime you want."

"I appreciate that." Hardy walked past Luke on out of the building. "But I don't want to impose on you. It's enough that you provide lunch for me every day."

"I don't mind." Luke stepped out and stood beside him. "I cook enough extra for both you and Holly to have for lunch." He chuckled. "I save a little more for you than I do her."

"I'll go to the diner anyway. Thanks just the same." Hardy turned and pulled the large door closed. He double-checked the lock, having been told of past vandalism. Nobody would spray paint or slash tires on his watch.

"Just come on up to the house if you change your mind." Luke slapped the side of his leg. "Come on, Clarence."

Hardy watched as the man and his dog walked toward the house. There was a friend Hardy would like to keep. Luke was who Hardy might have been if he hadn't been hardened by years of duplicity and criminal activity. And although Luke was on the taller and broader size, like Hardy, the farmer seemed gentle. He was determined to see the good in every person and situation.

Not Hardy. Years of seeing people lie, cheat, steal . . . he wasn't sure if he'd ever lose the cynicism.

He grimaced when he looked in the mirror a few minutes later. His sand-colored hair and healthy skin tone were somewhere under the layers of rusty-gray dirt.

Taking a shower in the mobile home was an adventure in and of itself. He was too large to comfortably fit in the small space curtained off, so he'd fixed up a larger space, rigging a raised mat, and stretched the shower curtain. The problem with his solution was it pretty much took up the entire bathroom floor. So, he ended up acting like a contortionist trying to take his shower without falling on top of the stool or out the door. He figured if anybody were to ever see him, they would laugh themselves silly. Thankfully, his showers were taken in private.

An hour later, he sat down at the table he'd gotten into the habit of occupying when he ate at Wilkins Diner, which was nearly every evening. Nancy Shepard, the regular second-shift waitress, smiled as she placed his usual glass of soda in front of him.

"Meatloaf is good today, Hardy." Nancy stood poised with her pen over the pad she was holding.

Hardy had already known what would be "good" this evening. "I'll take meatloaf then, Nancy." He grinned at the sixty-something-year-old woman, whose cheeks turned a soft shade of pink. How a woman her age managed to work in a busy restaurant and be shy at the same time was beyond him.

He hid another smile by taking a drink. While it wasn't the only restaurant in Shadow, the diner was comfortable. During the evening, which was when he frequented it, the place was never over crowded. And the food they served was tasty, even if the menu was predictable.

Mondays were meatloaf. Tuesdays, it was fried chicken, Wednesdays, beef stew, Thursdays pork roast, and Fridays all-you-can-eat fish. On weekends, or when the urge struck him, Hardy would mix things up and order a burger and fries or even a steak, but most of the time he stuck with the specials.

Nancy set a steaming meatloaf dinner in front of him just as Mitch Landon sat on the chair across the table.

"That looks good, Nancy." Mitch smiled at the waitress. "Bring me one just like it, please."

Hardy felt his hackles rise as he looked at the other man. "What brings you to the diner, Sheriff?"

The red-haired ex-football player who stood at least an inch taller than Hardy, took a long drink of his ice water before he answered.

"I know who you are." The words were spoken so quietly Hardy wasn't sure he'd heard them.

"I haven't ever tried to hide who I am." He casually sliced his baked potato open. "I'm Beau Harding. I'm a simple man making an honest dollar working on a farm. I'll be moving on as soon as my boss is back to work. That's all there is to know about me, Sheriff."

He scraped the butter from its container and proceeded to work it into the potato with more vigor than was required.

"I won't tell anybody." Mitch kept his voice low. "But I know you're Harding Davis, and I know what you did."

Hardy put his fork down and looked squarely into the other man's eyes. "Harding Davis is dead. I'm Beau Harding. Nothing more, nothing less. Is that a problem?"

Mitch gave him a measured look as Nancy placed his food in front of him. Neither man said a word until she left.

"I'm not trying to make trouble for you." Mitch had something to say, and it didn't look like Hardy would be able to stop him.

"Just tell me what you need to, Sheriff. My food is getting cold."

"It was on television last night. One of those shows about unsolved past crimes. There were clips of you on it." Mitch wasn't pussyfooting around the subject. "I knew you looked familiar, but I hadn't connected you to Harding Davis."

Hardy took a long drink and hoped the sheriff was finished. Apparently, he wasn't.

"I understand why you don't want people to know who you are, but what I'm trying to tell you is I won't be the only person around here who watched that show."

Hardy made himself calmly resume eating, even though his appetite had disappeared." How long do you think it'll take for things to be stirred up?"

Mitch sighed deeply. "It depends on who saw it. I don't think Luke or Holly did, or they'd have called me."

"Can you do me a favor?" Short of a call directly to his emergency phone number, there was only one solution that Hardy could come up with. "Can you let me know if people start calling you? Give me a chance to clear out?"

"I know you've got yourself a problem, but you'd be leaving one of my best friends in the lurch if you just up and disappeared." Mitch was obviously not in favor of that plan, but Hardy had to make him see reason.

"Sheriff, think about what could happen if I stayed." Why had his past caught up with him like this? "What would Luke and Holly's lives be like if the wrong people find out who I am and that I work for them? They'd be better off finding another person to help them these last few weeks."

The sheriff seemed to consider his words. "Okay. I get it." He leaned forward and spoke firmly. "But don't cut and run yet. Maybe nobody who knows Beau Harding will have seen Harding Davis. And, if it's possible, I'll contain the information as it comes in. Please just try not to disappear on Luke and Holly."

"I'm not a quitter." No matter which name he was going by. "I signed on to work for six months, and I'll do my best to stick to it. I'll only leave if it's better for them. You have my word."

Mitch nodded, his expression grave. "That's all I can ask." He looked at the plate in front of him. "I'll have Nancy fix this to go. I'm sure you'll enjoy your meal more without my company."

There was no sense in holding a grudge. "I'd welcome your company, Sheriff. As long as we don't talk about Harding Davis."

"Then, I'll stay." Mitch picked up his fork and dug in. "How's Luke getting along? I've been too busy at the station to get out and see him."

"He's outside a lot, but I think he's still hurting." This was comfortable conversation. "Can I ask exactly how he got shot? He just said it was something to do with a kidnap attempt on his wife."

"It's no secret." Mitch's forehead furrowed. "One of our classmates—Luke, Holly, and I graduated together—"one of our former classmates was obsessed with Holly. He kidnapped her. Luke and I found them, and during my struggle with the kidnapper, his gun fired and Luke got hit."

The question came out before he could stop it. ""Do you feel guilty?"

Mitch's gaze leveled on him. "I did at first. If I'd have gone for his right arm, maybe I would have been able to get the gun pointed at the floor." A light appeared in his eyes. "But I prayed. I prayed a lot. And now I realize it could have gone a million different ways."

"You're human, though. You had to wonder why the whole thing happened."

"Looking at the what-ifs won't do anybody any good. Luke has never blamed me. In fact, he thanked me for saving Holly. He helped me see even though things didn't go the way I wanted, it worked out just fine. With Luke's support and God's presence, I could let go of my guilt and be thankful my friends are okay."

"That's all well and good." Hardy wasn't convinced. "But if God was there, why did he let Luke get hurt? Why did he let Holly be kidnapped in the first place?"

"That's not the way it works." Mitch seemed certain of his statement. "We all have free will, and I'm sure God is often telling us we shouldn't do something. But we don't listen."

God talking to him? Hardy didn't believe it was possible.

"Holly's kidnapper is a troubled man who either couldn't, or chose not to, listen to God. Instead, he believed he should have Holly just because he wanted her. We all have to deal with the consequences of his choice, but God is with us, and helps us every day."

Hardy knew what he was saying but in his case . . . "I'm sorry, but I just don't buy it."

Mitch's brow furrowed. "Maybe I didn't explain it right. Why don't you talk to Pastor Rollins? He's a lot better at making sense."

Pastors. "That's okay. I've done fine so far, and I'll keep doing fine." That was enough talk about God. "So, did I hear you're getting married soon?"

Hardy watched as the change in topic moved through the sheriff's eyes. He slowly smiled. "Not quite sixteen weeks."

"Have you been together long?"

"Tessa and I have known each other since junior high, and I'm pretty sure I've loved her that long. It just took me a long time to work up the courage to ask her for a commitment."

"You didn't date each other in school?"

Mitch shook his head. "I didn't date at all. I don't believe in dating simply for the fun of it. I decided to date only if I thought it would develop into something permanent. God has to be in the relationship with us, and I have to feel like it's what he wants. When I told Tessa how I felt and what I wanted, and she said she felt the same way, it was like God was right there, telling me our relationship has his blessing."

There he went with God-talk again. "Do you have any family here in Shadow?" And if Mitch Landon's father was a local minister, Hardy was getting up and leaving.

"Have you met Melissa?"

Hardy searched his highly efficient memory for that name. He placed it on a petite, auburn-haired beauty. "She's been out to the farm with Holly before. They went on a walk together." He remembered because Melissa, or Missy, as Holly had called her, insisted they walk on the gravel lane, to "stay away from the creepy crawlies and poison ivy."

Mitch's grin grew. "Believe it or not, that little gal is my twin sister. I'm a whopping seven minutes older than she is."

For the first time since the sheriff sat down, Hardy produced a real smile. "You're right. I'd never have guessed it."

"Our parents moved to Kentucky to manage a cabin rental business." He chuckled. "You want to see something funny, you should see Missy visiting Mom and Dad. She makes Dad or me go into the cabin with a broom to check for spiders or any other type of pest. And her idea of nature walking is the sidewalk between the cabins and lodge."

"Your sister sounds like a city girl."

There was that smile again. "Yes. A city girl getting married to the owner of the nature preserve." Mitch chuckled. "Joe Willis can't even get her to walk any farther than the pond with him. I wonder what it'll be like when their children play outside."

Listening to Mitch talk about his sister made Hardy think of Callie. "My sister and I aren't that close."

"Does she live nearby?"

"She and her husband live west of Chicago." And, he'd visited their place a grand total of two times.

"Does your sister have any children?" Mitch asked.

"She has a boy, Blake. He'd be . . ." Hardy had to think. "I guess he'd be five or six now. And her daughter is four, I think. Her name is Tabitha." Guilt filled him as he realized he hadn't seen his niece or nephew in over two years.

He had finished his dinner. Usually, Hardy would have a slice of whatever pie Maisie, the cook, had baked fresh that morning. Tonight, after the discussion with Mitch, he wasn't hungry.

"I'd better get going. Early start in the morning." He stood up and dug out his wallet.

"I'll see you." Mitch's voice dropped. "And you have my word. I'll let you know if anything I can't contain happens. I'll make sure you have plenty of time to clear out if it's necessary."

Thank you." Hardy dropped enough money for his meal and a generous tip for Nancy on the table before he turned and walked out of the diner.

It was probably too much to hope Mitch Landon had been the only person to watch that show and recognize him as Harding Davis. The agent in charge of his case must not have seen it, because if he had, Hardy would already be arguing about being relocated.

Despite Elliott's support, Rich Stephens, the agent handling his protection, had tried to move him to Boise, Idaho, of all places. Hardy flat out refused. He just couldn't bring himself to be that far away from his family.

Now, if too many people had seen him on that show and identified him as Harding Davis, he would have to move again, like it or not. Because if his past caught him, his life would end. And he wasn't ready for that to happen. He wasn't ready for that at all.

Chapter 2

"Hank, you there?" Haley Johnson absent-mindedly tightened the clasp in her ponytail as she spoke into the radio microphone of the base unit.

"Just got back in the car." Hank Snow, the youngest deputy in Shadow County, answered her.

"Betty Livingston just called. Her weekly complaint, a three-eleven."

Amusement was warring with frustration in Hank's voice as he responded. "If she'd quit peaking around the bushes, she wouldn't see Hubert." A deep sigh came over the radio. "I'll go talk to her. Maybe she'll be satisfied if I just warn the old guy. I hate to write him another ticket."

"Good idea. Base out."

Haley sat back in her chair. She had been the chief dispatcher for the Shadow County Sheriff's office for nine years, and most of the calls that went out were something similar to the one just made. Poor Hubert Belton was in his nineties and liked to take sponge baths in his front yard. There was plenty of foliage around the place, but about once a week one of his neighbors, usually Betty, would call and complain. An officer went out every time. They used to bring him in regularly until Mitch said it was getting ridiculous and told them to either give the old guy a warning or ticket. Haley was just waiting for the day when the elderly man showed up to pay his fine wearing nothing but a smile. That would make people talk.

The non-emergency phone rang and brought her out of her daydreams.

"Shadow County Sheriff's office."

"Is Sheriff Landon in?" The caller was a female, but Haley didn't recognize her voice right off.

"Yes." She looked through the glass separating Mitch's office from the rest of the squad room. He was looking at files on his desk. "May I say who's calling?"

"This is Jennifer Ewing. It's important that I speak with Mitch." The woman, who Haley knew tended to be a bit of a busybody, seemed to be growing agitated.

"Just one moment." Haley put the caller on hold and paged Mitch. He looked out the window at her as he picked up the phone.

"What do you need, Haley?"

"Jennifer Ewing is on line one. She says it's important she speak to you. Should I put her on through?"

Mitch groaned. "She probably wants to tell me about Craig Reynolds' new car. He's been pushing that Corvette right to the limit. Just take a message, and tell her I'll call back."

"Okay." Haley didn't think this would go over well at all. She pushed the button to open the line. "I'm afraid you'll have to wait until he can return your call."

"But this is . . . Oh, never mind. Tell him I saw a man on TV Sunday night, and he looked familiar. I just figured out who he is, and he's living right here in Shadow under a different name."

She'd need more information than that. "Please tell me which show you were watching and who you're referring to." The woman had probably been watching too many forensics shows and let her imagination get away from her.

"Just tell Mitch to call me."

Jennifer Ewing hung up before Haley could get any further information out of her. As daffy as the call seemed, Haley's job wasn't to analyze complaints. She just made sure they were reported. She pushed the button for Mitch's office again.

"Let me guess. Reynolds blew dust on the clean laundry she had hanging on the line." Mitch spoke drolly.

"No. I'm not sure if I completely understood her, but it's something about somebody in town not being who he says he is. She thinks she saw him on a television program. That's all she'd tell me. I told her you'd call her back."

Haley was totally unprepared when her boss abruptly told her he'd take care of it and hung up. She watched in disbelief as he looked up a number and dialed it. Evidently the message made more sense to Mitch than it did her.

"Hey, Blondie." Haley looked up to see Wayne Daniels, one of the deputies, heading her way.

"Hi, Wayne." The tall, black man was one of the nicest people Haley knew.

He paused in front of her desk, a big grin on his face. "I heard the radio chatter. Hank's visiting Hubert Belton again."

She returned his smile. "Don't be too smug about it. You're up for the next call on him." Since none of the deputies liked to confront the elderly man about his bathing habits, Mitch had come up with the solution of rotation. So far, it had worked well.

"Maybe Mrs. Livingston will stay on her own side of the hedges for a couple of months." Haley laughed at the hopeful expression on the man's face.

"You can dream."

Wayne's smile returned. "I didn't stop by to jaw about our outdoor bathing problem. Lori wanted me to invite you to dinner this evening."

Wayne and Lori Daniels regularly invited Haley to their house for dinner. In the past few months, they seemed to have had ulterior motives.

"Who else would be joining us?"

The sheepish expression on Wayne's face told Haley she'd hit a ringer. "Just one of the men Lori works with."

Haley mentally ran through the list of employees at Shadow State Bank. "Wayne, the only men who work with Lori are either married or old enough to be my father."

His smile widened as he explained. "Wyatt is new. He's only been there a couple of weeks."

And the poor guy was already being set up on a blind date. "I doubt if he'd want to meet me. You know with my work schedule, it's next to impossible for me to date."

"Lori already told him all about you." Wayne looked altogether too pleased with himself. "He can't wait to meet you."

"I don't like to be set up," she reminded the deputy. "And that's exactly what this sounds like."

"It's for your own good." Wayne wasn't giving up easily. "It's not right for you to be alone all the time. You need a social life."

"I have a social life." Haley wasn't quite ready to surrender just yet. "I belong to the ladies group at church, and I'm starting to teach the kindergarten Sunday school class next weekend. I have lots of friends at church."

"That's good," Wayne acknowledged, "but you need more than work and church. God didn't put you on this earth to turn into an old maid."

She burst into laughter. "I don't think very many people would classify a thirty-year-old woman as an old maid."

He sighed. "Just come to dinner tonight. If you don't like Wyatt, you'll never have to see him again—except at the bank. Please say you'll come."

The leftover tater tot casserole she'd been planning to warm up wasn't something she would necessarily mind missing. "What time should I be there, and what should I bring?"

"Six-thirty and a positive attitude. I believe Wyatt Millan might be just what you need."

Wayne had just said his goodbyes and left for traffic supervision duty when "Haley, can you come in here for a minute?" As was often the case, Mitch didn't bother with the intercom. He just yelled.

She looked at him, only to see him studying something on his desk. The last time he'd called her to his office had been to instruct her to write an official reprimand for one of the dispatchers she supervised. She warily walked over and opened the door to his office.

"Come in and close the door." There was definitely something bothering her usually easygoing boss.

As soon as she'd sat down, Mitch lifted his gaze to her. "This stays between us." His tone of voice brooked no room for argument. "The call we received from Jen Ewing . . . We might get more calls like that. Knowledge of them has to stay within the department, and I need you to make sure I'm notified of every one of them. It's crucial." The last time Haley had seen him this serious was when Holly Walker was being stalked.

"Can I ask what's going on, or is it secret?" Although it rarely happened, Haley was always aware that Mitch could decide to keep things from her.

He studied her face for a moment before he spoke. "All I can say is we're protecting one of the county's residents. There aren't any laws being broken. I just need to be aware of calls like Jan Ewing's."

"How do you want me to handle the other dispatchers?" They both knew what Haley was really asking. Ray Fine and Mavis Shepard would follow orders and keep everything under wraps, but Crystal Stanley was another story. She was one of the biggest gossips in the county and had been written up for sharing official information outside the office more than once.

"I hadn't thought about that." Mitch sighed as he ran his hand down his face. "I'll talk to all three of them, and I'll lay it on the line for Crystal. If I find out she's breathed one word about any of this to anybody besides me, she'll be job hunting."

Something occurred to Haley. "Mitch, Jan Ewing didn't identify the man she was talking about, but other callers might. What am I supposed to do if you don't want me to have that information?"

He closed his eyes, and as she saw his lips move, Haley knew he was praying. When his eyes once more met hers, determination, or possibly resignation, was evident. "The person they'll be calling about is Beau Harding, the man working for Luke and Holly Walker. All you need to know is I'm aware of the situation, and it's being handled. Fair enough?"

"Yes."

A few minutes later, though, back at her station, Haley's mind was troubled. She hadn't exactly met Beau Harding, or Hardy, as most people called him. But she'd heard from several people that he was stand-offish. Haley was prepared to like him if for no other reason than he was helping the Walkers.

She pictured the tall, muscular man with grayish-blue eyes and couldn't stop the shiver that shot up her spine. Haley wasn't the type of woman to be attracted to a man because of his looks, but she wasn't blind, either. And Beau Harding was easy on the eyes.

"Hey, Haley, I'm going to need you to sign for this."

The male voice startled Haley out of her musings. She looked up and smiled at the man standing there.

"Hey, Will." She stood up and walked the few yards between the dispatch station and counter. "Have a package for us?"

The mail carrier, William Baxter, held up a shoebox sized box. "It's special delivery."

Haley waited while he placed the package on the counter and prepared his hand-held computer for her signature. "How's the weather out there, Will?"

The burly man who somehow always made Haley think of Barney Rubble, looked up as he held out the device. "It's pretty warm for an October morning, but it seems like the leaves are falling like crazy. I lost count of how many people are burning them today."

She wrinkled her nose as she signed her name. "I hope my neighbors don't burn theirs. My apartment will smell like smoke for two weeks if they do."

Will nodded. "The city needs to come up with an ordinance. Most towns don't allow leaf burning within city limits." He tucked the computer back in its holster and adjusted the bag on his shoulder. "It's too bad I don't have your side of town on my route anymore. I could drop off your mail with the sheriff's."

"That's okay." Haley picked up the letters beside the package. "I'm not in that big of a hurry to see my bills."

"I know what you mean." His eyes practically disappeared under his brows. "Those doctors are killing me."

"How is your mom?" Haley felt guilty. She should have asked about Lydia Baxter first thing.

He shrugged. "As well as can be expected, I guess. I think she's getting used to the nursing home. They take better care of her than I could at home."

She smiled gently. "Is the money a problem again? I know your mom's insurance ran out, and it's been nearly six months since we had the fundraiser. We can have another one if you need it." Bone cancer was an expensive disease.

"No." Will's face was flushed as he answered a bit abruptly. "I mean, we're doing okay. Thank you, though."

"Well, please let me know if things change." Haley had helped spearhead a very successful fundraising event for Mrs. Baxter.

"I will." The mail carrier produced a forced smile. "Any outgoing mail today?"

"Oh, I forgot." Haley turned and walked to her desk and picked up the stack of envelopes that needed to be mailed. "Good thing you reminded me." She handed them to him.

"Have a nice day."

Haley watched as Will walked away. The door had just closed behind him when Hank Stone pulled it open. Hubert Belton, clad in a pair of bib overalls, walked into the building in front of him.

"Hi, Hank. Mr. Belton." She wondered what was going on.

"Don't 'hi' me, missy." The older man huffed. "It's a crime when a man can't take care of himself in the privacy of his own yard."

Hank's steady gaze met Haley's. "I had to arrest him. He refused to stay dressed if I left." His freckled face suddenly developed red blotches. "I need a prisoner uniform if any are clean."

"I washed both of them not too long ago." Did he think the old man was going to try an escape?

Hank must have seen her curiosity. If possible, his face turned even redder. "All he has on are those overalls."

"Oh." Haley felt her own face warm as she realized she was at a complete loss for words.

"I'll just go process him." Hank steered the older man toward the heavy door that separated the station from the small booking room and their only cell. "Could you let Mitch know what's going on? Tell him I tried everything."

Still somewhat shocked by the knowledge the man in front of her was barely clad, Haley nodded.

She waited until the two men had gone on into the other part of the building before she pushed the button to page the sheriff. He looked up from something that had him engrossed enough he hadn't noticed Hank and Mr. Belton.

"Hank wanted me to let you know he's processing Hubert Belton."

Mitch sighed. "Does he need help?"

"I don't think so. Mr. Belton is unhappy, but he's not putting up any resistance." She just hoped he kept his suspenders over his shoulders until Hank had him in one of their two lovely neon pink uniforms. A couple of women on the county board had them specially made and then donated them.

"Go ahead and call Samantha. She may as well come down here and bail him out." His eyes were already back on his desk.

"Okay." After placing the receiver in its cradle, Haley picked up the phone book. Maybe she should make an effort to memorize Samantha Belton's phone number since the woman had to routinely pick up her grandfather.

After she finished speaking with the beleaguered woman, Haley finally had time to sort through the mail.

There were several pieces of junk mail, offering everything from the newest vacuum to a specially crafted porcelain statue. She'd never understand why companies weren't able to keep police stations off their sales lists. It was highly unlikely that a sheriff's office would purchase a porcelain doll, even if it was a limited edition.

After filing the junk mail in the round plastic container, Haley set about dividing the rest. It was part of her job to classify mail as urgent, routine, and staff-handled. Mitch would receive the urgent and routine mail, and take care of it accordingly. She would deal with the staff handled mail.

One envelope was addressed to the station, and she placed it in her stack. Something about it caught her eye, so she stopped to take a closer look. There was something unusual about the envelope.

It took her a minute to realize it wasn't postmarked. How had a letter been delivered in the mail without being postmarked? She decided to go ahead and open it.

Her first thought when she pulled the paper out of the envelope and unfolded it was this had to be a joke. But, there it was. A phrase comprised of words cut out of magazines and crudely pasted on a sheet of unlined paper.

We will get even.

Without thinking, Haley carried the letter and envelope straight to Mitch's office. She opened the door and walked in.

He looked up, surprised by her unannounced entrance.

"Look." She placed the two items on his desk.

Mitch frowned as he picked them up. "What in the world?" He looked incredulously at Haley after scanning the sheet of paper. "This came in the mail?"

She nodded. "It's not postmarked, but I found it while I was sorting the mail Will just delivered."

He looked at it again. "It's probably a joke. Kids daring each other to do something foolish. Put it in a folder and hang onto it for a while, but I doubt if anything will come of it."

"Okay." She accepted the letter from him and picked the envelope back up. "You don't suppose any of those boys who just got back into town would be up to something, do you?" For their sakes she hoped not.

Mitch shook his head. "I'm pretty sure four months behind bars put the fear in all three of them. Besides, they worked hard to get out after only four months of their six-month sentences. I can't see them throwing away that length of good behavior on a silly joke."

"I'll file this then." Haley turned and walked back to her station. The boys she was worried about were three of five young men who unknowingly helped Holly Walker's kidnapper. While they hadn't known how big of a crime they were committing, they had used a stolen key to break into a storage room in the high school. They ended up with over fifteen-thousand dollars' worth of equipment they used to "keep Luke Walker busy," as their boss instructed them.

It was only because all the equipment was returned and that Luke and Holly went to bat for them, the boys got off as easily as they did. The two who were still seventeen at the time of the crime were sentenced to three months of juvenile detention, while the three who were tried as adults received six months in jail, and all five of them were placed on a year's probation.

Sammy Lewis, Trevor Bayne, and Rod Hirsh had all recently returned to Shadow after being released early for good behavior. While Trevor and Rod quickly found jobs and settled into seemingly normal lives, Sammy was still struggling.

Haley supposed it would be the most difficult for him to adjust since he'd had the most to lose. As one of the best high school quarterbacks in the state, Sammy had been looking at a football scholarship to allow him to play college ball. There had even been speculation that he would go pro. But, after his arrest, the offers disappeared, and he was left with no plans. It was sad.

Luke and Holly exemplified true Christian forgiveness when they requested leniency for the boys. They were positive the boys were duped by a man more devious in nature than any of them had ever been exposed to before. Poor choices were the result. While the Walkers in no way condoned the boys' actions, they forgave them.

Haley could only hope she would have been as forgiving had she been in their shoes. Her heart was troubled by the mere thought one or more of the boys might be responsible for the strange letter. Because, if the boys betrayed the trust the Walkers had placed in them, they were evidently in need of harsher consequences.

She said a prayer for the boys and the individual who had sent the letter as she finished her mail sorting duties. For the first time in a long while, Haley would be glad when five o'clock arrived, and with it, the beginning of Mavis Shepard's shift. This had turned out to be a crazy day, beginning with Jan Ewing's phone call.

Her mind went back to Beau Harding. She pushed the attraction she felt aside and focused on her curiosity. What was his real name, and why wasn't he using it? She most likely would never know.

Chapter 3

Hardy was going to die. Not in any gun-shooting blaze of glory. Nope. He was going to die from a bad fall caused by his legs being tangled in a shower curtain—while he was trying to get to his phone. And when his body was found…That simply wasn't going to happen. He braced his hands against the wall and pulled hard.

He reached for his phone just as it stopped ringing. It was a good thing nobody could see him—a fully grown man with shampoo in his hair and a torn shower curtain draped around his body like a Roman soldier. Dripping all over the floor.

Since it was too late to answer his phone anyway, he went ahead and finished ridding himself of the clinging curtain. Very few people had his number, so caller ID would show which one. The caller hadn't used the emergency signal of two rings, a pause, and an immediate second call. He'd take enough time to get decent.

Callie's name and number came up as a missed call when a dry and clothed Hardy checked a short while later. Wondering why his sister would be calling, he pushed the buttons that would speed dial her. She picked up on the second ring.

"I'm glad you called me back, Beau." There was an edge of fear in his sister's voice.

"What's going on?" If there were something wrong, he wasn't going to bother with casual conversation. He and his sister weren't chatty siblings anyway.

"It's Dad."

"What about him?" He hadn't meant to sound so sharp.

A shaky breath came across the phone. "He's had a stroke. He's holding his own, but it was touch and go for a while."

And this didn't constitute an emergency? Now wasn't the time to bring that up, though. "How's Mom?"

"She's doing okay, but I think she needs you, Beau." Her voice had grown stronger as she spoke.

Hardy drew a deep breath. "You know I can't come up there. It would make it worse for both of them if I did."

"Nobody has to see you." His little sister wasn't giving up without a fight. "Elliott will make sure you get in and out of town without being noticed."

"I can't let Elliott risk his job." His brother-in-law had already taken enough flak.

"He won't be." Callie sounded satisfied. "He has special permission from his boss. He can use whatever means necessary to get you in to see Dad."

Elliott had permission from the regional director of the Federal Safety Agency to sneak Hardy in and out of Chicago.

"Is Dad that bad?" Hardy didn't want to ask the question, but he needed to know the answer.

There was silence on the phone for a moment. "Please come, Beau."

Hardy held the phone away from his ear, thinking. If anybody recognized him, it would make far more problems for his parents than whatever benefits they would receive from him being there. But if his dad . . . He couldn't lose his father without even telling him goodbye.

"I'll need to set things up with Elliott, and I'll only be able to stay for an hour at most. It's all that's safe, Callie."

"Thank you, Beau." He could hear her relief. "Here's Elliott."

"Beau, how is everything downstate?" Elliott's businesslike facade rarely cracked.

"So far, so good."

"You were on TV the other night. That show about unsolved crimes. They had some pretty clear footage of you, shot from the store's surveillance cameras."

"I heard." Why didn't the place where Harding Davis "died" use a typical cheap camera system that produced footage so grainy the subjects looked like aliens? His life would have been much easier.

"I had to talk myself in circles to keep you there." If Elliott didn't sound too upset by his confrontation with Rich Stephens, Hardy knew it was because there was no love lost between the two men. "Stephens wanted to move you out of state immediately. I told him you wouldn't go. Was I right?"

"As rain." Hardy appreciated his brother-in-law's efforts to help him stay close to home. "The local sheriff knows who I am now, and he's watching out for me. If there's too much notice taken, he'll let me know so I can get out of here. But Stephens better understand I meant what I said about my location."

"I keep reminding him you don't want to be farther than a few hundred miles from Chicago. The man is still stuck on

Boise, though, so if we move you, it might be a battle." For the first time in their conversation, humor crept into Elliott's voice. "I think Stephens has something going with one of the field agents in Boise. She's a few years younger than he is, and their names have been linked. If you were out there, he'd have a valid excuse to get in touch with her more often."

"Wonderful." Hardy couldn't keep the sarcasm from his voice. "My safety comes in a distant second to his love life."

"I won't let it," Elliott assured him. "You're going to stay hidden for as long as it takes."

"Speaking of hiding, how are you planning on getting me in to see Dad?"

Elliott immediately became the experienced agent Hardy knew him to be. "Hal Gunther is in Pattinton, less than twenty-five miles from your location. You're to meet him in the parking lot at Mercy General Hospital, there in Shadow."

"I suppose he'll have one of those cars that may as well post a sign saying this is a government car."

A dry chuckle came from the phone. "No Crown Vic; he'll be driving a blue Impala."

"That's okay." And at most, a step away from the Vic.

"He'll drive you to Central City Hospital, where your dad is. I'm sending a couple of experienced agents to meet you at the hospital. Just stay with them and follow their instructions."

"What time do I meet Gunther?"

"In two hours. Can you make it?"

That would give him time to come up with some kind of cover story for Luke. He was technically off work for the day anyway and would be back in plenty of time to take care of his morning chores. He figured a total of seven hours in transit, with a stay of no longer than two hours, would be okay.

"I'll be there." Hardy had one more question for his brother-in-law before they said goodbye. "What's the word on Dohner?"

"Undercover says he still thinks you're dead. There hasn't been any hint that he's interested in your family, so they're all safe, too. If there's the slightest chance he's coming after your parents or Callie and my kids, they'll disappear faster than you did." Elliott spoke assuredly. "You have my word I'll keep your family safe, Beau."

"If I didn't believe that, I would be there instead of here." Hardy spoke the truth. His brother-in-law would use every means at his disposal to protect his family. "Thank you."

"Just be careful," Elliot advised him. "Your family needs you."

As Hardy hung up, for the first time in a long time he wished he were a praying man . . . like he'd been before Kari. But he just didn't believe God listened to him anymore.

After he took a few minutes to rehang his newly duct-taped shower curtain, Hardy went in search of Luke. He didn't like bothering his boss in the house, so he was relieved when he saw Clarence cavorting about in the field toward the pond. Luke wouldn't be too far away.

Hardy stood still as the dog ran to him and shamelessly rubbed against his legs, begging to be petted. Luke was barely visible in the twilight as he walked steadily toward him.

"I think my dog likes you," Luke observed when he was within a few yards of Hardy.

Hardy scratched behind Clarence's ears. "I think he likes anybody who'll pet him. Have you ever thought of getting a real watchdog?"

Luke's grin belied his stern words. "I'll have you know Clarence has chased off bad guys more than once. And heaven help you if you ever try to hug my wife. He won't even let my dad do that. In fact, I feel fortunate he lets me."

Clarence's tail thumped the ground as his owner talked about him. Hardy looked at the dog for a moment before addressing Luke again.

"I have some personal business I need to take care of tonight. I'll be back in time for morning chores, but I didn't want you or Holly to worry when you saw my truck was gone all night."

Concern filled Luke's eyes. "Is something wrong?"

Hardy wasn't sure how to answer him. Even though he had spent nearly five years living a lie, he wasn't by nature a dishonest man. But he didn't want to do anything to place Luke and his wife in danger.

"I just have something I need to see to."

It appeared like Luke wanted to ask more questions, but then he slowly nodded. "Just let me know if there's anything I can do to help you. You've done me a solid, working the farm as well as you have."

Hardy returned his gaze. "That's what you and your dad pay me for."

Luke shook his head. "We don't pay you nearly enough. You've done as fine a job as I would have." A wry grin formed on his face. "In fact, you patched the west side of the barn roof better."

"It's a good thing you weren't out here to see me do it." Hardy couldn't help but smile at the memory. "The wind caught a wide sheet of tin, and I had to do quite a little dance to keep from being blown right off the roof."

"Too bad we didn't have a video camera pointed at you." Luke chuckled. "Holly could have taken it to school and showed it to the kids."

"She could let the science class figure out how fast the wind was blowing." Hardy joined in with Luke's kidding.

"Next time you get up on the roof, let me know." Luke patted his leg. "Come on, Clarence. We're keeping Hardy from leaving."

"I'll be back for morning chores," Hardy reminded his boss.

"I can call my dad to come do them if you get held up." Luke didn't seem the least bit concerned about the possibility. "So, if you need to be away longer, go ahead."

Hardy was once more touched by the kindness and consideration the other man was showing to somebody he really didn't even know. "Thanks, but I'll be back in time."

He watched for a few moments as Luke and Clarence headed for the house. Then Hardy walked over and climbed into his truck. He didn't have to meet Hal Gunther for a little over an hour, but he had some preparations he'd need to make before then.

The drive into town seemed to take twice as long as the actual twenty minutes. He was pleased when he pulled in at the drugstore and saw only one other vehicle. He wouldn't have to worry about curious people paying too much attention to his purchases.

"Good evening." The young lady at the cash register greeted him as he walked through the sliding door.

He nodded in response and headed toward the aisle he wanted. He soon had a box of men's hair color that would wash out with a couple of shampoos, a pair of nearly clear reading glasses, and a baseball cap. He had just turned the corner to head to the magazines when he nearly mowed somebody over.

"Excuse me." The woman in front of him was upset by their near collision. "I wasn't watching where I was going."

Hardy gave her a cursory glance. "Neither was I." She looked vaguely familiar, but he didn't have the time or inclination to figure out why. He started around her to his right.

At the same time, she moved to her left. This time he hit her with enough force the things she'd been holding dropped to the floor.

"Oh, I'm so sorry." She rushed to apologize as she bent to retrieve the items, even more flustered.

Hardy sighed. "It was my fault. Let me help." He tried to shift his items into one hand so he could help her but nearly dropped them. "I guess my hands are too full."

She looked up at him and smiled, displaying startling blue eyes and the biggest dimples he'd ever seen. Had he ever seen a woman more exquisite? "H—"No. He didn't have time to appreciate a woman, no matter how attractive he found her. His life was in enough of a mess without adding a female to the mix.

He mumbled something he hoped passed for an apology and stepped around her. The magazines in front of him became his main focal point as he steadfastly ignored the woman behind him.

After mindlessly scanning magazines for nearly every interest imaginable, Hardy finally remembered what he was looking for. He carefully examined variety puzzle books, looking for ones he knew his mom would enjoy. If he knew her, she wouldn't leave his father's side any longer than necessary, so she would need something to pass the time. Flowers or balloons would draw too much attention to him anyway, so he'd settle for the gift of a puzzle book.

Hardy breathed a sigh of relief when he saw the dimpled beauty walk out the door. The fascination he fought wouldn't be tested.

He forced his gaze back to the bubble gum-popping clerk.

"You're a sweet man." She picked up the hair dye. "I bet your grandpa will be tickled like a pickle."

Hardy fought the urge to ask if she had to return to the "home" after she got off work.

"Yeah."

"Men usually aren't so thoughtful, so you are an original. My ex-boyfriend, Rudy, thinks he's an original, but— "

"Grandpa's waiting."

His blunt statement worked. She stopped talking and resumed ringing up his purchases.

As he accepted his change and picked up the plastic shopping bag, her motor kicked back in.

"So, I don't have a boyfriend right now. Do you have a girlfriend? Do you drink coffee?"

Hardy thought of how his mom would say to handle this situation. Speaking as kindly as possible for him, he said, "Miss, you can't be much over twenty. I am thirty-four. You don't know me at all, and you're set to meet me somewhere for coffee."

"You're a good guy. I can tell."

"Not that you can safely make that call, but if I am, it doesn't mean the next guy you flirt with will be."

A few moments later, as he left the drugstore, he glanced over to see his gum-popper seemed subdued. Maybe he hadn't helped her, but at least he tried.

As he drove, he thought of girls like that getting into trouble. To keep from blowing his cover, he had to sit back and watch members of the Dohner "family" seduce young women, then toss them away like a well-read newspaper.

Soon, he pulled into the only gas station in town that offered an exterior-doored bathroom which remained unlocked unless occupied. While it wasn't as clean as he would have preferred, it suited his purposes just fine.

Twenty minutes later, a man appearing to be twenty years older than Hardy, with graying hair and glasses, walked out of the bathroom. He pulled his baseball cap down low on his head to change his profile. Anybody looking at him closely would recognize him, but at a glance, it would do. He purposely slowed his stride as he stepped into the guise of an older man.

Becoming someone else was nothing new to Hardy, but he found it didn't have the same appeal it had in the past. Maybe the normal life he'd lived the past five months had changed his outlook. Given the situation, Hardy wasn't sure if that were a good thing.

Looking around and seeing nobody paying any attention to him, Hardy climbed back into his truck. He would be a little early for his meeting, but it wouldn't hurt to have a look around the parking lot before he pulled in. Though he'd never admit it to anybody, the television program featuring his death had put him on edge. He'd just be a little more watchful now. That would have to be enough since he wasn't ready to give up his life as Beau Harding just yet.

In fact, he found himself liking this life a little too much. As quickly as he had the thought, he shoved it away. Thinking like that could get him killed.

Chapter 4

"And so I told him to count it again if he didn't believe me." Wyatt Millan laughed at the story he had just taken twenty minutes to share. Unfortunately, none of the other three people present were able to manage much more than a polite chuckle.

He looked at Haley. "So, tell me about yourself." What? He knew there were other people there besides him?

"I'm just a small-town girl." Not the type of woman he was familiar with.

"What is there to do for fun around here?" Well, she'd held his interest a long time.

Wayne answered. "We have several good restaurants and a pretty big movie theater. Or if you're physically active, we have a bowling alley and skating rink."

Wyatt looked disbelievingly at Wayne before returning his focus to Haley. "What does a lovely woman like you enjoy?"

Haley exchanged pointed looks with her friends, who appeared to regret trying to fix her up with Wyatt. She decided to answer honestly. "I am very active in my church. God has given me all I have, so I try to do my best to use it for His glory."

Wyatt looked at her as though she had just announced she was from the planet Mars. "I didn't take you for one of those people."

She had never been particularly fond of being dismissed as a strange duck simply because of her faith. Haley felt a spark of energy light her heart and travel to her mouth.

"Well, if you mean a Christian, then I am. I believe in God the Father, the Son, and the Holy Ghost. I believe Jesus Christ suffered on the cross and died for me, to take away my sins. I know I'm saved by grace alone since there's nothing I can do to deserve it. I will mess up and do things that break his heart, but there is nothing I can do that will make God stop loving me. I believe in doing my best to see my fellow brothers and sisters as God wants me to." Even when the person was aggravating her beyond belief. "Any questions?" Haley hoped he did; she would be happy to set him straight. From the corner of her eye, she saw Lori hiding a smile behind her hand and Wayne just outright grinning.

Wyatt Millan sat there with his mouth hanging partially open. It seemed that Haley's witnessing had taken him enough by surprise to make him speechless. She silently apologized to God when she couldn't help but wish she'd witnessed to him four stories earlier.

"Uh . . . up in Chicago, at least the people I hung out with, weren't church-goers. I've never heard it put that way before." The too-handsome man seemed sincerely taken aback.

Haley immediately felt ashamed of her attitude. "I'd be happy to tell you all about my faith. Jesus died just as much for you as He did for me."

Wyatt seemed to have regained some of his equilibrium. "I suppose lots of people go to church. I mean, do most people around here go?"

Lori answered him. "You'll find nearly everybody you work with goes. Nanette and Polly go to the same church Wayne and I attend." She looked at Haley. "Mr. Houston and his wife still attend your church, don't they?"

The bank president had been the church council president for the past four years. "Every Sunday." If Wyatt's boss attending church didn't impress him, she didn't know what would.

A speculative look came to his eyes as he seemed to consider Haley's statement. "Would it be possible for me to go to church with you sometime?"

While the expensively dressed, not a dark brown hair out of place, self-centered man didn't seem to be a person Haley would choose to build a relationship with, she couldn't refuse to help him find God. "Just let me know when you'd like to go."

"You're welcome to go with us, too." Wayne gave Haley an apologetic look. She doubted he and Lori would be fixing her up on any blind dates for a while. "We go to a different church than Haley. You can try both of them if you like…to see which one you feel most at home in."

"Thank you." Wyatt's smile didn't quite reach his eyes, and, when he shifted his attention back to Haley, there was something about his expression that made her uncomfortable. "What about your job? You work with Wayne, right?"

Work was a nice neutral topic. "Yes. I'm the chief dispatcher for the Shadow County Sheriff's office."

Interest showed in his eyes. "I imagine that's an interesting job. Are there many crimes in Shadow?"

Haley thought about the type of calls she regularly fielded, and for just a moment the image of Beau Harding popped into her head. She'd practically run him over in the drug store after work and was mortified when he started to help retrieve the feminine hygiene products she dropped.

"What types of crime do you have in town?" Wyatt's repeated question jolted Haley out of her thoughts.

Reckless driving, possible domestic violence which usually turned out to be Mrs. Turner dumping Mr. Turner's alcohol down the drain, minor thefts, very rarely shoplifters, and of course, the routine indecent exposure complaints. "Probably not what you would consider real crimes. Do you agree, Wayne?"

Wayne chuckled. "Let's just say they'll never have one of those true-life police shows following any of us around with a camera."

Wyatt perked up. "Speaking of those shows, did any of you see the episode of Last Run Sunday night?"

"No." Haley answered while Wayne and Lori shook their heads. "What was it about?"

"I guess I found it interesting because it happened just north of Chicago." Wyatt sat forward in his chair. "Almost a year ago, an undercover cop was involved in a hostage situation. The hostage was killed, and so was he. They showed footage from the store where it happened, and it was wild. The cop and the hold-up guy killed each other, but not before the hostage ended up shot in the head."

Haley didn't care for those types of television programs. "That sounds perfectly dreadful."

Wyatt's enthusiasm didn't wane. "The guy with the gun was the shooter, but according to the detective they interviewed, there was another man who got away. That's why they had it on Last Run. They're hoping somebody with information about the shooting will come forward so they can catch him."

Wayne caught Haley's eye and winked before he spoke to Wyatt. "Well, we don't have anything like that happening around here, I'm happy to say. Shadow will be a big change from Chicago for you."

"We'll never be on television," Haley agreed, glad to shift the discussion away from the violent event.

"Although, if we were, they'd have to black out part of the picture if they followed us on one of our routine complaints." Confused by Wayne's statement, Haley looked at him. When he mimicked someone washing themselves, she knew what—or who—he was referring to. She had to laugh.

"I don't suppose the viewing public would receive Hubert very well," she commented.

Wayne had noticed Wyatt's curious expression. "We have a gentleman in town who likes outdoor sponge baths. He claims they're why he's still alive."

"So, you have to arrest him?" Wyatt didn't seem very amused by the idea. "Just how many officers are there in the department?"

Haley exchanged a puzzled glance with Wayne, uncertain why Wyatt would respond so dismissively to Hubert's story when most people found it amusing. "Since the county isn't that large, the sheriff's department takes care of the city, too. Mitch Landon is the sheriff. The board just hired two new deputies, so he has five now—Wayne, Jeff Fielding, Jerry Young, Tom

Winkler, and Hank Stone." That was common knowledge, so Haley didn't see any harm in answering his question.

The banker's brows shot up. "Six police officers for the entire county? That doesn't seem sufficient to me."

Wayne spoke up. "When we get something big, the state police over in Pattinton send officers to help us out. We've only had to call them in for support a handful of times."

Wyatt's eyes narrowed. "So, there are more than just the six officers in the sheriff's department to keep us safe and sound."

Haley wondered if he could be concerned about his own safety in Shadow. "If we need them."

"Would anybody care for a piece of cake?" Lori stood up, effectively ending the police-related conversation.

"Please." Wyatt had an inscrutable look on his face for a moment before he smiled. "It's not often I get homemade desserts."

"I'll help you," Haley told Lori as she stood up and followed her into the kitchen.

"I'm sorry." Lori spoke softly enough her voice wouldn't carry into the living room. "He doesn't act like that at work. I've never heard him tell stories at all, let alone carry on about himself."

Haley shrugged. "Maybe he's lonely. I shouldn't have been so hard on him."

"It was considerate of you to agree to his visit at your church." Lori appeared troubled as she sliced the pineapple-upside-down cake in front of her. "But, what if he thinks of going to church with you as a date, Haley? That could become uncomfortable quickly."

"I hadn't thought of that." Haley picked up two plates of cake and headed into the dining room. She wondered if she should clarify that attending church together would in no way be a date. But, how would that be done in a polite way? "Maybe she was overthinking; maybe nothing would come from it at all.

Thankfully, Wyatt didn't seem inclined to make a late evening of it, so it was relatively early when Haley pulled into her parking space. Her heart lifted when she saw the car parked in the visitor's spot and the woman standing there.

"What are you doing out this time of the night?" Haley asked Missy Landon.

Mitch's twin sister returned Haley's smile. "Joe and I set the date. We're getting married in May. That's only seven months away." She leaned over the hood of her car and straightened back up, holding a stack of magazines. "I wanted you to help me look for a dress since yours will have to match mine."

Haley's heart felt lighter than it had all evening. "That sounds fun. Come on in."

It was really too late in the evening to begin the search for a wedding dress, but somehow, the thought of it offset the disquieting evening she'd spent with Wyatt Millan.

The two women were soon sitting side by side on Haley's sofa, the magazines spread on the coffee table in front of them.

"Will your parents be able to come home for your wedding?" Missy's mom had severe arthritis, and when it was at its worst, she couldn't get around at all. So, Missy and Will had talked before about having a simple ceremony with Mitch giving her away. Then she and Joe would follow it up with a trip to see her parents before they went on their honeymoon.

Missy's smile brightened. "Mom's doctor is trying a new medication, and she's much better."

"That's great." Haley had good memories of the kind carpenter and his wife.

"Yes, it is. They're planning to come. Dad says he'll be here no matter what. If anybody gets the pleasure of giving one of his kids away, it's going to be him." She giggled. "Although he says he'd rather give Mitch away since he's the one responsible for all the gray hair on his and Mom's heads."

Haley pointed to a picture in the magazine on her lap. "Here you go. This dress is for you."

Both women laughed when Melissa took a good look at the dress with an enormous puffy bow over the posterior.

"How on earth would a woman sit down wearing that?" Missy shook her head. "I'd have to stay standing for the entire reception. I can see it now. Everybody's sitting down, and there I am standing at attention." She gestured toward the picture. "Not to mention how large my tush would look."

"They don't show a picture of this dress from the front." Haley could imagine her friend in it. Missy would be sure everyone knew why she was standing and probably end up having all her guests do the same.

Missy seemed skeptical. "It's most likely because the bow sticks out so far you can see it."

That sent both women into peals of laughter.

"I kind of like this one." Melissa showed a picture to Haley a few minutes later.

"It's strapless." It was Missy's wedding, and as maid of honor, Haley was obliged to wear a matching dress, but Haley did not want to wear a strapless dress. "Wouldn't it be uncomfortable when you dance?" And heaven help them if one of them sneezed.

Melissa sighed. "You're right." She leafed through the magazine. "Have you thought about who you're asking to Mitch and Tessa's wedding?"

It was Haley's turn to sigh. "Just because the invitation is for Haley Johnson plus one, doesn't mean I have to bring a date."

Her friend looked into her eyes. "But you should." Her eyes brightened. "And I know who you should ask."

Haley raised her hand. "I've met Wyatt Millan, thank you, and he is not my type."

"Wyatt Millan?" Missy's eyes were perfect circles. "Don't tell me Wayne and Lori tried to set you up with that Romeo wannabe."

"Lori said he doesn't tell stories at work like he did this evening." Haley felt the need to defend her friends.

A very unladylike snort erupted from Missy. "That's because Lori is his boss. Believe me, those of us at the teller windows with him have heard it all. The man has a split personality, one minute all kissy face and friendly, and the next patting himself on the back for being such a wonderful person. And I'm pretty sure he'd hang a mirror in his space if he could figure out how."

"Well, at least we agree I shouldn't ask him to Mitch and Tessa's wedding." Haley turned the page and began looking at another dress.

"I think you should ask Beau Harding," Melissa announced matter-of-factly. "He's single and very handsome. He must be lonely, too. It would be nice to invite him to join in something like a wedding."

"Beau Harding?" Dress forgotten, Haley examined her friend's face. "You're kidding, right? Because I don't even know him. Just this evening, I practically knocked him silly in the drugstore. He looked at me like I was an amoeba. Even if I did ask him, he'd say no."

Missy looked up from the magazine with a piercing expression. "Are you telling me you've decided to avoid him because of one event? He might have been in a hurry or had a hundred different things on his mind."

Expecting Missy's usual follow-up, Haley wasn't surprised by her next words.

"You're too pretty for him not to notice you unless something had him distracted. Those dimples of yours alone stop men in their tracks."

Haley's face grew warm, and she knew she was blushing. "Not every man thinks dimples are attractive." She relied on her usual rebuttal. "And besides, I never see him. How can I ask him if I don't see him?"

"We'll go out to the farm after church on Sunday, and you can ask him." Before Haley could protest, Missy held up a picture. "Do you like this one?"

Haley looked at the dress. "It's pretty. What does the back of it look like?"

It wasn't until after Missy had gone home, and Haley was lying in bed that she remembered her friend's ridiculous suggestion to invite Beau Harding to the wedding. His first response would be to ask her who she was. No, she didn't think she'd ask him. She would just go by herself as she'd planned. If Missy wanted to invite him, she could ask her brother for a special invitation for him.

Haley turned over and plumped her pillow. When she closed her eyes, she found herself looking into silver eyes that seemed bottomless. Missy was right about one thing. The man was very handsome.

But, even if she knew who he was, he had no idea Haley Johnson was alive.

Chapter 5

Hardy walked silently into the hospital room. His eyes immediately concentrated on his father and all the tubes and wires hooked to him, with machines beeping and humming. The man lying in the bed was a mere shadow of the strong, sturdy dad Hardy had always looked up to and tried to emulate. Until Kari, he planned for a relationship like that of his parents. He prayed for someone like his mom, who understood the reality of being a police officer's wife and not only accepted it, but supported it.

"Beau?" The most familiar voice in the world to him drew his attention to the woman sitting on a chair by the window. "Is that really you? I'm not dreaming?"

He redirected his steps and walked over to her. "I'm here, Mom." Before he was barely finished speaking, his mother was standing, held tightly in his arms as she softly sobbed.

"We almost lost him." She finally managed to speak. "The doctors didn't think they were going to be able to save him." Sharon Davis pulled back and looked into her son's eyes. "Your father almost died. It was only through God's grace he survived."

Hardy carefully supported her as she sat back down before he settled himself in the chair next to hers. She held on to his hand tightly, as if she were afraid he'd bolt. Once they were sitting side by side, he looked at his dad.

"What happened?"

Her breathing was ragged as she spoke. "He was watching a football game at a friend's house. He was all right when he left home, Beau, so I don't know how this could happen." Her fingers tightened on his. "Phil told me he had come back to the room after visiting the bathroom. H.B. began to say something to Phil, and then he just collapsed. Thank God John was there." Hardy knew John Tarp was a retired physician.

"I shouldn't have let him go." Her tear stained eyes looked into his. "I should have seen that something was wrong with him."

"You couldn't have, Mom." Hardy wasn't about to sit there and listen to his mom blame herself. "If none of his friends thought anything was wrong with him, why should you?"

Sharon looked twenty years older than her age of sixty-four. "I'm his wife. Even though H.B. spends a lot of time with his friends, I'm still his wife. I should have known."

Hardy slid his hands out of hers and framed her face. "Stop it, Mom. You have to stop blaming yourself and just focus on Dad getting better."

His mother slowly smiled through her tears. "Thank you. I needed to hear you say that."

Hardy lowered his hands and impulsively kissed her cheek. "I'm sorry I wasn't here for you, Mom. I'm sorry I still can't stay. It's just not—"

"I understand why Harding Davis had to die. Your dad understands." Sharon had regained her composure and spoke firmly. "Elliott did a good thing to get you here, and I won't soon forget it."

"Neither will I." He looked over at his dad. Not that it mattered, but he was curious anyway. "Besides Dr. Tarp, who did you say was with Dad?"

"Phil Welsh and Rob Weston. You remember Phil. I know. He retired from the force just before H.B. did. He and your dad are still fishing buddies." The corners of her mouth curled slightly. "Rob was on the force with your dad when you were a baby. He moved away before Callie was born, so you probably won't remember him."

Hardy tried to picture it—four retirees, probably close to his dad's age of sixty-seven, watching a football game—and his dad just dropped. He didn't take his eyes off H.B. as he spoke. "Does he sleep most of the time?"

Sharon reached over and patted his cheek. "Yes, but he can still hear you. It will mean everything to him to know you came. Just talk to him. Let him know you're here."

He rose and and found that his legs were shaking as he walked the few yards to Harding Beauregard Davis Senior's bed. The older man's hand felt like a piece of cold leather when Hardy took it in his.

"I'm here, Dad. I wish I could stay with you and Mom." Hardy felt his dad's hand twitch. "I know you understand why I can't. But you need to get better so you and Mom can be there for each other. She needs you."

"B...Beau..." Startled, Hardy looked at his dad's face. H.B. had his left eye open. Hardy noticed for the first time the entire right side of the older man's face was drooping and motionless.

H.B.'s speech was so slurred it was difficult to comprehend him. Nevertheless, Hardy knew his dad had said his name.

"I'm here, Dad. I came to see you." He was suddenly transported back to the day when a seven-year-old Beau stood in front of his dad at the police station, saying those exact same words. Instead of getting on the bus to return home from school, Hardy had decided he'd just walk the twelve blocks to visit his dad at work. He hadn't understood why, since everybody was so delighted to see him, why H.B. severely scolded him. A little boy had wanted his dad.

"Beau." While still greatly slurred, his name was a little easier to understand this time. H.B.'s hand turned under his son's, and his fingers grasped Hardy's hand. "He feel turtle." He drew a ragged breath. "Jesus water."

Hardy looked at his mom, completely at a loss for what to say. Something about feeling a turtle and Jesus? His parents were devout Christians, but his dad's words simply didn't make sense.

"Jesus water." The strain of moving the muscles needed in order to speak showed on every surface of his face. "He feel turtle."

"I'm sorry, Dad." Hardy looked helplessly from his dad to his mom, who smiled sadly.

"It's the lack of oxygen, Beau. He isn't able to say what he means."

He looked back, and his eyes searched his dad's open one. The seemingly pointless words seemed too important to his dad for them to not have some kind of meaning. Hardy wasn't a doctor, but he didn't think his father would be repeating the same thing if he wasn't aware of what he was saying.

H.B. sighed and closed his eye. Hardy had just about decided he'd fallen back asleep when his dad's hand tightened once more, and he spoke again. "He feel turtle. Be careful."

"Dad?" Hardy had understood the last two words. "Don't worry about me. I'm being careful. Nobody in Shadow knows who I am. I just wish you 'd take care of yourself and get better. Please."

There was no response this time. Hardy felt his dad's hand go limp and saw his breathing even out.

"He's fallen back asleep." His mom spoke quietly from beside him. She put her hand on his arm. "He was just telling you, he's worried about you. The words that came out weren't the ones that left his brain. Dr. Gillespie explained that to me."

Hardy gently placed his dad's hand on the bed and pulled his own away.

"Come sit over here and tell me what it's like to work on a farm again after all these years." His mom smiled gently. "I know it's been a big change for you."

He shrugged as he returned to his chair. "Luke had three good kids working for him all summer. What I didn't remember from Pop's, they reminded me of. I was back on top of things within a few weeks."

"We've all been praying for you." Sharon reached up and placed her hand on the side of his face." I know what happened shook your faith. But just remember, Beau. God never moves away from you. He's right where he's always been, waiting for you to come back to him."

"Mom, I wish I could . . . " He didn't want to have this conversation with his dad lying so deathly ill less than ten feet away. "I'll remember." That was the only thing he could give her.

She patted his cheek before lowering her hand. "Callie will be glad to know your dad woke up while you were here."

Hardy was relieved his mom had switched the subject. "Has he been able to speak to her?"

"A couple of times." Sharon's eyes were on her husband. "He was able to ask about the kids. At least that's what we think he asked."

"How are they?" Hardy felt the familiar twinge of guilt as he thought of the niece and nephew who probably wouldn't even recognize him.

A genuine smile lit his mom's eyes. "Blake won the first grade spelling bee—out of all four classes. He's quite a reader, like his mom. And Tabby's preschool teacher told Callie that Tabby was going to be bored in kindergarten next year since she already knows most of what they'll be taught."

Hardy thought back to the last time he'd seen the kids. "Does Blake still look so much like his mom?"

Sharon nodded. "It's ironic, isn't it? That Blake would have his mom's brown hair and coloring while Tabby ended up with Elliott's blonde hair. At least they both have Callie's brown eyes."

"I should have gone and seen them more when I had the chance." Hardy spoke the words before he'd thought them out.

"You would have been exposed." Sharon seemed genuinely perplexed. "If those men who thought you were Joe Ryman had ever found out about your family, the kids would have been put in danger. Beau, you unselfishly kept all of us safe."

For the first time, Hardy saw the last five years of his life through the eyes of a son and brother. "I shouldn't have done it, Mom." His eyes met hers. "I should have never gone undercover. Living a lie for that long made me miss too much of my own life."

"You did a good thing," his mom assured him. "If it weren't for you, Teddy Dohner would still be running a network of drugs that were killing people. Think of all of the lives you saved."

Hardy could only think of the one he hadn't. "I'd better go, Mom. I don't want to take any chances of being spotted."

Sharon looked like she was going to press her point about his achievements, but then she smiled. "Thank you for coming. I'll make sure to let you know if your dad's condition changes."

"I love you, Mom." Hardy stood up. "Don't forget the emergency signal."

"Call and let it ring twice before I hang up. Then call right back, and you'll answer," she recited.

Hardy nodded. "I'll see you when I can."

"I love you, Beau." His mom started to cry. "Stay safe."

"I will."

The two FSA agents looked uncomfortable on their chairs when Hardy walked into the hall.

"Ready, Mr. Davis?" The one named Warburton asked.

"As ready as I'll ever be."

After fifteen minutes of cloak and dagger moves worthy of a James Bond film, Hardy found himself once more in an FSA car.

The agent driving him to Shadow told him his name was Tyler Rawlins, but then remained silent, leaving Hardy to his thoughts.

Five years. For five years, he spent the majority of his time being Joe Ryman. "Joe" had started at the bottom of the Dohner organization, and made it to within one step away from working directly for Ted Dohner himself.

Then, his son, Teddy, had discovered a way to ensure even more money on the lucrative drug trade he ran. He laced his drugs with additional ingredients, simply to stretch the product further. And if those ingredients had deadly side effects, Teddy didn't care. He had enough customers; what did the death of a few dozen people mean to him?

By the time Hardy discovered what the young Dohner was doing, Teddy had his pushers marketing the contaminated drugs in schools. Children died before Hardy could do something about it.

Of course, he'd let his handler know as soon as he had the chance. Then Hardy had waited for what seemed like forever to see how Teddy would be stopped. Someone above Hardy's pay grade made the wise decision to take the son down before he killed any more people. Joe Ryman had even been arrested in the bust, so Hardy's cover was still viable.

Then the trial began. Ted Dohner's money had bought a very fine lawyer with very low morals, and it looked like Teddy was going to get off. The prosecution was built on circumstantial evidence. The only hope had been eyewitness testimony, which came from known drug addicts and pushers—not exactly the most credible.

So, the decision had been made to bring Hardy in to testify. He'd blown his cover and became a wanted man the moment he entered the courtroom. They kept him in protective custody and safe houses during the trial, and his testimony had put Teddy Dohner away for the rest of his natural life.

Then, after the trial, Hardy reluctantly assumed a new identity and settled in a small city just over the state line in Wisconsin. His new name was Beau Knox, and he lived in a small house on the outskirts of town. He was just settling into the routine of his new life as a grocery store clerk when disaster struck.

He was nearly home when he realized he was out of coffee. Instead of driving clear back across town to the store he'd just left, Hardy decided to stop at the convenience store on his way. The coffee can hit the counter just as a gunshot rang out.

His police training immediately kicked in, and he'd gone for cover behind the counter, where the store employee crouched, crying. Hardy looked at the young woman and spoke softly. "Just stay down. It'll be okay."

"Stand up or I'm going to start shooting." The calm matter-of-fact voice sounded about twenty feet away. Instead of taking a chance on the store clerk being shot, Hardy chose to stand up. Just as he moved, the young lady pushed something into his hand. He glanced down to see a pistol.

"What do you want?" he calmly asked the man, who looked like someone he'd pass on the sidewalk without a second glance. With his short-cut hair and standard jeans and T-shirt garb, there was nothing about him to indicate that he was a thief. Hardy figured he'd want him to empty the cash register for him, though.

"Take care of the girl!" A second voice came from the back of the store, followed by the dull thud of a heavy door slamming shut.

"You heard him." The man waved his pistol. "Stand up, doll-face, or I'll just have to come over there and get you."

Hardy put his free hand on the woman's head to stop her from rising. "Listen, I'll give you whatever you want. Here. We'll empty the register." He made a movement toward the machine.

"Freeze." The crook's gun stabilized, pointing directly at Hardy.

Hardy stood still. "What do you want?" he repeated.

The other man sneered. "I want that girl to stand up right now, or you'll both look like Swiss cheese."

"Stay down," Hardy urgently instructed the woman. "Just stay down."

The young lady moved her head out from under Hardy's hand and slowly stood, her legs shaking so badly her entire body was quivering. "I-I can't open the safe. It's-It's on a timer." A tear ran down her cheek.

"Who told you I want money?" The crook kept his gun trained steadily on Hardy. "Maybe I just came in to see you, Sweet Cheeks."

Hardy gripped the pistol tighter. "Listen. You can have all the money in the register. Just take it and go."

"But then I won't have done my job."

Job? "What are you talking about?" Hardy had an idea of what the man planned, but he hoped he was mistaken.

"I have to do what I've been paid for." The man could have been discussing the weather, he was so calm and cool.

"What are you going to do to me?" The woman's voice shook as she asked, tears now streaming down her face.

The crook looked at her as if she had just asked the most ridiculous question in the world. "Shoot you."

Hardy saw the gun swivel to aim at the woman and instinctively went into action.

He raised his gun and stepped in front of the woman, pushing her behind him. He felt a knife slice through his abdomen at the same time he heard the shot. Barely able to stay on his feet, Hardy fired his gun. The other man went to his knees, but he didn't lower the gun.

The next part would be forever frozen in Hardy's mind. The woman stepping forward. The man firing his gun. Hardy simultaneously firing his weapon. Seeing there was a hole in the man's chest as he fell. Turning to the woman to find her lying completely still, a bullet wound in the center of her forehead telling him he hadn't fired in time.

He'd dropped to his knees beside her.

"Why'd you stand up?" The world started spinning around him as the pain from the gunshot set in "Why?"

The next thing he'd been conscious of was waking up in a sterile hospital room with FSA Special Agent Harold Binkley standing with his back to him, staring out the window.

"What…where am I?" Hardy had been able to ask.

Binkley turned around. "You're in a hospital in Racine. The shot you took missed all of the important parts, so the doc says you'll be just fine after you mend."

"The girl…What about the girl?" Hardy hoped by some miracle, she was alive.

Binkley shook his head. "Her name was Jeffries. Kari Jeffries. A student at the University of Wisconsin, only twenty years old. Her mother is driving down from Green Bay."

Thinking about it now, Hardy was once more filled with the pure anger he'd felt at the death of the college student. He hadn't been able to meet her mother or attend her funeral because he "died." After recuperating for six long months in a safe house, the deal with Luke Walker had come up and he once more left Chicago.

The crime itself continued to be a mystery. There had been no robbery, and no further sign of the second man who was there. In fact, other than a glimpse of his profile on the state-of-the-art security camera, there wasn't even proof he'd been there.

Bile rose in his throat as he thought of all the news broadcasts he'd seen, showing footage from the convenience store and lauding him as a hero. He wasn't a hero. A hero would have died and left the hostage alive. Buzz from the undercover operation still in place reported Ted Dohner's desire for revenge died when Hardy did. There had been no indication at all that the man paid any attention to Hardy's family.

Thinking of his family brought his mind back to his parents. What might his dad have been trying to tell him? *He feel turtle. Jesus water.*

Maybe it was like his mom said and the words H.B. spoke weren't anything close to what he wanted to say. Hardy just couldn't shake the feeling he was missing something, though. He just wished he could figure out what it was

Chapter 6

It was time. The old man had found out too much and hadn't died; he could still tell his son the truth. Sadly, there was no way to finish off the snoopy, retired cop without setting off too many bells and whistles. At least not yet. Of course, if the ailing man improved enough to communicate with his son, plans would change. He couldn't allow H.B. Davis to tell his son what he'd discovered. He'd have to implement his plan right away.

And, after careful preparation he was ready. It had taken some creative financing, but he now had all the players in place.

He would still have to exercise some patience, though. If things moved too quickly, it could cast suspicion on him and ruin everything. He would bide his time until it was just the right moment to end everything. To end Harding Davis's pretense. To end Harding Davis.

He had a good plan. He picked up the phone and dialed it. It was time to set things in motion.

Chapter 7

"Shadow County Sheriff's office." Haley answered the phone. She hoped the early call didn't mean it was going to be super busy all day.

Her hopes were quickly dashed.

"This is Pete White. Joni and I just got to the salon, and it's been broken into."

Haley's dispatch training kicked in. "Pete, please leave the building and go somewhere safe. I'll send a squad car right over. Don't come back to the shop until you see an officer signal that it's safe."

"Okay."

Haley quickly disconnected the call and keyed the radio. She didn't have to look at the roster to know who was up.

"Hank, this is base. Do you copy?"

A few seconds later, the young deputy's voice came across the radio. "This is Snow. I copy."

"What's your twenty?"

"I'm at the Diner. Just stopped for a cup of coffee."

"There's been a four-fifty-nine at White's Salon over on Britton. Owner waiting nearby for all clear signal."

"Repeat." Haley could hear the disbelief in Hank's voice. They didn't get burglary calls every day.

She repeated it slower and as clearly as she could.

"Ten-four. I'm en route, ETA five minutes." Haley could hear the siren before the radio signal was off. The phone rang as she was writing everything on her dispatch sheet.

"It's Mitch, Haley." His tone of voice told her he wasn't calling to wish her a good day. "I heard the call on my radio. I'm fifteen minutes out. I'll be at White's as soon as I get to town. Just follow usual protocol if there are more call-ins for the same crime."

"Okay, Mitch."

The usual protocol was to write down the name of the person who called, the time the call was received, and as close to the exact words spoken as possible. The calls were recorded, but the notes would indicate where to listen to find a specific message. The police would have the information to investigate anybody who may have known too much too soon. Haley didn't know how other counties did it, but she thought Mitch's system was simple and thorough at the same time.

Twenty minutes later, she had five more calls written on her sheet. Three of them were by concerned passersby who saw the squad cars at the salon. They supposedly wanted to "make sure everything was okay," but it was more likely they were hoping for her to tell them why Hank and Mitch were at White's. The other two were citizens who had observed a strange vehicle at White's the previous evening. It might be nothing, but both callers described it as a dark blue or black older model panel van. Neither of them got the plates, but the second caller tried, only to discover they were covered in something, possibly mud.

She pushed the button on the radio.

"Base to Sheriff Landon. Do you copy?"

"Landon here."

"Ten-twenty-one."

She barely finished the code for him to use his phone when the one in front of her rang.

"Okay, Haley."

"Sheriff, two calls came in, reporting a strange vehicle in the vicinity last night. It's a dark blue or black older model panel van. Plates were obscured."

"Ten-four. Call the state dispatcher, and have them put out a BOLO. We want everybody to keep their eyes open."

Haley hesitated. While they attempted to run the station as professionally as possible, Shadow was a relatively small community. People knew and cared about each other. She had to ask.

"Nobody was injured, were they, Mitch?"

"No. I'm on my way back to base. Hank and Wayne have this under control out here."

"Ten-four."

Haley quickly called the state dispatcher and gave him the van's description, noting that the plates were most likely covered with paint or mud.

She had just finished writing information from the last of three more calls, with the last two describing the same van, when Mitch walked in.

"Any more calls?" He looked down at her paper.

Haley nodded. "Two more sightings of the van, both late last night, both unable to see the license plates."

He reached over and pulled a chair out before he sank onto it. "Haley, there's something I don't think I'll ever understand."

"What's that?"

Mitch took his hat off and studied the brim. "We've got people who call in if somebody is parked a couple of inches over the line. Yet, at least four people saw a strange van at or near White's last night, and not a one of them thought to pick up the phone and let us know. We might have caught the vandals before they completely destroyed the shop."

Haley thought about it. "I don't know, Mitch. I'd like to say even if I didn't have this job, I would have called, but the truth is, I don't know. If I were on my way home from work or a long day with kids, the oddity of the vehicle might catch my attention—until something else made me forget it. Then, I would put it out of my mind until something triggered the memory. Something like seeing the police where I saw the vehicle."

"That makes sense," the sheriff allowed.

"If you don't mind telling me, were there a lot of things stolen? I can't imagine Pete and Joni keeping much cash on hand." One of Haley's favorite things about her job was when Mitch sat and shared information with her. He claimed she was a good person to bounce ideas off of.

"That's another weird thing." Mitch leaned forward. "They only take their money to the bank once a week, every Friday morning. So, burglars hit it on a Thursday night, when the most money possible was there."

"Who would be aware of that?" They didn't even have any employees Haley knew of.

Mitch shrugged. "You tell me, and we'll both know."

"Will their insurance cover everything?" She hoped the Whites wouldn't lose their only source of income.

"Joni was on the phone with Clay Richmond when I left. He's their agent now since his grandfather retired and moved to Nevada."

"He should help." When Clay moved back to Shadow five months ago, many people in town had been less than thrilled with his taking over Richmond Insurance. Word on the street now, though, was that even though he appeared to be a little overly fond of himself and slightly pushy, he was an honest, fair-minded agent. He was rapidly developing a good business reputation.

Mitch stood up. "I'd better get to my office and try to catch up on some of that paperwork. I sure hope I'm wrong, but I have a feeling this robbery is going to cause us more problems yet." He took a few steps toward his office door before he turned back to face her. "Tell me right away if we have a caller who raises a red flag. I want to stay on top of this. Shadow doesn't need another drama."

Haley watched her boss walk into his office and sit down behind his desk. She knew he was referring to the kidnapping of Holly Walker. It turned out there were actually two men after her, for very different reasons. Mixed in with the whole mess had been a group of teenagers vandalizing Luke's farm. Poor Mitch had spread his three deputies as thin as he could, having to leave

Hank on protective detail for Holly a large part of the time. He was forced to do something that he tried not to—ask the state police to step in and help. At least the county board had been obliged to hire two more deputies as a consequence. The public outcry had seen to that. To placate their constituents, the board even set aside emergency funding to hire yet one more officer if the situation ever demanded it.

The ringing bell told her somebody had come into the station. Haley couldn't stop a genuine smile when she saw Matt Ashford walking toward her.

"Hey, pretty lady." The easy-going truck driver in his mid-fifties winked as he placed his hands on the counter.

"You big flirt." If Haley had been blessed to have an uncle, she'd want one just like the man in front of her. "What are you doing in town?"

His brows rose over his blue eyes as his grin widened. "Don't try to play innocent with me, Haley. That speed trap Jeff Fielding sets up southwest of town is your biggest moneymaker."

"You got another speeding ticket?"

His handsomely gray-flecked hair flopped onto his forehead as he nodded. "I'll have you know that on my complete route between St. Louis and Milwaukee, this is the only town I have to come in and pay parking and speeding tickets."

"That's because our department is so efficient." She accepted the paper he held out. "Let me pull this up on the computer."

"So, has Wayne found your prince charming for you yet?" Matt teased her as she typed his information on the computer.

She didn't take her eyes off the monitor as she answered. "I think I'll just wait for my prince charming to come along on his own."

"Well, you know if I were twenty years younger, I'd be right there on my white steed." Haley's eyes met his before she rolled hers.

"You probably have a woman in every city on your route you talk to like that."

He placed both hands over his heart and comically staggered. "You slay me! There's no way I could stop in every city on my route." She looked up in time to catch his wink. "So, I only have five or six regulars."

Haley pressed the enter key to print out the correct form for him. "You have a big fine this time, Matt. Why were you in such a hurry?"

Matt placed his wallet on the counter and withdrew some bills. "It's Luke's fault. He ordered that fertilizer he's trying for the university, and the silly stuff came in bags. Hardy and I had to unload them by hand. It took me three times as long as it usually does to make a delivery out to his farm."

She slid the sheet across the counter for him to sign. "That's the price you have to pay when your boss is good friends with a farmer." Sky Randolph, the owner of Sky Trucking, frequently had Matt make special deliveries to the Walker farm. When Sky and his fledgling company relocated to Shadow from

St. Louis five or six months ago, he'd lost no time in reconnecting with his old college buddy, Luke Walker.

"Hey!" Matt stopped writing on the form and looked at her, a broad grin on his face. "There's a prince charming for you!"

Haley was flummoxed. "What are you talking about? Sky and Bobbi Jo have three kids."

Matt shook his head. "Not him. Hardy." His smile grew even wider. "Beau Harding is about your age, and he's single. I know both of you, and I'm telling you right now you'd make a great couple."

Only Beau Harding wasn't really Beau Harding. Even if he did know she was alive, she had no interest in a man who wasn't even using his real name.

She pointed to the paper in front of him and tried to look stern. "Just sign it, please."

The phone rang before he could pop off again. Haley turned to answer it.

"Shadow County Sheriff's office."

"This is only the beginning." The line went dead the instant the unfamiliar male voice finished speaking.

Haley shook her head as she turned back to Matt. "I guess a telemarketer didn't realize he was calling the police station until I answered." What a cheesy sales pitch, anyway. "If this is the way they advertise, they may as well fold up shop and sell pet rocks."

She pushed the call out of her mind as she accepted the signed and dated form Matt handed her, along with enough cash to cover his fine.

"Just a second and I'll give you your copy."

"So, what about Hardy?" Apparently, Matt hadn't given up on his matchmaking quest. I'll put a bug in his ear to ask you out the next time I run into him. Okay?"

She sighed as she handed him the paper. "No, it's not. I don't want to be fixed up with anybody, Matt. When the right guy comes along, he and I will both know it. It will be as simple as that."

Matt gave her a skeptical look. "But how will either one of you know if you're right for each other if you don't try it first?"

"Look, Matt." She would just be as honest as she could. "Even if I were willing, which I'm not," she emphasized, "I ran into him just the other night, and he didn't even look at me twice. The man isn't interested in me at all. So, you're wasting your breath."

The ringing bell announcing somebody's arrival stopped whatever Matt was about to say. He glanced over his shoulder and then back at Haley.

"Okay. I give up for now."

"Good." She smiled at him as he left. He didn't mean any harm, and she really did like Matt.

"Hi, Mrs. Ewing. How may I help you?" Jennifer Ewing had taken Matt's place at the counter.

"I need to apply for a homecoming fundraiser permit."

Haley was soon involved in the business of her job, and her chat with Matt was all but forgotten until later that evening when she walked into her empty apartment.

She needed a pet, she thought not for the first time. But the only kind of pets her building permitted was fish. While Haley thought fish tanks were pretty to look at, she had absolutely no desire to clean one. Besides, the one time she had a goldfish, it had gone the way of the septic system a few days after she and her dad brought it home from the fair.

Her dad. She still felt like crying when she thought of her parents, despite that they had been gone for nearly twelve years. And it wasn't like she didn't know where they were. They had both accepted Jesus long before they became parents, and made sure their only child knew him as well.

With no other family, the three of them had been an exceptionally close unit. Larry and Julie Johnson were the best parents any girl could have asked for. Haley's dad had been a security guard at a factory in the small Ohio town where they lived, and her mom was a full-time wife and mother.

Between church and school activities, Haley experienced a nice, full life growing up. Then, to celebrate her high school graduation and acceptance to Kent State, they decided to spend a week on a beach in South Carolina. It had been one of the happiest times in Haley's life . . . until the day they planned to leave for home. At Haley's request, they decided to get back in the ocean just one last time. Then, her mom had gotten caught in what the officials referred to as rip current. When Haley's dad was trying to help her, he, too was pulled under. It was only because a burly man grabbed her and held fast that she didn't join them.

Even though the life guards were quick and efficient, they were no match for the ocean. They simply couldn't get her parents out of the water in time. Haley's final image of the beach was her parents' still bodies lying on it. She didn't think she'd want to be on a beach again for as long as she lived.

She made a few changes in her life after her parents 'deaths. Instead of entering into law enforcement, like her dad encouraged, she instead decided she wanted to dispatch. After earning her bachelor's degree in communication, Haley had gone on to receive certification to be a police dispatcher. When she came across the position for Shadow County Dispatcher posted on a website, she applied and was hired.

So, a small town girl from Ohio ended up living in a slightly smaller city in Illinois. And while she didn't have any family, many of the people she'd gotten to know during the nine years in Shadow had taken her under their wings. Haley didn't really feel like she was left alone.

Except times like this, she thought as she placed a container of leftover crock pot pizza in the microwave. She could only pray what she'd told Matt was true. That when the man she was meant to be with came along, they would both know it and it would work out. And, no matter how attractive she found Beau Harding, there was no way anything could work out between them. Not with him already lying—even if he were interested.

Maybe next time she fell at his feet, she'd be holding something a bit more glamorous. "Oh, excuse me I didn't mean to drop my earrings on your feet." Giggle, giggle. Of course, that would happen.

Put him out of your mind, she instructed herself sternly. There was no sense in dreaming about a man who was wrong for her in so many ways. He may not even be a Christian, which was her number one criteria for a romantic interest. In fact, if he were living a lie, he probably wasn't a believer.

Haley shifted her thinking back to the robbery at White's Salon. Of all the places in Shadow, why would a criminal choose a salon to rob and vandalize? It was right across the street from a strip mall, where any one of the stores probably took in more money in one day than Pete and Joni did a week. Was there something personal motivating the robber?

Not for the first time, Haley thanked God the scope of her job was to take messages and make calls. She'd hate to be in Mitch's shoes right now.

Chapter 8

"If we can put that sofa against the north wall, won't those two chairs fit by the window?" Holly Walker looked critically at the furniture and spaces in question.

"Sweetheart, I just don't think we can fit two houses worth of furniture into one." It wasn't the first time Luke had pointed that out.

She sighed. "I know." Her gaze swept from the sofa Hardy and Barney Nettles, an EMT for Mercy General Hospital and friend of Luke and Holly's, had moved at least a dozen times, to the other one. In Hardy's opinion, the dark green sofa did not coordinate with the lavender striped one they were carting all over creation. Besides, who needed two sofas?

"Why don't you sell your house furnished?" Holly's good friend and Mitch's fiancée, Tessa Lincoln, suggested. "You can pick and choose what you like from both households and put the rest in your house. No offense, Holly, but with it being so small, being furnished might make it more appealing to buyers."

"That's a good idea." Luke pounced on the suggestion. "And since I don't care which we keep, as long as I have a place to sit, I'll leave it up to you to decide which stays and which goes."

Hardy looked at Barney, at the other end of the sofa, and nearly laughed at the other man's exasperated expression. The two of them had loaded two borrowed panel trucks with every piece of furniture from Holly's house in town and driven them to the farm. Now, it looked like they would be taking two loads back—if Holly ever decided what she wanted.

"I guess we'll keep the solids in here." Holly looked skeptically at the striped sofa. "My stuff just doesn't seem right for a farm house, does it?"

"I like your bedroom suit better, Holly," Luke was quick to say. "My bed here matches your dresser and chest of drawers, so we can keep the king-size bed and put the rest of your furniture in the bedroom."

"Oh, for cryin' out loud." The muttered words came from Barney's end of the sofa.

"What did you say, Barney?" Holly looked at him apologetically. "I'm sorry I wasn't paying attention."

The EMT's face turned beet red as he stammered, "I thought I saw a rain cloud."

Hardy had to bite his tongue hard enough that it hurt to keep from cracking up when both Holly and Tessa peered intently out the picture window. Although Luke didn't say anything, the smile on his face and the fact that he wouldn't make eye contact with the other two men told Hardy he'd heard Barney's exact words.

Then it became even funnier when Tessa turned to Holly. "It must have blown over. I don't see a thing."

"The window is dirtier than I thought." Holly reached up and wiped the glass with her fingers before turning back to Barney.

"I think you must have seen that dirt on the window, Barney. The sky is clear."

"So, did you want this sofa back on the truck?" Hardy not only felt sorry enough for Barney to rescue him, he didn't plan on being at this job until midnight. The day had already seemed too long and was an end to a seemingly interminable week. So far he hadn't heard any news of his identity leaking out. He had to trust Mitch was staying true to his word and taking care of it.

"I guess we'll have to get everything out of the trucks." Holly bit her lower lip. "Then I'll decide what goes back to town."

Luke looked at his watch. "It's one o'clock, sweetheart. The guys have been at this since six this morning. I imagine those pancakes have worn off by now."

Hardy hadn't even thought about food. He just wanted to be finished with this task. Why hadn't he come up with a viable excuse when Luke asked him to help? If Luke hadn't hired his teenage employees to come and spend their Saturday morning doing chores, Hardy would've had the excuse of farming.

His mind wandered as the others discussed lunch plans. Something about Barney's muttered words had given him an idea. What if he had misunderstood his dad's words? He needed to hear them aloud again. Maybe if he wrote them down and read them repeatedly, something would click, and it would make sense. Of course, it was more likely wishful thinking. His mom was probably right, and his dad's words were misfiring between his brain and mouth.

"What about you, Hardy?" Luke's voice pulled him back to the real world. "Would you rather have a submarine sandwich or pizza for lunch?"

"Whatever everybody else wants is fine with me." He just wanted to be finished moving furniture.

"That won't cut it, Mister." Tessa walked over and stood in front of him. "You are the tie breaker. Holly and I want subs, and the men want pizza. So, what's it going to be?"

Hardy thought about the end results. "Which would be quicker?"

"Subs!" Holly and Tessa both declared.

"Then subs sound good to me."

"Fine. Side with the women. He hasn't looked at the color of my eyes, has he, Barney?" Luke batted his eyelids which, given his size, sent both women to laughing.

"The subs were Hardy's idea in the first place." Holly gestured toward him. "We're just the front people for the job. He's behind it all."

Hardy just wished they'd all quit kidding around and get lunch. "I'll just go out and start emptying the back truck while we wait for food to get here."

"I'll go with him." Barney looked as relieved as Hardy felt to be getting out of the house.

"Women," Barney muttered as they headed for the truck. "I don't think I'm ever going to get married. What about you?"

Hardy could give an honest answer to that question. Given the lifestyle and secrecy necessary to be Joe Ryman, it was a no-brainer. "The thought never crossed my mind."

The two men were just hauling the dining room table out of the back truck, amazingly emptying the vehicle, when the women pulled up.

"That's just peachy." Barney was muttering again. "They're multiplying."

Hardy looked at the car to see what the other man meant. Holly and Tessa got out of the front of the car, and an extremely attractive woman with long, blonde hair got out of the back. She looked vaguely familiar, but he couldn't quite place her.

"Look who we found!" Holly was speaking to Luke, who had come out of the house to greet her. He was supposed to have been resting inside, but Hardy heard furniture scooting. He had no problem remembering the last three or four weeks of his recovery and how it was so hard to follow the doctor's advice.

"What?" Luke was talking to their newest arrival. "Mitch let you out of the dungeon?"

She had the most melodious laugh Hardy had ever heard and those dimples . . .

"This is my Saturday off. Mavis is on duty today."

Mitch. Sheriff Mitch Landon. And this woman was talking about being on duty. "Is she a police officer?" he quietly asked Barney. He hadn't heard of a female deputy in Shadow.

Barney had admiration on his face as he looked at her. "She may as well be. Haley Johnson is the best dispatcher in the state, as far as I'm concerned. We never have any problems making ambulance calls when she's on the radio."

Haley Johnson. Hardy remembered her now. He'd seen her around town, and she came out to the farm with Holly one day before the Walkers moved. Holly had politely introduced them, and then the two women disappeared into the house.

Hardy hadn't even seen them leave. They were gone when he came in from the south field.

He didn't remember her being this attractive, though. His defenses went up like a brick wall. Harding Beau Davis did not have even a sliver of life he could devote to a relationship. Women, particularly one who affected him like Haley Johnson did, were dangerous and to be avoided at all costs.

"Come on in and eat!" Holly called as she linked her arm with her husband's and started for the house.

"Yes, Hardy." Barney stuck out his arm. "Come on in and eat. We'd better hurry before Holly decides she wants this table and chairs in the house to eat on."

Hardy looked at the other man's arm and the comical expression on his face, and for the first time in a long time, laughed.

Chapter 9

Beau Harding had what Haley's mom would call contagious laughter. Even though she had no idea what he found so funny, she had a hard time not joining in and laughing right along with him.

She looked at him as he took a seat across from her at the breakfast bar. Not counting their literal run-in at the drugstore, this was the closest she'd been to him—and she couldn't help but notice what a handsome man Beau Harding was. His sand-colored hair touched his collar and was just shaggy enough to tell her it needed a trim. When he looked up from his sandwich and into her eyes, her heart skipped a beat. His gray eyes seemed to see into her very being.

Haley needed to get a grip. For one thing, she wasn't so desperate for a husband she was reduced to hunting one. For another, and still the most important, Beau Harding wasn't who he said he was. Even if they somehow connected, she would never be able to trust a single word he said. One lie led to others, and if he lied about who he was . . . No. She mentally placed a big red X over his face

Neither Holly nor Tessa said a word about him helping move them when they invited Haley. Of course, they may have assumed Haley would realize the man who worked for them would naturally be there. Either way, from now on, Haley would just stay away from the stranger who called himself Beau Harding. That was the best plan.

"Hardy, do you remember Haley?" Holly had caught them looking at each other and smiled craftily.

"Yes." Well, wasn't he the talker? Maybe Haley should just grunt at him. Just because she had decided to avoid him didn't give him cause for rudeness. And somewhere in Haley's mixed-up mind, that reasoning was logical.

Barney Nettles very impolitely snorted. "Holly, Haley, Hardy . . . I don't guess the rest of us can join your club."

"Club? Why we're going to take our act on the road!" Holly gestured toward her "H-name" cohorts. "We'll be Triple H, and we'll play in the main coliseums around the country."

"Play what?" Luke's brow shot up. "Because I hope you're not threatening to sing to people, sweetheart. It's bad enough when the people at church look at us like they think I'm hurting you."

"Oh, I sound like I'm in pain?" The twinkle in Holly's eyes belied her stern voice. "At least Clarence doesn't sit outside the bathroom door and howl when I sing in the shower."

"Okay. I give. I sound like a quartet of tone-deaf frogs with sore throats." Luke grinned and took a big bite of his sandwich.

Hardy was laughing again, and Haley found herself enjoying the sound entirely too much. "I've already had my lunch, Holly. How about if I go ahead and start putting the clothes away?"

"Are you sure you don't want half my sub?" Holly held it out.

"I had warmed up lasagna. If I eat another bite, I won't be able to help you at all." She stood up. "Which room am I working in?"

The sound of the doorbell kept Holly from answering her question. Instead, she asked Haley to see who it was.

Haley opened the door to find Will Baxter on the top step, a package in his hands.

"Hi, Will," Haley greeted him.

"You mean Mitch let you out of the office?" Will grinned at her.

"Oh, I break out every once in a while." She looked at him standing there in his postal uniform. "What are you doing working on a Saturday? And not even your route."

He shrugged. "Slim called in sick, so I'm getting some overtime. I forgot how far out of town Luke and Holly Walker live, though." He glanced toward the large trucks he'd parked behind. "Looks like they're officially moving in."

"Yes." Haley felt the need to explain the furniture scattered across the lawn. "Holly is deciding which furniture she wants to keep here and which she's moving back to town."

Will frowned. "Who's moving this stuff? Has Luke been cleared for that kind of lifting?"

"Barney Nettles is here, and Beau Harding is helping."

"Hey, Will!" Luke spoke from beside Haley. "Oh, good. My new cookbook is here." He had apparently noticed the package in the mail carrier's hands.

Will handed it to Luke. "It wouldn't fit in your box, and I thought it was silly to leave a pick-up slip when you were here."

"Thank you." Luke stepped out onto the porch. "Have you been fishing out at Bertrand's lately?"

"Excuse me." Haley wasn't even sure the two men heard her as she left them talking about the joys of fishing. She'd just ask Holly where to work.

A few minutes later, Haley found herself alone in one of the extra bedrooms, folding Holly's summer clothes and putting them into a large chest of drawers. With the faint scent of jasmine on the fabric, she found herself relaxing as she took care of a mundane task. With all the details about the White's robbery making work more hectic than usual, she needed a break.

A shuffling noise brought her attention to the door, where Beau Harding stood, holding a large box.

He was obviously surprised to see her there. "I'm sorry. I didn't know anybody was in here. Holly asked me to bring this. It's full of psychology books or something. She wants them on the bookshelf." His eyes scanned the room and settled on the shelves taking up the entire north wall. "I guess I'll just put them on it for her."

"You can set the box down in front of them, and I'll take care of it as soon as I finish with these clothes." Haley didn't like the idea of working side by side with this man.

He appeared unsure of what he should do. "If you're sure you don't mind, then I can help Barney move more of the heavy stuff. I think Holly finally figured out which pieces she's keeping here and which ones are going back to town."

Before she could stop it, Haley yawned. "I'm sorry." She felt her face warm and knew she was blushing.

Hardy looked like he'd rather be walking barefoot through fire than socializing with her, but he spoke again. "You're a police dispatcher?"

"Yes."

"Been at the job very long?" He stepped over to the wall of shelves, carrying what had to be an incredibly heavy box with no visible effort.

"Nine years." Clarence was more sociable than Haley was at the moment. "It's usually a calm job, but, this past week was pretty rough."

"It's all over town about the beauty salon being robbed."

Of course, it was. "Pete and Joni White own the salon. They're very nice, and I guess we're all frustrated that no new leads have come in."

He seemed to be reluctantly interested. "Was much taken?"

"A week's worth of money. The burglars totally trashed the place, though."

A strange look came over Hardy's face. "Personal vendetta? Vandalism, with a spontaneous robbery?"

"We're not sure." Hardy reminded her of someone.

"Any leads? Suspicious people hanging around the last few days before it happened? Vehicles that shouldn't have been there?"

"We're asking everybody to keep an eye out for an older model dark blue or black panel van. We've had several people report seeing it in the vicinity of the salon the night before." Why did she feel like she'd already had this conversation?

Hardy shook his head. "It's a shame when people don't call something suspicious in when they see it. There'd be a lot better chance of catching the criminals."

Haley suddenly realized why this was all so familiar. Talking to Hardy was just like talking to Mitch. Hardy sounded like a—

"Are you a police officer?" The question came out before she could stop it.

He froze, a deer in the headlights look on his face. Then, shutters came down over his eyes, and his expression went decidedly neutral.

"I'd better help Barney." He turned and strode out of the room before Haley could say another word.

She set the top she'd been folding on her lap and looked at the empty doorway. She was ninety-nine percent sure she'd just discovered something the man calling himself Beau Harding didn't want to be known. He was, or at least had been, in some type of law enforcement. He slid all too quickly into the smooth pattern of knowing which questions to ask to elicit the most information. Why would a police officer live under an assumed name? Could he be some kind of fugitive? The subject of an internal investigation getting away from the area while he was under the gun?

She was still puzzling over her discovery thirty minutes later while she placed books on the shelves. Mitch had assured her there weren't any laws being broken, but it wouldn't be illegal to help a fellow officer get away from a messy investigation. And as for the calls concerning him, there had been about a dozen during the two or three days after Mitch gave her a heads up, and then they stopped.

Why couldn't Haley have been one of the people who saw that television program? She'd come awfully close to asking callers more specific questions, but that wasn't her job. In fact, it would have been very wrong since she'd only be asking to satisfy her curiosity. So, all she knew from the calls was a man who looked just like Beau Harding had been on a television show.

"Wow." Tessa's voice drew her from her thoughts as Haley looked at the other woman standing there with her gaze on the bookshelves. "You've been busy."

Haley slid the book in her hand into the space she'd opened for it. "I tried to put them in some kind of order, but when it comes to Holly's psychology books, I have no idea how to sort them."

Tessa leaned over and looked closely at the top shelf of books nearest her. "Built Up, not Let Down, Using Our Assets. Let's Go!" She giggled. "These sound more like exercise books than ones she needs for counseling."

"Well, I'm down here getting jealous right now." Haley pointed to the books she was kneeling before. "She has the most Brandilyn Collins and Terri Blackstock books I've ever seen outside of a library. There are at least five of these I haven't read."

"She likes Christian suspense." Tessa wrinkled her nose as she sat on the edge of the bed. "They give me bad dreams. I collect Mary Connealy and Karen Kingsbury, myself."

Haley looked at the book in her hands. "I like them all. I think I've read everything the library has. I'm waiting on the newest one by Liz Curtis Higgs to come from another library in the system right now." She had never felt the need to own books; she'd always used the library.

"I'm sure Holly would let you borrow any of these, and you're welcome to mine, too," Tessa graciously offered. "Mitch is having more shelves put in the office at his house so I can fit my books in it. He told me at first he thought he'd just build a new room."

"Are you ready for your wedding?" Haley went back to putting books on the shelf.

Tessa's smile lit up her entire face. "Mitch told me he'd marry me tomorrow. Just get a license and rings and have Pastor Rollins marry us on the spot. He doesn't care how we do it. He just wants to marry me."

"He loves you." Haley fought back the envy she felt. If she were meant to be married, the right man would come along. "He has your picture in so many places at the station Wayne told him visitors probably think you're a wanted fugitive."

Tessa's smile dimmed. "I just hope he catches whoever robbed Whites soon. I'm not sure if he'll enjoy our wedding while he's still worried about it. Mitch is very frustrated that there hasn't at least been another sighting of that van."

"I know." He'd been keeping all five officers on the road most of the time, as well as having Haley frequently contact the state police for any updates. Cheryl Higgens, one of the state police dispatchers, had asked Haley if maybe they shouldn't string tin cans between their offices. Even though the state police would notify county if there was any news, they understood

Mitch's need to check for himself. Things like this just didn't happen in Shadow.

"Has he been okay at work?" Tessa's voice was soft, as though hesitant to ask the question.

Haley glanced at her friend and nodded. "Like you said, he's frustrated, but he's got a good head on his shoulders. He has the deputies and state police working the county in grids. I couldn't have ever organized it as efficiently as Mitch did." If the van was still in the vicinity, they would find it.

Tessa knelt beside her and pulled a book out of the box. "I'm not sure if I'll be a good sheriff's wife."

"What makes you say that?" Haley was stunned. Tessa Lincoln was the most confident woman she knew.

"I know Mitch is in God's hands, and he knows what he's doing." Tessa's smile was shaky. "But I'm still afraid. When he wrestled the gun away from Kevin Tripp, it could have been Mitch who was shot instead of Luke." She rushed to qualify her statement. "Not that I want Luke to have been shot. I guess I've seen too many television programs where the person trying to take the gun away from the criminal gets shot with it. My imagination gets away from me."

Haley sat back on her heels and looked into Tessa's eyes. "You have every right to be afraid. But, you're right about whose Hands Mitch is in." She searched for words to help the other woman. "Lori Daniels has been a police officer's wife for nearly fifteen years. I'm sure she struggles with fear for Wayne, too. Maybe you could talk to her and see how she handles it, because they are one of the most secure, happy couples I know."

Hope shone in Tessa's eyes. "You're right. I forgot Wayne and Lori. She's a good wife—the kind I want to be. I'll call her tomorrow afternoon and see if we can get together one evening next week."

"Good." Haley pulled the last book out of the box. Then she had a thought. Mitch told Tessa everything. How would it hurt to ask a general question? "What do you know about Beau Harding?"

"Other than the fact that he's not hard to look at?" Tessa was back in her usual cheerful mood. "I think he's from up north somewhere."

Haley had heard he was from Wisconsin. "Do you know what he did for a living before he came to work for Luke and Holly?"

Tessa frowned as she thought. "I guess I don't." Her brows lifted as she looked at Haley questioningly. "Isn't that strange? He's been living here nearly six months, and I don't think anybody has ever said a word about what he did before he came here."

Holly's voice calling Tessa's name came from the living room.

Tessa stood up. "I'd better see what she wants. She's probably trying to decide whether to let poor Luke keep his favorite recliner. The old thing is a horrendous shade of green, but Luke loves it."

Haley shared a smile with her friend before watching Tessa leave the room. She slowly stood up and looked once more at the bookshelves. She had learned something else.

Whatever Beau Harding's secret was; it was important enough Mitch hadn't even shared it with his fiancée. The man was even more of an enigma. Why was she so drawn to him? Why couldn't she just forget he was even there?

I know I have too much curiosity sometimes, Lord, but this time, I'm more intrigued than I've ever been before. If I'm supposed to leave this alone, then help my thinking shift. If I'm supposed to find out about Beau Harding, please help me do so. And You know I'm troubled by the feelings he's causing—even though I don't know him and don't feel like I can trust him. If he's a bad guy, open my eyes before it's too late. Keep me away from him. Please. I have a feeling about him that I've never had before, and I'm not sure I like it. I'm putting myself in Your hands and asking for your protection and guidance. Amen.

Chapter 10

He hung up the phone and sat back in his chair. It was as he'd been told; Harding Davis didn't seem to have settled in Shadow. It might be that he hadn't been in Shadow long enough to care about anybody yet. The former police officer would, though.

And when Davis did, he would be right there to take everything Davis loved away from him. It wouldn't do to simply end his life. Not if he wanted to continue the charade he'd been involved in during the past several months. If the wrong people discovered his real motives for ridding the world of Davis, everything would fall apart. There was already one weak component as it was, but he'd been assured it was under control.

He still had to stay informed of any progress H.B. Davis made. If it were necessary, he would be the first thing Harding Davis would lose. And it wouldn't be as difficult as he first thought.

Chapter 11

Hardy lifted the second giant bag of dog food onto the counter.

"Clarence Walker's favorite brand," the friendly woman at the register observed as she rang up the price.

"He eats enough to keep a small kennel in business." Hardy had found himself reluctantly drawn into the habit of making small talk. He'd soon realized it was much easier to just respond than draw attention by being rude. It was really just another undercover technique when all was said and done.

Wilma Ebhart, the co-owner of the grocery store, chuckled. "Luke has spoiled that dog since Clarence was a pup. I have to special order this brand just for him." Her smile dissipated as concern replaced it. "How is Luke? When will he be able to work on the farm again?"

"The doctor released him yesterday for light duty. Two more weeks until he's back to his usual routine." He didn't know who had been happier about his boss's recovery—Luke or his wife.

Since the couple moved to the farm, things had changed. With no visitors stopping in to see him, Luke was bored to tears every day.

To pass the time, Luke had taken to watching cooking shows on TV. Holly never knew what kind of cuisine she might come home to. And unfortunately, the Walkers still insisted on saving leftovers for Hardy's lunch. Just today Hardy had eaten something called cheesy Italian tortellini and a Tiramisu Brownie bar. Fancy food was something Hardy had never grown accustomed to, even while undercover. Spending a large portion of his childhood in a rural area conditioned him to be a strictly meat and potatoes man.

"What are you going to do when Luke's able to get back on the tractor?" Wilma didn't strike Hardy as a gossipy woman; she merely appeared curious. "Do you have another job lined up around here?"

"I haven't made firm plans for anything yet." And if he had, he wouldn't be able to share them. When it was time, Beau Harding would have to disappear just like Harding Davis had.

A look of deep sadness appeared on Wilma's face. Hardy was uncertain what to think until he realized she was looking past him at somebody outside the window. "That boy had it all, you know, and he just threw it away."

Hardy considered picking up the dog food and acting like he hadn't heard her, but his mother had raised him with better manners than that. "Who is he?"

Her gaze left the young man and refocused on Hardy. "That's Sammy Lewis. He was all set to go to college after he graduated last spring. He was one of the best high school quarterbacks the state has ever seen. Most folks thought he'd go pro for sure. But he didn't even graduate."

"Why not?" The sooner she told him, the sooner he'd get out of there.

"He got mixed up with the man who kidnapped Holly Walker. He and some other boys stole some pretty expensive property from the school and vandalized Luke's farm. The teenagers all ended up in jail. I guess Sammy earned a GED while he was in there, but now, he can't even get a college to look at him. I heard Mr. Randolph over at the dry cleaner's just hired him."

She had managed to pique Hardy's interest. Without going into the specifics, Luke had told him there had been a series of bizarre pranks played on him, and the farm was vandalized. He hadn't said anything about it being connected to Holly's kidnapping. "He couldn't have received a very harsh sentence if he's already out."

Wilma smiled proudly. "Luke and Holly spoke to the judge. They thought the boys were taken in by a person much different than anybody else they'd ever known. The Walkers believed the boys really only saw what they were doing as being paid money to pull pranks." She patted the bag of dog food as though it were Hardy's shoulder. "While they didn't condone it, they didn't want the young men placed into situations that might result in them changing for the worse."

Unfortunately, that was too often the case. What his squad used to call toe dippers were tempted by more experienced criminals. Law breakers on the borderline frequently ended up with worse behaviors, sometimes needing to be like their fellow inmates to stay safe. The despondency of the young man Mrs. Ebhart called Sammy woke something up Hardy had considered long gone. He wanted to help the boy.

He needed to tune back into the real world. She was still talking.

"They all ended up with some kind of sentences, but Sammy was let out after four months for good behavior. He'll be on probation for another year, now, I think."

Luke hadn't shared that information with Hardy either. He and his wife apparently not only forgave the teenagers; they went to bat for them. Who did something like that?

My mom and dad would. Even though his father was a retired police officer and had dealt with just about every type of crime imaginable, he managed to come through with a strong faith in place. Hardy once foolishly believed he'd be able to do the same.

"That was kind of them." Hardy would only bring danger to the young man; he shoved the idea of helping the boy clear out the window. He moved the top bag of dog food to the cart and threw the second one over his shoulder. "I'd better get this to the farm before Clarence realizes he's run out."

"Take care of yourself, Mr. Harding." Wilma sounded sincere. "And I hope you know you're welcome to attend our church. I go to the one across the interstate."

"Thank you." Hardy turned to leave and about mowed down the man who had walked up beside him. "Excuse me. I didn't see you there."

The man with blonde hair and a dark tan that were both too perfect to be natural smiled at him "It was my own fault. I should have realized you wouldn't be able to see me."

Hardy tried to smile as he started to leave.

"You're Beau Harding, aren't you?"

Hardy stopped pushing the cart and left one hand on it as he turned back to the other man. "Yes., but I don't believe I've had the pleasure."

"Oh, of course. I'm just so used to everybody recognizing me." He stuck out his hand and then must have realized Hardy had his hands full. "I'm Clay Richmond. I run the insurance agency at the end of the block."

Insurance salesmen were right up there with root canals on Hardy's list of things to avoid whenever possible. "It's nice to meet you." He turned and headed for the door.

"Please come by the office sometime soon." Clay Richmond's voice came from behind him. "It's never too late to get good coverage. I can beat whatever policies you have on your truck and camper."

Hardy looked over his shoulder and nodded. He didn't own the truck or camper, and no matter how good of an agent this Richmond guy was, the FSA wouldn't be hiring him. Anyway, Hardy would be out of the area in two weeks. After over five months without running into Clay Richmond, he could surely avoid him for another couple of weeks.

The door opened just as he reached it, and Matt Ashford walked in." Hey, Hardy, let me help you with that."

"Thanks." If Hardy had made any friends in Shadow, Matt was one of them. He drove a truck for a company based right there in town. Matt's route took him from St. Louis to Milwaukee, but he seemed to gravitate toward Shadow. Hardy had met him when Matt dropped a load of supplies off at the farm.

"Let me guess." Matt lifted the bag of dog food off the cart and dropped it over the edge into the bed of Hardy's pickup. "Clay Richmond can beat whatever insurance you already have."

Hardy dropped the bag he was carrying beside the other one. "Who told you?"

Matt snorted. "Oh, he'll beat their cost all right. And then he'll sit there and talk in circles until you end up with nearly twice as much coverage as you need and spending even more than you had been."

Hardy turned and leaned against the truck. "He's that bad?"

His buddy shook his head. "He's that good."

"You talk like a man with experience."

Matt shrugged. "I'm covered for just about any kind of calamity you can imagine. I'm pretty sure I even have hurricane insurance."

"Now you're pulling my leg." Matt's sense of humor was one of the things Hardy liked about him right off. The other was Matt had no roots and seemed to be content. Hardy had pulled his up and could no longer allow himself to settle in one place for very long. Matt lived that way by choice. The only home he had was the cab of his semi-truck.

Matt's grin faded. "Have you given any more thought to my offer? Luke's going to be back in action soon, and you'll be out of a job."

"I don't know if truck driving is for me." Hardy had thought long and hard about accepting the job of driving a route between Springfield, Missouri and Milwaukee, Wisconsin. He'd be able to swing by Chicago for short visits with his family, and nobody would be looking for Harding Davis to be driving a semi. The thought of what the agency might do in response to that job concerned him. He might be able to make it without their help, but he couldn't leave his family without it. "Can I let you know next week?"

"Sure." Matt smiled genially. "Sky says it's yours if you want it."

"Joe Ryman" had kept a CDL, which Beau Harding managed to inherit, so the necessary licensing wouldn't be an issue. "I'll let you know."

"Why don't we check out the diner and have a piece of pie?" Matt gestured toward the building across the street. "I can stop back by for the groceries I need afterward."

Hardy checked his watch. "Okay, but I won't be able to stay long. I have some work to do on a silo, and it's starting to get dark earlier."

The two men walked across the street and to the diner. They were soon seated at Hardy's regular table. A waitress with a remarkable resemblance to Andy Griffith's Aunt Bee and a nametag reading Sandra waited on them.

Hardy had just taken a bite of peach cobbler when the hair on the back of his neck stood up. He knew the feeling well. He was being watched. The spoon next to his saucer hit the floor loudly after he unobtrusively knocked it off. Then he used the movement of picking it up to scan the room, which was more crowded than he was used to.

"Clumsy much?" Matt kidded, apparently unaware that anything was amiss.

"I guess." Hardy hadn't seen anybody who stood out. One man had been looking at him, but Hardy was pretty sure it was simply because he'd caught his attention by picking up the spoon. At least he was sure of one thing. He hadn't seen any members of the Dohner organization. And unless Ted had done some recruiting, Hardy was familiar enough with the men who would come after him to recognize them. It must have just been his imagination.

"So, what do you have to get done during your last two weeks on the farm?" Matt asked.

Their conversation resumed, and Hardy pushed the incident out of his mind, certain he was safe.

Chapter 12

He put the phone on the table. It appeared that Harding Davis was making friends after all. But his time in Shadow was coming to a close, and that simply wouldn't do. There would have to be a reason for him to choose to stay. Something that would pique his interest. A woman? Maybe, but two weeks wasn't really enough time. That would come after Hardy made Shadow his home. Davis needed something else . . . something that would tempt him enough to bring him at least partially out of hiding. And he had an idea of what might work.

He smiled as he picked up the phone. He had his players, such as they were, in place; it was time to set his plan in motion.

Chapter 13

Haley automatically checked the time as she answered the emergency phone. Seven-thirteen.

"Shadow County Sheriff's station."

"Haley, you've got to send Mitch over here right away. It's terrible." The caller's voice was unrecognizable beneath the panic.

"Okay. Slow down and tell me your name and where you're calling from." She spoke clearly and firmly.

"It's Tina Foster, and I'm at the clinic. Haley, they tore everything up and they . . . the dogs . . ." Tina broke into sobs.

"Sit tight, Tina. I'll have somebody there as quickly as possible. Just stay on the line."

Haley shoved the idea of what Tina was saying out of her mind and signaled Mitch on the radio.

"Base to sheriff. This is a code three. Repeat, code three to Shadow Animal Clinic."

"Landon here. Details." Mitch's deep voice came over the radio.

"We have a four-fifty-nine with possible multiple ten-ninety-one-D." They had a burglary, possibly with multiple dead animals. Codes Haley had never imagined using together.

"Ten-four. En route. Estimated ETA seven twenty-five. Radio Snow and Daniels for assistance."

"Ten-four."

Haley signaled the two deputies and repeated the codes. Then she picked up the receiver and pressed the lit button. "Tina, are you still there?"

"Who-who would do something like this?" The sheer horror in Tina's voice told Haley everything she needed to know.

"Mitch is on his way. He'll be there any moment. Are you still in the building?"

"No." Tina was crying again." I brought the cordless phone outside. I just couldn't stay inside with the—"

Haley heard the siren through the phone and knew Mitch had arrived. "Mitch is there now, Tina, so you can hang up. He'll take care of everything." The sound of Tina's sobbing stopped abruptly when the line went dead.

Somebody had broken into the animal clinic and not only trashed the place; they had also killed defenseless animals. Haley could only imagine what images Tina would have emblazoned on her brain.

"Landon to base." Mitch was calling on the radio.

"Base here."

"Call Dr. Waters at home. He needs to come down here ASAP."

"Ten-four."

Mitch's voice was softer. "Prepare him for multiple ten-ninety-one-Ds. Every one of them."

"Ten-four."

It wasn't often Haley heard her boss sound upset, but she heard deep dismay and disbelief in his voice. It must truly be a terrible scene.

She quickly located the veterinarian's phone number and dialed it.

"Good morning. Harold Waters speaking." The man spoke in his usual cheerful manner. Haley wished she didn't have to give him such bad news.

"Dr. Waters, this is Haley Johnson from the sheriff's station. I'm calling to inform you there's been a break-in at the clinic. The sheriff needs you there as soon as possible."

"A break-in?" Shock resonated in his voice. "What on earth would somebody want to steal from an animal clinic? Did they get into the medication?"

This was the hard part. "I'm not sure about theft, Doctor. I'm very sorry to tell you, though, there were no animals left alive."

"No animals . . . alive . . . Oh, my." Haley didn't speak as she gave the man time to gain control of his emotions. "I'll be there in a few minutes. This is just terrible."

"Yes, it is."

Haley sat at her station, unmoving, for a few minutes after hanging up. What was going on? Things like this didn't happen in Shadow. First, somebody had broken in and robbed the beauty salon and now this?

She took a few moments to pray for God to be with everybody at the animal clinic. They needed his strength and comfort.

Then there was one more phone call she needed to make. She picked up the phone and dialed a number from memory.

"Good morning. This is Pastor Rollins." The voice that had offered Haley instruction, redirection, and comfort during the past nine years nearly brought her to tears.

She took a deep breath to get her emotions under control. "Pastor, this is Haley Johnson."

"Well, hello, Haley. How are you this beautiful October morning?"

"Not so good right now. I'm calling to request the prayer chain be started."

His jovial manner was immediately replaced by concern. "What do you need?"

Confidentiality wasn't an issue with the pastor, as he knew how much he could share with his parishioners and what would need to be kept to himself. "There's been a break-in at the animal clinic. Tina discovered it when she got there this morning." A shiver ran up her spine. "The thing is, all the animals were…none of them were left alive. We can't provide details to others, but I think we need to pray for everybody who has to deal with this."

"We certainly do." There was a moment of silence. "Let's not forget to pray for the people who did this, Haley. They need God's help to set them straight."

This was a concept Haley struggled with, even though she understood it. "Okay."

"I'll get it started right away. Do you know where Tina is? I would like to go see her."

"Just a minute and I'll find out for you." Tina would undoubtedly appreciate a visit from Pastor Rollins. She was most likely frightened and horrified beyond words.

Rather than bothering the sheriff, Haley signaled for Wayne to phone the office.

"It's me, Haley." She couldn't remember the last time the jovial man had used her given name. This was going to be terrible for all of them.

"Wayne, I have Pastor Rollins on another line. He'd like to know where Tina is so he can visit her. Can you tell me?"

"She's gone home. Her husband came and took her home with him. She's pretty shaken up."

"It's that bad?" Haley was certain she knew the answer, but had to ask anyway.

"Haley, this is the stuff nightmares are made of. Nobody should have to see something like this."

"Any leads so far?"

"Not really. Jeff should be back at base any moment, though. He'll fill you in."

"I'm sorry for any of you who had to look at it. Thanks for calling, Wayne."

She pushed the button for line three. "Pastor, her husband took her home. The deputy said she's in pretty bad shape."

"Thank you. I'll get the chain started and get over to her house as quickly as possible."

They said their goodbyes and hung up.

Haley had just finished writing up the report on the call-in when Jeff Fielding walked through the door. One look at the pasty color of the usually robust man's face told Haley he had seen something awful.

"I got sick." Least sociable of the squad, he surprised Haley by sinking onto the spare chair. "I've seen car accidents and victims of abuse, but Haley, I've never seen anything like this."

"Let me get you something to drink." Haley left him sitting and staring into space while she went to the refrigerator in the back room. They kept it stocked with several different kinds of soft drinks and bottled water, and they used the honor system to pay for it. She took two dollar bills out of her jeans pocket and stuffed them into the jar on top of the appliance before she pulled out a bottle of soda and another of water. She wasn't sure which would help Jeff at this point.

He reached out and accepted the soft drink when she offered him his choice. The bottle was half empty when he pulled it away from his mouth.

"The thing is, I don't think Wayne or I saw the worst of it. There was something in one of the kennels Mitch wouldn't let anybody look at. He took the camera from Wayne and was in there for quite a while. Then he had Wayne working on paperwork with Doc Waters, and he sent me back here." His eyes had a haunted look in them as they met hers. "If what he was looking at was worse than the rest, I'm glad he didn't want me to see it."

"Are there any leads?"

Jeff shook his head. "Not yet. Once this makes the news, we'll probably have everybody and their grandma seeing strange people around town. Don't be surprised if Mitch pulls one of the other dispatchers in here to work with you for a while."

"That'll be fine." Haley reached over and placed her hand on his trembling arm. "Jeff, is there anything at all I can do to help you right now?"

He looked at her, his eyes still broadcasting his feelings all too well. "Does God care about animals?"

Another diametrical statement from the man who occasionally swore there was no God. "He cares about his entire creation." Maybe she could witness and offer him comfort at the same time. "The Bible tells that after God created the animals, he saw his creation was good. If he didn't care about them, he would have let them drown instead of insuring their repopulation by putting them on the ark."

The usual skepticism was absent on his face as he looked at her. "Then, pray, Haley. Pray we catch whoever did this before something else happens. Maybe something even worse."

The fact it was he who asked her to pray nearly brought tears to her eyes. God was at work with the officer.

"Would you like me to pray aloud?"

He didn't speak for a long moment, but then said, "Yes."

Pray. She could do that. She bowed her head and did as he asked.

Chapter 14

Hardy had just cleaned the last bit of pork roast from his plate when he heard the scrape of the chair across the table. Somehow, he wasn't surprised to see the sheriff sitting there.

"Afraid you'll have to eat alone this evening, Sheriff." He took a drink of his cola. "I was just about to leave."

"We need to talk, Davis." This was a different Mitch Landon than the one who had confronted him before. "And we can do it in here where we're liable to be overheard, or you can come to the station, and we'll have a private discussion in my office. But either way, we are going to talk."

Harding Beau Davis knew for a fact if he didn't want to go with the man sitting across the table from him, he wouldn't be going. One thing he'd learned during his years on the force was size didn't always matter. So, even with Landon's taller height and additional fifteen or twenty pounds, the sheriff wasn't going to get him to cooperate by intimidation.

The two men sat, looking into each other's eyes for what seemed like an hour. Neither was backing down. Hardy was impressed, despite himself.

"I'll go with you," he finally agreed, "but you've got five minutes, and then we're through."

Mitch nodded warily. "We'll see how you feel about that once we've talked a little."

Hardy didn't feel any differently about it when he sat on a chair in the sheriff's office, and he certainly wasn't inclined to extend his visit when Mitch told the dispatcher to notify him of emergency calls only, and then shut the door and locked it. The closed vertical blinds didn't tickle him pink, either.

"Just say what you have to say." He wasn't in the mood to channel his inner Jack Bauer.

Mitch opened a drawer and pulled out a folder. He placed it on his desk and stared at it as he began to talk.

"Yesterday morning, a break-in was discovered. The animal clinic out on the edge of town was totally trashed." He raised his eyes and looked directly at Hardy. "There were six dogs, two cats, and a rabbit being housed there. Not one of them was left alive."

"I'm sorry, Sheriff, but I don't see what that has to do with me." Hardy had a thought." You're not thinking I had something to do with it, are you?"

"You tell me." The sheriff slid the folder across the desk. Hardy opened it and immediately wanted to close it again. Instead, he steeled himself and looked. The folder was full of pictures of carnage. As he looked at them more closely, his trained eyes began to take in details. Things were not exactly what they appeared to be. He looked back up at the sheriff. "I still don't see what this has to do with me."

"Look at the last two pictures. Closely."

Hardy flipped through until he came to the bottom of the stack. At first, he couldn't make out anything different about the picture. He leaned closer and took a good look . . . and his heart kicked into overdrive.

Somebody had written something in blood. *For Davis.*

"Now, any ideas?" Mitch reached across and took the folder back. "Because your name is the only real evidence I've been able to find at the clinic. So far, there is nothing else of substance."

"Different Davis." Hardy sat back in his chair and leveled his gaze at the sheriff. "I guarantee you they haven't found me."

The sheriff's skepticism showed. "How can you guarantee that?"

That was an easy question to answer. "Because I'm still breathing."

Landon's gaze went from Hardy to the folder before finally resting back on Hardy's face. "I don't believe you're directly responsible for this, but I do have to consider the possibility somebody is trying to get your attention. A part of me wants to tell you to pack up and get out of town, but I'm not going to do that."

"Why not?" If the situation were reversed, he'd be packing Mitch's suitcase for him.

"Because you're a human being, and I'm not chasing you away from people who can help you. I know you ran from Chicago, and I understand why. But this is Shadow. We take care of our own, and like it or not, you've become one of us."

"For another week." This incident was all the more reason for Beau Harding to disappear.

The sheriff gave him an assessing look. "We'll see, Davis. We'll see."

Hardy stood up. "Yes, we will."

He felt the other man's eyes drilling holes in his back all the way out of the room. As Hardy stepped aside to miss the man standing outside the door, he automatically excused himself as his mind stayed on the animal clinic. Had somebody found him? If so, who? It couldn't be any of the Dohner organization. If anything, it had to be an individual or small gang he'd managed to irritate. That opened the door to too many possibilities to even consider.

Ideas swarmed his mind as he drove to the farm. As Joe Ryman, he caused several people and smaller organizations grief. His actions were solely to help build his cover, and he had forced himself not to look back. When Harding Davis "died" and been proclaimed a hero, it hadn't taken the press long to link him to his undercover past and crucial testimony against Teddy Dohner. So, pretty much everybody in the country knew Harding Davis and Joe Ryman were one and the same. But, how would they know him as Beau Harding?

For Davis could mean a myriad of things. Had the sheriff even considered locals in the area with the name? Or had he automatically jumped the gun and placed the blame on Hardy?

Heaven knew many things could be blamed on Hardy.

Besides Kari's death, the one thing he felt the guiltiest about was Audrey Dohner. As Ted's niece, she had been Hardy's ticket into the inner circle. Even though she knew their relationship wasn't real and used it to suit her own purposes, she had no idea he was a police officer. Hardy had no way of knowing whether her uncle would have believed that, though.

He tried not to think of what Dohner might have done to her--niece or not.

Before Kari Jeffries, the nearly four years he and Audrey had been "together" were the most dangerous to his faith. They had never taken their act past public displays of affection, but it felt more wrong to Hardy than anything else he'd ever done. As a young adult, he had vowed to wait for the woman he loved before partaking of so-called romance. So, when he kissed Audrey, or held her tighter than was comfortable, he felt like he was cheating on his future wife. And even though they meant nothing, his actions had somehow cheapened something precious.

His handler, who was also a Christian, tried to comfort Hardy by reminding him at least he wasn't having to play the field or fool a woman into what she thought was a real relationship. It hadn't mattered, though. It just felt wrong.

The next time Hardy spoke to Elliott or Stephens, he was going to pull his head out of the sand and ask if they could find out about Audrey.

He pushed the thought away as he pulled into the Walkers' drive. The lights were on, and the Walkers' farm house looked warm and inviting as Hardy drove to his camper. The thought of Luke and Holly happily ensconced in their home, enjoying each other's company, brought a hollow feeling to his chest. When he was in his twenties, he'd planned on being married by the time he was thirty. He'd have a family by the time he was thirty-five. Now he was thirty-four, and didn't even have a chance at any kind of a relationship with a woman.

An image of sparkling blue eyes and dimples on a smiling face flashed in his mind. Haley Johnson. She was dangerous to him in more ways than one. Not only did he find himself greatly attracted to her; after less than fifteen minutes, she had known he was a police officer.

He parked his truck beside the dark camper and got out. Rustling leaves announced the dog's arrival moments before Clarence appeared under the nearest security light.

"What are you doing out here?" Hardy asked him as he scratched behind the dog's ears. "I figured you'd be in the house with Luke and Holly, eating popcorn and watching a movie."

Clarence cocked his head and looked up at him as if he were contemplating Hardy's words. The dog's responses to people were uncannily human-like most of the time. Hardy could understand why people found themselves talking to him like he was a person.

"Well, I don't have any dog food out here, and Luke will kill me if I give you people food." Hardy opened the door to the camper. "You'd better get on back to the house, boy."

Luke's whistle caught Clarence's attention right at that moment. The dog seemed to nod his head as if to say, "see you later" before turning and galloping toward the house.

The camper was too small, too quiet, and too empty when Hardy walked in. Was this how his life was going to be from now on? Living alone in whatever home the agency found him, uncertain from day to day what might happen to change things. No deep friendships. No real relationships, because nobody would know who he really was.

God, I know you're probably not even listening to me anymore and I don't blame you. I've been mad at you for a long time now. But if you are, I . . .

Hardy couldn't even think of what to ask for, what to tell God. He picked up the paperback he'd bought at the drugstore and sat on the sofa. He'd just forget everything and get lost in the story of Texas Ranger "Tex" Callow and the cattle rustlers he was after. He hoped Tex had better luck at catching his rustlers than Hardy did at catching the senior Dohner.

Chapter 15

"What are you doing, you fool?"

The voice on the other end of the phone was too confident. "Your way is taking too long. We need to get his attention. So we did. We even left his name. His real name."

"Davis?"

"Yes." The caller sounded quite proud of himself.

He should have known better than to agree to hire these barbarians. "Has it ever occurred to you that nobody there knows who he is? You wrote his name, and nobody will even put it together with Beau Harding." His voice was growing in volume, right along with his anger. "You killed those animals for no reason!"

He softly swore. "If we aren't patient and stick to the plan, we'll all end up in prison. I understand prisons aren't particularly comfortable for men like you. Now, am I understood?"

"What if next time we put his whole name?"

"No!" He wanted to punch something, but the only thing close enough was a very valuable painting, which meant too much to him to destroy. "We will stick to the plan and give him a reason to make his home in Shadow. My way. No more killing. Not even a rodent. You may burglarize and vandalize to your heart's content, but leave no more than similarities behind. We want him to realize something is going on, and that he needs to stay and help fix it. The police officer in him is too strong not to want to help. Do you understand?"

"Fine. We'll do it your way." Of course, they would. The fools thought they had found a relatively easy way to become wealthy. Once

they had served their purpose, they would be expendable. But until then, he needed to keep them on the path he so carefully plotted.

"Don't call me again unless you have new information about Davis."

"Okay."

He hung up. This plan had to work. He had come up with it and ironed out every last detail. Harding Davis was a dead man. He just didn't know it.

Chapter 16

Leaves on the trees were in beautiful fall colors. Haley took a deep breath of fresh air and admired her surroundings.

Coming here had been a wise choice. Holly had noticed Haley's mood at Bible study Wednesday evening. She hadn't even asked Haley to explain; she simply told her to come to the farm and go for a walk when she got off work today. Then, there had been yet another break-in this afternoon, making her job even more stressful, so Haley was doubly grateful for Holly's offer.

She looked to her left, at a field of soybeans. To her uneducated eye, they looked ready to pick. Soon, Luke would be the one out there on his tractor taking care of his fields. And Beau Harding would be a name she'd once heard.

Expecting him to be there, she'd braced herself and been prepared to be polite. Only when she arrived, Luke and Holly had left for an evening spent at her parents' farm, and there was no sign of Beau Harding. She had the place to herself.

Could she ever be a farmer's wife, like Holly? The role seemed made for the farmer's daughter to step into. But Haley couldn't even keep a cactus alive, let alone an entire vegetable garden like the one planted closer to the house. She'd probably pull the edible plants and fertilize the weeds.

Her thoughts came back to Hardy. If, as she highly suspected, the man was some sort of law enforcement officer, how was it that he was so good on a farm? Holly had commented numerous times Luke was as pleased with Hardy's work as he would be if he'd done it himself.

And, if Hardy was a crooked law man, she couldn't imagine Mitch sanctioning his employment by two of his best friends. So, what was his story?

She sighed. He'd be gone in another week, and she would never have to worry about it again.

A particularly pretty shade of orange drew her attention to a bush a few yards from the trail. She'd just walked over for a closer look when what sounded like a herd of cattle came crashing through the brush.

"Clarence!" The male voice was stern. "Get back over here."

Haley laughed as the friendly dog cocked his head as though he were studying her. "What are you doing out in the woods, Clarence?"

Beau Harding stepped into sight, standing on the path Haley had just left.

"I'm sorry. He wanted to be let out, so I thought I'd take him for a walk. I didn't know anybody was out here." His displeased tone of voice belied the polite words.

Haley's feathers were immediately ruffled. "Didn't you see my car?"

"I figured whoever was here had ridden to the Morris's with Luke and Holly. I didn't think anybody would be here with them gone."

She was liking his attitude less and less. Did he think he owned this farm?

"Holly invited me to come and enjoy a walk. I can assure you I have permission to be here." She reached out and broke off a sprig of the leaves she'd admired, determined to ignore the brute. They felt like satin against her face.

His soft laughter drew her attention right back to him.

"What's so funny?" Clarence was looking at him, too.

He looked altogether too handsome with that smile on his face. "Call it a hunch, but I'm guessing you're not exactly a country girl, are you?"

Well! "What makes you say that?" Surely the way a person stood in the woods didn't depict the level of her experience with nature.

"Because," His grin grew wider. "You're standing there rubbing poison oak. Unless you're not allergic, you're going to be covered with a rash in a few hours."

Haley let go of the leaves and took a quick step back, embarrassed beyond belief. "I'd better go."

She walked back to the path a little closer to the house than he was, but he was there before she'd taken two steps.

"Wait." His hand on her arm stopped her. "I'm sorry. I shouldn't have laughed. Some people get sick from poison oak."

"Well, I'll go home and . . . " She realized she had no idea what to do. Sit around and wait to break out, she supposed.

"You need to take a shower and get into some different clothes right away. You'd better come on back to my trailer with me." He took her arm and started to lead her on the path.

"I can't take a shower." She stopped in her tracks. "I don't have anything to change into, and I'm not . . . I can't . . . It's not proper!"

He glanced at his watch. "I figure you have about twenty minutes to wash that stuff off before it does its damage. You can use the shower in my camper while I stay outside with Clarence. I'm sure you'll be okay in a pair of my sweats and a T-shirt. You have my word I will be a perfect gentleman."

"But, I—"

"Getting closer to fifteen minutes, and my water pressure isn't the greatest."

She turned and started up the trail. "I guess I don't have any other choice."

"Sure you do." She turned to see a wide grin on his face as he walked beside her. "You can break out and be miserable for a week or so."

"What about you?" She looked at his hand. "You touched my arm. Won't you break out?"

"I might if I were susceptible to it." He reached down and petted the dog trying to edge between them on the narrow path. "I've never broken out from any kind of poison in my life, and I've been exposed to them all at one time or another."

Well, aren't you special was on the tip of her tongue before she reminded herself he was only trying to help. The grudging attitude he'd first displayed had been replaced by a pleasant, even friendly, one.

Fifteen minutes later, she was unsure if he had truly been friendly at all. His shower was a convoluted creation put together with a torn shower curtain hanging on what looked like might be old metal clothes hangers. And instead of simply hanging it around the shower area, he had rigged up a mat on a board of some sort so it would drain back into the stall and hung the curtain around the whole kit and caboodle.

Her first problem came when she turned the faucet on only to have nothing happen. She studied the apparatus and finally figured out she had to turn a dial on the shower head. Only when she did that, she didn't get her face out of the way fast enough, and was nearly drowned in the flood of water that shot out.

Then she realized she'd have to use his soap and shampoo. And it smelled good—like clear, fresh air with just a hint of musk. She became embarrassed when she realized she was standing there sniffing a bar of soap.

It would have been nice if he'd warned her that the hot water didn't last very long. She had barely worked the shampoo into a lather when the comfortably warm spray became ice cold needles pounding on her skin. She was certain he'd heard her yelp of surprise because Clarence howled.

The man could make a living teaching contortions, too. When Haley started to get out of the shower, she found herself entangled in the curtain. Somehow, she ended up abruptly landing on the stool. She just gave up and stayed there as she dressed. How he could possibly shower and dress in the tiny un-curtained area of the already small room, she couldn't imagine. At five-seven, she wasn't a small woman, but he had to be every bit of six-two or more. Not to mention his build—all those muscles.

What was she doing? Standing in a closet masquerading as a bathroom, wearing a shirt that came down to her knees and a pair of sweats she could probably have gotten around her waist twice, mooning over a man's muscles! A man that A—didn't like her very much and B—was living under a false name. Not exactly her dream man.

Only, if that were truly the case, why had her heart felt like it might pound out of her chest when he'd taken her arm? And why had she stood, mesmerized, looking into his eyes? What was it about this man?

Okay, Lord, I know You have a sense of humor. Please don't let me go all silly over a man I shouldn't be with. He's lying, and I know that's wrong. And I'm pretty sure I annoy him. Could you just wait and give me these feelings when there's a good, honest man who will be just as interested in me?

That's right. All the guys Wayne and Lori had tried to fix her up with, and the first time a man ever really interested her, it was this one. She should have her head examined.

"If you give me your clothes, I'll throw them into the washer. You don't want to handle them until the poison is washed out." Hardy held out his hands to accept the clothes she was timidly carrying as she stepped out of the camper.

"How can you throw them into the washer? Are Luke and Holly already home?"

He flushed guiltily. "I have my own key. They let me do laundry and use their stove. And I have to let Clarence out for them."

Why would he feel guilty about having his own key? Wait a minute. "I could have taken a shower in one of their bathrooms!"

The guilt disappeared into a lazy smile. "But it wouldn't have been as much of an adventure, would it?"

"An adventure?" She angrily stomped her foot on the ground, which wasn't so smart since she didn't have any shoes on. "I nearly killed myself using that concocted accident waiting to happen you call a shower!"

"Okay." Hardy held up a hand in supplication. "The truth is; I didn't think of you using a shower in the house until you were already in mine. I'm sorry."

Haley didn't think she believed him. "Just put my clothes in a garbage bag. I'll take them home and dump them into my washer."

"How will you drive without your shoes? Your sneakers will need to be washed, too."

"I'll drive barefooted!" She was about to stomp her foot again. Why was it so easy for him to rile her like this?

He looked at her, the expression on his face telling her he was considering the merits of continuing their arguments, but then he answered her. "Okay. Just a minute."

She watched as he disappeared into his trailer. He came out the door a few minutes later carrying a large plastic shopping bag.

The bag was just about in her hands when he pulled it back. "Go out for dinner with me tomorrow night."

Now she was hearing things. "What did you just say?"

"Will you please have dinner with me tomorrow evening? You . . . you intrigue me."

Hardy wanted to take the invitation back as soon as he'd issued it. Haley could see it in his eyes. Maybe that was what compelled her to give him the answer she did.

"I'd love to. What time should I be ready?"

Conflicting emotions warred in his eyes as he held her clothes out to her. "Six-thirty. You'll have to tell me where you live, though."

She gave him her address and the general directions for how to get there.

It wasn't until she was halfway home when it sank in. She was going on a date with a man she knew absolutely nothing about. What was she thinking?

She would talk to Mitch first thing in the morning. He knew what was going on with Hardy, and even if he wouldn't tell her why, he'd tell her if she shouldn't go out with the man. She felt better immediately.

Haley had a date.

Chapter 17

"Now why'd you let me go and do that, Clarence?" Hardy asked the dog. "You just stood there and let me ask her out when I had absolutely no intention of doing so. You could have jumped on me or stepped between us, or I wouldn't have even cared if you bit me. You know why I can't get involved with anybody, especially a woman like Haley."

Instead of hearing Clarence's excuse, the sound of a car reached Hardy's ears a minute before the squad car pulled to a stop right in front of him. He stood, warily waiting, as Sheriff Landon got out of the car.

"I still can't help you with your animal clinic." Hardy had thought long and hard and convinced himself it was merely a coincidence. It was like he'd told Mitch before. If he had been located, he wouldn't still be breathing air.

Mitch stopped and stood in front of him. "I'm not here just about that. I came to pick your brain about something else."

"What's that?" He didn't feel like he had much brain left to pick, but if the sheriff wanted to try, who was Hardy to throw water on his sandcastle?

"We had another break-in. This afternoon, while Clay Richmond was at a meeting, somebody broke into his office and trashed the place. The cash he kept on hand and a few expensive pieces of art were taken."

"What do you want from me?" Hardy was going against the strong inclination he felt to help.

"Shadow is a quiet town. We've had maybe five break-ins over the past five or six years. Now, I'm dealing with the third one in less than two weeks. I need somebody outside my circle to take a look at this and tell me if I'm seeing something that isn't there. Because I'm wondering if somehow, we're dealing with the same people in each case." Mitch shifted his feet and stared into Hardy's eyes. "You've got a strong background in organized crime. Do you see any red flags here?"

Hardy wasn't sure what he'd expected, but it wasn't this. He fought his work-honed instinct and shook his head. "You want to talk to a man who doesn't exist anymore, Sheriff."

"I'm not asking you to announce who you are to the world." Mitch's gaze didn't falter. "I'm asking you to look at what I have and give me your honest opinion. We can meet somewhere outside the office . . . where we won't be seen. I'll show you what I have. Then you can tell me what you think. That's all I want."

No was on the tip of Hardy's tongue, but there was a major factor keeping it from being spoken. He had been an officer of the law for too many years to simply look the other way when his help might be useful. And the sheriff was only asking for his take on the crimes that had occurred. But a clandestine meeting just didn't feel right. He came up with an alternative.

"You get me the files. I'll keep them overnight and give you my opinion when I give them back."

Mitch frowned. "That's not how we do things around here."

"It is if you want my help." Hardy was in charge. "You're asking me to do something I've quit doing. If anybody finds out in what capacity I'm helping you, it could open the door to my identity being discovered by the wrong people. This offer is the best you're going to get from me. Take it or leave it."

Hardy thought from the look on Mitch's face, he was going to leave it. Then the sheriff slowly nodded. "I'll have copies of everything out here to you in a couple of hours. I don't need to tell you this stays between the two of us."

"That's my condition as well," Hardy reminded him.

Mitch looked at the farm around them before directing his attention back to Hardy. "I just don't get it, Davis. Why would anybody destroy a hair salon, trash an animal clinic—killing every animal in it, and now break into an insurance agency? The only commonality I see is they're all being done in Shadow within a short period of time."

"Sometimes, things are just coincidental." Hardy felt like he needed to caution the sheriff. "I won't have preconceived ideas in my head when I look at your files. I'll tell you what I think, not what you want to hear. It's how I operate."

"I've looked into your professional history a little since I found out who you are." Mitch didn't look the least bit apologetic about it, either. "Your reputation is what made me ask you in the first place."

His reputation. Hardy had worked hard to be known as a good cop. But one day—one incident—made the value of a reputation seem worthless. What good had his reputation done Kari Jeffries? He mentally shook himself out of the memory. "If that's all you need; I have some chores to get to."

It was while he stood watching the squad car disappear down the long lane the reality of what he had just agreed to do sank in. He looked at the dog standing beside him.

"Well, Clarence, don't things just keep getting better?" He couldn't help but chuckle when Clarence appeared to nod. "I went from keeping to myself for not even another week to having a date and helping the police. What do you suppose is wrong with me?"

When the dog provided no answer, Hardy turned and headed for the barn. He still had a little daylight left to clean up the area of the barn he'd noticed needed it. Rakes, shovels, axes, and several assorted tools were piled haphazardly in a corner of the building. Since he hadn't paid that close of attention, Hardy was afraid the boys left the mess. And Luke would have enough on his plate with his body getting readjusted to the hard work of the farm without having to take care of this.

As Hardy moved the lawn tools around, his mind wandered to the problem the sheriff was facing. With only six officers on the county force, if he were looking at a single person or group of people committing these crimes, he was going to have his hands full. Hardy purposely steered his mind in a different direction when reasons to believe they were the same perps started forming. Like he told Mitch, he wanted to look at the files with an unformed opinion. That would be the best.

No matter whether these crimes were committed by the same individual or different ones, Mitch Landon had better be prepared to use every resource available to him. Hardy hoped the county sheriff wasn't like some officers he'd known; he hoped Mitch would call in the state police if they were needed. One thing Hardy learned in Chicago was the value of teamwork.

Not that it had done him any good when it came to the most crucial moment in his life. His reputation and teamwork had been useless, and even God had seemed absent from the situation.

Hardy wished he could go back to being a man with strong faith. He knew the doubts he had right now disappointed his parents. Not that either one of them had been pushy. It was almost worse when his mom smiled sadly and told him they were both praying for him to find his way again. She had even said that when he'd gone to the hospital to see his dad.

His dad. Callie hadn't called, so there hadn't been any change in their father's condition. Hardy wanted his dad to be his normally healthy self again, full of life and enthusiasm. Not a man who uttered nonsensical phrases.

What had H.B. said again? He feel turtle. Jesus water. Be careful. The final phrase made perfect sense with what was going on in Hardy's life. The other two, though…He remembered the theory he'd come up with Barney and the cloud statement. Could it be possible his dad had said something completely different than what Hardy and his mom heard?

"He feel turtle. He feel turtle. He makes sense. What could feel be?" His mind searched for a word. "He kill turtle. He will…"

Hardy looked at Clarence. "He will something, Clarence. He will turtle . . . He will tur . . . tle . . . He will bur . . . He will girl . . . He will hurt. . ." His heart sped up. "He will hurt you! He will hurt you." For just a moment, Hardy tried to figure out a way he could high five the dog.

"Okay, Clarence." Hardy thought he was finally onto something. "He will hurt you. Jesus water. Be careful." He tried using different words to replace the second phrase, but nothing fit.

Still, it was obviously a warning, most likely about Ted Dohner. Hardy sadly shook his head. His dad was worried about the Dohner organization coming after his son. That was all he was trying to tell Hardy.

Yet, he still had a strong urge to speak to H.B. again. He'd have to wait at least a couple of days, though. It would take him a while to get things arranged with Elliott, if his brother-in-law could even set it up again. Within a couple of hours, he'd have three cases to review and see if they were linked. And tomorrow . . . Tomorrow he had a date with Haley Johnson.

What had he been thinking? Even though there was something about Haley—something that enticed and intrigued him like no other woman had before—Hardy wasn't even remotely close to a point in his life where he could have a romantic relationship. He shouldn't be starting something that was ultimately impossible.

"Maybe I'll call her and cancel." He grasped the handle of a shovel and leaned it against the wall. "That might be best for both of us."

That probably would be best for both of them. In fact, Hardy knew it would. He was going to call Haley at the station first thing in the morning and tell her . . . what? "I can't take you out because I will only be here a few more days, and then you'll never see me again." Or how about, "I am not using the name I was born with because I'm not ready to check into a coffin.

He was still mulling his options over when he heard Luke's truck. Clarence charged out of the barn, intent on getting attention from his owners. Hardy placed the wheelbarrow in the corner and looked around the area he'd straightened. It was as neat as a store display. Even if his mind had been stuck on his dilemma, he had somehow managed to accomplish the task he set out to do.

His mind was still unsettled about the date with Haley as he walked out of the barn. He raised his hand in greeting when Luke and Holly both called out to him. It was only because of the security lights they were able to see each other. Hardy had worked longer than he realized, for it was dark.

Mitch should be there with the files any time. Hardy would let the sheriff decide how to handle the Walkers' curiosity about him visiting Hardy this late in the evening. Hardy had enough to think about.

He took a deep breath and dug down into the nerves of steel he'd been known for on his job in Chicago. He would just take one thing at a time. Starting with the case files. The rest, he would work out when it was time.

Chapter 18

"Shadow County Sheriff's office." Haley fought to keep the frustration out of her voice. It wasn't the citizens' fault Karl King had somehow discovered details about the animal clinic break-in. It wasn't their fault the reporter for the *Shadow Sundown* thought with the local paper's circulation of a little more than three thousand, the *New York Times* would be on his doorstep any day in search of his investigative reporting skills.

"Another one?" Mitch had stopped by her station on the way to his office.

Haley finished writing the last sentence of the caller's information before she answered the sheriff.

"Christine Connors knows it was her next door neighbor, Fred Lancaster, who, in her words, butchered those animals."

Mitch sighed. "What brought her to this conclusion?"

Haley looked at the note she'd written. "He called her dog Ralphie a worthless, flea infested, fur covered pile of bones."

"And that would be the dog Lancaster regularly reports to animal control for chewing up his landscaping and defecating all over his lawn," Mitch steadily commented.

"That would be the dog." Haley placed the ridiculous accusation on top of the growing pile beside her phone.

"I knew the phone would be ringing off the wall when I saw the paper this morning." Mitch looked at the offending publication lying folded on the table behind Haley." Go ahead and call Mavis in to help you. I'll argue with the board about overtime, to keep the workload manageable for my dispatchers."

Haley noticed the way Mitch emphasized that Mavis was who to call in." Mitch, I know Crystal likes to talk, but do you really think she's the one who gave Karl the information?" As the chief dispatcher, Haley was considered Crystal's immediate supervisor and hated to think the other woman was responsible for this mess.

Mitch looked steadily at her. "Haley, besides the victims, there aren't even a dozen people who know the details of these cases. Can you honestly tell me you believe any other one of them would have talked to a reporter?"

"No." Haley turned around in her swivel chair and looked at the headlines once again. "Bloody Slaughter at Animal Clinic," and below, "Police have no leads." Haley had read the article with growing horror as Karl King described in great detail how the animals had been found.

She swiveled back around when the phone rang and picked it up with dread.

"Shadow County Sheriff's office."

"I know who killed those animals." The voice sounded like that of an elderly lady, and Haley didn't recognize it.

"I'll need your name and telephone number, please."

"It was those men. I saw them."

"Ma'am. Please tell me your name and telephone number." If a caller wouldn't give the dispatcher that information, it put the validity of the call in question from the start.

"I can't say who I am. They'll get me."

Mitch caught Haley's eye and nodded, giving her permission to go ahead and take the woman's report. He was able to hear enough of the call to know what was being said.

"Okay, ma'am. Who did it?"

"I don't know their names, but there were three of them. They flew by my house in a blue ship. I saw them come out of the clinic and get in before they lifted off."

Haley put her thumb and forefinger on her forehead and squeezed. *Lord, please give me patience with this woman.*

"If you'll tell me your name, the sheriff will do all he can to keep you safe." After all, how difficult could it be to protect her from spaceship travelers?

"I can't. They'll know. He'll know. He sees everything."

"Okay." Haley sighed. "I'll write down the information. Thank you for calling." The line was already dead, the caller having hung up. She turned to Mitch. "Caller ID shows Hilda Crowe. I'll run her address just for the records."

"Call Mavis," Mitch reminded her before he turned and walked into his office.

Haley opened the program she needed and typed in the woman's name and telephone number. Immediately, an address popped onto the computer screen. She started to write it on the report when she realized something. She opened a new tab on the computer and pulled up the files on the animal clinic break-in. Her heart sped up as she scribbled both its address and that of Hilda Crowe. Then she pulled up a satellite feed and typed both addresses in.

"Mitch?" She spoke loudly enough she didn't need the intercom. "You might want to see this."

The sheriff walked out of his office, to her desk, and looked over her shoulder at the computer. It wasn't very often his dispatcher asked for his presence.

"Look." Haley pointed to the red mark indicating the location of the animal clinic. Then she pointed to the one marking Helen Crowe's address. "If I'm reading this right, she's less than a sixteenth of a mile from the clinic. The back of her place would face the back of the clinic."

Mitch leaned down closer to the computer screen. Haley moved her hand away as he reached for the mouse and moved the cursor. The screen was soon enlarged by two-hundred percent.

"Crazy or not, this woman might have seen something." Mitch straightened. "Call and see who's closest to that property. I want to know what's in the field between the caller's house and the clinic. We need to see if there's a clear line of vision between the two places."

"Yes, sir." Haley keyed the radio and asked for the deputies on duty to call back with their locations. Hank was nearest to the house in question. She gave him the code to use a phone to reply.

"I want to talk to him." Mitch stepped over and picked up the ringing phone. "Hank, this lady is skittish, but I think she may have seen our guys. Keep her calm and try to get as much detail as you can from her. Find out if there's a clear line of vision between the two locations, and do your best to get a rational story from her. If need be, I'll come out myself. Let me know what you find out ASAP."

"Do you really think she could have seen them?" Haley still found it hard to believe the confused woman she'd spoken with might have been telling the truth as she saw it.

Mitch smiled grimly. "I'm going to pray she did. We're going to have to keep her off the grid, Haley. We can't have Karl King find out about Helen Crowe. A story about her could put her in danger if those guys are still around here."

"I won't tell anybody, but won't everybody here have to know?"

"Not Crystal," Mitch bit out. "I'm going to do a little side investigating, Haley, and if I find out she had anything to do with this story," He straightened and picked up the newspaper, "there is nothing that will save her job."

"I understand." Haley felt sorry for Crystal as she watched her boss walk resolutely back to his office. If Crystal was indeed the leak, she had done something very wrong. Haley just felt bad that the other woman evidently needed attention to the point she would risk a police investigation and her job.

The phone rang just as she started to pick it up to call Mavis.

"Shadow County Sheriff's office."

"I saw it all!" a man shouted. "I saw those foreigners go into the animal clinic, and I told Trudy they were up to no good."

When Haley heard the name Trudy, the voice was immediately recognizable. "When did you see the people you're talking about go into the clinic, Zane?"

It took her the better part of twenty minutes to figure out what was going on. Zane Danziger and his wife had taken their pug in for his shots and some people of Mexican-American heritage were in the animal clinic waiting room. It seemed that anybody not completely Caucasian was a "foreigner" and Zane didn't trust them. He even accused Chen Lee, who'd been born right there in Shadow, of being a secret spy for China. It was most likely that Chen used his position as owner of Shadow Inn to smuggle even more "foreigners" into their county. Zane wouldn't even be surprised if Chen weren't letting the suspects stay in his hotel, free of charge.

Haley had a splitting headache by the time she finally placed the receiver on the hook.

Lord, I know there are lots of people in the world who need extra help. I'm asking you for extra help myself, now, to deal with some of them. Losing my patience isn't going to be productive, but I don't know how much more I can listen to without blowing my stack. Please.

She felt calmness settle in her heart after her prayer. God wasn't leaving her alone to deal with this. In fact, He had worked through Mitch when he told her to call Mavis.

Fifteen minutes later, Haley leaned back in her chair and took a long drink of her now lukewarm soda. Mavis would be there in less than a half hour. She took a deep breath and picked up the ringing phone to answer it.

Chapter 19

Hardy walked into the police station and came to an abrupt halt. Haley was working at the computer while another female dispatcher manned the phone. Haley was deeply immersed in whatever she was working on. Why did this beautiful woman have to attract his attention while he was dealing with the mess his life had become? Of course, he had no idea when, or even if, he'd ever be able to return to a normal life. There were too many factors to consider.

"Excuse me." He watched Haley's eyes widen at the sight of him before she spoke. He hoped she wouldn't ask about the contents of the plastic bag he was carrying. It hadn't been the ideal thing to put the case files in, but he didn't want to walk around with them in plain sight.

"I'm not supposed to have visitors at work."

Hardy hadn't thought of her assuming he'd stopped in to see her. He didn't want to embarrass her, but he had to tell the truth in this case. "I'm here to see the sheriff."

Her lovely blush confirmed she was indeed embarrassed by her misassumption. "Just a minute. I'll see if he's available."

Before Hardy could stop himself, he reached out and placed his hand on her shoulder. "Not that I don't want to see you. I'm looking forward to this evening."

Her blush increased as she returned his smile. Instead of responding to Hardy, she picked up the phone and called the sheriff. The other woman, a spike cut blonde who appeared to be about the same age as Haley, stared curiously at him.

"He said for you to come right in." Haley gestured to her right, where Hardy knew Mitch's office to be. He smiled at Haley once more before he turned and walked in to see the sheriff.

"Close the door," Mitch instructed from his seat behind the desk.

Hardy obligingly closed it before he sat down. He leaned forward and placed the sack of files on Mitch's desk.

"So, what do you think?" It appeared the sheriff wasn't going to beat around the bush.

"I'd like to summarize what I discovered about each case individually before I explain my findings." Hardy had spent most of the night awake, caught up in the familiar challenge of investigating a case.

Mitch nodded. "Go ahead."

"Okay." With his excellent memory, Hardy hadn't needed to write notes. "The salon break-in wasn't about money. There are just too many sites in that area, some which would have yielded the thieves ten times the money they stole from the salon. The items they took aren't exactly things they can fence, either. There's not much of a market for hair care supplies or tanning products. I imagine if you check dumpsters or the city landfill, you'll find the stolen items there."

Mitch wrote something on a piece of paper. "I'll have the trash checked out. I'm pretty sure the dumpster would have been emptied since the robbery, but if it has, maybe we'll have some luck at the landfill." He frowned. "If robbery isn't the motive for the break-in, what do you think is?"

"To get your attention." That was the only explanation Hardy had come up with. "They may have just wanted to see how you respond to a burglary."

"You don't think it's something more personal than that?" Mitch appeared unconvinced. "It was awfully violent for an attention getter. I don't think there was one piece of equipment or furniture not damaged or destroyed."

"Look at the crime scene photos again." Hardy waited while Mitch retrieved the folder containing the pictures he'd spoken of. "These aren't signs of rage. It's controlled destruction. The dryer chair was torn apart and dropped where it stood, not thrown all over the room. The pieces broken off the tanning beds, as well as the cords that were cut off, were all right next to what they came from. Imagine somebody in a rage, Sheriff. He's going to break things and throw them. This destruction is calculated and methodical."

Mitch seemed surprised when he looked back up at Hardy. "I see what you mean. It's not as violent as it appears at first glance."

"I'm going to skip the animal clinic right now. I'll come back to it later." He reached over and indicated the folder containing the insurance agency break-in files. "Look at these photos again, Sheriff. Remember what you just figured out about the hair salon."

Hardy sat quietly while Mitch did as he'd asked. The sheriff slowly sat back in his chair and looked at Hardy. "This looks staged. Just like the salon. They wanted it to look worse than it was, like an act of rage."

"That's what I think."

Mitch's brows rose. "So, they're connected?"

Hardy slowly nodded. "If I were a gambling man, I'd put my money on it."

"Then what about the animal clinic?" Raw emotions raged in the sheriff's eyes. "Those animals were tortured. If that's not rage, I don't know what is."

Hardy wanted the sheriff to realize what he was seeing. "Shut off your emotions and take another look at the photos."

Reluctance was apparent on Mitch's face, but he slowly opened the file and slid out the pictures. "This is horrible. The perps were furious."

"That is what they want you to think. I noticed something the first time you showed me those pictures." Hardy reached across the desk and slid one out to show the sheriff. "This dog is in the middle of a blood-covered carnage. But if you look, the only visible injury to the dog is a single stab wound. You'd have to check with the vet, but I'm fairly sure it would have hit the dog's heart. You can look at all of the dogs, and you'll see the same thing."

He waited while the now interested sheriff looked more closely at some of the photographs. Hardy noticed Mitch was examining a picture of a cat. "I can't tell from the pictures how the cats or rabbit died," he admitted, "but I believe it was the same way."

Mitch looked up from the picture he was holding. "What are you saying, Davis?"

"I'm saying the intruders killed these animals with however many stabs it took to get to their hearts; it doesn't look like more than a couple. Then they took the blood and bodies, and created the nightmare that was discovered." Hardy had thought long and hard about this case. "As bad as it looks, there is no real rage here. It's set up to appear as there is, but it's just like the other two."

"So, you think we're looking at the same person . . . people . . . for all three crimes."

Hardy nodded. "It looks that way to me."

"But why did they go to the extreme of killing the animals? They could have trashed the clinic without killing the animals." Mitch slid the photos back into the file folder as he looked at Hardy.

"I don't know," Hardy admitted. "It may have something to do with the message they left."

"You mean it might be somebody after you?" Mitch grimaced. "But you told me that was impossible."

"And I still think it is." He had good reason to believe that. "You said you read up on me. So you know exactly who's after me." Mitch nodded. "Then you have to know if they've found me, they're not the kind of people to play games to get my attention. I was responsible for their golden boy's life sentence being spent at the federal penitentiary in Tucson, and anybody Dohner sent would be instructed to either grab me or kill me on the spot."

"You're sure about that?"

"I told you, Sheriff, I know that organization inside and out. I was one of them until I had to blow my cover,"

The sheriff appeared to consider Hardy's words carefully. "Why'd you do it, Davis? Everything I found out about you says you're not the kind of guy to quit. So, why did you blow your cover and testify when you were so close to catching Ted Dohner himself?"

"I didn't do it by choice." At least Hardy could honestly say that. The man Hardy was looking at couldn't possibly imagine what it had taken to get Hardy to blow his cover. "You had to have read about Teddy Dohner's drugs killing all those people. The prosecution was going to lose the case on technicalities. I couldn't sit by and let those people win. Not that time."

Memories assailed him as his gaze focused on the sheriff. "I testified against seven members of the Dohner organization before I was finished and barely made a dent in it. Except when it was Teddy. Once he was sentenced, word came down through our undercover ops that the big man himself was out to get Harding Davis. He wasn't about to let a cop get away with pulling the wool over his eyes for the better part of five years, and then putting his son away on top of that."

Mitch leaned forward in his chair, his face full of empathy. "And so you disappeared."

Hardy nodded. "They gave me a new name and moved me to a new town."

"And that's where the robbery happened," Mitch commented, "when you died."

The robbery was one thing Hardy was not willing to talk about. "I'm here now. At least Beau Harding is. And I don't believe the Dohners are looking for me at all anymore."

"But if they should find you?" Mitch's voice was soft as he asked the question.

Hardy took a deep breath. "Then I'll fight with everything I have in me, and if that's not enough, I'll die."

Mitch's gaze was troubled. "And you're leaving Shadow at the end of next week."

"Don't you think that's best for all concerned?" Hardy quickly pushed a flash of disappointment away. "Dohner may not have found me, but I can't guarantee smaller organizations aren't responsible for the break-ins. I stepped on a lot of toes to get as far into the organization as I did."

The sheriff looked out the window of his office for a minute before returning his attention to Hardy.

"Let's say you're right," he agreed. "Then, what are you doing with Haley?" Hardy followed Mitch's gaze to the chief dispatcher busily working on the computer before settling back on Hardy. "She asked me this morning if it were safe to date you. She only knows you're not using your real name. I had to tell her that much so she could help me field the television viewers who saw you. And this morning she tells me you've asked her on a date. You're leaving in seven days. What are you hoping to accomplish with her in seven days?"

Guilt flooded Hardy. "You're right. I just . . . I'll tell her something has come up. I won't start anything. I knew I couldn't, but there's something about her. I'll tell her."

Mitch gave him an appraising look. "If you're going to leave, it's better to hurt her feelings now than to possibly hurt her worse in a week. Haley is alone, Davis. Her family is all gone. She has nobody but her friends, so we have to look out for her. If she thought something was developing between the two of you, and then you cut and run...Well, I don't want to think about how that would hurt her."

Hardy felt something that had barely started to take wing crash to the earth. "I understand. I'll tell her now."

"Thank you." Mitch stood up with Hardy. "And I appreciate your take on the crimes. I still don't know who's committing them, but I have a clearer perspective. I can focus on finding the motive." He looked steadily into Hardy's eyes. "You're a good police officer, Davis. It's a shame you have to give it up."

"Thanks." Hardy turned to leave. "Life doesn't always work out the way we want it to, though, does it?"

Before Mitch could answer, Hardy walked out of the door and over to the dispatcher's station. He felt lower than a snail's belly when Haley looked away from the man she'd been talking to and smiled shyly at him, her cheeks once more a rosy pink.

"Haley, something has come up." Her smile faltered. "I don't think . . . I can't take you out. I'm sorry."

Before she could respond, Hardy turned and headed for the door. He didn't even take the time to apologize to the mail carrier when he nearly knocked him over. He just wanted to get away before he had to look at the face of another woman he had hurt, even in a small way.

Chapter 20

"You're gonna like this, Father. He's interested in a woman in Shadow."

He gritted his teeth. "And what caused you to believe this? Did he stop and exchange views on the weather with a female?"

"He was gonna take her on a date. He told her he couldn't, though. I think she was sad."

He rolled his eyes. "If he broke it, I'd say he's not overly interested in her. Is this all you called about, you imbecile?"

There was indignity in the caller's voice. "I'm a man, Father. I'm not a baby."

"You're not a . . . Are you really that stupid, or have you been abusing your medication? I said imbecile, not infant, you fool!" It was all he could do not to hang up the phone. With his genius of a son on the job, he may as well walk into the nearest police station and confess.

"I think Davis isn't taking her out because he's leaving town."

"What?" He walked over to the window that looked over a busy street. "You can't let him leave Shadow. You have to intensify your efforts." He had to think.

"Father, Davis was gonna take out the woman who works at the sheriff's office. He was in there talking to the sheriff for a long time, and when he came out is when he made her sad."

It was a good thing the man on the other end of the phone was not within arm's reach at that moment. He could have cheerfully throttled him with his bare hands. "If he is speaking with the sheriff, there's a good chance our employees' pitiful attempt to get his attention *by leaving his name may have worked." He thought for a moment. "Go ahead and have them leave a message at their next site. But they are not to kill animals to do it. They can use their imagination instead."*

"Yes, Father."

And the sky would be lime green before he would talk to this fool again. "From now on, you'll only communicate with me through James. It will be safer that way." Especially for his own sanity.

Disappointment sounded in the voice on the phone. "Yes, Father."

He hung up before his son could say anything more idiotic than he already had. If his plan to take care of Harding Davis didn't work, it would be because of the fools he was forced to work with. The situation had severely limited his options.

He couldn't fail, though. He paced around his desk, thinking. He would need a backup plan if his first one fell apart. There must always be a backup plan.

Chapter 21

Haley sat back and smiled as she watched the six children with their Sunday school lesson sheets. That hadn't been so hard. She had read them the story of Noah's Ark, and now they were coloring pictures of it.

She stood up and walked around, looking more closely at their artwork.

"That's nice, Jeremy. I see the dogs you put in the ark." At least she hoped the four-legged stick animals were canines. His nearly toothless grin told her she was close enough.

She made a few more observations until she came to Denny Allen's paper. On his paper was something she couldn't identify.

"Did you draw some fish in the water, Denny?" There was a shape in the blue space next to the boat.

The energetic, red-headed, freckle-faced boy shook his head. "That's my sister's cat. I don't like him, so I'm throwing him off the boat."

"But . . ." Exactly what could Haley say to that? Before she could come up with something, Carter Danes started scribbling furiously in the blue water he'd colored around his ark.

"I'm going to throw my grandpa's bull in there. He's mean." The little boy's tongue peeked from the corner of his mouth as he colored.

Haley felt like she was watching a runaway train as the children began throwing things from their boats. She was just about to try to regain control of the situation when she noticed the figure Emmy Wyler was coloring. It was an unusual stick figure with a yellow ball on one end. She just had to ask.

"What animal are you throwing overboard, Emmy?"

The little blonde girl turned and smiled angelically. "That's Miss Simms. I don't want to take piano lessons anymore."

"Boys and girls." Haley waited until she more or less had their attention. "Noah didn't throw anything off the ark; he saved animals and his family just like God told him to. Please stop drawing animals and people in the water around your arks."

She could see it now. Tara Wyler asking her daughter about the Sunday school lesson, only to be informed her daughter no longer had to take piano lessons because she'd thrown her teacher out of the boat. At this rate, this would be both the first and last day she taught the kindergarten class.

When she saw the children continue to create shapes in the water, she sat back down at the table. It appeared the damage was already done. At least their lesson hadn't been Daniel in the Lions' Den. She could only imagine a five-year-old's depiction of an animal eating their sister's cat or piano teacher.

Maybe she would color the extra lesson sheet sitting in front of her. Within minutes, she had a brown ark with dark blue water below it. The light blue around it appeared to be a lovely sky. It had already stopped raining on her ark. Her mind drifted as she worked on putting animals in the windows of the vessel.

"Miss Johnson?"

Haley looked up. "Yes?"

Lacey Jones pointed at Haley's paper, "Who did you throw off your boat?"

"I didn't . . ." Sure enough, she had, indeed, drawn a figure floundering in the water. While she was by no means Rembrandt, it was plain to see it was a person with light brown hair, clad in blue jeans and work boots. The familiar black T-shirt told her what she'd already known. She had thrown Beau Harding out of her ark.

The buzzer signifying the end of Sunday school saved her from having to explain. "Remember to try and learn your Bible verse this week. If you can say it next Sunday, you'll get a sticker for your book." Haley had chosen something simple for them to memorize.

She had given them slips of paper with Psalm 145:9 printed on them. *The Lord is good to all.* Hopefully, their parents would be so caught up in helping the children learn the Bible verse they would overlook the fact they'd all been tossing living creatures out of Noah's Ark.

The students picked up their papers and noisily left the room. Their parents would meet them in the fellowship hall, where they would enjoy a pastry and milk. Then, most of them would go to the Sanctuary for the worship service.

Haley had skipped breakfast, hoping she'd have a few minutes to eat a donut. She looked at the crayons strewn across the table and chairs scattered about the room. It appeared that the time between Sunday school and worship would be spent tidying up her classroom.

The sound of heels hitting the floor preceded Tessa Lincoln's arrival. "How'd your first day go?"

Haley gestured around the room. "Did they leave it this much of a mess when you taught?" Tessa had asked for a replacement since she had tons of wedding preparations.

Tessa walked in and began helping pick up crayons. "You need to keep them for a minute after the buzzer goes off. They know they're supposed to clean up their areas before they leave. They're just testing you."

Haley straightened from where she'd knelt to retrieve a crayon from under the table. "Would that testing include throwing animals and people off of Noah's Ark?"

"Who? The kids or you?" Tessa was looking pointedly at Haley's artwork. "Either you colored that, or one of the students in this classroom has become an overnight prodigy."

"It's nothing." Haley quickly picked up the paper and folded it twice before throwing it into the trash can. "I was just doodling."

Tessa's voice was soft as she touched Haley's arm. "That was Beau Harding in your picture, wasn't it?"

Haley shook her head. "Don't be silly. It was just an idle scribble."

"I don't think so." Tessa put her hand on Haley's shoulder and gently pulled her around, so they were facing each other. "Mitch told me about the broken date."

"Great." Haley felt her face warm with embarrassment. "Does the entire population of Shadow know Beau Harding broke a date with me?"

"As far as I know, Mitch and I are the only people besides you and Hardy who know about it." Tessa spoke consolingly.

"And Mavis." Haley remembered the moment all too well. "Wyatt Millan was standing there, and Will Baxter was delivering the mail, so I'm pretty sure they heard him, too. At least Matt Ashford was gone. He's so kind; I probably would have cried if he'd said anything to try to make me feel better."

"You had a busy morning at the station," Tessa observed.

"Of course, we did." Haley couldn't even remember why some of the people had been there now. "It was too much to hope for that I could be humiliated in private."

"I have to ask you," Tessa picked up a crayon off the floor "Why did you agree to a date in the first place? You don't date. You've never made a secret out of the fact you won't date until you think there's a future with the man. Haley, how can there be a future with a man who's set to leave town at the end of the week?"

Haley sank onto the chair nearest her. "I don't know, Tess." She raised her eyes to look into her friend's. "I don't know why I told him yes. I've never had trouble telling a man no before. We'd even been arguing about his pitiful excuse for a shower, and he laughed at me because I was holding poison oak." She needed to stop seeing his eyes and smile. She should be angry. "The brute tricked me into using his rigged shower when he had keys to Luke and Holly's house all along. And then he asked me, and I just said yes. I don't know why."

Tessa held up her hand. "Whoa. You took a shower in Hardy's trailer?"

Out of everything Haley had just told Tessa, that's what she picked up on? She took a calming breath before she spoke again. "I touched poison oak. Hardy warned me if I didn't take a shower and get into different clothes shortly, I would break out and be miserable for days. There wasn't time to go home. So, he gave me a pair of his sweats and one of his T-shirts to wear and waited outside while I showered. Nothing inappropriate took place."

"I see." Tessa slowly smiled. "And then he asked you out, just like that. Out of the blue."

"Yes." Haley glanced at her watch. "We need to get into the Sanctuary, Tess, or we'll be late for worship."

She noticed the smile still on her friend's face. "What are you so happy about?"

"Oh, I was just thinking." Tessa's smile grew wider. "Maybe Mr. Harding isn't as dead set on leaving Shadow as he'd have us think."

Before Haley could ask Tess to clarify that statement, the church bell began to ring. She hurriedly picked up her purse and followed the other woman out of the room, switching off the lights as she left.

She didn't have any idea what Tessa could think might have changed Hardy's mind about sticking around. Since he didn't want to take her out even one time, it sure couldn't have anything to do with her.

Chapter 22

Hardy looked out the window at the scenery flying by. It had been a little harder to get his visit arranged this time. He had to tell Luke it was necessary personal business, and inexplicably found himself feeling guilty when Luke had to ask his dad for help. Then, Elliott hadn't been able to arrange a drive back and forth, so "Steve Scott" purchased round-trip Amtrak tickets from nearby Pattinton to Chicago. The FSA had taken care of everything else, and Elliott assured him he'd be able to remain incognito. The same agents were to meet him when he got off the train.

His mom had been confused when he called to tell her he planned to come and see his dad again. She told Hardy that H.B.'s condition hadn't changed, so there was no sense in endangering himself to visit.

Hardy's dad had understood, but he didn't think his mom realized there was pure evil in the Dohner Family. She couldn't comprehend the depth these criminals would go to for revenge, or how people from the Dohner family enjoyed torturing their victims. His stomach rolled over at just the thought of an attack on his mom. Though he had started to tell her what the Dohners were capable of, he couldn't bear giving her a glimpse into the life he lived for five years. He hadn't murdered, but what he did was bad enough.

Besides, the Dohner family may have given him his initial reason for leaving, but it had taken what happened with Kari

Kelley to cause his "death." He agreed to take advantage of the agency fueled misconception Harding Davis had died trying to protect the woman who worked at the convenience store.

Thanks to Elliott's influence, his family was kept out of the spotlight. And Hardy's supposed heroism finally slid into the archives of the news. Until that TV show broadcast the incident. Hardy may not know what the man looked like, but he would never forget the cold voice ordering the gunman to take care of the woman.

Hardy didn't think he'd ever understand why she stood up. The man may have shot, or even killed Hardy, but he for sure would have taken the hoodlum with him. Of course, she had no way of knowing Hardy wasn't an ordinary citizen, so terror controlled her. He didn't think he would solve this mystery.

He had wanted to attend her funeral, to apologize to her family for not being able to save her. But, of course, it was totally out of the question. Even if the agency could have come up with a plan for a supposed dead man to remain completely unrecognizable at a funeral, Hardy doubted Kari's family would have welcomed him with open arms.

He purposely shifted his thoughts away from Kari Jeffries. In the past, he would have used this quiet time to pray and meditate. Now, he was afraid to talk to God. He feared the depth of anger he felt. How Hardy wanted to tell him how unfair he was, that people like Ted Dohner walked the earth while innocent—No. He had to put that out of his mind.

He shifted his focus to Shadow. From all appearances, Mitch Landon had a real problem on his hands. And all of

Hardy's instincts told him it was going to get worse. One thing he hadn't brought up with Mitch, but puzzled him, was the step the burglars had taken when killing the animals. If the culprits wanted to appear like they were growing increasingly violent or aggressive, the natural thing to do would be to stage each scene progressively worse. But, instead, the last break-in was actually the least destructive of the three. Whoever was doing this might have a plan, but Hardy didn't think they were doing very well at following it.

The conductor's voice announcing the next stop pulled him from his musings. He could already see the unremarkable gray sedan parked in the lot as he exited the train. Warburton's nearly imperceptible wave signaled it was clear for Hardy to continue with the transportation plan. It appeared he was once more going to safely visit his father.

"How was the ride?" Fletcher, from behind the wheel, asked politely once they were on the road.

"It didn't take me long to remember why I don't like to ride the train," Hardy replied. "It's hard to just sit there and watch the scenery pass."

"I know what you mean." The giant in the front passenger seat sympathized. "I took the metro-link everywhere when I lived in St. Louis."

"That was when Warburton tried out for the Rams." Fletcher chuckled. "They were looking at him as a wide receiver. A very wide receiver."

Hardy laughed with the men. The two agents, who told him had been partners for over ten years, were about as different as day and night. Fletcher looked like a hard-working man who might have just walked out of a factory after putting in a full eight hours. Warburton strongly resembled former pro football player Reggie White. In fact, if Hardy didn't know better, he might suspect Mr. White had changed his name and joined the agency.

Warburton sobered as he turned in his seat to look at Hardy. "We have a message from Tom Fowler. He thought you'd like to know, there's still nothing on the radar indicating the Dohners suspect you're anything but dead."

"And my family?" Although he admired his Chicago PD handler, Tom Fowler was known for forgetting the witnesses' families.

The large man chuckled. "Your brother-in-law never lets anyone in the agency forget your family."

Hardy could easily visualize how Elliott reminded them.

Warburton's smile disappeared. "Fowler has a source he trusts keeping him informed, and he'll make sure you know if there's the slightest indication the organization has found out you're alive."

Fowler was responsible for at least five other undercover detectives working the case—that Hardy knew of. For all he knew, they could have a dozen agents infiltrating the organization by now. He still felt frustration that he'd gotten so close to taking down Ted Dohner and failed.

The large man must have read it on Hardy's face. "It's hard to remember sometimes, but we're all on the same team. If one of us wins, we all win. You did a lot of good when you testified, so now it's somebody else's turn to have a crack at Ted Dohner."

"You're right," Hardy had to admit. "It's hard to remember that, though."

The three of them sat in silence for a few minutes, leaving Hardy to try to remember and believe he was indeed a part of a larger group.

"Is your dad worse?" Fletcher's eyes met Hardy's in the rear view mirror.

"No." He didn't want to explain why he felt the need to visit. "I just wanted to see him again. It's rough not being able to spend time with my parents while he's so bad."

"Well, today you'll be in scrubs." Fletcher spoke the words matter-of-factly. "You're Fletcher Warburton, and you're a nurse's aide."

Hardy saw Fletcher's eyes roll. "Yeah, we're real original around here. You should know, though, Warburton suggested Harry Chesterman."

Hardy found himself grinning at the agents. He'd never seen partners this in tune with each other.

"Stephens is afraid you'll draw too much attention if you go in as a visitor," Warburton informed him.

Hardy shook his head. "Draw attention? If anybody thinks I'm really a nurse's aide and asks me to do anything, you may as well stick a neon sign with my name on it over my head. I don't even know how to use a tongue depressor."

"My nephew built an entire road system with tongue depressors," Fletcher said. "He has it on a big sheet of plywood, and he puts his toy cars, trees, and lots of stuff on it. He even has a railroad track crossing the depressor road. Used toothpicks for that."

"I saw a--"

As the three of them shared stories about race cars, Hardy was grateful for the normal conversation. It helped ground the otherwise surreal experience.

There was nobody in the room with H.B. when Hardy walked in. Hardy looked closely at the machine monitoring his dad's heart and took comfort in the steady, strong rhythm of it.

"I'm here, Dad." He murmured as he took his father's hand in his. "I know you're tired, but I need to talk to you. Can you wake up for just a few minutes?"

"B-Beau." One brown eye was open as his name came from his father's mouth. The right side of his mouth moved slightly as he spoke. "That shoe main."

"Okay, Dad." Hardy took his time and considered his dad's words carefully. "I know you want to tell me something. I'm going to do my best to understand you."

"Glad shoe main." The corner of H.B.'s mouth lifted in a lop-sided smile.

Glad shoe main. "Glad you came." Hardy tightened his hand on his dad's. "Is that what you said? You're glad I came?"

"Chess." The older man appeared relieved Hardy understood him.

"Dad, can you help me understand what you meant the last time I was here?" Hardy didn't like seeing the smile disappear, but he didn't have much time and had a feeling this was important. "You said He feel turtle. Jesus water. Be careful. Remember?"

Determination shone through H.B.'s weak eye as he managed a small nod.

"Okay. Did you mean He will hurt you? Be careful?" Hardy's mind raced as his dad once again nodded.

"So, there's somebody I should know who will hurt me. Are you talking about Ted Dohner?" Finally, Hardy knew his dad did indeed have something he considered crucial to tell him.

"Jesus water." The words were slurred, but Hardy still understood them.

"Jesus water?" He thought for a few moments. Jesus water—what did that sound like when he heard it aloud.

Suddenly a loud noise blasted from the monitor as his dad's face went from colorless to bright red. Within seconds, medical personnel had surrounded the bed, with one of them looking at him strangely before asking him to step out of the way.

Hardy stood back, frozen, while they worked on his father. Shortly, one of the men injected a liquid into H.B.'s IV. Almost immediately, his heart rate slowed down and returned to its steady rhythm.

"Are you new to this floor?" One of the women asked.

Even though he was supposed to be a nurses' aide, he decided he simply couldn't pretend at that moment. "I'm his son. Is he all right?"

"Yes, but he needs to sleep." She put a hand on his arm. "That's the best thing your dad can do right now—sleep. I imagine he overdid it, visiting with you. You can stay in here, but please don't disturb him." If she had any questions about his garb and nametag, she didn't seem inclined to ask them.

"What happened?" Sharon Davis rushed into her husband's room. "I heard the code and was afraid it was H.B."

"He's okay now, Mrs. Davis." The nurse spoke soothingly to Hardy's mother. "He just overexerted himself. He needs to rest."

His mom's gaze narrowed in on Hardy. "You're here." Her smile was shaky and didn't quite reach her eyes.

She waited until the hospital staff left the room before she spoke to her son again.

"What did you do, Beau?" Hardy hadn't seen that steely look in her eyes since he was a teenager.

"I was just talking to him." He didn't want his mom involved in whatever his dad was trying to tell him. Ignorance was too often safety in these situations.

"Harding Beauregard Davis, look at me." She hadn't spoken to him like that since he'd driven his motorcycle into the neighbor's pond and tried to blame it on an errant dog. She had known he was speeding. "You came to see him out of the blue when we both know how dangerous it is. Then you speak with him about something that upset his condition." Her eyes were lit with determination. "I suppose you were telling him about the weather, or how the soybean crop is doing this year."

"I'm sorry, Mom." He didn't know what else to say. Endangering his dad's health was the last thing he intended to do.

She pulled on his arm until they were across the room from H.B.'s bed. "That's not going to cut it this time, Beau. Something is going on, and I have every right to know what it is. So you are going to tell me right now."

Hardy looked into his mother's eyes, eyes that had so often been his comfort in the storm. Maybe if would be better if she did understand how the Dohners worked.

"Okay, Mom." He took her hands in his. "The Dohner people are completely heartless. No regret, remorse, or humanity. If they came after you or Callie and the kids . . . Mom, I can't even let myself think of what Dohner would order to be done." He didn't see any signs indicating his mom was upset. "For sure he'd have his men kill you--all of you. In fact, Ted Dohner would think it was poetic justice if he took someone away from me like I took his son away from him. Dohners' men would do what they're ordered, and not bat an eyelid. That's just the way it is."

It surprised him when his mother nodded. "I figured it was something like that." Her eyes narrowed. "But what does that have to do with seeing your father?"

She probably wasn't going to believe this, but he'd try. "I know you think Dad isn't making any sense when he talks to me, but he is. I've figured out most of what he's been saying to me. It has to be important, or he wouldn't be so determined to tell me." His gaze didn't waver. "But he hasn't told me enough for it to completely make sense. I wanted him to tell me more."

"What have you figured out?" His mom was uncharacteristically calm.

"He's said 'he will hurt you,' 'Jesus water, 'and 'be careful'." Something niggled at his mind, but he was too focused on Sharon at the moment to think about it.

"He's talking about those hoodlums coming after you." His mother nodded. "And I imagine he's reminding you that Jesus is still with you."

It clicked into place. "You're right, Mom. Dad is confused. He's warning me about Ted Dohner. He wants to hurt me, and I need to be careful. Dad is saying something about Jesus in the middle of that."

Sharon smiled sympathetically. "I'm sorry, Beau. It's good that it's not another completely different problem, though, isn't it?"

"Yes." He saw her calmness and decided she hadn't processed what he'd told her. "Mom, you have to be careful. The police have a source monitoring the Dohner family, and so far they still think I'm dead. But if you and Dad or Callie catches his attention . . ."

"I understand." His mom's blue eyes were lit from deep within. "But you need to know something, Beau." She squeezed his hands tightly. "Neither your father nor I am afraid to die. We're not in an all-fired hurry to do it, but we know it won't be the end. It will be the beginning of our real lives. This life is a blink of the eye in God's plans. So, don't worry about me."

"You say that." Evidently blunt speaking about the Dohners hadn't made much of an impact on her. "But it's not just the fact you'd die; it's how it could happen. They wouldn't make it easy for you." He studied her nearly serene appearance. She needed to know. "I've seen grown men, healthy and physically larger than me beg to be shot. Please, just think of your grandchildren being in their hands."

"Elliott will keep them safe." Sharon spoke with calm assurance. "And, I understand why you fear those monsters getting their hands on any of us. But, I refuse to let those evil men have even the slightest control over my life."

Where were the tears or pale face? She understood, and believed what she was saying.

"I can see how your faith gives you strength," Hardy acknowledged. "But, please don't do anything foolish. If somebody calls or comes by asking about me, you don't want to talk about it. Maybe you're even a little ashamed your son wasn't able to save that woman." Heaven knew it shamed him. "Hopefully, one day soon they'll get enough on Ted Dohner to take him and his organization down. And then we can go back to life as usual."

"I will never say I'm ashamed of you." His mom spoke firmly. "But I will do everything else you've asked." She slid her arms around his waist and hugged him.

Hardy found himself wishing once more that he was a praying man. He wished he could trust God enough to take care of his family. He just couldn't, though. Not now and maybe not ever again.

Chapter 23

"He went to see his father again yesterday. I think he might be talking." Excitement filled the caller's voice. *"Is he going to have another stroke?"*

James tended to be too eager sometimes. *"Do you have any idea of what he told his son?"*

"Couldn't have been much. Davis hasn't gone to the sheriff." James must have realized he wasn't going to get to murder anybody right away, for he now sounded disappointed.

"From what I've heard, the prognosis on the old man is good. We don't have to rush into anything." He had his ways of keeping abreast of the situation, which his caller would do well to remember.

"What do you want me to do?"

Jump off the highest building in town was on the tip of his tongue, but he needed this person—more than he needed the others working on this project for him. *"Let's wait. Unless he starts telling Davis things he shouldn't know, we'll let the old man get better. Then we'll take him out. It'll hurt his son more that way."* And inflicting pain on Harding Davis was of utmost importance.

"Are you sure we can't just kill him?" Now the man was definitely unhappy.

He bit back the retort on the tip of his tongue. *"You know we can't. Unless you'd like to take the chance of being caught."*

Silence met him before James hung up. It would be okay, though. This man, in particular, knew what was necessary.

Now he had to call an employee. Restructuring communication had been a wise choice. He didn't have to talk to a complete idiot.

His phone's ring startled him. According to the caller ID, an "unknown" from Tuscaloosa. Right.

"What?" He wasn't in the mood to talk to this person, but since he didn't want any one of them to know more than the others, it was necessary.

"Mr. —?"

"Do not use my name!" Maybe he needed to rethink his decision after all. "I've told you before."

"Sorry, sir." This man was much more eager to please him than the previous caller had been.

He made his tone civil. "That's okay."

"What are my instructions? What do you want us to do next?"

"You can hit a couple of places in one night and make sure to leave a clear message for Mr. Davis."

"Yes, sir."

He started to hang up but then thought of something. "Remember there is to be no killing. I don't want to hear about any more dead animals."

"Will do."

He placed the phone on the desk in front of him. Killing animals. He did have some scruples, after all.

Chapter 24

"Base to Sheriff Landon." Haley tried to keep the panic out of her voice, but for the first time in her career, she found it nearly impossible.

"Landon here." He sounded irritated, which was to be expected since he was investigating a break-in at the grocery store. However, she had no choice but to call him.

"Sheriff, we have a possible ten-fifty-four, looks like a ten-seventy-one, at In and Out Convenience store." For the first time in Haley's career, she had just reported a possible dead body, most likely due to a gunshot wound.

"Haley, you sure you're using the right codes on this one?"

"Yes." She had taken a few moments to double check them before she called.

"Call the state dispatcher and see if they can send a few cars to town. I'll need one of them at Ebhart's and the others at the convenience store. I'm on my way there right now."

"Ten-four." She couldn't quite keep the quiver out of her voice. Shadow was a relatively small community, and chances were the body Dennis Ewing had stumbled upon would turn out to be that of somebody she knew.

Haley quickly contacted Cheryl Higgens and had to repeat her request twice before it was understood. A gunshot victim in Shadow was impossible for anybody to imagine.

Father, we all need Your help in this one. Be with everybody involved. Be with the family of that victim and the officers working the scene. Please help those still working at Ebhart's, too. We need to figure out what's going on in our town. I'm asking for your guidance. Amen.

She set up her workstation, prepared for an influx of telephone calls and radio conversations. Maybe she should call Mavis or Ray. No. Mitch would let her know if that's what he wanted. Haley was an experienced dispatcher and good at her job. She could handle this.

The phone rang at the same time Mitch's voice came from the radio.

"Sheriff, one second."

She quickly answered the phone, thankful it was on the non-emergency line, and placed the caller on hold. "I'm back, Sheriff. Phone call at the same time."

"Ten-four." Mitch's voice was strained. "We need an ambulance, and you'll have to call Doc Tindell. He's acting coroner until the election."

"Ten-four."

"Call Mavis in." Mitch spoke again. "Hey! Seal that off until Doc Tindell gets here!"

Haley held the phone away from her ear and could still hear her boss chewing someone out.

Thankfully, he was back to his normal voice when he spoke to her. She wasn't too sure she wouldn't cry if he yelled at her like that. "This appears to be a one-eighty-seven. The phone will be ringing off the wall, and I need you to be clear to stay on the radio."

"Will do." It was a one-eighty-seven—a homicide. "Should I make any other phone calls yet?"

"Negative. We have no positive ID on the male subject at this time."

Haley felt relief and guilt in equal measure. It wasn't likely to be somebody she knew, or Mitch would have recognized him, but that shouldn't matter. Whoever he was had a family and friends who loved and cared for him.

"Let me know what you need, Sheriff."

"Will do. Call Mavis." It wasn't Haley's imagination that he had stressed Mavis's name on the last instruction. He hadn't been able to prove Crystal was their leak, but he was certain she did it. And they didn't need word of this getting out—at least not that the police didn't control.

She suddenly remembered the caller she'd placed on hold. "Sheriff's office."

So began a seemingly endless flurry of phone calls and radio chatter, eased markedly by Mavis's presence. Mavis had taken over answering the phone as Mitch instructed, while Haley manned the radio and computer. She finally gave up and pulled the code sheet out so she could check when one of the deputies or state police officer used an unusual one. While Haley knew every number-letter combination on her cheat sheet, a mistake could waste valuable time.

It was with shock she saw Wayne usher a very displeased Beau Harding into the station. A quick look told her he wasn't in any restraints, but if the scowl on his face were any indication, this visit wasn't by choice.

"Mr. Davis will be in the interrogation room." Wayne spoke as he led the other man past Haley. "If you have a minute, could you bring him something to drink? I had to pull him out of the field, so I imagine he's thirsty."

"Sure."

A few minutes later, Haley walked into the small area christened the multi-purpose room. Interrogation was rare, so they had never needed a room with it being the sole purpose. When she walked in, Hardy was alone. A snarl and his look of anger stopped her in her tracks.

"I brought you a soda." She held out the bottle, half expecting him to smack it out of her hand onto the floor.

His gaze softened. "I'm sorry. This isn't your fault."

"What are you doing here?" She kept her voice level. "You haven't been arrested."

Frustration appeared on his face. "I have no idea. Barney Fife out there showed up at the farm and told me the sheriff wanted to see me at the station. I could either come peacefully or with his help." He smiled grimly. "I'm not in the mood for a fight today."

"I'm glad." Haley wouldn't want to see a fight between Hardy and Wayne. They were both large, well-muscled men, and she couldn't see it having a pleasant outcome for either of them. "Can I get you anything else while you wait for Mitch?"

He gestured to the soft drink she'd let hang by her side as he spoke. "No, but I'd appreciate that bottle. I'm as dry as the desert."

She felt her face warm as she handed him the forgotten soda. "I have to get back on the radio. It's a crazy day."

"Thanks for the drink." He held up the bottle and produced a small smile.

"You're welcome." Haley turned and hurried out of the room and back down the hall. Wayne was just coming out of the men's room.

"What's going on?" She was too curious to abide by her self-imposed "wait until they told her" rules.

Wayne shrugged. "All I know is Mitch wants to talk to him. It's a command performance, too. I was told to get him in here no matter what it took. Thought for a few minutes it was going to be a chore getting him to comply, but he came peacefully enough."

What on earth could be so important Mitch needed to talk to Beau Harding? They were just now wrapping up the scene at the convenience store, with Jeff Fielding staying behind to keep curious bystanders on the right side of the crime scene tape. And the robbery at Ebharts was all but wrapped up, with Hank finishing the last details on it. Bringing Beau into the station surely didn't have anything to do with either crime.

Her blood ran cold. Did it have something to do with the crimes? Granted, the robberies hadn't started until after the man had already been here nearly six months, but could he somehow be connected? Or was it worse? Was he linked to the homicide? Criminals might know as much about the law as an officer. Was that why he'd reminded her of Mitch?

She shook her head as she sat back down at the radio. It was probably nothing to do with either. She was letting her imagination get away from her. Because, even with the unknown identity and secrets he was keeping, Beau Harding just didn't seem like a criminal to her.

But, was she seeing him clearly?

Chapter 25

Okay. If Sheriff Mitch Landon wasn't in this room in the next five minutes, Hardy was walking out. He'd walk all the way back to the farm if he had to. If Landon thought he'd soften Hardy up by making him cool his heels, he'd forgotten he was dealing with a seasoned Chicago police officer. There wasn't an interrogation trick in the book Hardy hadn't seen or used, himself, at one time or another.

What in the world could the sheriff have to ask him about, anyway? Hardy had been sticking to the farm, minding his own business and staying out of the public eye. He had three days to go before he could leave this town behind. Elliott had called to give him his moving instructions. A small town near Terre Haute, Indiana was going to be his new home. He wasn't about to make waves at this stage of the game.

Solid approaching footsteps announced Mitch's presence a few moments before he walked through the door.

He sat down across the table from Hardy and leveled his gaze at him. "I'm sorry I had you brought in like I did. I have to talk to you, and I don't have time for the niceties today."

"I've been waiting for nearly two hours." Hardy kept his voice controlled, even though he wanted to raise it. "I could have just about finished the west field instead of sitting in this closet nursing a bottle of soda. So, get to it already."

Mitch slid the top folder he was carrying across the table. "They're not very good, but I had Linda rush them so you would see what I'm talking about."

Hardy opened the folder, half expecting to see photographs of more dead animals. Instead, he saw what, at first glance, appeared to be blood covering a shelf full of canned goods. However, he knew from experience it was too red to be blood.

"Ketchup," he murmured. He looked at the next few photos and slowly looked up at the sheriff. "Somebody trashed the grocery store."

"Keep looking." Mitch nodded at the file.

It wasn't until Hardy reached the sixth picture he knew what the sheriff wanted him to see. For Davis was scrawled across the meat case in what appeared to be a purple substance. His brows rose as he looked questioningly across the table at the other man.

"Grape jelly. Out of one of those new squeeze bottles." Mitch nodded. "Pretty creative, I guess."

His expression grew more serious as he slid the second folder across the table.

Another break-in on the same day? Hardy opened the folder and immediately saw the message that had been left. This time, Ask Davis was written in ketchup, spread across a wide window. Gas pumps were visible outside.

He looked up at the sheriff. "Where is this?"

"In and Out Convenience store—out by the interstate." Mitch nodded at the pictures Hardy was holding. "Keep looking."

The eighth picture was one Hardy was all too familiar with. A man, obviously dead, was lying next to a large soda display. The cause of death was probably the gunshot wound clearly visible on the back of his head.

His eyes met the sheriff's. "This was the same place?"

Mitch nodded. "Still so sure you haven't been found? We now have a homicide in the same location as a message that was most likely left for your benefit."

"Who's the victim?" It was impossible to tell since the man was flat on his stomach, arms and legs outstretched.

"We're not going to get a clear look at his face until his exit wound is cleaned up, and we couldn't find any ID for him. The state police are running his prints through CODIS to see if they can find a match, and I just had my dispatcher get on the computer to see if there are any reports of a missing person who fits his description."

Roughly five-eleven, one-seventy, brown hair, no face to go by—they'd better hope they matched his prints. Then Mitch's last words sank in.

"Haley's still here?" It was after seven o'clock. Surely she didn't work this late.

"No. My night guy is here." Mitch seemed to shake off the question. "So, do you have any idea why a homicide and message to you ended up at the same place?"

Hardy considered the possibilities. "One thing I'm still sure of, Sheriff. I lived, ate, and breathed the Dohner organization for five years, so I know what I'm talking about. If any of them have found me, I promise you I'd be dead. They wouldn't play games like this. Ted Dohner would consider this juvenile and beneath him. He imagines himself in a class all of his own."

"Then, what is going on in my town?!" Mitch demanded angrily. "It has something to do with you, and we both know it."

"What do you expect me to do?" Hardy wasn't going to take this sitting down. "I told you I have no idea what's going on, and I don't."

"Okay." The sheriff visibly calmed. "I have a proposition for you."

Hardy most certainly did not like the sound of that. "What?"

"You have a strong background in organized crime. I need your expertise on this, Davis. I'm not foolish enough to try and pretend Shadow County is equipped to handle what's been going on, even with the state's help. I'm offering you a badge."

"Are you crazy?" The sheriff had to be certifiable. "If somebody really has found me, somewhere down the line it will eventually get back to Ted Dohner that I'm alive. Then, he'll come after me. And if you think you've got a mess right now, let me assure you, it's a walk in the park compared to what that man and his 'family' are capable of."

"I said I'm not foolish," Mitch reminded him. "Why would anybody in Chicago notice a new deputy being hired in a small county downstate? We would make sure your real name didn't come out. I'd be hiring Beau Harding. It's that simple."

Hardy shook his head. "It's not going to happen. I'm not risking my family like that. I'll be gone in three days. Sooner now. I'll tell Luke I have to leave early and be out of here first thing in the morning. Then, whoever is doing this will give up and go away."

Mitch's disbelieving expression didn't falter. "We both know that isn't how it will work. If somebody is trying to get your attention, they might just amp things up even more if you leave. To try and get you back to town." He glared at Hardy. "Only you'd be gone and wouldn't even know it was happening. The man who left everything he knew and cared about to do what's right would never run out and leave an entire community in danger because of him."

Hardy took a deep breath. "Listen, I'm sorrier than I can ever say. I didn't mean to bring trouble with me. But you're asking for too much. I can't--I won't put my family at risk for anything. Like you said, I gave up everything in part, to keep them safe, and I just won't throw that away."

"Then we'll compromise." Mitch sat forward in his chair and tented his fingers on the table in front of him. "Come to work for me as a consultant. We'll make sure you stay off the radar, even though it's clear somebody knows who you really are. I'll even arrange for you to have a gun, for your own safety. Just help me fix this." He looked accusingly at Hardy. "You just admitted you brought this trouble with you. Stay at least long enough to help me fix it."

"I can't." Did the man not understand what he was asking Hardy to do?

Shades came down over Mitch's eyes, and all traces of friendliness were gone. "Then I have no choice but to hold you here for suspicion of criminal conspiracy. I'll come up with more charges as they're needed. You're sticking around Shadow one way or another, Mr. Davis."

Anger took hold of Hardy, but years of retaining a calm demeanor in trying situations kicked in." You forget who you're dealing with. I can have the FSA here with one call. I'm leaving town first thing in the morning."

The sheriff didn't hesitate. "You forget where you're at. This is a small town in a small county. We have one of the snoopiest reporters in the state. All it would take is one little phone call. Karl King would dedicate the entire front page of the paper to an article about a hero like Harding Davis living under our noses for six months. And he wouldn't be shy about letting big city papers—like Chicago—have his article. I believe that would make it difficult for you to remain in the area, no matter what name you used."

Hardy stood up so abruptly his chair toppled over backward. "Are you threatening me?"

The door behind Mitch swung open, and a young deputy stood there with his hand on his gun. "You okay, Sheriff?"

Mitch held up his hand as he stood. "Everything is fine, Hank. Mr. Harding needs a few minutes." He turned his attention back to Hardy. "For the record, Harding, I don't make threats. I keep promises. And I promised the people in this county to do my best to keep it a safe place to live. I've told you what I need from you to make that happen."

He turned and followed the deputy out the door, closing it softly behind them.

Hardy's first instinct was to pick up the chair and throw it as hard as he could. What was he going to do? Landon wasn't heartless; he wouldn't put Hardy's family in danger by revealing he was alive. Should Hardy call his bluff?

But, what if the sheriff were desperate enough to follow through? Even the slightest hint that Harding Davis was alive would ruin everything. He'd be out in Boise, Idaho before he could sneeze, and his family would be in more danger than ever. Not even Elliott would be able to keep them safe.

The small-town sheriff had him caught between third base and home plate. Because it all came down to one thing. What would Harding Davis do to protect his family? The answer was easy. Anything he had to.

"You'd better be able to keep me off the radar." Because if the sheriff didn't, matters would quickly become worse than they were—for everybody.

Chapter 26

Pure rage filled him as he read the newspaper article again. This was not part of the plan and therefore intolerable.

He nearly picked up the phone and threw it through the plate glass window when it rang.

"Hello," he bit out.

"Roscoe's dead." The person who was extremely fond of himself sounded frightened. He was probably afraid he'd shoot the messenger.

"I read the paper." He took a deep breath. "Not that it matters, but what happened?"

"I'm not sure myself," James admitted. "It looks like Roscoe and Brockman got into an argument about something. Harve said he didn't even know Brockman had his gun on him until he pulled it and shot Roscoe."

"Explain to me why he was shot in the back of his head. The paper calls it execution style." There was no way the story he'd just been told was the truth.

"Would you like to hear my idea of what happened?"

"Much more than the cockamamie story those worthless men made up."

"I think Roscoe got to mouthing off about the money again. He thought since he was the one we made initial contact with, he should get a bigger share of the pay-off. I think he spoke out one too many times, and the other two took him out, plain and simple. They probably figured it would make their statement for Davis more effective to leave a dead body there, and if they could fool us, then no foul."

He made an immediate decision. "Tell them an anonymous tip will find its way to the sheriff's office if anything like this happens again. Remind our employees there is no proof linking them to us, so we have nothing to lose."

"Okay."

"Just remember what you're there to do, and don't disappoint me." James should know by now; disappointments were not tolerated.

Chapter 27

Haley lifted the end of her small sofa and shoved the vacuum cleaner head under the front leg. She couldn't remember the last time she expended this much energy on housecleaning, and she still felt like an overcharged battery.

It was Saturday, so Beau Harding—or whatever his name was—had left Shadow this morning. It wasn't like she hadn't known he would. And it wasn't like there was any reason for her to care what he did, anyway. But she did! Was the interest he'd shown in her an act? Had she totally misread the situation?

She shouldn't even be thinking about the man. For one thing, she still didn't know who he really was. For another, he had been brought into the station for Mitch to "talk to" on the very same day a robbery and homicide occurred. For all Haley knew, he was the prime suspect.

No. The man who'd teased her about fondling poison oak, and then been considerate enough to help make sure she didn't suffer the consequences of her ignorant actions, simply wasn't capable of crimes like burglary or murder. For some reason, she was sure the man she'd seen that day was the real Beau Harding, no matter what he called himself.

The doorbell brought her out of her reverie. She quickly shut off the vacuum and headed for the door. Before she opened it, she tightened her ponytail and hoped she didn't have dust on her nose.

She wondered if she was hallucinating when she discovered Beau Harding.

He smiled. "Hi."

Haley was struck speechless for a minute. Then she sputtered. "I thought you were leaving town this morning. Did Luke suffer a relapse?"

"No." His smile didn't dim. "Can I come in?"

Where were her manners? "Please." She backed up so he could walk through the door. "I've just been cleaning." There were signs of her efforts all over the room, from the dusting spray and rag she'd left on the table, to the small stepladder she climbed on to clean ceiling fan blades.

His amused gaze scanned the room before settling on her face. "I can see that."

"I thought you were leaving this morning," she repeated, completely taken aback by his presence.

"Things changed." His smile faded. "Can we sit down and talk? Or if you'd rather, we can go for a walk or something."

"You want to talk to me." Was this man bipolar or something? "What about?"

Troubled gray eyes looked into hers. "I'm sorry about our date. I know I hurt you, and I wanted to explain."

"Mighty fond of yourself, aren't you?" Haley mentally stiffened her spine. "What makes you think anything you say or do could hurt me?"

"I saw it in your eyes." As if of its own volition, his right hand rose and gently traced her cheekbone. "You have the most expressive eyes I've ever seen."

Haley's first instinct was to lean her face against Hardy's hand, but thankfully, rational thought took over.

She stepped back, out of his reach. "Why don't you say whatever you feel is necessary? I have a lot of work to do."

"I need to tell you why I broke our date." Apparently, Hardy wasn't going away until he had his say. "Please, just sit down with me for a few minutes and let me explain. Then, if you want me to leave, I won't bother you again."

What should she do? Haley had never felt drawn to a man like she did the one in front of her. Maybe she owed it to herself to at least listen.

"Okay." She walked over and sat on the chair, indicating he could sit on the sofa.

Once they were sitting and facing each other, Hardy suddenly appeared to be searching for words. Haley waited patiently until he finally spoke.

"I have never reacted to a woman like this." Her heart sped up in response to his calm, firm voice. "I want—No. I feel a need to get to know you better." He looked into her eyes as if willing her to believe him. "So, I asked you out."

"And then what?" If Haley hadn't remembered she was an adult in the nick of time, she would have chucked the can of dusting spray at him. "You just decide you don't want to get to know me better? You see me at work, and what? I look hideous sitting at the dispatch station? Did I have on a color that didn't go with my complexion? Maybe you didn't like—"

"Stop." Hardy's command halted her harangue. "There is nothing wrong with you. It's me. I couldn't take you out because of who I am."

"And who might that be?" She was on her way to being good and angry.

He looked steadily into her eyes. "I'm Beau Harding. I—"

"I know that's not your real name." Haley's voice rose as she sprang to her feet. "Look, whatever-your-name-is, you don't have to explain. You're a man passing through town who I'll never see again. Except for a mutual attraction I can't explain, there is no reason for either of us to remember the other."

Hardy stood up and stepped over to her. "Do you think I want to be merely passing through? Do you think I want to have secrets I can't tell you?" His eyes were full of pain and frustration. "I'm going to be in town longer than I thought. I know I should stay as far away from you as possible, but here I am anyway. Tell me you don't feel the same way I do, and I'll leave and never darken your door again."

"I don't . . ." Haley had never been a liar. She covered her face with her hands and turned away from him. After she had regained control of her emotions, she turned back and lowered her hands to look into his eyes. "I feel it, too, but I have to be strong and stay away from you. I don't think I can start a relationship when there's no way it will last. We don't have any chance at all of that happening."

He seemed to consider her words before he spoke. "Then, what about being friends? We won't date. We'll just be friends.

Then, when this is over, and I leave, we'll say goodbye and have fond memories of friendship."

She came to her feet, forcing him to step back. "When what is all over?"

Hardy's brows lowered for a moment before he appeared to come to a decision. "You'll know anyway. My exact role won't be public knowledge, but I'm helping the sheriff with these cases he's dealing with."

"But why would you—?" Then she knew. "I was right. You are a police officer."

"I was." He reached out and gently placed his hands on her shoulders. "That's all I can tell you . . . for your own good. You'll have to trust me on that."

Haley's mind whirled with the implications of what she was learning. "You're a police officer pretending to be a farmer. Are you in witness protection?"

His hands tightened slightly on her shoulders. "Please, Haley. Don't ask me questions I can't answer."

He'd just answered her question. Her eyes widened as she looked at him. "Then you can't help Mitch. People will talk, and then Karl King might find out and put it in the paper. Whoever is after you will find you. You can't do it."

"Listen, Haley, it started out not being my choice," His gaze didn't move. "But I thought about it, and the sheriff is right. I owe it to everybody here to help fix this." He let his hands slide down her arms and take hold of hers. "And it looks like it's my fault in the first place."

"How can it be your fault?" She was growing more confused by the second. "Please, Har—I don't want to call you Hardy. Can I at least know your first name? I won't use it in front of anybody."

He smiled gently. "I won't tell you my first name, but you can call me Beau. That's what my family calls me."

"Beau is your real name?" That surprised her.

What looked like relief was in his eyes. "Part of it."

She readjusted her thoughts from his name back to what they'd been talking about. "It can't be your fault. Please...Beau...explain it to me. It won't go any further."

"I was undercover for a very long time, and then I had to die. Some dangerous people would love to get their hands on me if they knew I was still alive." Silver eyes seemed to search hers. "I'm certain it's not them, but it could be somebody else I've made angry in the past." He tightened his fingers around her hands. "And I've made a lot of people angry."

"Somebody is doing all of this...robbing...killing...to get to you?" She leaned closer to him. "I don't understand."

"Neither do I," he admitted. "That's why I'm sticking around to help the sheriff sort this out." He dropped her hands and backed away from her. "I understand if we can't even be friends. It may not be a good idea to be my friend right now."

Everything shifted in Haley's mind and became apparent. "You need me—a friend. You can talk about it, and your secrets will be safe with me." And she would pray every day that God would protect her heart from becoming involved in their relationship.

Hardy looked uncertain for a moment before a small smile appeared on his face. "Thank you."

Haley shoved back her wayward thoughts and smiled as brightly as she could. "As your friend, I'm inviting you to come to church with me in the morning."

His smile immediately disappeared. "I don't really go to church."

Her heart sank as she frowned. "You're not a Christian? Or do you just not like to attend church?"

"I believe in God." Hardy looked as though the words were being wrenched from him. "But I'm pretty mad at Him right now, and I don't see that getting better anytime soon."

Haley may not know why Hardy was angry with God, but she was familiar with the emotion.

"I was mad at God, too, Beau," she admitted. "I blamed him when my parents died. They were all I had. I didn't think he really loved me because he took them away from me."

"How did they die?" Hardy took her hands in his again.

A shaky laugh emerged from Haley's throat. "I was eighteen, fresh out of high school. Mom and Dad took me to a beach in South Carolina for my graduation present, one last family vacation before I went away to college." She could still hear her mom's laughing protests as her dad sang horribly with the radio during the long drive there. "We had been at the beach for four days. It was our last day there. Mom wanted to go swimming one more time before we left." Tears came unbidden to her eyes.

"You don't have to tell me." Hardy spoke gently.

She shook her head. "I want to. We went into the ocean—not really swimming, more like standing and being buffeted by waves. The tide was out so we could walk clear to the end of the pier." The memory Haley was envisioning now was one she would never forget, no matter how hard she tried. "Mom got caught in what they called a rip current. Dad was close enough he tried to get her. They were both pulled under. I tried to go help, but a lifeguard stopped me. The lifeguards tried, but the current was too strong. They both drowned."

"I'm sorry, Haley."

A smile broke through her tears. "It's okay. Because even though they were taken before I wanted them to be, I know where they're at, and Who they're with. I'll be with them again someday, too. It took me a long time to realize that, but I did. And whatever you're mad at God about, if you let him, he'll help you accept it." She framed his face in her hands. "You just have to let him."

Hardy reached up and wiped an errant tear from her face. "I'm glad you found peace, but my situation is different. I don't think there's anything anybody could say or do to make me accept what happened."

"God isn't just anybody." She could see pain underlying the anger he was sharing with her. Whatever happened had deeply hurt this man, and he needed to let God help him heal. "Please just come to church with me tomorrow. You can sit and watch. You don't have to sing or pray or anything."

He gave her a measured look. "I'll think about it. That's the best I can do."

She smiled brightly. "And I'll pray about it. Church starts at ten. I go to the one across from the park. Do you know which one I mean?"

"Yes. But don't hold your breath waiting for me to get there."

"I'll save you a seat." Her eyes twinkled as she gave him a quick hug. "Now, I hate to run you off, but I have to get my housework finished."

A few minutes later, after Hardy had left, Haley sat down on a chair. What was she opening herself up to by being Beau Harding's friend?

First of all, even though she now knew he was a police officer in some kind of witness protection program, she still had no idea what his real name or situation was. Second, he had no intention of staying longer than it took to help Mitch catch the people responsible for the crime wave in Shadow. Third, she was very drawn to the man romantically, making it dangerous to establish any kind of a relationship with him. And finally, he was struggling with his faith.

If it's wrong for me to be his friend, Lord, why does it feel right? Even with all the reasons making it seem like a bad idea, I still feel like I have to do it. Are You drawing me to him, or am I letting other things control me? I'm asking now for your guidance. Please use me to help him come to grips with the pain he's suffering and ease the doubt he's feeling about you. If that's all I can do for him, that's enough. Amen.

Chapter 28

Hardy and Matt Ashford paused at the front door of the police station. "You'd really rather take pictures of dead animals than drive a truck?" Matt still seemed surprised by the answer Hardy gave him over an early dinner.

"I told you, I'm not cut out for sitting in one place." No matter how much Hardy liked Matt, he couldn't share what he was really doing. As much for his friend's safety as his own.

Matt shook his head. "Better you than me, son." He gave a small salute. "Got to get back on the road. I still have a long way to go before I call it a night."

"See you later, Matt." Hardy watched a moment as the other man walked down the sidewalk to where he'd parked his semi-truck, before turning and heading into the police station.

He walked back to the dispatch area, where a man way too dressed up for a visit to a police station stood talking to the woman behind the counter.

"I'm Beau Harding," he told the dispatcher with Crystal on her badge. "Sheriff Landon is expecting me."

Mitch appeared before she could respond.

"Hey, Millan," Mitch addressed the other man before turning his attention to Hardy. "Come on back. We're all set up and ready for you to get started."

Hardy followed the sheriff down the hall to the room in which he'd been "talked to," which was now set up as a conference room. He sat on the chair Mitch indicated.

Hardy looked at the other men sitting around the room. Other than the sheriff standing at the corkboard, the tall, black man who had brought Hardy in was leaned back in a chair, nursing a bottle of lemonade. Hardy remembered his name was Wayne Daniels. The other four sat at attention, waiting for Mitch to begin their Saturday afternoon meeting.

"Men, this is Beau Harding." Mitch gestured toward him. "Hardy, I think you remember Wayne." The black man nodded amiably. "And the man sitting next to him is Jeff Fielding." The man with coal black hair, probably about Hardy's age, casually saluted. "And the young man sitting there writing down every word I say is Hank Stone." The young, red-haired deputy's face flushed as he looked up from the pad of paper he was industriously writing on, to smile at Hardy. "The duo sitting in the back are Tom Winkler and Jerry Young, our very own Tom and Jerry." The men, who reminded Hardy of people he couldn't quite place, nodded.

"You men will have to trust me when I tell you Mr. Harding is highly qualified to work on cases like the ones we're dealing with in Shadow right now. He's been kind enough," Mitch looked pointedly at Hardy, "to agree to act as a consultant. For reasons I can't go into, the depth of his involvement stays in this office. His name stays out of the paper."

"So, he's going to look at case files and tell us who's doing it?" Deputy Fielding looked less than impressed. "If he's like that FSA profiler, why don't we just ask him for help instead of this guy?"

"He's not a profiler, Jeff." Mitch's tone of voice was enough to cause the deputy to squirm in his seat. "He'll be on site with us. I'm giving him a gun. For all intents and purposes, he's a deputy acting as a consultant. We're just not letting the public know."

Wayne set his soda on his leg. "Won't people wonder why he's at crime scenes with us?"

"You can thank my fiancée for this one." Mitch appeared to be pleased with whatever Tessa had come up with. "Beau Harding is now our official crime scene photographer."

Wayne sputtered on the swallow of lemonade he'd just taken. "I'm sorry, Mitch, but we have a total of six...seven, if you count him, on staff, and you expect people to be okay with one of us doing nothing but take pictures?"

"I'll handle any flak we take," Mitch assured his deputy. "And just so all of you know, Harding is the man who linked the crimes together for me. You all asked me how I figured it out. Well, I didn't. He did."

The attitude of the deputies changed immediately. Hardy could now see a mixture of respect and admiration on their faces.

"So, let's bring Harding up to speed. Hank, dig into your notes and tell us about our witness."

Hardy wasn't aware there had been any witnesses, so his interest immediately heightened as the young man stood and walked to the board.

"Hilda Crowe, eighty-seven, lives alone on River Junction Road. The back of her house faces the back of the animal clinic. With the corn down in the field between the two buildings, it's a clear view of sight between them—both ways. She says on the night in question, she observed our perpetrators."

"In their spaceship," Tom dryly observed.

Hank's face colored. "In a blue vehicle. I believe she saw a dark blue panel van, like the one seen at one of our other crimes. She kept saying one of the men was important, which I finally figured out meant he was wearing a uniform."

"A police officer?" Hardy hoped not. Bad cops were worse than the lowest criminals in his book.

Hank shook his head. "She waved me off when I showed her photos of ours and the state uniforms and claimed it was something different.

Hardy mentally filed that information away to consider later. "How many people did she see?"

"Three, and she was certain they were all men."

"Okay. So, the blue vehicle further supports our premise it's the same perpetrators in all three of those crimes." Mitch looked at Hardy as though he expected him to comment.

"You're looking at the same perps in all of your cases, Sheriff. I can say that with certainty because of the lack of rage and obvious staging at each scene."

"Even the shooting at the convenience store?" Hank was the one who asked.

Hardy had taken a closer look at the crime scene photos. "I don't think the shooting was planned. I think your victim is one of your criminals. It was a double cross, or maybe he managed to make his partners mad enough one of them waited until his back was turned to shoot him in the head. I believe they were finished and ready to leave when it happened."

"So, do we have an ID on the victim yet?" Wayne asked Mitch.

The sheriff shook his head. "His prints aren't in CODIS. No missing person reports matching his description. The coroner supplied me with a picture of his face after he got him cleaned up, though. I may have the state lab fix it up to show to the public." Mitch pulled a sheet of paper from the envelope in front of him and tacked it to the board as Hank sat down.

Hardy started to give the photo a cursory glance but was immediately drawn back to it. He stood up and walked to the board for a closer look.

"You recognize him, Harding?" Mitch asked.

What could the presence of this man mean? Hardy nodded. "His name is Roscoe Callen." He shook his head. "Sheriff, this doesn't make sense. Callen is a small-time thief who has been arrested more times than I can count. His prints should have shown up in CODIS right away."

"You sure you got the right man?" Mitch's voice was quiet.

Hardy carefully again before he answered. "That's either him or he has an identical twin I've never heard of. I don't know why his prints didn't come up, but that man is Roscoe Callen."

Mitch seemed to accept Hardy's word as fact. "Okay, then. Any idea who he might be working with?"

Another puzzle. "He was a loner. He had the personality and social skills of a turnip. Even other criminals disliked him."

"Apparently one of them disliked him enough to shoot him in the back of the head," Jerry dryly observed.

Hardy slowly nodded. "I can see that. Roscoe somehow pulled in on a team job. Mouthing off like he always did, until one or more of the other guys got fed up with him." That theory made more sense than anything else he could come up with.

The sheriff sighed. "We're still back to square one. Unless this guy had it out for you." He looked expectantly at Hardy.

"I don't know why he would," Hardy honestly admitted. "I've never even arrested the guy. I was at the station plenty of times when he was hauled in, but I'm not sure how he'd even know who I was."

"So, maybe it's not you after all." Hardy didn't know whether the sheriff looked relieved or disappointed. If he wasn't the "Davis" the messages were being left for, they were really in the dark.

He felt pretty sure of one fact, though. "I think there's a good chance it's me. I just haven't figured out exactly what's going on or who's behind it."

"Could this Callen guy be hired muscle?" Hank asked.

"I don't know," Hardy had to answer. "He was money-hungry. The man tried to rob a restaurant at the Navy Pier while over two hundred recruits were on leave from the Great Lakes Naval Base. I guess he didn't figure a sailor would try to stop him." Hardy smiled wryly at the memory. "It made the paper because three female recruits took him down." As far as Hardy could remember, Callen hadn't been identified, other than as "an escaping thief."

"You're a Chicago cop." Hardy realized too late he'd said too much when Wayne spoke.

He exchanged looks with the sheriff before he reluctantly nodded. The two of them had wondered if it would come to this.

"He's a Chicago cop with a large syndicate out for his blood. He disappeared and is living here under an assumed name. He's doing us a solid by helping us out. That's all you need to know." Mitch's expression dared any of his deputies to object.

"You're Harding Davis." Jeff spoke flatly. "You're supposed to be dead." He looked at Wayne and then back to Hardy. "I read about the trial. It was your testimony that put Teddy Dohner away for good."

Hardy didn't know what to think when the deputy stood up and walked forward to offer his hand. "You have guts. Most men would have denied knowing anything to save their own hides, but you showed up in court every day and testified. I'll be proud to work with you."

"Nobody will find out who you are," Wayne assured him as he stood. "We'll protect your secret, and we'll protect you." The two deputies in the back row offered similar sentiments.

Hank stood and spluttered around so much Hardy nearly offered him a tissue to dry off with. Before the embarrassed young man was finished fawning over him, Hardy halfway feared Hank was going to ask for his autograph.

It was a much more cohesive unit that sat back down to listen to their sheriff.

"Thank you." It was all Hardy could think to say. "I'm sorry I brought trouble to Shadow, but I'm going to do my best to help get rid of it before I leave."

"You aren't responsible for what others choose to do." Mitch looked him straight in the eye. "I was wrong to try to force you to stay, and I won't try to stop you from leaving again."

Hardy shook his head. "I'm not leaving until I know this is taken care of." He thought of the people he'd grown to care about. Luke, Holly, Nancy, Matt, Tessa, Barney, and certainly not least of all, Haley, as well as others he'd met in passing. "I tried not to care about people in this town, but some of you just wouldn't let me get away with it. So, let's put our heads together and figure out our next step."

Mitch smiled at Hardy before he looked at his watch. "We have a couple of hours since the state boys are helping us out. Let's brainstorm."

"Where do we think the next break-in might be?" Wayne asked. "Is there a pattern?"

Mitch flipped the corkboard to show a map of the county on the other side. There were red pushpins at five points on it.

"I have the site of each incident marked." He pointed to a pin. "This is the salon." His finger indicated corresponding pins as he spoke. "Then next was the animal clinic all the way out here. The insurance agency, Ebharts, and the convenience store was our last—so far."

"They're all over the place," Jeff observed. "I don't see any kind of a pattern."

Hardy's mind was working, and he'd come up with a different angle. "What about where our perps are staying?" The other men stopped and looked at him. "Roscoe didn't live here in Shadow. He had to be staying somewhere. What about motels, or the bed and breakfast?"

Hank leafed through his notebook before he spoke. "There haven't been any guests at the bed and breakfast for eight weeks, and no guests at any of the motels or the inn who stayed longer than two nights."

"Okay." Hardy looked from Hank to Mitch. "So, where are they staying?"

"Someplace where they won't be noticed." Mitch spoke confidently, but then he frowned. "I just don't see how they could blend into the community without somebody noticing them. Haley and the other dispatchers have been answering some pretty ridiculous calls."

"What about the campground out at the nature preserve?" Hank hesitantly offered the suggestion. "It wouldn't be busy this time of the year, would it?"

Wayne gave Hank a pat on the back. "They could have a tent on one of the primitive forest spots, and nobody would see them, not even Joe. He only goes that far out for maintenance, and I doubt he'd be mowing in October."

The deputies exchanged looks of growing conviction. They clearly liked Hank's idea.

"Okay." Mitch looked around the room. "Let's go check this out. Wayne, you and Hank follow my car. Davis—Sorry, man." He smiled apologetically at Hardy. "Harding, you're riding with me, and Jeff, I need you to patrol. We don't want the community to think we've forgotten them." He nodded at Winkler and Young. "You two go home and get some sleep. I'm going to need you on your toes every night from now on."

The men were quickly organized, and Hardy soon found himself sitting beside Mitch in the sheriff's squad car. They were running with lights, but no siren.

"Feel like old times?" Mitch glanced over at Hardy to ask.

"Very, very old times," Hardy had to admit. "I've been in an unmarked too many years to remember what it feels like to drive a cruiser."

"What's it like to go undercover?" Mitch seemed almost embarrassed by his own curiosity, but evidently not enough to keep him from asking. "I've always wondered."

Hardy searched for a way to describe his old job. "It's rough. You can't just tell people you're somebody else; you have to be that person. I was Joe Ryman for nearly five years while I worked the Dohner case." It felt very strange to be talking about it. "I probably still would be if it hadn't been necessary to testify against Teddy."

Mitch glanced over at him again. "What made your bosses decide it was more important to put you on the stand than stay undercover? To be so close to taking him down and ending it so abruptly had to be tough."

While Hardy hadn't liked it, he understood the decision. "Teddy Dohner managed a network of people who sold drugs to kids. And he didn't care about quality, only quantity, so the drugs he was moving were very dangerous. Kids were dropping like flies from using stuff his people sold. And he couldn't care less, as long as the money kept coming in."

"I read about him when I checked up on you." Mitch's wry smile was probably as close to an apology as he would give. Seems like every article had a different body count, though.

"There's no way of knowing the exact total, but the number they came up with for trial was fifty-two. Fifty-two kids, some as young as twelve years old, died so Teddy Dohner could have a larger profit margin."

Hardy fought back the rage he had dealt with for more than a year. "They were leaving me in place until the prosecutor realized he was losing. The witnesses he called were drug pushers and people who bought from them. He needed something solid to take Teddy out of business." He shrugged. "That was me. Joe Ryman had access to evidence that would lock Teddy Dohner up for good, but it wouldn't hold up without my testimony. So, they called me in and blew my cover."

"So, to take down the son, you had to sacrifice your chance to get the father." Mitch's brows lowered in a frown.

"That about sums it up."

"That's a bad situation, no matter how you look at it." Mitch's knuckles were white on the steering wheel. "The FSA must have hated losing their only chance to take down the ringleader."

"The media was purposely misinformed; I wasn't the only chance we had to get to the old man, but I was further in than anybody else had ever made it." Hardy trusted the man sitting next to him. "There are others."

"Agents? In the Dohner network?" The sheriff's gaze left the road to look at Hardy.

"Yeah. There are agents from the FSA and Chicago PD working the case. I recognized a couple of them, but I never knew how many other officers were undercover in the organization, or how deep they were."

"So there's a good chance they'll still bring the man in?"

Hardy nodded. "The good guys haven't given up; they just suffered a setback."

"Is there any chance this Callen has anything to do with the Dohners?" Mitch turned the car onto a blacktop road.

"My gut says no." Hardy had thought long and hard about the possibility. "Dohner has a lot of money, and Roscoe Callen was a petty thief. If Ted Dohner found out I am alive, he would send somebody with what he considers class. He'd want the right people to know he'd gotten even with me, and he wouldn't want somebody with Callen's lack of pedigree sullying his reputation. Does that make sense?"

Mitch nodded. "Perfect." The sheriff squinted as a ray of sunlight hit the rearview mirror. "Can you think of any other people you've put away who would be angry enough to do all this?"

"The Dohner case was all I worked for the last five years of my career, and I don't think I ever arrested anybody who would hold that much of a grudge before I went undercover." Hardy's mind went back to the last crime he'd been involved in. The man who'd slipped out of the convenience store had gotten off scot free and would be foolish to risk being caught just to get even with Hardy. Before his thoughts traveled the inevitable path to Kari Jeffries, he pushed them out of his mind and focused on what they were doing. He pulled his gun out of the holster strapped to his shoulder and checked it.

"Is the nine millimeter okay?" Mitch nodded to the pistol in Hardy's hands. "It's what we all carry."

"It'll work." Hardy lifted it and familiarized himself with the weapon's weight. "Holding a gun feels strange."

"Well, hang on to it now, because we're almost there." Mitch pulled into a long tree-lined lane that was nothing more than two strips of gravel with grass growing between them. "We'll have to go on foot for the last five hundred yards or so. Be on the lookout for any vehicles. According to Joe Willis, there shouldn't be anybody out here."

There were no vehicles in the graveled parking area when Mitch pulled the squad car in. Hardy couldn't help but admire how he and Wayne automatically angled the cars so anybody trying to drive out would find it impossible to get through.

"Wayne, Hank, you two go around and come in from the south side. Hardy and I will approach from the north. There are lots of places a car could be stashed." Mitch looked at his deputies. "Remember, at least one of these guys killed his own partner. He won't have any qualms about shooting an officer."

Hardy felt the adrenaline flow as he headed into the wooded area. He and Mitch were following a nearly invisible trail, but Mitch indicated he wanted them to each remain a few yards from either side of it. It seemed like it took longer than the five minutes it did to reach the first of the primitive campsites.

"How many sites are there?" He kept his voice down so only Mitch could hear him.

"Fifteen individual and one large group site that will hold twenty tents. Local churches use it for youth outings." Mitch grimaced when he stepped on a pile of fallen leaves. "That would have told a hearing impaired person we're here."

They both kept their guns drawn as they slowly made their way through the sites. It was at the seventh campsite where they found something.

"Somebody's been here recently." Mitch spoke as he looked around. "You can see where a tent has been pitched." He knelt by the fire pit. "Charcoal's been dumped in here lately. No leaves have fallen on it."

The fading sunlight sparkled off something. Hardy leaned over to investigate. "Sheriff, I've got a gun here."

Mitch quickly joined him. He picked up a stick and lifted it by its trigger guard.

"It looks like a thirty-eight," Hardy observed.

"The same caliber Doc Tindell thinks killed Callen." Mitch pulled a handkerchief out of his pocket and gently grasped the gun by the end of its barrel. He looked around the site as he stood up. "Whoever was here is long gone. Why do you suppose they left this behind?"

Hardy shook his head. "No idea." This whole case was one giant puzzle that was becoming harder to solve with every clue they found. "No idea at all."

Chapter 29

Haley looked at the empty place beside her and sighed. Hardy had told her not to expect him, but she had hoped he'd come to church this morning. Missy Landon, sitting on Haley's left, smiled sympathetically. Haley regretted telling the other woman she invited Hardy to join her.

"Am I too late?"

Haley looked at the man who had quietly sat beside her and forced back her disappointment. "No, Wyatt. It hasn't started yet."

He smiled his too-charming smile at her. "Thank you for saving me a seat."

"I . . ." What exactly was she going to say to him? I was saving it for somebody else? That would be intolerably rude, and Haley could never intentionally make anybody feel unwelcome here.

Missy leaned around Haley. "Hi, Wyatt."

"Melissa." He graced her with a smile. "I didn't know you'd be here."

Joe Willis, who was sitting on the other side of Missy, leaned forward and gave a half wave to Wyatt. Haley got a distinct impression neither he nor Melissa were overly thrilled to see Wyatt there. Well, this was God's house after all.

She pasted on a smile. "I'm glad you decided to visit."

His attention was on something in front of them. "Is that Clay Richmond?" He nodded his head to the left.

Haley looked. "Yes. Do you know him?"

Wyatt shook his head. "No, but I'd like to."

As usual, Pastor Rollins led a compelling and rewarding service. Of course, Haley would have appreciated it more if she hadn't repeatedly found herself distracted by the man sitting beside her.

Wyatt reminded Haley of a little child as he leaned and looked around throughout the service. From what she could tell, he was looking at their fellow parishioners. He even turned to look behind them a few times. At one point, she found herself wondering if perhaps he needed to use the restroom. After all, children squirmed in their seats when they had that problem. Of course, she couldn't very well ask a grown man if he needed to potty. Just the thought of doing so nearly induced a fit of giggles.

"What's his problem?" Missy's whisper as they waited to exit the pew was soft enough even had Wyatt been paying attention, he wouldn't have heard her.

He stepped into the aisle and moved back to let Haley walk in front of him. She needn't have worried about what to say to him since he was still mimicking a lighthouse beacon, staring shamelessly at everybody.

"Who is our guest?" Pastor Rollins smiled genially as he looked at Wyatt.

"Pastor Rollins, this is Wyatt Millan. He's new to town." Haley stood back so the men could shake hands.

"Welcome, Wyatt." If the minister noticed the other man was looking past him at other people, he was too polite to react to it. "What brings you to Shadow?"

Wyatt finally gave the pastor his full attention. "I decided to get away from the big city. Some of my friends visited here a couple of years ago, and they told me it would be a good place to live. I came down here and applied for a job, and when I was hired, I packed everything and moved here." It sounded like he was reciting frequently used lines. Knowing how he liked to talk about himself, that didn't surprise her

"Well, I'm glad you chose us," Pastor Rollins replied. "And I'm glad Haley invited you to church. I hope you plan to come back and visit us again."

"Oh, I will." Wyatt once more scanned the crowd. "This is the kind of place I want to join."

A place he wanted to join? Haley felt uncomfortable as Pastor Rollins finished speaking with Wyatt and moved on to the next person waiting in line.

Once outside, she found herself at a loss for what to do. She really didn't want to encourage a friendship with Wyatt Millan. But she needed to see him as God's child.

"I love this church," Wyatt announced.

Haley turned around, the question of exactly how he'd know, since he spent the entire service gawking, on her lips. Instead, she managed a smile. "I'm glad."

There he went again, looking around. He gestured toward a group of people standing and talking. "That's Mike Tucker with Aaron Houston, isn't it?"

Haley looked where he indicated to see Mayor Tucker laughing at something the bank president had said. "Yes."

Wyatt nodded before he looked to his left and indicated another group of people. "That's Paul Handers in the blue suit, isn't it?"

She was beginning to feel unsettled by his blatant curiosity, but she nodded. "Yes. That's his wife Hannah in the yellow dress, and they're talking to Dennis and Jennifer Ewing." She took a step. "Why don't I introduce you around?"

"That would be great." Wyatt took Haley's arm and nearly pulled her off her feet when she paused to introduce him to the Carmichaels. It seemed there were specific people he wanted to meet.

Twenty minutes and several awkward greetings later, Haley found herself thoroughly embarrassed. After only a few introductions, she realized Wyatt only wanted to meet the wealthy residents of Shadow. He had been dismissive of people of middle class, even though there were several conversing with the ones he wanted to meet.

"Would you go to lunch with me?" He was exuberant as he asked Haley.

Haley quickly scanned those standing around, but none of the friends she often spent Sundays with were still there.

"Where do most of these people go to eat?" Wyatt grasped her arm again. "I'll take you there."

"I believe Haley is going to join me for lunch today." Pastor Rollins spoke from behind them. "You're welcome to join us, Wyatt. We'll be eating a delicious casserole Mrs. Dunning prepared yesterday." His smile grew. "I just have to put it in the oven for thirty minutes, so I can't mess it up."

"You're not going out?" Wyatt seemed perplexed.

Pastor Rollins shook his head. "You'll find that most of our church family enjoy Sunday lunches at home. Would you like to join Haley and me?"

"I don't think so." Wyatt practically wrinkled his nose. "I'll just find something."

Haley could have hugged her minister as the two men said polite goodbyes. Wyatt turned to her before he left. "Maybe I can take you out for dinner one night this week."

"I'm sorry, Wyatt, but I don't date." She at least could tell the truth to escape further involvement with this man.

It appeared as though he might question her, but instead he said a stilted goodbye before he turned and left.

Haley turned to Pastor Rollins. "Thank you, but you shouldn't have lied for me."

His brows rose. "Just when did I lie?"

"When you said I was joining you for lunch. We didn't have any plans."

Pastor Rollins lifted a finger and swayed it from side to side. "No, I didn't. I said I believed you were going to join me for lunch, and I did. You looked miserable, young lady, and I just felt moved to rescue you."

Haley chuckled as she realized what the minister had done. "You're sneaky. I'd never have guessed you had it in you."

He led her to the parsonage next door. "Believe it or not, I was once a teenager. If my parents were alive, my father would tell you I was forever getting away with too many hijinks." His sky blue eyes sparkled as he looked at her. "My mother would inform you that I was an expert at using my words to get out of trouble." He opened the front door of the house for her to enter. "It's amazing, our English language. It's a tool like none other if we choose to learn how to use it, and then use it wisely."

Haley had never thought of it that way before. "It can build people up or knock them down."

The older man nodded as he led her through the living room. "Come into the kitchen and have a seat while I put our casserole in the oven. We'll continue our discussion while it's warming."

She found herself fascinated by her pastor's perspective on spoken language and enjoyed their conversation so much, she couldn't believe it when he said it was time to eat lunch.

It was during their meal when Pastor Rollins asked her a question.

"Haley, is something troubling you? I mean something about that young man." He rushed to qualify his statement. "I'm not asking you to gossip, but you're one of my children. If I can help with anything, I'd like to."

Haley had prayed for help with Hardy's situation, and here it was. She could tell Pastor Rollins everything and know it would go no further. She breathed a sigh of relief.

"I have a new friend who I'm worried about," she confessed. "Not Wyatt. His name is Beau Harding."

Pastor Rollins nodded. "He's the young man who's been working the Walker farm while Luke was mending."

"Yes." Haley thought once more of how at home he appeared on a farm. "The truth is, he's a police officer in some kind of witness protection program. Somebody is after him, so he's using a false name and hiding."

"Oh, my." The minister put down his fork. "And you're worried he may be in danger."

Her thoughts were jumbled up again, but she'd try to sort them out so she could share them with him. "I'm worried because the break-ins and murder may have something to do with him. He's going to help Mitch with them. Mitch is telling everybody he's their new crime scene photographer, but he's still going to be getting out there. And if the wrong person sees him . . ."

"I understand why you would be concerned." Pastor Rollins reached across the small table and placed his hand over hers. "But if he's working with the police, he'll be in a safe environment--surrounded by police officers. I imagine Mitch will see to it he's armed."

The image of Beau holding a gun did nothing to soothe her nerves, but Pastor Rollins didn't seem to notice Haley's concern as he continued.

"If Hardy is comfortable helping Mitch with the investigation, we need to trust he knows what he's doing. He's in God's hands, anyway, remember?"

"That's another thing I'm worried about." Haley could still hear Beau's declaration of anger. "Something has happened in his life or maybe even to him. He blames God for it, and when I invited him to church, he said he's too angry with him to worship. I hoped he would come, anyway."

"Do you feel more than friendship for this man?" The pastor's voice was gentle.

Haley closed her eyes tightly. "I'm frightened by my feelings." She looked up at her minister. "I feel drawn to him. He told me he feels the same way about me. But since I won't date when I know our relationship can't grow or last, and he's leaving town as soon as these cases are solved, we don't have a chance."

"So you're going to avoid each other entirely?"

"Do you think we should?" Haley hoped for a definite answer. "Because right now we're going to try to be friends."

Pastor Rollins eyebrows went up. "Is there a reason you shouldn't be friends?"

Now she was embarrassed. "Because of how I feel about him. What if I'm drawn to him so much I forget how I choose to live?"

Haley was totally unprepared for her minister's response. He chuckled. "Haley, you are a confident and determined person with a good, solid faith to stand on. Just the fact you're concerned about the situation tells me you can handle it." He sobered. "Of course, that doesn't mean you should put yourself into situations where temptation might be too great."

She knew what he meant. "Where things could get out of control."

He nodded. "It sounds like Beau Harding needs friends like you. I can't imagine what it must be like to give up your life in order to keep it."

Again, Pastor Rollins had given Haley a new perspective. Tears welled in her eyes as she thought it through. "Beau gave up more than his job. He gave up his home, family, friends . . . He can't even go to his favorite restaurant again. He couldn't go to the church he went to even if he wanted to." A lone tear escaped and trickled down her face. "What a lonely life."

"From what I've seen, Hardy isn't doing too badly here." Pastor Rollins took a drink of water. "He may not have made any close friends, but I see him speaking to people when he's out and around. Our community has welcomed him."

"That's not the same as having real friends, though, is it?" She already knew the answer to her question.

"At least he's found one." The minister smiled warmly before picking up his fork and returning to the casserole on his plate.

Haley picked up her fork and dug into her food. She would be Beau Harding's friend if it killed her. And there was no way she'd give up on getting him back to God. Her stubborn genes kicked in when it came to sticking to her faith. Beau Harding may as well just give up now. Because she wasn't about to.

Chapter 30

"I was able to remove your men from the system," Weiss assured him.

"How long can you keep them out?" He knew there was a limit to the other person's resources.

"I don't know." The caller rarely failed. *"but I'll do it as long as I can without getting caught."*

"That's all I ask." He had to be careful how he handled Weiss. This man was crucial to the success of his plan, and unlike his other players, irreplaceable. *"I trust the other records are still missing."*

"Of course."

"Thank you." He didn't want Weiss to think he doubted him. *"I trust you implicitly."*

A humorless laugh came out of the phone. *"I'm sure you do."*

Before he could respond, Weiss disconnected the call. It was okay, though. Weiss knew he would only get his money if his plan succeeded.

He picked up his phone and dialed a special number.

"Father?" His son's annoying, whiny voice answered.

"I've told you not to answer like that." And he could tell him ten times a day and not get through to him. *"How is the situation coming along?"*

"Something might have happened." Now he could hear the panic in his son's voice. *"Jim was going to call you later to tell you."*

He drew a deep breath, trying to hold onto his temper. *"But since I'm talking to you, you can tell me."*

"Oh." There was a brief pause as the younger man must have considered his father's words. "We don't know where the men are. When Jim went to meet them, they didn't show up."

"What do you mean?"

"Jim's here, Father." Relief was evident in his voice. "He wants to talk to you."

He stood and began to pace. There had to be a mistake. James's voice was strained when he spoke.

"I saw Weiss's man at the campground, and then all the stuff was gone when I got to the site. And I almost got caught."

"You what?" He froze in his tracks. "What do you mean?"

Annoyance was now in James's voice. "I heard somebody coming, trying to be all quiet, and at first, I thought it was the men. But I hid, just in case. It was the sheriff and Davis. I think Davis is a deputy now, and they found the meeting place."

His mind raced as he considered the implications of what he'd been told. "You're certain you weren't seen?"

"Davis found a gun, and they were so interested in it, they didn't hear me. I walked right by them." As usual, James's overconfidence annoyed him.

"What do you mean, Davis found a gun?" This was starting to sound worse.

"I think it might have been Brockman's," James informed him. "I think Harve and Brockman might have skipped town on us. And I'm telling you, the tent and everything were gone. The van's not where it's supposed to be, either. What do you want us to do now?"

"Let me think," he ordered James. What would have enticed those two men to drop the plan and leave town? The answer was "nothing." They wanted, no needed, the money they'd been promised too badly to simply quit. Tendrils of dread entered his stomach. No. He couldn't operate based on assumptions. He'd continue on with the plan. "Harding Davis is doing what we wanted him to do; he's a deputy now. Let's sit quiet and let him get comfortable. We'll let him become even more attached to the residents of Shadow."

"Okay."

He hung up the phone and sat down behind his desk. Something unexpected had to have happened with Harve and Brockman. They would show up with an explanation. Until then, things would continue. His plan would still work.

But just in case... He picked up the phone and dialed it.

"I thought we just said what we had to say." Weiss's cold voice answered.

"It's time to make Davis start to hurt. My son needs to see him be hurt."

A sigh came out of the phone. "What do you want me to do?"

"I want H.B. Davis to die."

"Consider it done." The line went dead.

It wouldn't be to his advantage to question Weiss about his employee conveniently turning up at the same time his own two men disappeared. He had a feeling Weiss had been having his man check on things in Shadow himself. And since Weiss stood to lose everything if they were caught, he couldn't really blame him. For now, he'd stick to the plan.

Harding Davis Sr.'s death would solve two problems for him. It would show his son they were indeed, going to hurt the younger Davis, and it would remove the possibility of the old man talking. Yes. He *should have already done this. It was time for Harding Davis to feel real pain.*

Chapter 31

"So, how's your great photography job going?" Matt Ashford took a healthy drink of iced tea before putting his glass back beside his plate. Hardy had been expecting the question since he walked into the diner and joined his friend at the table.

"Thankfully, there haven't been any crimes to photograph, so it's been pretty boring." Hardy had been on the force for three days now, and there hadn't been any more break-ins reported yet.

Matt waved his hand dismissively. "I don't blame you for taking that job. If I had a choice between sitting behind the wheel of a truck watching the same scenery pass by, or the excitement of taking pictures of the crime scenes we've had around here lately, I'd have done the same thing you did."

"It's not that." Hardy had to be careful with his words. "I'm still only here temporarily. When the sheriff catches whoever's responsible for these crimes, he won't have any need for a crime scene photographer. I'll be out of here in a heartbeat."

"You say that now," Matt smoothly replied, "but who knows how you'll feel in a few weeks? You might just decide to switch to becoming a full-time deputy." He looked pointedly at the radio clipped to Hardy's belt. "Looks like you're already on call."

Hardy shrugged. "The sheriff needs pictures right away if something happens."

"The beef stew looks good." Nancy's pleasant voice interrupted their conversation. "Can I bring you some, Hardy?"

He smiled at her and nodded. "I'll take a soda, too, Nancy. Thank you."

The older lady returned his smile and headed for the counter.

Hardy turned back to face Matt. "How's your route been going?"

Something resembling anger flashed in Matt's eyes but was quickly replaced by forced casualness. "My job is the same as it ever was. It never changes."

"Do you ever get lonely?" Both men waited until Nancy set Hardy's glass on the table.

Matt dipped a French fry in ketchup. "Not really. I've had jobs where I worked with other people. They never lasted long." He smiled self-depreciatingly. "I guess I'm not a team player."

Hardy found it hard to believe the easy-going man in front of him had trouble getting along with others. "What kind of jobs have you tried?"

"Nothing that paid very well." Matt's frown grew. "I've done everything from bussing tables to managing an apartment building. All gigantic flops."

"Managing a building?" Hardy sat back while Nancy placed a plate of beef stew and saucer stacked with bread slices in front of him. "Thanks, Nancy." He acknowledged the friendly waitress before turning his attention back to Matt. "How did that come to be?"

Matt swallowed the last bite of his hamburger before answering. "A friend. The guy's uncle owns several buildings, and he knew I needed a job."

The beef stew was hot; Hardy was going to have to let it cool for a minute. He shifted his attention to Matt once more. "That's not a team job. Why didn't that work out?"

A crooked smile appeared on Matt's face. "I don't have the temperament. Do you know how many things there are for apartment tenants to complain about?" He didn't give Hardy time to answer. "Too cotton pickin' many. You wouldn't believe how many air conditioner vents don't cool rooms enough, or how many spider infestations occur." He shuddered exaggeratedly. "And I won't ruin your meal by talking about clogged drains."

"Thank you for that." Hardy grinned at his friend before he pierced a large chunk of beef with his fork.

"But I will tell you it's possible to flush a soda can down a toilet if it's crushed enough, and you flush several times." A wide grin appeared on Matt's face. "Gives a whole new meaning to going to the can, doesn't it?"

Hardy groaned at Matt's joke. "Who do you entertain while you're on the road? You can't let that sense of humor go to waste."

"Oh, I don't," Matt assured him. "I'm on my CB a lot. My handle is Snickers."

Hardy shook his head as he took care of a large forkful of stew. "I'll have to buy a base radio just so I can hear you in action."

"Anything else, Matt?" Nancy stood beside the table, an order pad in her hands.

"Just the ticket." Matt winked at her. "Unless you want to meet me for a movie after you get off, you gorgeous chunk of lady."

The poor woman turned three shades darker red as she wrote on her pad. She appeared speechless while she tore out the ticket. Before she could place it on the table, it slipped out of her hand and fluttered to the floor.

"I've got it." Matt leaned over to pick it up.

Hardy glanced at his friend, and his attention was immediately caught by a horribly discolored area showing beneath his shirt tail. He waited until Matt sat back up and Nancy left before he addressed the issue.

"That's a nasty bruise on your side, Matt. How'd you get it?"

Matt shrugged. "I'm not sure. It probably happened while I was inspecting freight. You know, one of those things where you don't notice it until the bruise shows up."

"That's an awfully big bruise not to have noticed." Hardy couldn't hide his skepticism. "You didn't get into a fight with somebody, did you?"

"Me?" Matt waved the thought away. "Who would I need to fight with? I'm a joker, not a fighter."

Hardy couldn't quite get the image of a large fist, or even a kick, landing on his friend's lower rib cage out of his mind, but Matt was right. He just wasn't the kind of guy to drive somebody to strike him.

"Well, be more careful," Hardy advised him. "You'll hurt something important."

Matt stood up to his full six feet plus and saluted him. "Yes sir, officer." He pulled a wallet out of his pocket and threw a few dollar bills on the table. "And as much as I appreciate your advice, Hardy, that tip is for Nancy. Not you." He winked before he walked away.

Hardy chuckled as he went back to eating his meal. When the time came for him to move on, Matt was one of the people he would miss.

"Is this seat taken?" The soft, hesitant voice brought his eyes from his food to the woman standing there.

"Haley." He stood up. "Please join me."

She smiled and stood back while Nancy quickly cleaned Matt's place off. Then Haley sat across from him.

"Can I just have a chef's salad, please?" she asked Nancy. "French dressing on the side."

"Be right out, Haley." It was apparent Nancy not only liked Haley, she felt comfortable with her. It was the first time Hardy had ever seen the waitress interact with a customer without turning nine shades of red.

"So, what brings you out on a Wednesday evening?" Not that Hardy was about to complain.

"One of the dispatchers called in sick, so I got stuck working half the next shift." She seemed more comfortable with him somehow. "It's too late to go to Bible study, and the vegetable soup I heated for lunch is a memory, so here I am. You eat here a lot, don't you?"

"Just about every night," he admitted. "You've seen my trailer, so I don't have to tell you cooking is pretty much out of the question."

She frowned. "Where is your camper since you don't work for Luke anymore?"

He took a drink of his soda. "It's still out at the farm. They were nice enough to let me stay there until I figure out what I'm going to do."

Hope was written all over her face. "You might stay here after all?"

"I can't." Hardy hated to see the way her face fell. "I'm only sticking around until this mess is cleared up. Then I have to go."

Her smile looked forced. "I understand." She studied her hands for a moment. "I missed you at church Sunday."

"Sorry." He figured his smile looked more like a grimace. "I just can't do that. I have to be honest and tell you I'm not sure if I'll ever be able to again."

"I believe you will," she stated adamantly. "I'm praying for you, and I won't give up."

He needed to change the subject. "I want to know more about you. You told me you lost your parents. Do you have any extended family?"

"No." She sat back while Nancy placed a large plate of salad in front of her. "Thank you, Nancy. That looks good."

"You're welcome, Haley." Gone was the blushing, shy waitress Hardy was used to. "I hope you save some room for dessert. There's a big piece of Maisie's coconut cream pie with your name on it back there."

Dimples appeared in Haley's cheeks as she smiled. "I'll take that even if I can't eat it now. I can always have a midnight snack."

"I'll box it up for you." Nancy turned her attention to Hardy. "Would you like dessert? There are a couple of pieces of cherry or apple left."

"I'll take a slice of apple pie if you'll add a scoop of ice cream on top of it." Hardy waited until the waitress left to go fetch his pie before he spoke to Haley again. "So, how is it you rate a huge slice of coconut cream pie while I only qualify for cherry or apple?"

Haley looked even prettier as her cheeks turned pink. "I told you I don't have any family. There are people—lots of people—in Shadow who are like family to me. They care about me and look after me." She poured salad dressing over the lettuce. "Once, when I missed an entire week of work because I had pneumonia, a different person showed up at my apartment every day. They took care of me. Nancy came one day, and she baked a loaf of homemade bread while she was there." Her eyes sought out the waitress for a minute. "I couldn't taste very much of anything, but the smell of baking bread...I ate three slices of it, fresh out of the oven."

An idea that had just begun to creep up on Hardy came tumbling to the ground. "You'd never leave Shadow for anything, would you? This is more than your home. These people are your family."

She seemed to carefully consider his question before answering. "I would go if I believed it was what God wants me to do. But right now, I feel like this is where I'm supposed to be. Why?" Her face colored a shade brighter. "Are you asking me to go with you?"

For one split second, that was exactly what he'd wanted to do, but reality reared its head. "I couldn't take you with me. It wouldn't be safe for you."

"I imagine adding a second person would make it hard to disappear." Haley pushed salad around on her plate, not really eating it. Before he could comment, she smiled a little too brightly. "Can you tell me about your family, Beau? I mean, not their names, but about them as people."

That, he could do. "My parents are great." He had always been proud of them. "Dad is a retired police officer, and Mom is his wife."

"She never worked outside the house?" Haley finally took a bite of her salad.

Hardy shook his head. "She made a career out of raising her kids and being a cop's wife. I always thought I'd find a woman just like her someday." The phrase that was beginning to be his mantra slid right past his lips. "Some things just aren't meant to be."

"You said kids. You have siblings?" Haley seemed willing to gloss over his poor choice of words.

"I have one sister." He would forever regret he hadn't taken the time to be closer to her when it was possible. "Callie's four years younger than me. She's married, and they have two children. Blake is six, I think, and that would make Tabitha four."

"Is your brother-in-law a police officer?"

"FSA." Hardy had always been thankful his sister married a good, stable man like Elliott Lawrence. "He helped me disappear, and he helps me when I need to see my family from time to time."

"Wow." Haley's blue eyes were as round as silver dollars. "You don't believe in a boring life, do you?"

"I think I'd like to try one out sometime and see how it fits."

"How often do you visit your family?" Concern was etched on her forehead.

His throat tightened. "I've had to go a couple of times lately. My dad had a stroke."

Haley reached across the table and touched his hand. "I'm sorry, Beau. It must be terrible to know he's sick and not be able to see him whenever you want."

"They'd like you." Hardy knew it was true as soon as he said it. "My parents, sister, they would all like you." He grinned as he thought of something. "My dad would call you Dimples."

And that was what appeared on her cheeks in response to his words. "Why do you say that?"

He shrugged. "I know Dad. He'd take one look at your pretty smile and see those dimples, and that would be your name."

"Was he a cop like you? Undercover, I mean."

"No." The mere idea made him smile. "Dad looks too much like a police officer to ever have passed for anything else. I think you could have dressed him in a clown costume, and people would have recognized him as a cop."

Haley was back to pushing her salad around. "What made you decide to be an undercover officer, then?"

"I'm good at it." It was as simple, and yet as complicated, as that. "I slid completely into my character. I became another person. The guys I was after couldn't tell I was pretending, because in a way, I wasn't."

Her eyes were clouded as they met his. "Did you have to do things…drugs, girls…that you wouldn't have done otherwise?" She looked more disappointed than embarrassed by the thought.

"I've never used drugs," he could answer honestly. "The head of the ring I was trying to bring down didn't like his guys to use them." Hardy laughed derisively. "He's responsible for roughly thirty percent of the drug trafficking in Chicago, but doesn't want anybody close to him using the stuff."

"And women?" Her voice was small.

Hardy had always tried to consider he would one day need to answer this question while he was making decisions as Joe Ryman. Now that it was time, the answer he'd thought so good seemed dishonorable.

"The first year was the hardest. There were a lot of women around, and to fit in, I had to act interested." He'd found himself feeling nothing but sympathy for the women he met. "I kept things on the surface. I flirted, but never followed through." And had his face slapped more than once. "I earned a reputation for being too choosy when it came to women."

Haley was staring fixedly at the plate in front of her. "What happened after the first year?"

He wished more than anything she hadn't asked that question. This was the part she probably would never be able to understand.

"There was a woman. Audrey was her name. Her uncle is the head of the organization, and he was always telling her what to do, how to live." Hardy kept his eyes focused on Haley, wishing she would look at him. "She was in love with one of the guys who worked in the organization, but he wasn't good enough to suit her uncle. One day, Audrey confronted me and told me she saw the games I was playing with women. She had a proposition."

Hardy took a deep breath. "We would be a couple in front of everybody else, but in reality, I was a cover for her relationship with Cass. In return, she made it appear as though I was in a committed relationship. It wasn't ideal, but it was better than the alternatives."

He wanted so much for Haley to understand—to accept. Before he could go on, she asked another question.

"So, you and she . . .?"

And here it was. "We acted like a couple when others were around. That meant holding hands, keeping an arm around her . . . kissing." He had to make Haley see how it was. "But, we never crossed the line. Never. Once we were alone, we never even touched each other."

Tears welled in Haley's eyes. "But for four years, you and she were together—only for show, but still acting as a couple." She picked up a napkin and wiped her eyes. "I'm sorry, Beau. I just can't—I can't—" She stood up and rushed away. The bell on the door sounded louder than usual as it closed behind her.

She had responded just like he feared she would. Before he'd gone undercover, he had practiced the same kind of faith Haley did now. Kissing, and even small intimacies like holding hands, were special, and saved for the person you thought you were supposed to be with. Even though he'd never gone any further with Audrey, Hardy knew he'd gone too far in Haley's eyes.

He dug his wallet out and threw enough money on the table for both their meals. He suddenly wanted to leave, to go away and never have to face who he'd been again. But first, he had to help stop the people terrorizing Shadow. He took off out the door and headed for the station. Maybe if he looked at the files again, he'd get some more ideas. The sooner the cases were solved, the quicker he could forget all of this. The quicker he could forget Haley Johnson, and how ashamed she'd just made him feel.

Chapter 32

Haley focused all her attention on the paper in front of her. If she kept busy writing notes, she could make herself forget that a glance to her left would be a view into Mitch's office. Nothing unusual, except Beau Harding was sitting and talking to the sheriff. Her feelings went all over the map just thinking about him, let alone while looking at him.

What had made her even think of Hardy with women, let alone given her the gumption to ask? It wasn't like she was now, or ever going to be, his girlfriend. And, if she had just used her brain, common sense dictated the necessity of doing more than announcing his undercover name.

She had to be honest with herself. There was a part of her wishing their relationship could become more. Her heart had foolishly soared during those moments she thought he wanted to take her with him—not that she could have gone.

No. She wanted him to make peace with God, somehow be able to safely make his home in Shadow, and build a life with her. She hadn't been prepared to face the reality of who he really was or who he had been before they met.

Sitting and listening to him talk about his family had added to her delusional fairy tale. If he had parents with a stable marriage, maybe he could have one too. Only he wasn't who she'd imagined him to be. He wasn't the man for her after all.

The non-emergency phone's ring drew her from her troubled thoughts.

"Shadow County Sheriff's office."

"Haley, this is Todd Warner over at the post office."

"Hi, Todd. How can I help you?" She picked up her pen; he would have license plates on cars parked in the handicap zone. His father was a quadriplegic, and Todd had been known to leave notes under the windshield wipers of wrongly parked vehicles. He surprised her this time.

"I have an employee who hasn't shown up for his last three shifts, and he's not answering his phone. He's usually reliable, so I gave him the benefit of a doubt. But today, he's not here again, and I'm worried that something may have happened to him. I thought maybe the police could check on him just to make sure he's okay."

"Which employee are you referring to?" She held her pen ready to write a name.

"William Baxter. He lives over on Timber Street. If you need his address, I can look it up for you."

"No, Todd, that's okay. I can pull it up on the computer." She scooted her chair to the keyboard and typed in the missing mail carrier's name. An address and phone number instantly popped up. "I have it in front of me. I'll have a deputy over there to check things out shortly."

"Thank you, Haley. Will somebody let me know what you find?"

Haley wrote herself a note. "I'll give you a call and let you know as soon as I hear from the deputy."

Her thoughts were on Will Baxter as she hung up the phone and keyed the radio microphone. She'd thought it odd that

Steve Peterson had delivered their mail the past two days, but hadn't gotten around to asking him where Will was.

She looked at the short list of officers on duty and their last locations. It looked like Hank was nearest Will Baxter's home.

"Base to Hank."

A few seconds later, Hank's voice answered. "Stone here."

"Hank, we have a possible ten-fifty-seven. A resident hasn't shown up to work for two days in a row, and his boss wants us to check on him." She gave Hank the address.

"Ten-four."

Hopefully, will was sleeping off a wild weekend or something similar to that. Haley realized that, despite the interaction she had with him during the fundraiser, she knew nothing about Will Baxter's personal life.

Haley turned back to her notes and resumed writing them more legibly. Waiting was one of the hardest parts of her job, and she had long ago learned to keep busy while she did so.

"Haley, can you come in here for a minute?" Mitch's voice came over the intercom.

For one brief instant, she thought about pushing the button and saying, "no." She didn't want to go into the office where Beau Harding currently sat. She wondered what Mitch would think if his usually reliable employee suddenly refused his request.

Not that Haley would find out. Her job was too important to experiment with, so she grabbed a pad of paper and pen before walking over to open Mitch's office door.

"What do you need, Mitch?" She deliberately avoided looking at Beau.

"I need you to help Hardy for a few minutes." Of course, he did.

She sighed before she could stop herself. "What do you want me to do?"

Mitch seemed totally unaware of her reluctance to comply with his instructions. "He has some ideas about our crime wave and wants to look at past records. I need you to put him on your computer and show him how to access our case files. He can tell you more precisely what he's looking for. Just give him a hand if he needs it."

Haley knew the three short hours of sleep she'd gotten the night before were insufficient when she had an inane urge to start applauding. That was the only kind of hand she felt up to giving Beau Harding.

She still hadn't made eye contact with him before she turned and led the way back to her station.

"Hey, you two." The male voice startled Haley. She hadn't heard anybody come in.

"Hey, Matt." Beau greeted the other man. Haley was a bit surprised by the pleasure in Beau's voice.

"How can I help you, Matt?" She turned to face the counter, all too aware of the man standing beside her.

Matt Ashford rolled his eyes and shoved a yellow slip of paper across the counter. "If your deputies aren't catching me in a speed trap, they're giving me tickets for parking where they say I shouldn't."

Haley smiled in spite of herself. "Where did you park your truck this time?"

"It's not like a bunch of kids are clamoring to go to the playground this time of year," Matt declared. "Nobody else wanted to park there."

Beau chuckled. "I take it from the way you two are talking, your parking habits aren't so hot." He addressed Matt.

Matt did a pretty good job of appearing affronted. "My parking habits are perfectly fine. It's just the deputies in this town are too cotton pickin' particular about where my truck is parked."

A soft laugh escaped Haley before she could stop it. "You took up every space in front of Whites Salon with that semi, and I'm pretty sure it's a given that an alley isn't ever supposed to be blocked."

"You hear this?" Matt asked Beau. "Picky."

After a few more of Matt's teasing protests and retorts from Haley, Matt paid his fine and left.

Once more, Haley found herself standing alone with Beau.

"You and Matt are friends," he observed, a strange note in his voice. "Or are you seeing him? He's a little old for you."

For a minute, Haley had no idea what Beau was asking her. "I see him every time he comes in to pay a speeding ticket or parking fine." Then she realized exactly what Beau had meant. She refused to dignify his question with an answer.

"You can use that chair." She indicated the second office chair they kept for when two dispatchers were needed.

Beau looked like he wanted to say something else, but he only said, "Thank you," and sat down.

Determined to stick to business, Haley leaned down in front of the computer and moved the cursor. "Just go into this file. Normally, our last names are our passwords, but you're not in the system. You can use mine."

She moved out of the way while he typed Johnson and pressed enter.

"What kind of crimes are you looking at?"

She could see him looking at her in her peripheral vision, but she kept her eyes focused on the computer screen. "I want any petty thefts, shoplifters, penny ante crimes."

"Then type infractions and misdemeanors in the filtering field." She waited while he did that. "Now, type in the date range you want to search."

She watched as he typed in a date allowing him to look as far back as two years up through the current records. "And now, just click in the box signifying if you want city records only, or county records."

He chose county records. "Press enter, and you should have what you're looking for."

She waited until the screen was full of police records before she sat down in her own chair and returned to her notes.

It was so quiet as they both worked Haley could hear the large wall clock ticking away the seconds.

"Haley, can you tell me about Joe Brockman? He's in here for several offenses, all misdemeanors, and it looks like he's gotten off with a slap on the wrist every time."

She wanted Hardy to just sit quietly and tend to his own business and leave her alone. But Mitch had told her to help him.

"See the scroll icon next to his name?" She leaned over and pointed to it.

"Yes." He moved the cursor over the icon.

"If you click on it, you'll get a full data sheet on him. It will tell you more about him than I can."

"Thank you." The screen filled with information about Joe Brockman, including a very unflattering mug shot. Haley turned back to her own work.

They worked quietly next to each other for at least a half hour when the non-emergency phone rang, breaking the silence.

"Shadow County Sheriff's office."

"Haley?"

"Yes."

"This is Wyatt. Have I called at a bad time?"

"Wyatt?" What was Wyatt Millan doing calling her at work? At all for that matter? "What can I do for you?"

"I know you said you don't date, but could I talk you into joining the new guy in town for dinner this evening? We can go to O'Leary's. I hear they have the best steaks in town." The pleading tone in his voice wasn't attractive.

"I'm sorry." She kept her voice firm and steady. "I'm not supposed to receive personal calls at the station, and I just can't go out with you."

"Come on." Okay. He was moving from unattractive to annoying. "We won't call it a date."

"It doesn't matter what we'd call it. I'm sorry, but I'm not interested." She took a deep breath. "I have to go. Have a nice day, Wyatt."

She disconnected before he could say anything else.

"Another admirer?" Beau's voice startled her. She had actually forgotten he was there.

She glanced at him. "I don't think that's any of your business."

"I want it to be, though." He sounded like the words had been torn from his very being. "You don't know how much I want it to be."

Her heart did a little flip-flop before reality set in. "We've' had this discussion, and besides you're not . . . You're not . . . "

"Perfect?" he supplied. "Maybe I'm wrong, but didn't Jesus himself love sinners? I haven't been to church in a long time, but I seem to remember something about judging others and forgiving."

"I don't want to talk about this." Haley bent her head and looked at the blurred figures she knew to be written words on the paper.

"Good." His voice was closer to her. "Because I'd rather you just listen."

She looked up at him with disbelief. "What...I'm—"

"I know I've done things—acted in ways you don't approve of. I could try to justify them by saying it was part of my job, and it was, but I know it was wrong, too. You may not believe me, but I understand how precious kisses and touches are. It went against everything I believed to do those things with Audrey. The only way I could get through it was to be Joe Ryman when I was with her. I don't know how else to explain it."

"I'm...I..." She didn't know what to say. "I can't talk about this right now." Haley pressed the intercom button on the phone. "Mitch, I'm taking my break."

"Okay." Mitch's voice came out of the speaker. "I'll man the phones."

Haley stood up and walked away, Hardy's earnest expression etched into her brain. She mindlessly walked to the refrigerator in the back room and stuck a dollar in the jar on top of it before grabbing a bottle of soda.

The small settee felt harder than usual as she sank onto it. She felt his words whirling like a cyclone through her mind.

Was she judging him? Yes, she was. But, if she were honest with herself, wasn't it more jealousy than disapproval? She had always figured when the right guy came along, they would be on equal footing. He wasn't supposed to be...experienced.

Wait a minute. What was she thinking? Beau Harding wasn't the man she was supposed to be with. He couldn't be. Because he wasn't staying in Shadow any longer than he felt he had to. They had no future together.

With that unhappy thought fixed in her mind, Haley made herself look at the situation from Beau's point of view. He had found it necessary to behave in a way that conflicted with his beliefs.

Was what Beau and this Audrey woman did any different than actors on a movie screen? Who was she to sit in judgment over his actions?

She took a drink of her soda and stood up. Beau needed a friend, and that's what she would be. Haley dug another dollar out of her jeans and stuffed it in the jar. Maybe her friend would accept a soft drink as a peace offering.

Haley had a smile on her face as she headed back to the dispatch station.

Chapter 33

He hung up the phone and stood to look out the window. It seemed that not only was Harding Davis working for the sheriff's office, he was interested in a woman who worked there as well. His source told him they were starting to become close.

What would the old man's death do to a burgeoning relationship, possibly even a romance? Davis would have to leave Shadow at least long enough to pay his respects. Would that pull him away from the woman he was interested in, or stir up sympathy in her that might bring them closer?

It was times like this when he felt older than he was. He would never tell another living soul, but he sometimes wished he'd made different choices. In many, many past situations.

He stood straighter and stiffened his spine. Harding Davis had gotten himself into this mess. And if there were any way he could simply wipe Davis off the face of the earth without being caught, he'd do it in a heartbeat. With the way things were, that was simply not possible, though. Instead, he had to take it slowly and make Davis suffer. According to his plan, how things appeared were just as important as what was done.

He still needed to make up his mind about Davis's father. The plan had been set into motion, and if he didn't make a phone call within the next hour, it would be too late. He needed to decide soon.

But either way, Harding Davis would cease to exist. It wasn't a matter of if; it was simply a question of when.

Chapter 34

Hardy's cell phone rang twice, then went silent. He quickly rolled over in bed and picked it up, ready to answer the next ring.

"Beau, it's Elliott."

He'd used the emergency signal. "What's going on?"

Hardy heard his brother-in-law draw a deep breath. "He's okay now, but somebody tried to kill H.B. last night."

"What?" Hardy abruptly stood, his knuckles white as he grasped the phone. "Who? How?"

"Not sure who, but you have your mom to thank for stopping the how." Elliott's calm voice did little to slow Hardy's pounding heart. "Sharon walked in on a male nurse getting ready to inject something into your dad's IV. Your mom didn't recognize the man, and she knew it wasn't time for H.B. to be getting his meds, so she went at him and yelled for help. The guy knocked her down and ran out of the room. The doctor said the syringe he dropped was full of bleach. It would have killed your dad within minutes."

"But Mom and Dad are both okay?" Hardy needed to hear the words.

"Your mom has a pretty good bruise on her arm, and she's so mad she's spitting nails, but yes. They're both okay."

Hardy took a deep breath and pushed his personal feelings to the back burner. This was the time to think like a police detective. "I saw security cameras all over that hospital. The guy had to be caught on tape."

"We've already got the pictures, Beau, but the man knew what he was doing. He never gave a camera a clear shot of his face."

"What about Mom? Can she pick him out of a photo lineup?" Thinking like a cop was harder than he'd ever imagined when it involved his family.

"She yanked off part of a fake wig, so we know he was disguised. Our best artist is there working with her on a composite sketch as we speak. Besides the Chicago PD stepping up security around the hospital, the FSA is putting Fletcher and Warburton on the job. Your parents are safe."

"What can I do?" There had to be something. "Should I come up there?"

Elliott's voice was troubled when he spoke. "I think it's safer for your family right now if you stay away. Maybe this was a fishing expedition to see if you're still alive. Try and get you to come out of hiding to take care of your mom."

The idea his parents may have been used like pieces on a chess board didn't sit right with him at all.

Elliott's voice came across the line again. "Do you think we need to move you, Beau? What do your instincts tell you? Has Dohner found out you're still alive?"

Hardy forced his hectic thoughts to slow so he could think logically. "What does Fowler say about the undercover operation?"

"Still not even a hint the old man knows you're alive." Elliott sounded dubious. "We have to consider whether or not we have someone close enough to know everything he thinks."

"No information from Fowler"

"He has one agent working in Dohner's office, but most of the time she's fending him off. He couldn't tell me about anybody else."

Protocol. Hardy sat silently for a few minutes, considering his options. "Can you fax the sketch Mom comes up with down here to the sheriff's office? If I recognize him as one of Dohner's men, we'll have to consider relocating more than just me, Elliott."

"I know." Elliot sounded very unhappy. "But if it's not one of Dohner's men, we're shooting in the dark, Beau."

Shooting in the dark. That's the same way he felt about the cases he was working there in Shadow. "It seems like there's an awful lot of that in my life right now," he admitted. "Let's just sit tight until I see the sketch. I'll go down to the station and wait. Then I'll call you back just as soon as I see it."

"That sounds like a good idea," Elliott agreed. "Are you sure you still want to help the sheriff down there?"

Elliott hadn't liked it, and Rich Stephens had been nearly apoplectic when he told them about his decision to extend his stay in Shadow. But Hardy knew what he had to do. "Unless I know for sure Dohner is onto me, I have to stay and help clear this up. There's too much of a chance I'm the cause of it, and I'm not going to run off and leave a mess for other people to clean up. I feel like I already had to do that once when I left the Dohners."

"You did what you had to do," his brother-in-law reminded him. His tone of voice changed. "Why don't you take a minute to call your mom? It will make both of you feel better."

"I don't want to interrupt her work on the sketch." Hardy said.

"So, don't talk to her very long. Just hear her voice and know for yourself that she's okay," Elliott urged.

They made arrangements for what to do once Hardy saw the sketch. Then after Elliott once more assured him that his family, including Callie and the kids, were safe, Hardy hung up.

His hands were shaking as he retrieved a soft drink from the small refrigerator of his camper. His mom could have been hurt, or if she hadn't shown up when she did, his dad would be...No. It didn't do any good to think like that. He opened the can and took a drink that left it half empty before picking his phone back up.

Sharon Davis answered on the second ring.

"It's me, Mom."

"Oh, Beau, I have never in all my life been as furious as I am right now." He had expected his mom to sound afraid, not outraged. "The nerve of that beast to come in here and try to kill a defenseless man. I'd have had a better grip on that big metal bedpan, he'd have a good knot on his head." Satisfaction filled her voice. "At least he'll have a shiner."

Hardy had to ask. "You blackened his eye with a bedpan?"

"Well, it was the only thing I could reach." Defiance laced his mother's voice. "I wish I could have stuck the IV pole—"

"Dad's okay, though, Mom." He knew his parent well enough to know she would be mortified later if he let her finish that declaration. "How's the sketch coming?"

"As good as it can." She seemed calmer. "I got a good look at him, and you know how I remember faces, Beau, but he was wearing a wig and beard that could have come off a cheap Halloween costume. I am sure he's not even six feet tall because I didn't have bend my neck to look up at him."

"What color was his hair?" Maybe a general description would jog his memory.

"The wig was black, but I think there was light blonde or white hair poking out from underneath it." She sighed. "I might have just imagined it, though." Confidence filled Sharon's voice. "But his eyes are blue. Not a pretty blue, either. An ugly, evil blue."

That told Hardy something. He was positive Dohner wouldn't have a man dressing in a cheap disguise. In fact, Dohner would be embarrassed, and he didn't handle that emotion too well. "How is Dad? Is he staying awake any longer yet?"

"He was awake off and on all day, but he slept through the whole thing. H.B. didn't even stir when that oaf knocked me over, and the bedpan clattered across the floor. I'm just thankful I came back into the room when I did."

"Me, too, Mom," he admitted. "I'm proud of you, by the way. You surprise me."

A low laugh came across the line. "Didn't know your mother had it in her, did you? Well, let me tell you this, Harding

Beauregard Davis. If a mother bear gets riled, folks best get out of her way. And I am officially good and riled."

"Just be careful." Hardy felt he needed to caution her, lest she start thinking she could take on an entire street gang armed with her bedpan. "Please do what the FSA agents tell you. They know the best way to keep you and Dad safe."

"Oh, you mean Charlie and Freddie."

"Who?" Elliott had told him two seasoned agents were taking care of his parents, not a couple of young rookies. "Elliott told me Fletcher and Warburton were taking turns."

"They are." His mother spoke soothingly. "Charlie is here during the day, and Freddie will come after dinner to spend the night. They're nice young men."

Even in this dire situation, Hardy felt himself fighting back laughter. He could only imagine how the two rough, seasoned agents handled being addressed as 'Charlie' and 'Freddie'. "Only you, Mom."

"And don't you ever forget it."

"I'll let you go so you can finish the sketch. Give Dad my love, and I love you, Mom." Hardy suddenly realized he wanted to see his parents with his own two eyes.

"I love you, too, Beau." His mom's voice was warm. "Stay safe."

"I will."

Hardy sat on the edge of his bed and stared at the phone in his hand for a few minutes, lost in thought.

He once thought his job was the most important thing he'd ever do with his life, but what had it cost him? Five years with snippets of stolen time spent with his family, no real friendships, the uncertainty as to whether this might be the day his cover was blown, casting aside his beliefs and morals so he could fit in with the gang he was infiltrating…He had given up too much.

And what would it still cost him? The people he loved and residents of Shadow were in danger, most likely because of him. And Haley . . . He would never know if his feelings for her would grow to be as deep and true as he thought. Because of his job.

Okay. You have my attention. Is that what you wanted? I don't even know if you're listening to me right now, but if you are, please don't take anybody else away. I still haven't gotten over Kari Jeffries' death. I couldn't bear it if one more person dies because of me.

What was he doing? He wasn't a praying man anymore, so why was he talking to God now? He hadn't said a prayer in over a year and he wasn't about to start wasting his time doing it now.

He put his phone on the table and quickly showered and dressed for the day. Picking up the phone, he dialed the number Mitch had given him if he ever needed to call him directly.

"Sheriff, I have a fax coming into the station within the next hour or so, and I don't want anybody else to see it. Can that be arranged?"

Mitch's calm voice came over the phone. "I'll let Haley know to watch for it. She'll make sure nobody but her sees it. What do you want her to do with it?"

"I'll be there in a half hour. If it comes in before I get there, have her keep it in a folder. The guy in the sketch they're sending tried to kill my dad yesterday."

"Have you been found?" Mitch's voice was sharp.

Hardy managed to keep his voice level. "That's what I'm going to find out when I see the sketch. Hopefully, I'll recognize him if he's one of Dohner's goons."

The two men spoke for just a few minutes longer, with Mitch asking for only a few details before hanging up.

It wasn't long before Hardy found himself walking into the police station. A man he recognized as having been in the station before stood at the counter speaking to Haley. Her face was beet red, and her eyes were blazing. She looked furious.

"Is everything okay?" he quietly asked as he walked around to stand beside her.

"No." She spoke curtly. "Wyatt was just leaving." She gave the other man a pointed look. "Weren't you?"

"You know you feel it too." The bleached blonde man in his expensive suit crooned to Haley. "Just come out with me once. You'll have a good time."

If anything, Haley's face became even redder. "I'm not interested. Now, please leave."

"But, babe—"

Hardy had heard enough. "I believe she asked you to leave. Do you need my help to find the door?" For the first time in a long while, Hardy used the bulk of his size to intimidate a smaller man. He had barely taken two steps to walk around the counter toward the other man before the man Haley called Wyatt turned and rushed away.

"Are you okay?" He gently placed his hand on her arm.

Haley turned wide eyes to him. "I'm not even sure what happened. He only walked in a couple of minutes before you got here. He started right off insisting I go on a date with him. Then, once you walked in, he started that nonsense about me feeling it too. I've never given him any reason to think I'm interested in him."

Hardy reached out and softly touched her cheek. "You just have that effect on every man you meet."

For just a brief instant, she seemed to lean against his hand before she straightened and stepped away.

"Your fax hasn't come in yet." Haley busied herself over a notepad on the counter.

"Haley." His voice was soft and hoarse. Her eyes slowly met his. "I wish things were different. I've never wished for anything more in my life."

A light shone from deep within her eyes. "I feel the same way."

Before Hardy could stop himself, he reached out and pulled her into his arms. She held herself rigid for a few moments before he felt her relax against him and slide her arms around his waist. He wondered if she could feel his heartbeat pounding with the side of her face resting against his chest. They fit together like they were made for each other, and nothing had ever felt more natural or right in his life than holding this woman.

A throat clearing behind him reminded Hardy where they were, but he was still reluctant to release Haley, so he drew away from her gradually before turning around to face the sheriff. Mitch did not look pleased.

"Wyatt Millan came in and upset me." Haley's voice was shaking as she spoke to her boss. "Beau was just comforting me. I'm sorry if I was behaving inappropriately in the office."

Mitch's gaze sharpened. "When did he come in? I was only gone for ten minutes."

Haley seemed more composed. "He came in a few minutes before Beau got here and started saying strange things. I'm sorry I let him upset me. It won't happen again."

"He was coming on to her pretty strong, and the man wasn't taking no for an answer," Hardy felt compelled to add. "It took a little friendly persuasion to convince him to leave."

The sheriff finally relaxed. "Then thank you, Hardy. Why don't you come on into my office while you're waiting for your fax? We have a new case you might be interested in."

"Sheriff? You wanted to see me?" Wayne had come in from the back door of the building.

"Yes. Both of you come in and sit down. I'll fill you in on what's happening."

Once they were all three in the office with the door closed, Mitch spoke to the other two men. "Nobody has seen or heard from William Baxter for four days now. Hank called twenty minutes ago to advise us he's located Baxter's car, with no sign of the man. The keys were in the ignition, and there was nothing in the trunk except a spare tire and jack. He's having it towed to the state impound lot, but there is no apparent sign of foul play."

"Who's William Baxter?" The name was unfamiliar to Hardy.

"He works for the post office. Delivers our mail here at the station actually," Mitch replied. "His mom has terminal cancer. I only know because Haley put together a big fundraiser for her last spring."

It didn't surprise Hardy in the least that the kind-hearted woman would take on something like that.

Mitch was still talking. "She had to move into the Parkside Nursing home when it got to be too much for Will to take care of her. I don't know how his financial situation stands right now. He's a nice enough guy, but when it comes right down to it, I don't really know much about him."

"Where'd Hank find the car?" Wayne asked.

"It was parked in the old drive-in theater out east of town. Hank said it was pulled up to the speaker stand just like somebody parked to watch a movie."

Wayne looked at Hardy and elaborated. "It would be hard to watch a movie since there hasn't been a screen standing out there for going on fifteen years. It's just an abandoned lot."

"How'd Hank find it?" Hardy would like to have seen it in the location it was found before it was towed, but hopefully he'd see photos of it.

"Mel Carmichael was picking his field of late corn and saw it sitting there. He didn't have any idea it was connected with a missing persons case; he just figured some kids had been fooling around and left it as a prank." Mitch stood and pointed to a spot on the map. "The drive-in is here, about ten miles from Baxter's house. We need to figure out how it got there and what happened to Baxter in between."

"Mitch, I know you've had to have already searched his house, but can I just check it out?" Hardy didn't want to step on any toes, but his instincts told him William Baxter's disappearance might be important. "I'd just like to get a feel for things."

A knock sounded on the door before it opened to show Haley standing there, a file folder in her hand.

She directed her attention to Hardy. "I'm sorry to interrupt, but your fax just arrived."

Hardy looked at Mitch, who with a slight nod indicated he understood what Hardy needed to do.

"I'll be right back," Hardy told the other two men before standing up and following Haley out of the room.

She turned and silently handed him the folder before speaking. "Nobody else saw it. Nobody else even knows it's here."

"Thanks." He waited until she walked over and sat back down before opening the folder. He couldn't let her distract him from looking as closely as he could at the sketch.

The man whose sketch Hardy found himself looking at could have been a scrawny version of Bluto from the old Popeye comic strips. The sketch artist had also rendered what he thought the man might look like without the excess facial hair, so that's the picture Hardy focused on. He carefully studied the thick face with a squared off chin, searching his mind for any signs of familiarity. But it didn't matter how long he looked at the picture; he had never seen this man before. Dohner liked his employees big and tough, and from his mom's description, Hardy estimated the criminal would be five-ten or five-eleven, tops, and of slight build. Hardy was all but certain he wasn't looking at a Dohner employee.

"I have to make a call," he told Haley, who looked at him questioningly. Even though his thoughts were once more in a turmoil, he managed to smile at her before he turned and walked down the hall to the back room.

Elliott answered on the first ring.

"I've never seen this guy," Hardy told his brother-in-law.

"And you're sure about that?" Elliott asked.

Hardy flipped the folder open and looked at the sketch again. "I'm positive. If this guy is one of Dohner's men, he's a new one."

"I'm not sure if that's good news or not." Worry filled the agent's voice. "If Dohner didn't try to have your dad killed, then that means we have a new player out there after you or your family. And this guy apparently knows about the Davis family."

Make that two new factions if Hardy's hunch were correct that the people committing the crimes in Shadow were also after him. He quickly came to a decision. "I'm staying here, Elliott. I don't see how running and hiding will help anybody at this point. But you have to promise if you're the slightest bit worried about my family, they'll disappear."

"Your family is safe." The voice coming from the phone was filled with determination. "I will keep them that way, too, Beau. If I have to hire private security for them, I'll do it."

Hardy often forgot his brother-in-law was an extremely wealthy man. "I appreciate that."

"They're my family too," Elliott said calmly. "Just a second, Beau. Sherry just handed me something."

The line was silent for a few minutes before Elliott spoke again.

"We ran facial recognition on the sketch, and it didn't turn up anything." He once more sounded worried. "Beau, I know you're capable of taking care of yourself, but be careful. I don't like the idea this guy who's probably after you is off the radar. It makes me think we're playing in the big leagues with a little league bat. Just keep your eyes open."

Hardy had already considered the idea that since the man who attempted to kill his father failed, he might come directly after Hardy. "I'll see him before he sees me." Hardy would just have to stay on his toes.

"Okay. If anything changes, call me and we'll get you away from there." His brother-in-law once more sounded like the professional he was.

"I will." Hardy pushed the button to end the call before sliding the phone into his jeans pocket. An idea came to him as he walked back to Mitch's office. When he started to speak to Haley, he realized she was talking on the phone, so he went on into the sheriff's office.

"Sheriff, before we go on about the Baxter case, can I ask a favor?" Hardy still held the folder in his hand.

"Sure." Mitch and Wayne both turned their gazes toward him.

"Is there any way we can have a BOLO out on this guy without giving any details?" He slid the sketch out of the folder.

Mitch's gaze sharpened as he looked at the picture. "Is that one of Dohner's men?"

Hardy shook his head. "I'm pretty sure he isn't, but he tried to murder my dad last night." Instead of keeping the situation a secret, Hardy had decided it would be beneficial to enlist the police department's help. "And now he might show up here—after me. I need to know if he does."

It wouldn't have surprised Hardy if Mitch requested more information, or even ordered him to leave town, but instead the sheriff's reply was instantaneous and certain. "We'll have the state issue a BOLO. We'll just say he's a person of interest in an ongoing investigation. That's all anybody needs to know."

"Can I see that?" Wayne, his eyes already focused on the sketch, held out his hand so Hardy could hand it to him.

"What?" Mitch asked his deputy curiously.

Wayne looked up from the picture to his boss. "I've seen this guy." His brows lowered as he thought. "I don't remember exactly where, but I know he was in town a few days ago."

"Can you remember what day it was?" A ton of questions filled Hardy's head.

"If I can think of where I was, then I'll be able to figure out when." Wayne shifted his gaze from Hardy back to the sketch, his frown deepening. "I remember thinking those whiskers had to itch like crazy. But where was I?"

Hardy kept his voice calm. "Think of the places you've been within the past few days. Maybe something will jog your memory."

Wayne looked back at Hardy. "Okay. I'm pretty sure Lori wasn't with me, so I need to remember where I've been alone." Hardy and Mitch both sat silently while Wayne thought. The deputy finally shook his head. "I'm just drawing a blank. Maybe if I forget it for a while, it'll come to me. That's worked before."

Mitch spoke before Hardy could. "That's probably a good idea." He turned his gaze to Hardy. "Why don't you ride with Wayne to the Baxter house? We don't want people wondering why our crime scene photographer is scoping out a house by himself."

Hardy had forgotten the missing man. He wanted to know exactly when and where Wayne had seen his dad's assailant. But, he knew the other two men were right. If a person tried to push too hard, it often made a memory even harder to retrieve. Besides, they needed to find out where this William Baxter had disappeared to.

Haley wasn't at her station when Hardy followed Wayne out of the office. That was too bad. He'd have liked to have gotten a smile from her—to get him through the day.

Chapter 35

Haley scrutinized the selection of cookies on the shelves, determined to at least try to find something healthier than the double chocolate chip she too often enjoyed. It was difficult, though, because even the pictures on the "low-fat" packages reminded her of cardboard. Not to mention they were priced a good twenty to thirty percent higher than the regular ones.

She finally gave in and picked up her favorite brand. It wasn't like she had to watch her weight or anything—yet. She supposed the older she got, the more difficult it might be to maintain her figure.

Her shopping cart appeared to have enough food in it for a small family, but since she only made one real grocery store visit each month, she stocked up. With a monthly salary, Haley had long ago learned how to best manage her money. Of course, that was after she tried to dole cash out weekly, which had been a certified disaster. She'd found herself taking money from the weekly grocery fund for a pizza and movie, or a blouse she just had to have. The month she had to subsist on macaroni and cheese and canned tuna for the last week and a half forever cured her of the weekly allowance method.

Haley had always hoped her husband would be good with money. She simply didn't like it enough to try to do anything like investing. In fact, she wouldn't mind one little bit if her husband put her on an allowance like couples did on those old black and white television shows. He could just pay the bills and give her whatever they could afford to spend. She liked that idea very much.

First, she'd need to have a husband. She sighed as she picked up a loaf of bread and placed it in her cart. Why did Beau Harding immediately pop into her head? When he'd held her yesterday, she felt more comfortable and secure than ever before. She could have stayed in his arms all day. It just didn't seem fair they were so attracted to each other when it couldn't work out.

"So, I hear you and Beau Harding are an item after all." Tessa Lincoln's voice brought Haley out of her reverie.

Haley must have been incredibly lost in thought because she was surprised to find her friend standing right beside her. Then Tessa's words sank in.

"What do you mean, Beau and I are an item?"

Tessa leaned toward her and lowered her voice. "Jennifer Ewing was walking by the police station yesterday and saw you and Hardy 'embracing,' as she put it."

Haley put her hands on her cheeks, which she could already feel warming with embarrassment. "Please tell me you're the only person she's said that to."

"Sorry, sister." Tessa smiled sympathetically. "She's telling everybody. Apparently she thinks it's wonderful the two of you have found each other."

"Is this a ladies' chat, or can anybody join in?" Matt Ashford's voice came from right behind them as he stuck his head between their faces.

Haley looked at him. "How much did you hear?"

His smile widened. "I've already heard about you and Hardy straight from Mrs. Ewing herself." He drew back and shook his finger at her. "Shame on you, demonstrating such public displays of affection."

"It wasn't like that," Haley automatically protested. "I mean; he was . . . comforting me. A man had come in and upset me, and Beau was just trying to make me feel better."

Matt's eyebrows waggled as he spoke to Tessa. "I sure hope *Beau* doesn't ever try to make me feel better."

Tessa laughed and shook her head. "You are incorrigible, Matt Ashford."

"I'm pretty sure I'll be insulted by that as soon as I get a chance to look it up and see what it means." He casually threw an arm around each woman. "I'm sorry, Haley. I shouldn't give you such a hard time. I think you and Hardy are perfect for each other."

Haley had managed to regain most of her composure. "We're not together."

"Are you sure about that?" It was Tessa who asked.

Haley pulled out from under Matt's arm and pushed her cart a few feet away. They were drawing curious glances. "I'm not having this conversation here. Apparently, there's already enough talk going around."

"Meet me at the diner in a half hour. Dinner's on me." Before either woman could respond, Matt turned and ambled away.

"Looks like you have a dinner date," Tessa observed.

"He invited both of us, didn't he?" That's what Haley assumed anyway. "He was speaking to both of us."

Tessa shrugged. "It doesn't matter. Mitch is taking me to Pattinton for the evening. We haven't had an uninterrupted date in ages, and he promised to leave his cell phone and radio both at home."

Even though Haley protested, she found herself, after having hurriedly taking her groceries home and putting them away, sitting at a table with Matt.

"So, tell me about the man who upset you." Matt unexpectedly broached the subject as soon as Nancy had left with their orders. "Who is he, and what did he do?"

"I doubt if you'd know him. He's new to town." Matt spent a lot of time in Shadow since the trucking company was based there, but it wasn't really his home.

"What's his name, Haley?" he asked in a firm voice.

She sighed. "His name is Wyatt Millan. He moved here from up by Chicago, to work at the bank."

An unidentifiable emotion flashed in Matt's eyes for an instant before it was replaced by concern. "What did he do?"

Haley drew a ragged breath and looked at her friend. "He asked me out and didn't want to take no for an answer. He was being really pushy and ignoring what I told him, and Beau made him leave. Then I was upset, so Beau . . . comforted me. That's what Jennifer Ewing saw. That's all it was." Even if it had felt like so much more.

Chapter 36

The first thing Hardy saw when he walked into the diner was Haley and Matt, huddled together, appearing to be deep in conversation. An unfamiliar feeling flared within him, and it took a minute for him to realize what it was. He was jealous. He was envious of the man sitting too near her and speaking privately to the only woman Hardy had ever felt drawn to like this. It was as though she were a powerful magnet, and he was a weak piece of metal, pulled ever closer to her no matter what he did to try and stop it.

He didn't have the right to be jealous, though, so he quietly walked past their table to his usual one. He had just pulled out his chair when he heard Matt's voice.

"Hey, Hardy, we've got room over here. Don't sit over there all by yourself."

Hardy looked up and directly into Haley's eyes. The look he saw in them nearly stopped his heart. It was true; she felt the same way he did. But he could do nothing about it. Not with the ever growing disaster his life was.

"I don't want to interrupt your evening." Before either Matt or Haley could speak, he turned and sat, facing away from them. He almost preferred jealousy to this frustration over knowing Haley wanted to be with him as much as he did her.

"Fish is good tonight." Nancy's voice drew his attention.

Hardy didn't look at her. "I'm not hungry enough for the special tonight. I'll just take a loaded cheeseburger and fries."

"And soda?" The hesitation in the waitress's voice caused Hardy to give her his attention. He had been horribly impolite.

"Yes, please." He forced a smile.

He found himself wishing he'd sat at a different table a short while later. One farther away from Matt and Haley. He could hear their voices, but not their words, giving their conversation an atmosphere of intimacy. It was too late now. He couldn't very well pick up his plate and drink, and make a big to-do about changing tables. It would be pretty obvious why he'd moved.

Instead, he focused on his hamburger and let his mind wander to the cases he was helping to investigate.

The break-ins and murder were no closer to being solved today than they had been when he agreed to help. So far there hadn't been any more of them, but there also hadn't been any further evidence pointing them toward the culprits.

And the missing postal worker, William Baxter. The one thing he found that had been overlooked the first time his house was swept had been some correspondence using a different name. After he and Wayne looked closer and did some good old fashioned investigating, they discovered William Baxter had gone by his middle name when in social circles. His partying friends knew him as Harvey or Harve. And it appeared Baxter lived a double life.

Will Baxter was a friendly, soft-spoken, all-American man. People on his mail route all described him the same. Even the word trustworthy was used more than once. Harve, on the other hand, liked to party. He hung out in a couple of pretty seedy bars and was known to have a soft spot for a good game of poker. Junior Biggs, the owner of Biggs Bar and Grill, had been very forthcoming. It seemed the evening before Baxter went missing, he'd been at the bar. According to Biggs, Harve had been more intoxicated than usual, and his mouth was in high gear. He'd been excited about some money he was going to come into soon. He was even going to move his mother to an expensive cancer center out of state. Nobody they questioned had any idea what Baxter was talking about. They had hit a dead end.

Then came the man who tried to kill his father. Wayne still hadn't remembered exactly when or where he'd seen him, but one thing was certain. The man in the sketch had been in Shadow days before he attacked H.B. And if he was after Hardy, why hadn't he even gotten close enough that Hardy saw him? None of it made sense.

Once again, Hardy felt like he was on the edge of something. There was a puzzle here, waiting to be solved, but he had no idea how to fit the pieces together. What was he missing?

"Can I join you?" Haley's soft voice brought him out of his thoughts.

He turned and looked for Matt, only to see an empty table. "Did your date already leave?"

Fire flashed in her eyes. "I wasn't on a date, and you know it. But if that's how you want to be, I'll leave you to enjoy your dinner."

She started to walk past him, but as though against his will, he gently touched her arm to stop her.

"I'm sorry." His voice was husky. "Please stay."

She slowly turned to face him, and he found himself looking into eyes full of emotion. He would never have trouble knowing what Haley was thinking. "Stay," he repeated.

For a few moments, he watched an inner conflict on her face. She slowly walked over and sat down across from him, though.

"Did you have a nice dinner?" he made himself ask.

Haley shrugged. "More like a lecture, but the food was good."

A lecture? That surprised him. "What would Matt have to lecture you about?"

"Us." She seemed interested in the paper placemat in front of her. "You and me, I mean."

"Us?" he echoed, feeling foolish. "What about us?"

Her eyes remained steadily focused on him. "It seems you and I are too caught up in our feelings to behave appropriately. Everybody is ecstatic that we've found each other, though."

"What?" Hardy was confused. "I'm sorry, but I don't understand what you're talking about."

Her cheeks began to turn pink as she spoke. "Yesterday, after Wyatt left, when we . . . when you comforted me, one of the biggest gossips in town happened to walk by the station. She saw us, and now it is all over town we're an item. Not only are we together, we're also not concerned if we make a public spectacle of ourselves."

Hardy knew there was more to address than this, but there was one thing he wanted to make perfectly clear. "I didn't hold you to comfort you, Haley." He reached across the table and placed his hand over hers. "I held you because I wanted to."

"I know," she whispered. Her eyes widened. "What are we going to do?"

"Be together." He had no idea where the words came from; they had just appeared. And now that they were spoken, Hardy found himself unable and unwilling to take them back. "We have to figure out a way for us to be together."

A tear trickled down her cheek. "You'll leave me. You won't stay here."

"We'll figure it out." He spoke with determination. Something—God pulled us together."

A tremulous smile appeared on her face.

Hardy wasn't finished. "We both want this, Haley. We'll make it work . . . somehow."

All sense of trepidation showing in her eyes was slowly replaced by wary joy. "Really? You won't break my heart?"

Hardy's voice gentled as he reached across and wiped an errant tear from her face. "I'll never intentionally hurt you."

Haley's dimples appeared with her slowly growing smile. "Then we're really together?"

It was too late for second thoughts, even if he wanted to have them. He had already made a commitment. "We're together."

Her smile faltered. "Will you come to church with me this Sunday? Just once, Beau, and if you can't again, I'll learn to live with it. I promise."

At that moment, if she'd have asked him for the moon he would have gone outside and tried to lasso it. "What time should I pick you up?"

His heart swelled as he realized he was responsible for the look of happiness on her face. "You can just come to the church at about nine-forty-five. I have to be there at nine to teach my Sunday school class."

"Okay." Hardy reluctantly slid his hand off hers, missing the contact of her skin as soon as they parted. "So, now what's this about gossip?"

"It doesn't matter now," she replied.

"Good." He found he couldn't take his eyes off of her. "I have tomorrow off. Can we spend the day together?"

Haley's eyes grew wide. "The entire day?"

Hardy enjoyed seeing her blush. "I want to make up for lost time."

"But what will we do?" She didn't look put off by his suggestion, just curious.

He searched his mind for an all-day activity and hit on what he thought would be ideal. "I'd like to surprise you. Okay?"

Her cheeks grew rosier. "Okay."

And for the first time in what seemed like forever, Hardy found himself feeling okay, too.

Chapter 37

"Get out of here before I shoot you myself," he ordered Weiss's employee before slamming the door in the man's face. He had paid good money—money he couldn't afford—for this man to kill H.B. Davis, and he failed miserably. A woman, in her sixties, had managed to stop him!

The phone rang, and he nearly dropped it in his haste to answer. He'd been expecting this call.

"It's working," James assured him. "Our actions are pushing the dispatcher right into his arms." He snickered. "Literally."

"And you're positive about this woman's family?"

"She's completely alone." Doubt crept into the caller's voice. "You promised she won't suffer, though. Right?"

"She'll serve her purpose by causing pain for Davis. There is no need for her to suffer." Other than the effect watching her writhe in pain would have on her new boyfriend. He couldn't tell this person that, though. The fool thought himself noble.

"Just keep making appearances to stir things up a bit," he instructed the man on the other end of the call. "We don't want the newly budding romance to fizzle out."

"If you'd have seen how he acted with her, you wouldn't be worried. I wouldn't be surprised if they didn't make it something official before too long."

"Just remember your job." He hung up before the other man could make one more self-serving comment. If it were left up to James, there would be a parade right down the main street of Shadow held in his honor.

He caught a glimpse of his reflection in the mirror over his desk. When had he grown old? Had it been only after everything fell apart, or had it been from the life he was already living?

It didn't matter now. He stiffened his spine and stood straighter. What none of the men in Shadow knew, was that he had his own way of helping the plan along. And tomorrow would be a good time to kick things into gear.

He'd better get busy. There were many preparations to make.

He picked up the phone and dialed a number.

Chapter 38

Haley grasped Beau's hand tighter and tried not to scream. Why she had ever let herself be talked into riding a roller coaster was beyond her.

"Here we go!" Beau yelled, just as they crested a rise and plummeted down the other side.

Fine. She had been okay with visiting Six Flags on one of the last open weekends of the season. She'd even been happy about it. She just failed to consider what they would do when once inside the park.

At that moment, she was thanking her lucky stars she hadn't eaten more than an orange for breakfast. Haley might just find herself being very embarrassed if there had been anything more in her stomach.

She nearly went to her knees to kiss the asphalt when they finally stepped out of the car a few minutes later.

"It's official." Beau tugged her along with him as he left the ride area. "We have now ridden all of the roller coasters here except the Batman."

Haley froze in her tracks. "Oh, no." She shook her head. "I'm not getting on anything that turns me upside down. No way."

His gaze swept over her face before he laughed. "You do look a little green around the gills." Beau reached over and pushed some hair that had escaped her ponytail back from her face. "Okay. It's your turn to pick a ride anyway."

"First, I need to visit the ladies room." Because she was too embarrassed to tell Beau before, Haley had "held it" much longer than she should. That crazy roller coaster had just about taken care of the problem for her.

"Good idea." He didn't drop her hand as they headed for one of the several buildings situated conveniently around the park.

"I'll see you in a few minutes," he told her before leaving her at the entrance to the women's side, so he could go around to the men's.

After hurriedly taking care of her most urgent problem, while washing her hands, Haley made the supreme mistake of looking in the mirror.

"Oh, my goodness." She looked worse than she did when she first got out of bed each morning. Part of the hair on top of her head was standing up, and she doubted very seriously if even half of it was still inside the elastic band she'd so carefully put it in. And her eyes! Why had she tried to wear mascara to an amusement park? "I look like a deranged Barbie doll!"

"Oh, honey, it's not that bad." Haley looked over to see an elderly woman standing at the next sink. "Would you like to borrow my hairbrush?"

Haley knew using another person's hair implements was generally not advisable, but in this case, the woman beside her appeared to be very nice—and clean. "Yes, thank you."

"Here you go." The older woman handed a bright pink brush to Haley. "I have some wet wipes in my purse if you'd like to wash that mascara off."

A few minutes later, thanks to the kind woman, Haley felt like a new person. "Thank you very much."

"You're welcome." Her benefactor smiled warmly. "You look lovely, and that braid will hold up much better than a ponytail."

Before she knew it, Haley found herself learning about her new friend. Ethel Bradbury had been married to Frank for fifty-three years. They had four children, nine grandchildren, and six great-grandchildren—four of whom they had brought to Six Flags for the day. The boys, ranging in age from four to seven, were currently sitting in one of the restaurants with their grandfather, enjoying a pizza.

"Oh, gracious sakes." Ethel looked around her. "I've kept you in here forever, haven't I?"

Beau! Haley had forgotten Beau! "My date is probably worried. It was really nice talking to you, though."

"I'm glad we met," the other woman agreed.

Haley practically ran out of the bathroom. Beau stood a few yards away, an anxious look on his face.

Before she could say anything, Haley found herself wrapped tightly in his arms and held against him. "I was beginning to think you'd been kidnapped or something." Beau's breathing was ragged. "If you hadn't come out when you did, I was going in there to get you."

"I'm sorry." Haley felt horrible. There he was, with somebody after him, and his date had seemingly disappeared. Of course, it disturbed him. "I wasn't thinking, Beau. I met a sweet woman in there, and we got to talking, and I just forgot where I was. I'm sorry."

Beau eased his hold so she could lean back and he could look into her eyes. "Please don't scare me like that again, Haley."

She impulsively hugged him. "I won't."

He took a deep breath and slowly released her. "Okay." His smile wasn't as bright as it had been earlier, but it was there. "What do you want to ride?"

"I'm kind of hungry." Now that she was off those crazy rides, her nearly empty stomach was starting to protest. "Can we eat something?"

"Sure." His hand once more claimed hers as they started walking. "What are you hungry for?"

Twenty minutes later, Haley found herself sitting at a relatively secluded picnic table, across from Beau, with burgers and fries between them.

"Are you having fun?" The solemnity of Beau's voice told Haley he truly wanted her to be.

"I haven't had this much fun since I was a teenager." And that was the truth. "When was the last time you were here?"

Beau seemed to consider her question for a few moments. "I guess it was right before my sister graduated from high school. She asked for a family outing as part of her graduation present, and this is what our parents came up with."

That sounded very nice. "So, was it just the four of you, or did you and your sister bring friends?"

"It was just my family." A pensive expression appeared on Beau's face. "You know, I think that was the only time my sister and I spent the day together. We've never really been close."

Haley had often wished she had a brother or sister, especially since her parents were gone. "What is your sister like?"

A small smile came to his face. "Callie is a lot like our mom. She always wanted to be a wife and mother—nothing else. She married right out of high school, and slid right into the life she wanted."

"How did she and her husband meet?" Haley wanted to know more about Beau's family. "Did they go to school together?"

He shook his head. "Elliott is six years older than Callie." The french fry he was holding came perilously close to being dunked in his Coke as he spoke. "He was at a fundraising dinner my parents attended. Callie didn't want to go, but Mom made her. It was for a good cause, and they were all going to support it."

"So, it was love at first sight." How romantic!

Beau swallowed his fry. "Not at all. In fact, Elliott mistook Callie for the drug dealer he was there undercover to bust."

Haley's hand froze with her soda halfway to the table. "What happened?"

"My sister was standing by herself out on the veranda, pouting because Mom made her go. She had no idea it was the place where Elliott had arranged to buy drugs." From the smile on Beau's face, this must be an amusing story. "Elliott walked up and asked her if she had what he needed. Callie thought he was hitting on her, so she hauled off and slapped his face. He was shocked speechless." Beau chuckled. "My sister has Mom's temper, too. She told him in no uncertain terms what she thought of a man who would try to take advantage of a woman, merely because she had the misfortune to be standing outside alone. Then she got started about being forced to be there in the first place, and Elliott got chewed out for that, too. He says she was drawing too much attention to them, and he didn't know how to shut her up, so he finally kissed her. I guess Callie liked it because they've been together ever since."

"That is amazing." Haley smiled at him. "What a remarkable story."

His brow lifted as he looked at her over his burger. "You mean like the story of a man rescuing a woman from poison oak?"

Haley's heart sped up. "That's a good one, too." She couldn't help but laugh. "Especially if you include the shower." Her cheeks immediately warmed as she realized what she'd said. "I mean, not that you saw me in the—" She dropped the fry she was holding back onto the tray and buried her face in her hands.

The sound of his soft laughter brought her eyes slowly over her hands to peer at him.

"You are even prettier when you blush." Beau shook his head. "I don't think I'll ever get tired of seeing it."

She made herself pull her hands away from her face and focused on her sandwich. "That wasn't the first time we met, you know."

"I remember when we both helped Luke and Holly move in," he assured her.

Haley shook her head. "Still not the first time. We ran into each other once." She couldn't stop her smile.

"What?" Beau looked confused. "I think Holly might have introduced us once, but I'm not sure if either of us really noticed the other."

"You almost knocked me over." If he didn't have any memory of it, maybe she should just forget it.

His eyes studied her face for a minute before they lit up. "That was you! I literally ran into you at the drugstore, didn't I?"

"Yes." She was already having second thoughts about reminding him. What if he'd noticed what she was purchasing? That could be embarrassing.

"Tell me about your childhood." She would just change the subject.

He gave her a puzzled look at the change in topic, but then a smile appeared as he spoke. "I had a wonderful life." Beau seemed surprised by his own words. "I guess you could say I had the best of both worlds. We lived in a suburb of Chicago, where culture and activities were available, and I spent every summer on my grandfather's farm. My mom insisted her children would know what her life was like before she married Dad. Then, we could make up our own minds whether to live in the city or the country."

"So, your sister spent summers on the farm, too?" Haley had experienced a good childhood, too, but Beau's sounded fascinating.

He nodded. "Only she was inside with Grandma, or outside at the horse barn. I think we'd see each other at breakfast and dinner, and not even know the other one was there the rest of the time. Callie learned to garden from Grandma."

"You were happy." It was a simple observation.

"I was happy," he agreed. "What about your childhood? Before you lost your parents, I mean."

Haley swallowed the last of her hamburger before she answered him. "My parents and I did everything together." Her memories were precious. "Most of my friends complained about their moms and dads, but I never did. I never had cause to. They made sure I knew who Jesus was and encouraged me to be as involved in church activities as I wanted." She could still see her mom and dad smiling and waving goodbye the first time she'd gone away to church camp. Most of the other moms were crying and acting all sad, but her mom was happy Haley was going to experience something special. She knew Haley would be home in a few weeks. "We went on a family vacation every summer."

"I understand if this is too hard for you to talk about." Beau's gentle voice reached her ears.

"It's not." And it wasn't anymore. She found herself wanting to share her life with the man sitting across from her. "Can you believe I've been in all forty-eight contiguous states? I mean, we only drove across the corner of some of them, but we made it to every single one."

"That's quite an accomplishment." Beau set his empty paper cup on the tray in front of him. "How did you end up in Shadow?"

"After my parents . . . I decided I wanted to be a dispatcher. So, I went to Kent State and earned a bachelors' in communication. Then, one day, I was searching online and saw the opening for a police dispatcher in Shadow. I sent in my résumé and credentials, and the rest is history."

Beau frowned. "What's the deal with Shadow, anyway? Do you have any idea where it got its name?"

That was actually one of Haley's favorite stories. "A man named Virgil Richmond and his wife Betsy spent months traveling west.

Haley went on to describe the way Betsy outsmarted her husband. As the community grew, Virgil named it Shadow. It stuck, I guess."

Beau appeared to be amused. "You wouldn't be a descendant of Betsy, would you? Because I can just see you shoving a man under a tree and telling him that's where you were staying."

"Nope." Haley laughed at the thought. "But Clay Richmond is a direct descendant of Virgil. If you ever get the chance, ask him to tell you the story. He's actually much better at it than I am."

"I don't know." Beau reached over and picked up her last french fry. "You did a pretty good job of it."

Haley immediately felt her face grow warm and knew she was blushing again. "Let's go. I'm going to drive you around the track in one of those antique cars."

"You're going to drive?" Beau's brow shot up. "I'm not sure if I can handle that kind of threat to my masculinity." The teasing smile belied his words.

"Then just wait until we ride the bumper cars." Haley looked into Beau Harding's eyes and felt her heart being tugged a little closer to his. This was good, and best of all, it was real.

Chapter 39

Hardy nearly tripped over Clarence as he stepped down out of his camper the following Friday afternoon. "Whoa, there!" He barely managed to stay on his feet. "What are you trying to do, Clarence? I just showered." He scratched behind the dog's ears. "I don't intend to roll around in the dirt with you."

"Clarence!" Luke's voice came from the side of Hardy's camper a moment before the man appeared. "I told you to wait for me, didn't I?"

It was hard not to laugh when the dog appeared to nod. "Are you sure Clarence is really just a dog?" he asked Luke.

Luke reached down and petted the animal. "I'm not too sure sometimes. He's always been like this, though, ever since I brought him home.

"You haven't trained him?" How could Clarence act this way if he weren't trained?

Luke chuckled. "He plopped onto his stomach and wouldn't get up the first time I tried. The second time, he grabbed the trainer's soda out of her hand and ran like the wind."

Hardy had to laugh at the image Luke described. "I take it you didn't try that again." Luke shook his head. "Well, then, if he's not trained, how does he know to act like this?"

Holly says it's because I talk to him like he's a person. He thinks he is one."

"She may have a point." Hardy took in the dirty jeans and jacket the other man was wearing. "How does it feel to be back at work?"

"Good." Luke touched his side. "I can still feel my wound, though. I'm blessed that the bullet missed my vital organs and passed right through."

"I know what you mean." Before Hardy really considered his actions, he lifted his jacket and shirt, showing a scar on the right side of his abdomen.

Luke's eyebrows shot up. "That looks just like my...Have you been shot, Hardy?"

Hardy decided he trusted Luke and didn't care what the so-called rules of anonymity were. The Walkers should know enough to stay safe. "Yes. I was just given a clean bill of health right before I came here."

"What happened?" Luke asked, "If you don't mind telling me."

"You can't tell anybody except Holly, and it has to stop with her." Hardy suddenly realized this was the right thing to do.

Luke nodded. "You have my word."

"I was an undercover police officer in Chicago. I had to blow my cover to testify in a trial that put the top dog's son away for the rest of his life." Hardy found it oddly freeing to tell Luke. "The kid's father was after me, and he runs a big organization, so when I was shot during an unrelated incident, the Chicago Police Department and FSA decided it would be a good idea if I died. After I recuperated I came here."

"These robberies and the murder." Luke cast a worried look around them before returning his gaze to Hardy. "Do they have anything to do with you?"

"I think they do," Hardy admitted. "And even though I'm all but sure the syndicate hasn't found me, I don't know who has. I'm staying, though, and finding out. I won't run off and leave a mess I'm responsible for." He should have thought of this long before now. "If you want me to pull my camper out of here tonight, I understand. I don't want you and Holly to be in any danger because of me."

"You can stay here as long as you need," Luke replied without hesitation. "If somebody knows who you are, they most likely already know where you live. Nobody's going to come down my long lane without drawing attention."

The entire quarter-mile rocked road was in view; Hardy had liked this job even more when he saw that.

"I believe this is the safest place for you right now, and I'm not going to worry about Holly and me. I know she'll say the same thing."

Hardy was moved by the kindness and friendship of the man in front of him. "Thank you. I might relocate before long, though, but you'll be the first to know if I do." He actually had the germ of an idea he was giving serious thought to.

"So, you and Haley." Luke was changing the subject. "You've taken her out every night this week, haven't you?"

"Yes." Hardy couldn't read the expression on the other man's face. "Is there a problem with that?"

"Not as long as you plan to stick around and not break her heart." The farmer was serious. "She's been through a lot, and deserves a man who appreciates her."

"I know what she's been through." It felt good to be able to say that. "And believe me, I appreciate her more than you know."

Luke seemed to consider Hardy's words before slowly nodding. "Good."

Hardy glanced at his watch. "Speaking of Haley, she's expecting me for dinner. If I don't get going, I'll be late."

After Luke told him goodnight and walked away with Clarence, Hardy wasted no time in getting out of there. It was the first time Haley had invited him to her apartment for a meal, and he didn't want to keep her waiting.

As Luke observed, Hardy and Haley had spent every evening this week together. They were going to church again on Sunday, which still gave Hardy a funny feeling in the pit of his stomach. But he'd told her he would, and he wasn't going to start off their relationship with lies. He had more than enough of those in his life the way it was.

Tonight was a culmination of a complete week of dates. He'd taken her bowling on Monday and to what had to be the sappiest love story ever put on film Tuesday. Just last night, they'd gone to a surprisingly enjoyable Bible study. It pleased him when she suggested they stay in tonight. It seemed Haley liked to cook. Since Hardy liked to eat, he figured that was one more thing that made them ideal for each other. She laughed at him when he shared that sentiment.

He quickly discovered Haley had an excellent sense of humor and was loyal to a fault. He'd never met a person more determined to see the good in people. Something was going on with one of the other dispatchers, and Haley expressed dismay that Mitch might have to fire the other woman.

The most amazing thing was after only one week, he knew in his heart he'd found the right woman. Haley Johnson was the person he wanted to spend the rest of his life with. Hardy had never given much stock to love at first—or if he were technical, third—sight, but he was pretty sure she'd stolen his heart when he first saw her standing there caressing the leaves of poison oak.

The ringing of his cell phone rudely pulled him from his thoughts. He pulled onto the shoulder before looking at caller ID. It was the sheriff's personal number.

"Harding here," he answered.

"Hardy, I'm sorry to bother you, but I need you to take care of something for me," Mitch was brusque.

"I have a date with Haley." Besides, he'd already put in his eight hours that day.

"You can call her and let her know you'll be running late." Evidently, Hardy's new boss wasn't going to take no for an answer.

Hardy sighed. "What do you need?"

"There's a situation at the station I need you to take care of." Mitch sounded more like himself now. "Crystal just called to let me know somebody's there to see me. A young man named Sammy Lewis. You've probably never heard of him, but he just got out of jail a short while back."

Hardy immediately remembered Wilma Ebhart explaining what the boy had done. "I actually do know about him. Do you know what he wants to see you about?"

"Crystal says he'll only talk to me." Mitch cleared his throat. "Hank and Jeff are on duty right now, but I don't think Sammy will respond to either one of them, and I'm over in Pattinton, up to my eyeballs in china patterns and place settings. Tess will kill me if I try to leave right now."

"If he won't speak to Hank or Jeff, what makes you think he'll talk to me?" Hardy was confused.

A deep sigh emanated from Hardy's phone. "Hank is too easy going, and Jeff will scare the kid half to death. You've dealt with people like him before, haven't you? You know how to talk to a person his age?"

Hardy thought of the kids he'd managed to persuade not to join Dohners. "I guess." He couldn't help but be skeptical. "But, what are we going to do if he just clams up or leaves?"

"We won't be any worse off." Mitch's statement was blunt. "Just say you'll try. That's all I'm asking."

It appeared Hardy had no choice. "I'll give it a shot, but I'm not making any promises."

After Mitch had assured Hardy he'd understand if Sammy Lewis walked, and they said their goodbyes, Hardy quickly dialed Haley's number.

Even though she said she understood, Hardy could still hear the disappointment in her voice when he told her he'd be late. After she promised to keep dinner warm for them, he reluctantly ended the call. The sooner he got to the station, the sooner he'd be at Haley's.

A buxom brunette was standing behind the counter when Hardy walked into the station. So, he was finally seeing the Crystal Stanley he'd heard so much about—none of it good. Mitch made no secret of the fact he wanted to fire her, and would do so if he had the slightest bit of proof to back his suspicions. Hardy looked around but didn't see anybody else.

"Well, you must be Beau Harding." Even the woman's simpering voice was annoying. "I've been looking forward to officially welcoming our newest officer."

He didn't like the way she was looking at him, nor that she appeared to be walking toward him. Beau had dealt with women like this before, or at least, Joe Ryman had. Sharp and to the point worked best.

"I think you better back off. I'm in a committed relationship." Just saying it made his heart beat faster.

She tilted her head and posed in a style she probably thought was attractive. In reality, she reminded him of the women so hungry for love, they took all the verbal and even physical abuse. The only pleasant aspect was she stopped walking. Unfortunately, it seemed her mouth was still running. "I'll share."

Hardy tasted bile. "It's not going to happen." She was one of the most desperate women he'd ever met—and he'd met plenty. "Where is Sammy Lewis?"

His words brought Crystal up short. She wrinkled her nose. "Oh, I sent him back to the break room. He was giving me the creeps, just sitting out here looking around."

That was brilliant. Just leave a teenager alone in a room full of police equipment. Without another word, Hardy walked past her toward the back room.

When Hardy walked into the room, a young man with shoulder-length blonde hair sat at the table. A huge frown filled his face when he saw Hardy.

"Sammy Lewis?" Hardy kept his tone of voice friendly.

"Who are you?" The boy's eyes were full of suspicion. "I told that woman I'd only talk to the sheriff."

Okay. Hardy had to be careful how he handled this. "My name is Beau Harding. Sheriff Landon is out of town, but he asked me to come and see you. Can I get you a soda? I need one."

Without waiting for a reply, Hardy walked to the refrigerator and opened the door. "Looks like we have a few bottles of root beer if you like that better, or we can get into Deputy Daniels' lemonade." He stayed bent over, looking into the appliance.

"I like cola." Sammy sounded slightly less hostile.

"Me, too." Hardy grabbed two bottles and turned around, letting the refrigerator door close behind him. "Here you go." He handed the boy a bottle.

Sammy accepted the drink and looked uncertainly at Hardy. "Thanks."

"No problem." Hardy casually pulled out a chair at the end of the table instead of across from the boy. He leaned back and took a long drink of soda before returning his attention to the teenager. "So, Sammy, I hear you're a football player. I met Roger Weiss once."

The boy's eyes practically bugged before he remembered to play it cool.

"Have you heard of him?"

Sammy was fighting a losing battle trying to act unimpressed. "He's the starting quarterback for the Chicago Bears." The teenager put his elbows on the table and leaned toward Hardy. "How did you meet him? Do you play?"

"No, I was never any good at football." He couldn't very well tell Sammy he'd met Roger Weiss during a dinner party Joe Ryman escorted Audrey Dohner to. "I just ran into him at a party once."

"Did you get his autograph?"

Hardy shook his head. It wasn't that kind of party. "I didn't have anything for him to sign."

Sammy's interest was replaced by an expression filled with despair. "I was going to be like him. I was going to play pro ball."

"Maybe I can help you out." For some reason, Hardy felt like he needed to do something for this kid. "The coach at Illinois Continental College is a friend of mine. It's not a big school, but players are scouted there anyway."

"They won't want me." The teenager's blonde hair fell across his eyes as he shook his head. "I only have a GED. No college will take me, let alone let me play ball."

"Illinois Continental will accept students with GEDs, and like I said, I'm friends with the coach. He owes me a favor, so I'll ask him to give you a chance. You get yourself into school next year, and I'll arrange for the opportunity to try out for them." Hardy was all but sure from what he'd heard, the kid would easily get a scholarship. "You'll have to be good enough, though. My friend isn't going to let just anybody play."

"That's something I do right—football." Sammy's face lit up, his earlier trepidation all but gone. "I'll apply for next year. You'll really talk to your friend for me?"

"I don't say something unless I mean it." Buck Swanson claimed he owed Hardy a big favor after Hardy kept Buck's son out of the Dohner organization. Buck would give this kid a fair shake. "Now, how about you? You wanted to tell Sheriff Landon something. Will you tell me?"

Sammy's excitement faded but was soon replaced by a look of determination. "I don't want to get in trouble again. I haven't done anything wrong, but I know something. Maybe something important."

"If you haven't done anything wrong, there's nothing for you to worry about," Hardy assured him.

"You know that van? The one the paper says the police are looking for?" He seemed uncertain. "I know where it is."

"Where is it?" If they found the van, they might find the perpetrators.

Sammy stared at the table, no longer meeting Hardy's eyes. "It's at the bottom of the reservoir."

The three boys who worked for Luke had mentioned the extremely unsavory hangout for teens and young adults. If Sammy had been there…Had Hardy been too quick in agreeing to help him? "How do you know it's there?"

"I wasn't doing anything wrong." The teenager seemed eager to convince Hardy. "It was in the afternoon, and none of the other people who hang out there were even around. I was alone."

"Sammy." Hardy waited until the young man was looking into his eyes. "Just tell me what happened."

Resolve appeared on the boy's features. "I was having a bad day, so I went out there to think. I was just sitting by the water, thinking things over, minding my own business. Then I heard a car coming. I thought it must be the police or somebody like that since nobody parties out there during the day, so I hid." His gaze didn't waver. "It was a van—a dark blue panel van like the one in the paper—the one the police are looking for. It headed right for the water, and for a minute I thought it was going to go straight in. But it stopped at the edge."

If Sammy were telling the truth, he had witnessed something important. "Go ahead, Sammy," Hardy prompted.

"A man got out of the van, and when he leaned back in, he must have done something to the accelerator. For a minute, it looked like the door hit him, and he was stuck. He got out, though before the motor revved, and the van just went right off the shore into the water. The guy stood there until it sunk. It's really deep, you know. Then he turned around and left."

"Hiding was a good choice."

"I waited a long time before I came out of the woods and walked home. I didn't know why he had done that, but I figured it wasn't for anything good."

"How did he leave? Was there a second car, Sammy?" Hardy once more thanked God for his excellent memory; he didn't want to interrupt the boy's train of thought while he ran to fetch paper and pen.

"He walked, but I think somebody might have been waiting for him out on the road." The boy frowned. "I heard a loud motor start just a few minutes after he left."

"And the man? Can you describe the man?"

"Not very good." Uncertainty was once more on the young man's face. "I was pretty far away from him. Maybe I should have snuck closer to get a better look at him, but . . . I . . .I was scared."

"That's okay." Hardy didn't blame him for staying hidden; it had most likely saved his life. "We all get fearful from time to time, and sometimes that's the best feeling to have. It's saved my life a time or two."

Hardy sat quietly while Sammy processed his words. He decided to go ahead and ask. "Just tell me what you can about him."

"Okay." Sammy studied the empty bottle in his hands for a moment before returning his gaze to Hardy. "He was white and pretty tall, maybe a few inches taller than me." Hardy estimated Sammy's height at just shy of six feet, but it was hard to tell with the boy sitting down. "He was wearing a baseball cap, so I couldn't really tell what color his hair was. And he had on really dark glasses. Those expensive ones you can see your reflection in."

"What kind of clothes did he have on?" If the man had been wearing a uniform, it would fit with the eyewitness's account of what she'd seen at the animal clinic.

"He had on old jeans and a black leather jacket. At least it looked like leather." Sammy's brows went down as he frowned. "It might have been that cheap stuff that looks like leather. I wasn't close enough to tell."

Hardy was starting to get a picture.

"Did he have on tennis shoes?"

"I don't think so." The boy seemed to be picturing them. "I'm pretty sure his shoes were brown. They might have been work boots. I was too far away to tell for sure."

"Okay." Hardy smiled at the teenager. "You've done a good job describing him, Sammy. I know you weren't very close to him, but do you think you would know the man if you saw him again? Like in a picture?"

Sammy looked dejected as he slowly shook his head. "Maybe if I saw him out walking around or something I'd recognize him, but I just didn't see enough of his face with the cap and those glasses on."

"That's okay," Hardy rushed to assure him. "You've given me some very helpful information. Just one more question. When did you see this?"

The boy's color heightened as he stared fixedly at the bottle again. "About a week ago. I don't remember for sure." He seemed near tears. "I know I shoulda come in and told sooner, but I was scared."

"I can understand that." This wasn't some big-city street kid sitting next to Hardy; right now he was a frightened teenager. "Why did you decide to tell the sheriff now?"

Sammy's eyes slowly rose until he was looking into Hardy's. "I don't want to let Mr. and Mrs. Walker down. They told the judge I was a good person, even after what I did to them. I knew they'd want me to tell. I wanted to talk to the sheriff because he's friends with them. I wanted them to know I did the right thing."

"I'll make sure they know." Hardy smiled at Sammy and stood up. "Come on. I'll give you a lift home."

"Thanks."

A little while later, after Hardy dropped Sammy off at a rundown house in a crowded neighborhood, he pulled into the parking lot of a closed shoe store. As much as he wanted to see Haley, he needed to let Mitch know about Sammy Lewis's news.

"That's just what we need! A van at the bottom of the reservoir. That thing is over one-hundred and twenty feet deep in places." Mitch grouched to Hardy. "Are you sure Sammy doesn't know who this man is? He's not holding out on us?"

"You asked me to talk to this boy because of my past experience with kids like him," Hardy reminded the sheriff. "I believe the boy is telling us everything. He wants the Walkers to be proud of him for doing the right thing, Mitch. That's what gave him the courage to come in."

"Well, I guess I'll be calling in the state boys again." Hardy could hear the sheriff speak to somebody he was with. "If Tessa doesn't murder me before we get there, I'll be back in town within the next thirty minutes. We'll have to set up lights, and get divers and a wench truck. This is going to be fun."

"Don't shoot the messenger, sheriff." Hardy felt sorry for the other man.

"I don't suppose you'd want to visit a reservoir with me tonight?"

Hardy thought of the evening he and Haley had planned. But if this van was the one involved with the break-ins, he should be there when they pulled it out of the water.

"You'll have to tell me how to get there."

Chapter 40

"That looks great on you." Missy Landon's eyes met Haley's in the three-sided dressing room mirror.

Haley looked at the shimmery blue top she had on. "I don't know, Missy. Isn't it too dressy?"

Melissa frowned. "You're dating now, not hanging out with a friend. It's okay to be more dressed up sometimes."

"But I'm cooking him dinner at my apartment tonight." This dating business was beginning to seem more complicated than Haley had anticipated. "He'll probably be wearing jeans."

"So will you." Missy crossed her arms in a stubborn stance. "That top will look fantastic with a pair of skinny jeans."

Wait a minute. "I don't own a pair of skinny jeans." And she wasn't sure she wanted to, either.

Determination was in Missy's eyes. "You will when we're finished shopping. Maybe more than one pair." She gestured toward Haley's reflection. "With your build, you'll look fabulous in them."

Over an hour later, Haley found herself laden with bags containing six new tops, including the blue one, and four new pairs of skinny jeans, as they walked along the concourse of the mall. She still couldn't believe she'd let Melissa talk her into buying them in different colors. But she had to admit, her legs looked even longer in them.

"Now, how about shoes?" The eager look in Melissa's eyes made Haley laugh.

"I have enough shoes." Who looked at feet, anyway?

Melissa clucked her tongue while shaking her head. "You can't wear just any shoes with those jeans and that blue top."

Haley started to protest, but one look at her friend's face told her she would be wasting her breath. "Lead the way." Her savings account was taking a beating.

They had just come out of the shoe store when a voice spoke from directly behind them.

"I'm glad you bought those heels, Haley. You look pretty in them."

Both women whirled around, Haley mortified, to find a grinning Wyatt Millan.

"Were you watching us try on shoes?" Melissa asked incredulously.

He slid his sunglasses down his nose and looked over them. The expression in them sickened Haley. "I saw Haley when I was walking by, and I couldn't take my eyes off her sexy feet."

Haley honestly couldn't think of anything for a Christian woman to say. She grabbed the gaping Melissa's arm and pulled her around. "Let's go, Missy."

"Stalk much?" Melissa muttered as the two women practically jogged away from the offensive man.

Haley cast a furtive glance over her shoulder and breathed a sigh of relief when she saw Wyatt walking in the opposite direction. "Is he acting like this just because I invited him to church? I've never done anything to lead him on, have I?"

"He's weird." Melissa was blunt. "Did you notice how he acted at church last week?"

"Not really." Haley had been so content sitting beside Beau she hadn't paid attention to Wyatt Millan. "What did he do?"

Melissa steered Haley down the hall leading toward the food court. "He practically knocked Evelyn Carmichael off the end of the pew, squeezing in between Mel and Clay Richmond. Then he kept whispering to Clay all throughout the service." She grimaced. "I tried not to let him distract me, but you know how it is. Once you notice something like that, it's hard to ignore."

"I'm glad I didn't see him." In all honesty, Haley hadn't worshiped very well herself; she'd been too busy silently praying Beau was getting something out of it. "Where are we going?" The bags in her hands weren't light, and if Melissa gripped her arm any tighter, the circulation was going to be cut off.

"I need a cookie." Missy came to an abrupt halt in front of Cady's Cookies and Coffee, causing Haley's bags to swing wildly in front of her.

Before Haley could stop her, Melissa ordered a giant double-chocolate-chip cookie and café latte for each of them. She started to ask Missy how she was going to fit into her new jeans after eating a late afternoon snack like that. But after seeing the look of sheer delight on her friend's face, Haley didn't have the heart.

They had barely sat down before Melissa had her cookie out. She moaned with pleasure as she took her first bite. "Thith ith good."

Melissa must have seen Haley hide her smile.

"My manners are atrocious." Missy now had nothing in her mouth. "You just try growing up with an ox. If I didn't grab what I wanted, Mitch would have eaten it."

Haley had heard many of Missy's giant twin woes. She broke off a piece of her cookie and put it in her mouth. Her friend was right; it was extraordinarily good.

The two women ate in silence for a few minutes before Missy spoke.

"So, Hardy broke a date last night."

"He had to." Haley immediately had to defend him. "Mitch needed him down at the reservoir. I think all the deputies were there."

Missy seemed satisfied with Haley's response. "So, tell me what it's like to date Beau Harding. What does he like to do?"

"I think he likes everything." If there was any dating activity Beau didn't like, she'd yet to find it. "I still can't believe he took me to Six Flags."

"That's not very romantic for a first date." Melissa blew on her hot coffee.

Haley had to object. "It was perfect. It was one of the last weekends of the season, so it wasn't crowded, and we talked a lot." She paused to catch her breath. "He took me on every roller coaster there except the one that takes you upside down. I refused to ride that one."

An amused expression was now on Missy's face. "You sound like a teenager."

"I feel like one," Haley had to admit. "We've gone bowling and roller skating. On Thursday night, he took me to the movies, and we went to the new Robert Harper film. You know, that love story."

Melissa sighed. "I'm jealous. Joe likes to watch action movies, and that's about all we ever go see." A wry smile appeared. "I probably know more martial arts moves than a black belt. And if you want to know about guns, just ask me."

Haley chuckled at her friend's woebegone expression. "Maybe we can double date sometime, and Beau will rub off on Joe a little."

"Joe said he's going to invite Hardy out to the pond to fish." Missy used a napkin to wipe off her latte mustache. "He says they need to get to know each other since you and I are best friends. They'll be stuck together anyway."

"Hey, I forgot to ask," Haley slid her coffee aside. "Did you decide on a dress?"

As usual, Melissa was excited to discuss her wedding. The two of them shared ideas and made plans as they finished their shopping trip. And before she knew it, Haley was at home waiting for six-thirty, and Beau, to get there.

Chapter 41

Hardy turned over and looked at the clock with disbelief. He hadn't slept this late since the early days of recovery from his gunshot wound. But since it had been nearly ten o'clock when he finally got home this morning, four-thirty didn't seem that bad.

As he took his shower a short while later, he found himself picturing the van as it came out of the reservoir, water gushing out. Mitch had called every single one of his deputies to be there, and the state police were there in full force. They all thought they would be close to solving the case when they looked in the vehicle.

As soon as it was possible, Mitch located the VIN and radioed it in. Then it didn't take long for everybody's hopes to be dashed. The van had been reported stolen nearly six weeks ago. It disappeared from behind the owner's plumbing business in a small town near Elkhorn, Wisconsin. The van was now at the state crime lab, but there was little hope of finding any viable evidence after sitting under water for days. It was another piece of a very confusing puzzle.

As soon as Hardy was dressed and ready to go, he set about taking care of an important task. It took him a minute to retrieve the small black notebook he kept hidden in a shoe, and another few moments to locate the number he needed.

Just when Hardy was sure he would be sent to voice mail, a woman answered.

"Anne?"

"Yes." A hint of uncertainty was in her voice.

"It's Hardy Davis."

"I don't know who you are, but Harding Davis is dead." Now Hardy could hear a touch of defiance.

"It's a long story, Anne, but it's me. I tricked Derek with the fake drug bust, remember?"

There was a moment of silence, and then a timid voice came back. "How do you know about that?"

Hardy sighed. While he hadn't expected this to be easy, he hadn't anticipated it being this difficult. "I know because I'm the person who set it up, Anne. Derek cried like a baby. I was the only person there to see him other than you and Buck. Nobody else knows what happened. We promised Derek we wouldn't tell. Remember?"

"But how...Hardy, is it really you?" Anne Swanson sounded shocked.

"Yes. I can't give you any details, and as far as everybody else knows, I'm still dead." Now if he could convince her husband who he was. "I need to talk to Buck. It's important, or I wouldn't have bothered you."

"Hardy?" Buck Swanson's ear-splitting voice boomed over the phone.

"Hi, Buck." Now he'd have to see if Coach Swanson needed convincing.

"Something told me you weren't dead." And if anybody were within four city blocks of the man, they knew Hardy was alive, too. "How are you?"

"I'm great." He may not be able to hear out of his right ear for a few days was all. "But I need to ask you for a favor."

"Anything." The older man hadn't hesitated. "Derek is a senior at Virginia Tech. He's going to graduate with high honors, and it's all because of what you did. I owe you everything."

"Like I told Anne, as far as everybody else knows, I have to stay dead," Hardy cautioned him.

"Of course, you do!" Buck declared. "You don't want that Dohner fella after you."

"I'm living in a small town in Illinois, and there's a young man here who needs some help. He made some poor choices and ended up serving some time in jail."

"How can I help?" The coach eagerly offered.

"I haven't seen him play, but the word is he's an excellent quarterback. He earned a GED while he was in jail, and finances might be a problem, but if he can get into ICC next year, will you let him try out for the team?"

"Give me his name and telephone number," Buck directed Hardy. "I'll see to it he starts school next semester, and then he can try out for football next season. If he doesn't qualify for financial aid or a scholarship, I'll finance him myself. Anne and I have been talking about becoming foster parents since Derek's gone, so I don't see much difference in helping a young man get a good start in life."

Hardy was deeply touched. "Thank you, Buck. But if he doesn't qualify, let me know. I'll take care of him."

They argued good-naturedly and ended with the decision that in the unlikely event Sammy Lewis wasn't a good enough player for a scholarship, the two of them would split the cost of his education down the middle. Hardy gave Sammy's phone number to Buck before thanking the coach and ending the call.

After making sure he had time, Hardy made another phone call.

"Hello?" His mom sounded tired.

"Hey, Mom."

"Hi, Beau."

"How are you?" Hardy once more found himself wishing he could see his parents.

"Your dad had a rough night." She then went on to describe twelve hours with frequent fits of nearly hysterical babble, none of which Sharon or the nurses could understand. It went in cycles all night. H.B. slept for twenty or thirty minutes and then awoke to carry on for as long as fifteen minutes. Hardy could tell it had taken a lot out of his mother.

After giving her as much emotional support as he could over the phone, he promised to come and see them soon. Even though Sharon protested, Hardy could tell she wanted him there.

Try as he might to get rid of them, the worries about his dad stayed with him as he drove to Haley's apartment a short while later.

The smile on Haley's face when she opened the door an hour later made everything else fade away.

"You look beautiful." Hardy was awestruck by the startling color of her blue eyes, brought out even more by the sparkling top she was wearing. And she had on a pair of jeans and high heels that made it look like her legs went on forever. She literally took his breath away.

Her cheeks turned a lovely shade of pink. "Missy and I went shopping. She picked this stuff out." She smiled shyly. "Do you think it's too much?"

He was pretty sure his mouth had been hanging open. "It's perfect."

Haley's smile was instant. "Thank you." Then she sobered. "I heard about the van. I'm sorry you didn't get more information from it."

"I'm sorry I had to cancel," he told her as she led him into the living room. "I just couldn't tell Mitch no."

Haley turned to look at him. "It's part of your job. I understand."

For some reason, Hardy had known she would. "Thank you." Then he smiled at her. "Can we talk about something besides work? I'd like to think about other things."

Haley didn't hesitate before she nodded. "I hope you like slightly overcooked garlic bread." She smiled wryly. "I kind of forgot to shut the oven off."

"I like it crispy." He smiled and followed her to the small dining area of her apartment. Something caught his eye. "Did you get a new fish tank? I don't remember this being here before."

Her eyes lit up as she nodded. "I wanted to have a pet, and fish are the only things allowed in this building."

Hardy looked more closely at the two fish swimming around. "What are they doing to each other?"

Haley laughed. "They're kissing fish. Ozzie and Harriett kiss a lot."

It seemed to him those fish had the right idea. He wasn't going to rush things with Haley, though.

He soon discovered the woman who had captivated him was a remarkably good cook. And best of all, while her food was delicious, it wasn't fancy or complicated; it was just regular spaghetti with homemade sauce. And slightly burnt garlic bread.

After they talked and laughed their way through dinner, Hardy found himself sitting comfortably across the table from the most beautiful woman he'd ever seen. He found himself fascinated by her. "What are you doing tomorrow?" An idea had come to him, and now he felt the need to make it happen.

Haley rolled her eyes. "Fighting with my vacuum. The silly thing tried to eat my bedspread last weekend."

Hardy carefully considered his words before he made a suggestion. With all that was happening, he couldn't see it hurting anything. "Will you come with me to meet my mom and dad?" He hurried on before she could respond. "We'll probably have to leave at a horrible hour, and who knows how they'll have us travel, but I want them to meet you."

"Really?" He could see tears welling in her eyes. "Why?"

He told her the truth. "Because you're the most important part of my life. I've never felt like this, and I want to share you with my family."

"I'd love to." Her eyes were glowing, and her smile would have lit the darkest alley.

Hardy looked across the table at the woman who was rapidly becoming the nucleus of his existence. For the first time in his adult life, he felt satisfied. He was doing what he wanted to do with the person he most wanted to experience it with. Everything would work out. It had to.

Chapter 42

Haley pushed the clear reading glasses more firmly on her face. She was starting to get a headache, due, she suspected, to the tight bun her hair was pulled into under the brunette wig.

"You okay?" Beau touched her arm to get her attention. "You're squirming around an awful lot."

She looked at him again, still not understanding his appearance. The FSA agent they'd met, Rex Towers, had insisted she dress in these ugly clothes and did everything she could imagine to make her look like a different person. And Beau appeared to be an older version of himself. "Why aren't you in more of a disguise?" she finally asked him.

"You only recognize me easily because you know it's me," he calmly explained. "A middle-aged man with gray hair isn't going to catch the attention of somebody looking for me."

Haley knew what he said was logical, but still . . . "I don't want to meet your parents looking like this! They'll think you've chosen to date a . . . a . . . bag lady!"

She nearly kicked his shins when he laughed. She was pretty sure he'd been holding back his laughter ever since they boarded the train and he'd gotten a good look at her. "Your bag is overhead, honey. You can change in a bathroom and get back to your stunning self before we see Mom and Dad. Okay?"

An annoying yawn surfaced before Haley could answer. She'd always thought five o'clock was early, but three-thirty in the morning was pretty much the middle of the night as far as she was concerned. "Won't your parents be sleeping when we get there?"

Beau shook his head. "They know we're coming, so Mom will be pacing the floor waiting for us. Dad sleeps for hours on end and then stays awake for a while. He doesn't abide by day and night rules right now."

"What did you tell your mom about me?" Haley still felt the urge to pinch herself to make sure she wasn't dreaming. That she had, in fact, gone from pure misery because she had no future with this man to being part of a couple looking ahead and planning a future.

A teasing light entered his eyes. "That I'm dating a bag lady."

She swung her left leg forward and brought it back sharply, her heel landing solidly on his shin. "You deserve that," she informed him when she heard his grunt of pain.

He reached out and captured her hand, lacing their fingers together. "I told her I'm bringing the most incredible woman I've ever seen--the person who makes me feel more alive than I've ever felt before, and who somehow managed to talk me into going to church."

Haley felt her face warm as she blushed. "I hope she's not too disappointed when she meets me."

"She's going to love you." Beau spoke confidently. "And if Dad's awake and can talk at all, I still think he'll call you Dimples."

He tugged her against his side. "Why don't you nap on the way there? I know you're still sleepy. I'll wake you."

She resisted for a moment before she realized this was okay. There wasn't anything inappropriate about leaning against his side and dozing with her head on his shoulder. The last thought she had before sleep claimed her was she hoped she didn't snore or drool all over him.

"Sleeping Beauty." The tender male voice near her ear coupled with a hand gently brushing the awful artificial hair back from her face awakened her. It seemed like she'd just fallen asleep.

"Hi." She found herself unable to meet his eyes, embarrassed that he'd seen her at her most vulnerable.

Beau reached over under her chin and tilted her head so they were making direct eye contact. "You sleep like an angel." He winked. "You make little dove cooing sounds instead of snoring."

"Oh, you!" She jerked away from him and sat up straight, all awkwardness gone with his teasing.

"We're just about there," he told her, laughter in his voice. His smile slowly faded, and Haley believed she was seeing the policeman, not her boyfriend. He seemed all business as he spoke. "We'll look out the window and wait for the agent picking us up to give us the all clear signal. Then we'll walk straight to the car and get in. You get into the back passenger side while I get into the front passenger seat. It looks more natural for two people to be in front and one in the back. The main thing is we don't do anything to draw attention to ourselves."

Haley's stomach rolled with nerves. "What if he doesn't give us the all-clear signal? Or what if I do something wrong? You'll get hurt, and it'll be all my fault."

"Shhh." He placed his finger over her mouth. "Nothing will go wrong. We're going to spend a couple of hours with my parents and have a nice visit. Then we'll go back home and get back to our regular lives."

Her heart went into overdrive. "You just called Shadow home."

Beau gave her a questioning look. "I guess I did, didn't I?" His gaze remained steady. "I intend to do everything I can to make sure it is my home."

"I'm falling in love with you, Beau." Haley couldn't have stopped the words any more than she could stop breathing.

Light glowed in the depths of his eyes. "I'm right there with you, Haley."

She suddenly felt very frustrated. This would have been the perfect moment for their first kiss . . . If she weren't wearing this horrendous outfit and wig. She just couldn't sully such a precious memory by remembering herself looking like this.

Beau seemed to know what she was thinking. "Later."

"Later," she agreed. For there would be many laters for them.

The next forty-five minutes seemed like a bad movie Haley was starring in. Seeing the tall, gray-haired man nod and then strolling to the car, when Haley wanted to do nothing more than run to it and hide as quickly as she could. Only Beau's firm hand on her arm kept her from bolting.

And the drive through the dawn lit streets. Again, she fought the urge to hunker down and hide, sitting straighter when Beau reminded her they didn't want to draw attention. She supposed a woman with a wild hairdo like hers trying to hide in the backseat of a car might attract attention. So, she kept counting her breaths and sitting upright.

At the hospital, two men stood just outside the door. One of them was huge, and the other, though probably a large man himself, appeared small next to him.

"Those are the agents protecting my family," Beau explained. "They'll make sure we get in and out safely."

Finally, after another forcedly casual walk into the hospital, Haley was shown into a bathroom off an unoccupied hospital room. She nearly jumped for joy when the dreadful tightness of the wig was removed. After changing into her top and jeans and brushing her hair until it hung straight, she felt ready to meet Beau's parents.

He was waiting for her in the hall. "You look beautiful," he assured her.

She let him take her hand and lead her down the hall to a softly lit room. They had taken no more than three steps inside before a woman rushed over and hugged Beau, jarring his and Haley's hands apart.

Haley felt out of place as the brown-haired woman and her son embraced, thinking maybe she shouldn't have come. Then, suddenly, she found herself swept into the woman's arms herself.

"I am so happy Beau has finally met someone." The woman pulled away and left her hands on Haley's shoulders as she searched her face. "He's waited a long time for you to come into his life, you know."

"Haley, this is my mom, Sharon Davis." The name he'd given had just sunk in when Beau continued his introduction. "Mom, this is Haley Johnson—my girlfriend."

Haley honestly didn't mean to be rude, but she couldn't help but ask Beau, "What is your real name?"

"Harding Beauregard Davis Jr., you'd better not tell me this lovely woman doesn't even know your given name," his mom chastised him. "That is certainly no way to start a serious relationship."

Beau actually appeared embarrassed. "I guess I just hadn't gotten around to telling her yet, Mom. She already calls me Beau, so I just forgot."

"Harding Beauregard Davis...Beau Harding." Haley observed. "You just switched your name around."

"It's the easiest, safest way to do it," he replied. "My friends on the force always called me Hardy, and my family calls me Beau. No matter which name people in Shadow use, it's familiar to me. It can be dangerous for a person not to recognize his own name."

Sharon Davis chuckled. "I imagine you're relieved." She was speaking to Haley. "Haley Harding doesn't have quite the ring to it that Haley Davis has, does it?"

They could have turned every light in the room off and shut out the dawning sun with the drapes, and Haley would have lit it for them. Her face had never felt so hot, and she was certain she had never blushed so hard before. "We're not. I mean, we haven't . . ."

"Don't scare her off, Mom," Beau gently chided. "We're just getting started. Give her at least a week or two to get used to the idea."

"Beau . . ." His dad's weak voice came from the hospital bed across the room. "Beau. Zat too?"

Beau grasped Haley's hand and pulled her along with him as he walked to the bed. "Yes, Dad, it's me. I brought somebody I want you to meet."

He pulled Haley closer to him. "This is Haley, Dad." Beau smiled gently at his dad and touched his hand. "This is H.B. Davis, my father."

"C'mere." H.B. seemed to be speaking to Haley, so she leaned closer to him, smiling hesitantly.

"Zimples!" H.B. sighed, the side of his mouth coming up in a half-smile. "Hi, Zimples."

Haley exchanged an amused glance with Beau before her smile grew as she looked at his father. "HI, Mr. Davis. Beau told me you'd call me Dimples."

A familiar teasing light came to the one eye H.B. had open. "His god good ates."

"I do have good taste," Beau cheerfully agreed, translating his dad's words in the process. "How are you, Dad?"

H.B. focused on his son, his smile fading. "Can't member. Need to tell a portent, but can't member."

Beau seemed to consider his father's words for a few moments. "You need to tell me something important, but you can't remember what it is?"

His dad managed a nod. "Sorry."

"It's okay, Dad," Beau assured him. "You'll remember soon, and then you can tell me."

At the sound of the doorknob, Beau swiveled quickly to face the door, pushing Haley directly behind him when it opened.

"Mrs. D, you and Mr. D. have company," the man Beau had introduced as Fletcher announced. "I told them it's awfully early, but they said they only have a few free minutes this morning, and they just want to check in and say hi to Mr. D."

"Who is it?" Haley had never heard Beau use that tone of voice before. He was in no way pleased by the unexpected visitors.

"They're on the list," Fletcher replied. "Phillip Welsh and Robert Weston. They said they're old friends of your dad's."

"Of course, they are," Sharon Davis assured her son. "If they hadn't gotten help for H.B. so quickly, he may not have survived his stroke." She turned her attention to the FBI agent. "They're welcome to come in. They both already know Beau's alive, and they won't breathe a word about him being here. I trust them."

Haley thought Beau still looked unhappy as he smiled apologetically at her. "I didn't hurt you, did I? I didn't mean to pull you so hard."

"I'm okay." Although she might have finger marks on her arm where he'd grasped it. "I understand you were keeping me safe."

A few minutes later, two men quietly entered the room.

"How is H.B.?" the first man, probably in his late sixties, asked Sharon after giving her a brief hug.

"He's much better, Phil." She gestured toward Beau and Haley. "I know you remember Beau. The beautiful woman with him is his girlfriend, Haley Johnson." Sharon smiled at the other man who'd entered the room. "Rob, the last time you saw Beau he was barely out of diapers, wasn't he?"

The man with salt and pepper hair, who at first glance had appeared to be in his forties, upon closer inspection was more likely around the same age as the completely gray-haired man, Phil. Something about him seemed familiar, but it had to be her imagination since she knew they'd never met before.

"Haley, Beau . . . This is Rob Weston. He was on the force with H.B. for years, until he moved up north. He only recently moved back to the area. Rob and Phil Welsh are two of H.B.'s friends."

Beau reluctantly dropped Haley's hand to shake with both of the older men.

"Hey, buddy." Phil looked past Beau to speak to his friend. "It's great to see you awake. You've been busy sawing logs the last few times I've been here." He looked apologetically at Beau. "I don't want to take up your time with him. Rob and I are only going to be here for a few minutes."

Haley could see Beau's reluctance as he slowly stepped away from his dad's bed to let the other two men move nearer.

"Phil stops by to see H.B. nearly every day, but this is only the second time Rob has made it," Sharon quietly explained to her son. "Just give them a few minutes."

"I'll be right back." Beau squeezed Haley's hand for a moment. "I just need to speak to Fletcher." He turned and left Haley standing with Sharon.

After watching her son walk out of the room, Sharon turned her attention to Haley. "So, Beau tells me you're a police dispatcher. Do you plan on doing that even after you're married?"

"After I'm . . .?" Haley was momentarily at a loss for words. "I guess I've never thought about it before."

"Well, let me assure you, being a police officer's wife is a full-time job in itself." Sharon's gaze was kind. "And my son will always be a police officer. It's in his blood."

"He's a good farmer." Haley didn't know why she felt the need to say that, but she did.

Sharon slowly nodded. "That's in his blood, too, but not like law enforcement. Beau will never be content unless he's a police officer. If you can't live with that, you'd better break things off right now. Before you both end up hurt."

"Beau won't hurt me." He told Haley he wouldn't, and she trusted him. "And I want to be with him, no matter how he chooses to make a living. I believe God wants us to be together, and if he is for us, nothing can stand against us."

A smile replaced the concerned expression on the older woman's face. "I believe that my son has found the woman God put on this earth for him." Sharon gave Haley a tight hug. "And bless you for getting him back to church. He's been holding on to some powerful pain for a long time, but I know if Beau lets him, God will give him peace."

"Can you tell me what happened?" Haley hesitantly asked. "What hurt him so badly?"

Sharon sadly shook her head. "That's for him to tell you. I imagine when he's able to share it with you will be the same day he's able to let go of it."

"Sharon?" Rob Weston stood right behind Haley, so she turned to face him, too.

"Yes, Rob." Sharon waited for the man to speak.

"I know insurance doesn't cover everything, and I just want you to know if there's anything you or H.B. need, all you have to do is say the word." Haley realized his clothes were an expensive designer brand. "I have more money than I'll ever spend in this lifetime and no family to leave it to. If I can't use it to help my friends, it doesn't mean much at all."

Haley couldn't help but notice the change in the other woman's demeanor. "Thank you, Rob, but we're doing just fine." Her words were stilted. "Any worthy charity would make good use of your money, but we're not one of them."

"Now, Sharon," the man began to back pedal. "I didn't mean to insult you. I was just offering—"

"You didn't insult me." Sharon's voice was soft and firm. "But you know how H.B. and I feel about gambling. The way I see it, you got that money without doing anything to earn it. Now, maybe you feel all right about spending it, but we never will. So, thank you, but we won't accept your offer."

"Are you over here flirting with these beautiful women?" Phil stepped up beside the now silent Rob and smiled smoothly at Sharon and Haley. "Don't let him fool you. He's all talk and no action. He hasn't had a date in over twenty years."

"He wasn't flirting with us." Haley felt the need to protest.

Phil put his arm around the other man's shoulders. "Then he's foolish. If you get tired of young Beau, come find me. I still remember a thing or two about dating."

"She's not going to get tired of my son." Now Sharon appeared unhappy with him, too. "They're in a serious relationship—something neither of you has ever understood."

Haley wished Beau would get back in there. It was evident Sharon and her husband's friends didn't see eye to eye on more than one thing, and she was growing more uncomfortable by the second.

"How long have you and Beau been together?" Phil asked her, all politeness now.

"Zimples . . ." The softly spoken word coming from the hospital bed was Haley's salvation.

"I need to go see what he wants. Excuse me." She turned and walked across the room to where Beau's dad lay. His eye was focused intently on her.

"You luz im?" The question, even slurred, was perceptible to Haley.

The answer struck her squarely in the face. "Yes," she said. "I love him."

"He luz you." Satisfaction shone in his eye. "You be happy gether."

"Hey, Dad, I would have liked to tell her that before you did." Beau's voice came an instant before his arm slid around Haley's shoulders.

"They finally left," Sharon announced as she appeared on the other side of H.B.'s bed. She frowned at her husband. "I'm sorry, H.B., but I'll never understand how you came to be such close friends with a gambler and flirt. Not to mention they both have enough money to buy everything we own five times over."

"Frenz . . . rough times gether." H.B. managed to smile at his wife.

"I know you're friends who have gone through rough times together, but . . . " She stood straighter and shook her head. "Never mind. You like them, and they like you. As long as you never let them sway you to their ways of thinking, I'll be satisfied."

"Nezer . . . allays luz oney you." He was starting to look tired.

"Dad, Haley and I are going to leave now," Beau said. "We need to get back, and you need to rest. You've had enough company for the day."

"Ztay while," his dad insisted. "I zeep zen we talk more."

Beau looked at his watch. "Okay, but we can only stay another hour. It's not safe for us to stay any longer than that. I have to think about Haley now, too."

He had to think about her now. Did she complicate his life even more than it already was? Maybe she was selfish to be with him. Butterflies hit her stomach, and she felt nauseous. Haley was in love with a man who would most likely be endangering himself to stay with her. What had she been thinking? She was asking him to risk his life to make her happy!

"I'm sorry, H.B., but I need to go home now." She ignored the confused look Beau gave her. "I'm sure Beau will be able to stay longer the next time he comes."

Haley felt like she was sleepwalking as she told Beau's parents goodbye, knowing she'd probably never see them again. She didn't even try to argue as Fletcher helped her back into the wig after she'd donned the ugly clothes. And she couldn't bring herself to speak more than one or two words at a time to Beau, so she leaned her head against the window and pretended to sleep during the long train ride home.

"What happened?" Beau's voice was firm as he stopped her from getting into his truck at the train station. "You were fine, and then you just shut down on me, Haley. Tell me what happened."

Tears filled her eyes. "I can't do this, Beau. I'm so sorry. I just can't do this." She couldn't let him risk his life so they could be together.

Pain radiated from his eyes for a moment before it disappeared behind a neutral gaze. "I see. I suppose I was expecting too much to ask you to live like I do. I should have known better."

"What?" Haley didn't understand what he was saying. "I don't care what I have to do. It's not about me! I can't let you take dangerous chances just so we can stay together. I can't be that selfish."

"Haley." Beau's eyes lit from within as he shook his head. "What am I going to do with you?" Before she could respond, he cradled her face in his hands and kissed her lips.

The kiss was everything, and more than Haley had ever dreamed her first real kiss would be. She leaned toward him as he slowly ended it and pulled away.

"Wow." That was all she could say. "You're good at that."

"Listen to me," he quietly instructed her. She was finally able to gather her senses enough to comply. "When I told you we'd figure this out, I meant it. I was making a commitment I have never made before. You have to trust me that I know what I'm doing. We'll both be as safe as possible. I will do whatever it takes to keep you safe."

"What about you? I'll make things harder for you." As painful as it was, Haley tried to be strong.

His hands swept back her artificial hair. "You make me alive, Haley. I have spent the last five years of my life pretending. Beau Davis didn't even exist anymore; not really. But now I do, and for the first time in a long time, I have a real life. But I don't want it unless you're a part of it."

Haley reached up and placed her hands over his before she started laughing and crying at the same time.

"What is it now, honey?" Beau questioned her.

She shook her head before hiding her face against his chest. "You gave me our first kiss while I look like this."

His laugh rumbled through his chest. "Just think of the story we'll have to tell our kids someday."

Their kids . . . Beau was definitely planning a future with her. And she trusted him. If he told her they would be safe, then they would be safe. Besides, she had forgotten the most important part. She believed God wanted them together. There wasn't anything or anybody that could stand in the way of that.

Chapter 43

"Sheriff?" Hardy stuck his head in the door of Mitch's office. "Do you have a minute?"

Mitch looked up from his desk and frowned. "Just the man I wanted to talk to. Come on in and have a seat. Close the door behind you."

Hardy shifted his holster a little further to the side as he sat down. It appeared he was going to have to listen to his boss before he had the chance to speak.

"What do you think you're doing, Davis?" Mitch demanded.

"What are you talking about?" The sheriff was going to have to explain himself. Hardy wasn't going to play twenty questions.

"I heard the rumors about you and Haley, but I ignored them. I thought you were just being friendly." Mitch's brows rose. "But then Tessa tells me the two of you are actually together. You're a real couple. You're going to have to explain yourself. I thought we had an agreement."

Oh. That's what this was about. "Things have changed," Hardy calmly answered. "In fact, that's what I wanted to talk to you about." He decided to lay it all on the line. "Haley and I are a couple because I plan on having a future with her. Since the people in this community are her family, I need to make this my home, too. I'd like to start off with a full time job as your deputy."

The big man looked comical with his mouth hanging open. He abruptly shut it. "What about the people who are after you? You're putting yourself at greater risk by staying in one place, and you're putting Haley in danger by being with her."

"Am I really?" Haley would probably be upset with him if she knew he'd been thinking about their future instead of listening to the sermon yesterday.

"Somebody has already found me. We both know that. And if I run, things will most likely get worse around here. Didn't you tell me that?"

Mitch nodded, uncertainty written on his face.

"Then, why don't I stay here and help catch them? And then Beau Harding can live a quiet life with the woman he loves."

"But what about Haley?" The sheriff gestured toward the dispatch desk, even though it wasn't her sitting at it.

"People have already linked us together." This had been his greatest concern. "We both know how gossip in a small town works. If anybody shows up, they're going to think Haley's with me whether she is or not. I can keep her safer if we're really together."

Mitch seemed to carefully consider Hardy's words. "You're sure about this?"

"I'm surer about this than anything else I've ever decided," Hardy assured him. "Now, do you want another deputy or not?"

A grim smile lifted the corners of Mitch's mouth as he opened a drawer and reached into it. Hardy barely raised his hand in time to catch the badge Mitch tossed to him. "Getty's carry our uniforms, and they should have your size. Unless they have to order, I expect to see you in one by Monday. You'll have to go plainclothes until then, but make sure people see that badge. Got it?"

In response, Hardy pinned it in plain sight on his shirt pocket. "I'd like to get started right away. What do you want me to do?"

Two hours later, as he paced the smelly alley, he found himself greatly regretting that question. Mitch had sent him to meet Sammy Lewis, to show the kid some mug shots. So far, all Hardy had managed to do was ruin a perfectly good jacket when he pressed himself against a dumpster to avoid a curious passerby's eyes.

Having told Crystal that Sammy had merely been at the police station on a dare, Mitch told Hardy the teenager's involvement would only be known to the three of them. Which is why he'd arranged for this meeting to be held clandestinely. Sammy was supposed to have come out the back door of the dry cleaners, where he'd been hired not too long ago. He was twenty minutes late.

Hardy had just about made up his mind to go around to the front of the building and make sure the teenager was okay when a door opened and the boy stepped out.

His eyes immediately honed in on Hardy. "Where's Sheriff Landon?"

"He thought you wouldn't mind talking to me again." Hardy walked a few steps toward the teenager. "Do you?"

Sammy shrugged. Then he took a deep breath and wrinkled his nose. "Is that you?"

The jacket was going to have to be pitched. "Yes. I had to get up close and personal with that dumpster over there." He indicated the offensive receptacle.

The boy's laughter surprised Hardy. "That belongs to the Chinese restaurant. With the scraps they throw away, you'll probably stink for a month of Sundays!"

Hardy found himself once more liking this young man. "So, did you get a phone call?"

The teenager's eyes lit up. "I'm going to start classes in January. Coach Swanson wants me to get started this year. I'll have to keep my grades up if I want a scholarship—even a football scholarship."

"What do your parents think about your plans?" Maybe Hardy should have spoken to them first.

Sammy's smile dimmed just a little. "As long as they don't have to pay for it, they don't care what I do."

Hardy felt the need to reassure him. "I'm sure they'll be proud of you."

"I doubt it." The boy shrugged. "I'll make sure the Walkers are proud of me, though."

"Good." At least Sammy had somebody he looked up to. "Has anything else happened?"

"No." Sammy's expression became serious immediately. "I've been keeping my eyes open, but I haven't seen that man again. Maybe he left town right away."

"Maybe," Hardy agreed.

"So, are those the pictures I'm supposed to look at?" Sammy pointed to the binder Hardy was holding.

Hardy held it out for the teenager to take.

Sammy took the book and opened it. Hardy watched as the boy took his time examining each page. He finally closed the book and shook his head.

"I'm sorry, but I just don't know." He handed the book back to Hardy. "I mean, I didn't see his face that good. There's some of those pictures that might be him, but I can't say for sure."

Hardy slid a small notebook out of his shirt pocket. "Just tell me the numbers on the possible matches. We'll check them out."

Sammy accepted the binder with a sigh and opened it. After he thumbed through and gave Hardy six possible matches, he once more closed it and handed it back. "I won't ever be able to pick him out in a lineup or anything, you know."

"You might be surprised." Hardy smiled encouragingly at the boy. "Sometimes you recognize people by the way they stand or walk. If we find the right man, you may remember things you didn't realize you knew."

"Am I in trouble if I can't identify him?" The young man wasn't quite able to pull off the nonchalant manner he was trying to exude.

"You haven't done anything wrong, Sammy." Hardy spoke firmly. "We know you're trying to help, and we appreciate it."

The young man warily nodded. "I have to get back inside. I have to keep this job a few more months, and Mr. Randolph will wonder why I'm not in the break room. Tell the sheriff I'll call him if I recognize that guy anywhere."

Hardy thanked the boy and waited until he was safely back inside the building before heading back to the squad car. Deciding it wouldn't do to stink up the vehicle on his first official outing, he reluctantly removed his smelly jacket and tossed it in one of the nearest dumpsters. Some odors wouldn't come out, no matter how they were cleaned.

He had just sat down behind the wheel when the radio crackled.

"Base to Harding." The dispatcher named Crystal was calling him.

He leaned down and picked up the radio mike. "Harding here."

"Sheriff Landon wants you to phone him asap. Use his personal number." Even the dispatcher's voice bothered Hardy now. When he'd gone out to get keys for a squad car, the svelte brunette had looked him over like a piece of candy. Then, she made very little secret of the fact that she was ready, willing, and able to entertain Shadow's newest deputy. Hardy had finally managed to tamp down his disgust with sympathy. Crystal wasn't really any different from the women he'd seen in Chicago. Many of them wanted a man's attention so badly, they hadn't cared what they gave up in order to get it.

"Ten-four."

It must be something pretty important if Mitch didn't want it on the radio. Of course, Hardy had to remember Crystal wasn't to be trusted. Maybe it was information the sheriff didn't want her to know.

"Landon here." Mitch's gruff voice answered.

"It's Harding."

"Good." Mitch sounded relieved. "Listen, Hardy, we might have been looking at our robbery situation all wrong. Let me tell you what I've found out and see what conclusions you might come to."

"Okay." This was the way Hardy preferred police work. He had never liked preconceived notions going into an investigation. It too often resulted in tunnel vision.

"Wayne remembered where he saw your man." He didn't give Hardy a chance to ask any questions. "He saw him at the rest stop just across the interstate. Wayne is certain he saw him as he was driving home from work. On the same day we found the gun at the campsite."

"So, you're thinking what? The man in the sketch has something to do with the gun—" The totality of the situation sunk in. "It's all tied together. The man who tried to kill my dad is somehow connected with the men we're looking for. And Baxter coming up missing when he did is a little too coincidental." Some of the pieces of the puzzle finally slid into place. "We're looking for one group of people who know exactly who I am. They set up the burglaries to get me to do exactly what I did—stay here. That's why they happened when they did. And if Baxter were involved . . . Could he be one of the men we're looking for? Could he have been partners with Roscoe Callen? Did he shoot him?"

He didn't realize he'd been thinking aloud until he heard the sheriff's dry chuckle. "We're on the same trail. Now, my question to you is, what is to be gained from keeping you in town? And if they're after you, why haven't they done something about it? It's not like you live in a high security area out there on the Walker farm."

"I don't know," Hardy admitted. "But I have a feeling if we can figure that out, we'll take a giant step toward knowing who we're after."

"Let's hope that's soon." Mitch's voice changed. "Any news from Sammy?"

Hardy glanced back at the alley. "He gave me half a dozen possible matches, but I don't think any of them will pan out. He just didn't get a good enough look at the guy."

There was silence on the phone as the sheriff processed the new information. "Well, I guess we'll have to accept whatever he can give us. I assume Sammy will let us know if he thinks of something or sees someone."

"He said he'd call you." And Hardy trusted the boy.

"That's good enough for me," the sheriff stated. Then his voice lightened. "Since this is your first real shift, and I hear you have a big date this evening, why don't you call it a day?"

"Thanks." He couldn't keep the smile from automatically coming to his face. He was taking Haley on a special date. "I'll leave the list of possible matches on your desk when I drop off the squad car."

"That's fine." Mitch cleared his throat. "I should have already told you, but I'm telling you now. I'm glad you've decided to make Shadow your home. We could use more men like you around here."

Hardy felt humbled. "Thank you. I just hope I don't turn out to be more trouble than I'm worth."

He sent a quick prayer out before he'd even realized what he was doing. It looked like his girlfriend was already starting to rub off on him. And that wasn't a bad thing at all.

Chapter 44

"I will never go on a date on my day off again, Ozzie," Haley informed her kissing fish. At least she thought it was Ozzie. It could have been Harriett. It didn't matter. She had been a nervous wreck since she rolled out of bed at six-thirty that morning. She wasn't off on Mondays very often. Maybe if she'd called Crystal, they could have traded. Although she highly doubted the part-time dispatcher would have been accommodating.

As it was, she had shampooed her hair not once, but twice that afternoon. She'd gotten it into her head that curly hair was more feminine, so she spent the better part of an hour meticulously curling her long tresses. In theory, she should have looked like a lovely woman straight off the movie screen. In reality, she looked like Clarence was her inspiration. So, out had come the shampoo again. Her hair now hung straight over her shoulders and down her back.

Then her clothes concerned her. Beau had only told her to dress for the outdoors. This time of year an evening outside might require anything from a pair of insulated coveralls to a light jacket. And what would they be doing? While she couldn't think of anything she'd need to be dressed up for, the idea of donning her favorite jeans and sweatshirt just didn't feel right. The end result was a mostly empty closet and her bed buried under discarded garments.

She looked in the full-length mirror on her bedroom door and scrutinized the outfit she finally ended up with. The hiking boots looked neither dressy nor sloppy, so she thought they would do. And her blue corduroy jeans fit the same criteria. She had chosen to top it off with a comfortable sweater, deciding how she felt was more important than how she looked. Now if she could only keep herself from changing her mind again.

By the time the doorbell rang, Haley had returned all of her clothing to the closet and straightened her apartment. She idly wondered if Beau realized he was dating a person with a bit of an obsessive compulsive lifestyle. That was something he probably needed to know.

"Hi." She found herself suddenly feeling shy when she opened the door to find him standing there.

He held out a bouquet of pink roses. "These are for you."

"Thank you." Haley awkwardly accepted them. "Nobody has ever brought me flowers before."

Beau seemed surprised. "Never?"

Her cheeks grew warm as she shook her head. "You're my first."

"Hey." His voice was soft as he touched her chin. "This-- our dating isn't a test for either one of us. We've already decided we want to be together. It's time for us to relax and get to know each other. To enjoy ourselves." He tilted her head so she was looking into his eyes. "Okay?"

She smiled shyly. "Okay." What was she supposed to do now? "I think I have a vase under the sink. Do you want to come in while I put these in water?"

"Sure." As before, Haley's already small living room shrank when Beau walked in.

"I'll just be a minute." Haley was still flustered, despite what he said. She didn't miss the amused gleam in his eyes before she turned and carried her roses into the kitchen.

Beau was standing and looking at a framed photograph when she walked back in.

"Are these your parents?" He couldn't imagine losing his mom or dad.

Haley set the vase of roses on the table and walked over to look at the picture hanging on the wall. "Yes. That's the last family photograph we had taken. It was right after my graduation."

His eyes met hers. "Your mother is beautiful." He took her hand in his. "I think you have her eyes."

"Thank you." Haley had always been disappointed she didn't favor Julie Johnson more. "I'm not sure where my dimples came from. Neither Mom nor Dad had them."

"I like your dimples." Beau's smile warmed her heart. "But your eyes were the first thing I noticed. You have the most startling blue eyes I've ever seen. They're stunning."

Okay. Either he was going to have to stop complimenting her or she was going to look like a Christmas ornament all evening. She decided to change the subject.

"Am I dressed right?" She stepped back so he could see what she was wearing.

His eyes traveled from her face to her feet before he answered. "Perfect. Are you ready?"

A few minutes later, Haley found herself experiencing yet another new feeling. Even though she had ridden in Beau's truck with him before, somehow it felt different now . . . more comfortable, like she belonged in it.

"Where are we going?" she asked, unable to remain patient any longer.

"You'll see." He smiled teasingly as he glanced at her. "We'll be there in a few minutes."

Okay. She decided talking would make time pass more quickly. "Did you speak to your parents last night?"

His frown instantly made Haley regret asking him. But then he relaxed. "Yes. Dad had a bad spell yesterday afternoon. Mom said he became really agitated and said a bunch of stuff that didn't make sense."

H.B.'s crooked smile flashed into Haley's mind. "He was happy when we visited. Did something happen to upset him?"

Beau shrugged. "Mom said the only thing out of the ordinary was when Rob Welton and Phil Welsh stopped in again. They brought their other buddy, John Tarp, with them."

Are those the three men who were with your dad when he had the stroke?" Might it have been some sort of flashback?" Haley still had trouble imagining the peaceful man who'd called her Dimples becoming irrationally upset.

"It makes sense, but we won't know for sure until Dad improves." He took a deep breath. "Can we talk about you for a while? We've only touched the surface, and I want to know you . . . everything about you. " Beau glanced at her. "Where did you go to school? What was it like when you grew up?"

Although Haley usually found it disconcerting to speak of her past, it felt natural to share it with him.

"I was born in Vinton, Ohio. It's a small town about fifty miles south of Cleveland. We had lots of neighbors."

"So, you are a city girl," Beau observed. "That's why you didn't recognize poison oak.

"Heat crawled up her neck, and if she looked in a mirror, her face would be beet red. She answered him, though. "Before I moved to Shadow, the closest I'd ever been to nature was a city park."

"We'll have to see if we can fix that." Beau turned onto the road leading to the interstate crossing. "I don't want you grabbing the wrong leaves when we visit Luke and Holly."

"I like to visit them," Haley said. "Their home is peaceful and relaxing."

"Yes. I'm going to miss it." He slowed to let a car pass them.

Fear struck her at his words. "You're leaving Shadow? But you said—"

"Hey, I'm not going anywhere." Beau reached across the bench seat and grasped her clenched hand. "I forgot I hadn't told you yet. I'm renting Holly's house until I find a place to buy."

Haley's breath left in a whoosh. She couldn't remember feeling this degree of relief before. "You're moving to Holly's old house?"

He laced his fingers through hers and squeezed. "Not that I have anything to move. It's more like I'll empty the camper into the house." His hand reluctantly left hers so he could make a left-hand turn. "You'll help me buy what I need, won't you? I'm not a savvy shopper."

Beau was staying; she was so ecstatic she would have agreed to just about anything. "I'll help you."

"Good." His eyes met hers for an instant before he looked back at the road. "We're here."

Haley looked out the window and couldn't believe where he'd brought her. "How did you know about the Fall Farm?"

"I saw it in the paper." He pulled the truck into the nearly empty parking lot and turned off the ignition. "Is this okay?"

Her heart melted when she saw the look of uncertainty in his eyes. He really wanted to please her.

"I love to come here." They exchanged a tender look that spoke more than any words either of them could have said at that moment.

A few minutes later, Haley once more marveled at the way her hand fit in his as they walked toward the barn.

"It's not very crowded tonight," Beau observed.

She stepped a little closer beside him. "That's the way I like it." Every autumn the Fall Farm opened to the public. There, people could take their pick of activities, such as walking through the corn maze, sitting on a wagon for a hayride, or enjoying hot dogs and apple cider. Haley's favorite activity was the "redneck" golf course, which actually began in the hayloft of a big barn.

"You two picked the right evening for a visit," the lady manning the admission table told them. "Since this is our last week open, you just pay one price, and then you can partake of as many activities as you want. The only things that cost extra are food and drinks." She smiled brightly as Beau pulled his wallet out. "And the items in the craft barn have been marked down for clearance, so be sure to stop in there before you leave."

"What is redneck golf?" Beau asked a few minutes later, as Haley tugged him to the clubs.

She laughed as she picked up a "club" made from a knobby branch with a slight protrusion on the end of it. "We start up there." She pointed to the hayloft.

Beau looked up from the club he was examining. "Okay. How do we get up there? I don't see any ladders."

"There's a staircase behind that wall, Mister." A young man with Fall Farm Fun written on his sweatshirt pointed it out.

"Thank you." Beau looked at Haley, his brow raised. "What were you going to tell me I had to do to get up there? Something tells me you weren't going to show me the stairs."

Haley laughed as she gestured toward the other side of the barn. "I thought maybe you could get creative with that wheelbarrow and pitchfork."

"You've got an ornery streak, don't you?" He picked up his club and pulled her toward the stairs.

"Is that okay?" She was suddenly nervous. What if, after Beau had spent more time with her, he decided she wasn't who he thought she was?

His hand tightened on hers. "Everything about you is more than okay. I already told you, honey; this isn't a test."

Nearly two hours later, Haley felt like her capacity for laughter had been tested. From watching a man Beau's size play miniature golf to having him abruptly lift her onto his shoulders so they could finally find their way out of the corn maze, she laughed. After a trip to Six Flags and now this active date, it was evident he had quite a sense of adventure. He also apparently loved to make her show her dimples. She couldn't remember ever having this much fun before.

They were soon seated side by side on hay bales, waiting for the tractor to start pulling them through the woods.

"Here. Let me hold your cider while you wrap that blanket around your legs," Beau offered, taking the cup from her hand.

"Thanks." It was getting pretty chilly as it got darker. Once she was tightly covered, she accepted her cider back. "Are you sure hot dogs and potato chips are enough of a dinner for you? I know how you usually eat."

Beau gave her a sheepish grin. "I'll probably swing by the diner and pick up a couple of burgers and fries after I take you home. I'm fine for now, though."

There were only a few other people on the wagon ride with them, and since they were all huddled together in their own pairings, Haley felt like she and Beau were alone.

"Look at the stars." She pointed through the tree limbs to the clear October sky as a tractor slowly began pulling them. "They're beautiful."

Beau leaned back and looked up. "That's one thing I missed in Chicago. With all the city lights around, you just don't see the sky anymore."

Her eyes met his. "Do you miss Chicago, though? Shadow is a far cry from a place like you're used to."

He touched her cheek. "I don't miss one single thing from my life in Chicago. I have everything I want right here."

Haley couldn't hold back her smile. She snuggled against his side when he put his arm around her shoulders and pulled her against him.

"Can I ask you something, Beau?" She tilted her head enough to make eye contact with him.

"Anything."

Haley remembered his mother's words. "Did you ever consider becoming a farmer? Or have you always wanted to be a police officer?"

His gaze was troubled when he looked back at her. "There's one thing about me you have to understand, Haley. I'm a cop. When my cover was blown, the one thing that drove me crazy was the knowledge I couldn't do my job anymore. This chance Mitch is giving me—I feel like myself again. If you're expecting me to be something else, I'll disappoint you."

"I care about you, and I know who you are. You've shown me. I don't expect you to change." It was as simple as that.

"Would you like to meet my sister?" Beau asked out of the clear blue.

"Of course, I would," Haley assured him, "but is it safe?"

"I'll have Elliott arrange something. It's been too long since I've seen my niece and nephew. They probably don't even remember they have an uncle."

"Beau?" This was as good of a time as any. "Not now, but sometime, will you trust me enough to tell me what hurt you so badly?"

He lowered his head and focused on his feet. Haley wasn't sure if he was even going to answer her for a minute.

"I'll try to tell you . . . sometime." His gaze was troubled as it met hers. "But I can't yet. Please understand."

It was more than she'd expected. "I do." Haley made herself smile. "Now, tell me, were you a mischievous child?"

They spent the rest of the hayride with Beau sharing stories about the hijinks he had been involved in during his youth. It seemed he had always been very enterprising, particularly in grade school. He tried to build an airplane out of an old wooden crate and a lawnmower his grandfather junked. It was a miracle he only ended up with a broken leg after he drove the contraption out of his grandpa's hayloft. And he hadn't fared much better with the boat he constructed from an old wooden rain barrel. It made it out to the middle of the pond and proceeded to sink quite rapidly. Haley decided it was just as well he'd found his calling in police work. He'd never have made it as an inventor.

The evening rushed by, and all too soon they were standing at her door.

"Thank you, Beau. I can't remember when I've had this much fun." She turned the key in the lock and opened the door.

"Haley?" She turned back to face him. "I thought we'd see if that wig made any difference in how we kiss. Okay?"

His lips met hers before her smile was fully formed. She felt him pull her into his arms and hold her snugly against him as they kissed. Her arms seemed to have a mind of their own as they slid up around his neck and held on tightly.

They were both breathing heavily when he slowly ended the kiss.

"Okay." His forehead rested against hers. "It was even better without the wig, don't you think?"

Since Haley was pretty sure the grip she had on his arms was the only thing keeping her from zipping into orbit, she could only smile and nod.

"I'd better go." Beau spoke with conviction.

Haley made herself release him and step back out of his arms. "I'll see you tomorrow." Was that soft, breathy sound her voice? "Goodnight."

"Goodnight."

She could have looked at the tender expression in his steel gray eyes all night, and it was what she still saw as she fell asleep a short while later.

Chapter 45

"Sheriff, I've got another body over here." Jeff Fielding's voice came from the other side of the enormous pile of wrecked cars and junk.

Mitch looked up from the corpse he and Hardy were kneeling by and muttered something under his breath. "It's hard to tell for sure, but since this looks like a postal employee's uniform, I'm pretty sure this is William Baxter. Let's go see if we recognize the guy Jeff found."

A man named George Gibbons had phoned into the station early that morning, hysterical. It had taken Haley a long time to calm him enough to make sense. He had been letting his coon hounds run the woods that separated his farm from the junkyard. One of them started having fits, and when Gibbons walked over to see what his dog was barking at, he found a body. It was partially concealed by an old car hood.

"What you got?" the sheriff asked his deputy as he and Hardy approached him.

Jeff pointed to a couple of old refrigerator doors lying on the ground. One was rusted through, and a hand was visible in the opening.

Mitch keyed his portable radio mike. "Landon to base."

Haley's voice came over the radio. "Base here."

"Haley, call the state dispatch. We've got two bodies out here at Sampson's Salvage yard, and unless they figured out a way to bury themselves under junk, we're looking at homicides."

Hardy knew Mitch was upset because the sheriff hadn't used any codes; he'd just spoken plainly to Haley. That would have been rewarded with a stiff fine back in Chicago, but this was a small town.

"Ten-four, Mitch. Do you want me to call Dr. Tindell?"

"Yes." The sheriff sighed. "We'll be turning this over to state, though. We don't have the resources to handle it."

"Ten-four. Anything else?" Haley's voice was unsteady.

"No. We'll stay here and provide what help we can."

"Ten-four."

Mitch clipped the microphone on his shirt pocket with enough force Hardy was surprised the cloth didn't tear. During the past few weeks, Hardy had gotten pretty used to reading the other man, and right now Mitch was frustrated.

"Sheriff, I don't know if it means anything or not, but I admire you." Hardy felt the need to tell his boss this. "I've seen too many men in your position too stubborn to step down and let somebody else take over, no matter what's best for the case. The people here are fortunate to have you."

Mitch grimaced. "It's hard to do, sometimes. I'd like nothing better than to catch whoever did this, but our department just isn't set up for crimes of this magnitude."

Jeff looked up from where he knelt by the door the hand was visible under. "Is the other guy William Baxter?"

"I think so," Mitch replied. "I wonder who that is."

"I'm pretty sure it's another man." Jeff leaned closer to the exposed hand. "His nails are filthy. Like the kind of dirt that hasn't been cleaned out from under nails for a long time, not fresh soil."

Hardy thought of something. "I wonder if he's our camper."

Mitch gave him a measuring look, interest visible on his face. "If he is, he's probably one of our burglars."

Hardy picked up the other man's train of thought. "And if that's the case, Baxter and Callen must be our other two."

Revulsion filled the sheriff's voice. "Then we've got somebody altogether different murdering our criminals."

Jeff looked back at them. "What about that guy Wayne saw? The one in Hardy's sketch?"

Hardy's pulse jumped and went into overdrive. "If this was him . . ."

"This is all connected," Mitch finished for him. "Okay." Jeff stood up and walked over to join them. "Let's just try this out to see how it sounds."

The two deputies waited for the sheriff to continue. "We've got three guys—Baxter, Callen, and whoever this is. They rob and vandalize the salon, animal clinic, insurance agency, and Ebhart's. Baxter would have done it for the money to pay his mom's bills. You said Callen worked for cash. Just for the sake of argument, we'll assume this guy did, too. Then something goes wrong at the convenience store, and one of these two shoots Callen." What he said was making sense. "Then this other guy who tried to kill Hardy's father showed up and took care of these two." His eyes met Hardy's. "It's all about you. But I don't understand why you haven't been a target. Are you sure nobody's tried anything?"

"Mitch, I've been even more careful since Haley and I are dating. I guarantee you, I'd know if there were somebody even so much as watching me. There hasn't been anybody in town paying any particular attention to me."

"Except Crystal." This wasn't the first time Mitch voiced his opinion, but to do so with dead bodies right there indicated his level of disgust. "I talked to her yesterday about the way she's been acting toward you. And I still think she's in contact with Karl King. He knows too much about police business."

Hardy had quickly learned to avoid the dispatch station if Crystal Stanley was working. She was growing more blatant as each day passed in her attempts to attract him. At least Jeff usually worked the evening shift, which significantly limited the time Hardy was forced to interact with the woman.

The blare of multiple sirens drew his attention as four state squad cars pulled in and stopped. The next three hours were spent helping the state police officers as much as he could.

While they were pretty sure the first body was that of William Baxter, positive identifications of both men were going to have to come from something other than facial recognition. Dr. Tindell estimated they'd been out there for three to four weeks, and the elements hadn't been kind. There were no wallets or other signs of identification found on or near the bodies. A cursory examination led them to believe in each instance the man had been shot in the back of the head with what appeared to be either a nine millimeter or forty-five caliber gun. The job of working the crime scene was extremely unpleasant.

It was nearly time for Haley's shift to end when Hardy finally walked back into the station.

"Was it bad?" she quietly asked him.

He looked at the woman in front of him and knew he'd do anything he could to shield her from the gruesome scene he'd just left. "I've seen worse."

"Are you okay?" Her voice was full of concern.

"I am now." Amazingly, the sight of her eyes, filled with loving concern, washed all the ugliness away. "Haley, I know my timing is lousy, but I can't wait one more minute to tell you—I love you."

Her eyes widened for an instant before her dimples appeared. He had never seen anything more beautiful than the smile on her face. "I love you too, Beau."

He groaned. "I want to kiss you so much right now, but sweetheart, I stink."

"You can kiss me this evening," she suggested, her smile not dimming. "Maybe even twice."

"I believe I'll take you up on that." He wished he had stopped by his house to shower before he came to the station, but Mitch had asked him to do something. He sobered. "Right now I need to take care of something on Mitch's computer. I have to get busy, or we won't have dinner before it's time for breakfast."

He softly laughed as her cheeks turned pink. "I'm not making any inappropriate suggestions, Haley. It was just a figure of speech."

Her face grew darker. "I know."

"I have to get busy now." It was all Hardy could do to turn and walk into the sheriff's office. Once inside, he sat in front of the computer.

Using a password he'd hoped to never use again, Hardy found himself on a very secure website. On it was everything the police and FSA had on the Dohner organization, including photographs. Mitch had asked him if there was some way to make sure he was right about the sketch not being a Dohner employee. Aside from finding the guy and persuading him to talk, this was the only way.

His eyes grew tired as he studied photographs. Those with people Hardy recognized were easy to bypass. It was ones with several subjects that were hard to look at. He took his time and examined them carefully, determined not to miss the man in the sketch if he were there. But when he finally closed the last file, he hadn't found anybody remotely close.

It was thirty-five minutes after he was supposed to get off when Hardy next looked at the clock. He couldn't believe he'd been at it that long. It seemed like just a few minutes ago Haley had stuck her head in and told him goodbye. He'd have to get going or be late for dinner. After spending hours studying photographs, Hardy felt confident the man in the sketch did not work for Dohner.

That opened up a whole new line of questions, though. Was the man himself behind everything? Or did he work for somebody else—somebody who wanted to hurt Hardy?

To hurt him . . . Wait a minute. If somebody wanted him dead, it stood to reason at least an attempt would have been made. But if he wanted to hurt him...What better way than to kill H.B.? But did that mean everybody Hardy cared for was in immediate danger? His mom? His sister and her family? Haley?

His mind raced. Would she be safer if he distanced himself from her? No. Nothing had changed. If somebody wanted to hurt him by hurting Haley, it was already too late. People in town already accepted them as a couple. If he broke things off, it wouldn't help her; it would just leave her on her own. At least he could keep an eye on her this way.

But he needed to warn her. He didn't want to scare her, but she needed to know what to watch for. He hoped she would still want to be with him. He could no longer imagine his life without her in it.

Chapter 46

"Lock my car doors when I get out and as soon as I get back in. Make sure my windows at home are shut tight and locked. Don't go outside by myself after dark. Don't answer the door without first looking through the peephole. If I see or hear anything strange, I'm to contact Beau or Mitch immediately." Haley stood in front of her fish tank, her hands on her hips. "Got that, Ozzie?"

She walked over and sank into the sofa, her head in her hands. Instead of the promised kisses last night, Beau told her about the suspicions he, and now Mitch, had. She glared at the sketch on the coffee table in front of her. The man had most likely been hired by somebody, his job to hurt Beau. And since it was common knowledge Beau cared about her, Haley was in danger.

Okay, Lord. I asked for Beau to stay and make his home with me. I asked for him to love me. I knew he was in danger, but I forgot. And now I'm probably in danger, too. I don't have to tell you how I feel about danger. So, I'm asking for a big miracle now, Father. I'm asking this man and whoever hired him be caught. While I'm at it, please make that Dohner person be caught, too, so Beau can go back to being who he really is. I love him, and I want him to be safe. I want both of us to be safe. Please.

Haley immediately felt better. Now, if she didn't get her purse and get out of her apartment, she was going to be late for work.

A scream caught in her throat when she opened the door a few minutes later, to find Wyatt Millan standing right there.

"Wyatt!" She put her hand over her heart. "You scared me half to death." Then she really looked at him. It looked like he hadn't shaved for days, and his clothes looked like he'd slept in them. Something was wrong. "What happened?"

He grasped her arm tightly enough it brought tears to Haley's eyes, and before she could even think, he shoved her through the door. "Your boyfriend has to help me. He killed those other guys, and now he's going to kill me."

Haley tried unsuccessfully to pull her arm free from his grasp. "Let go of me, Wyatt. You're hurting me."

"Listen to me!" He released her arm only to grab her by the shoulders and shake her like a rag doll.

"Stop!" Her mind raced. How could she get away from this madman?

Wyatt's face was close enough Haley could smell liquor on his breath. "I've been working for the man who wants to hurt Harding Davis. I was supposed to make him care about you. Now that I have, I don't think he'll protect me anymore. The Janitor is coming after me, and I don't know who sent him!"

"You . . . " She couldn't have heard him right. "I don't understand."

"Tell Davis if he wants to know who's after him, he needs to meet me at the abandoned warehouse over on Willow Street in an hour. I'll tell him everything, but he has to help me." His hands tightened on her shoulders. "Do you understand?"

"Yes." Blood was pounding in her head. She nearly collapsed when he finally released her and turned and disappeared.

Beau. She had to talk to Beau. She picked up the purse she hadn't even realized she dropped and shakily stepped back into her apartment. It took her three tries before she was able to throw the deadbolt and latch the security chain. She didn't need Wyatt Millan to come back and gain entry.

Her fingers were so unsteady she was afraid she wasn't going to be able to push the keys on her phone to call the station, but somehow she did.

Ray Fine, the night dispatcher, answered.

"Ray, it's Haley. I need to talk to Beau Da . . . Harding immediately. It's an emergency."

"He's on a call, Haley. Will Mitch do?" The older man's voice sounded worried.

No. She needed Beau. But maybe Mitch could get him. "Yes."

Haley heard Mitch's voice an instant later. "What's going on, Haley?"

"Wyatt Millan was here. He works for somebody who wants to hurt Beau and now they want to kill . . ." Kill. Was she really saying this? Had Wyatt forced his way in and threatened her?"

She vaguely heard her name, but the enormity of what had happened . . . danger . . . The room began spinning. Before she could ask for help, everything turned black.

"Haley . . . sweetheart." A deep voice spoke closely to her ear. "Please, my love. Wake up."

The light was blinding as her eyes somehow opened, causing her head to throb. Her mouth felt like sandpaper as she spoke.

"Beau?"

"I'm here, Haley." Relief was evident in his voice. "She's awake, Mitch."

What was going on? Why were Beau and Mitch at her apartment? Why was she still at her apartment? She'd been on her way to the station . . .

"Wyatt!" She tried to set up, only to find herself tightly cradled in Beau's arms. "Beau, Wyatt Millan works for somebody who wants to hurt you." Panic was once more setting in.

"Haley, listen to me," Mitch, kneeling beside them, spoke in a firm voice. "You have to calm down and tell us what he told you. If you want to protect Hardy, we need to know what Millan said. You can't tell us if you don't calm down."

He was right. Her eyes met Beau's as she drew several deep breaths.

"Can you sit up now?" Beau asked.

She needed to if she were going to think straight. "Yes."

With both men helping her, Haley was able to get up from the floor and find her way to the closest chair, where she sat.

Beau knelt in front of her.

"Now, Haley, please try to tell us everything Wyatt told you. Even if it doesn't seem important."

"Okay." Tears filled her eyes. She could still feel his hands on her arm and shoulders. She looked into Beau's eyes as she spoke, taking courage in knowing he was there.

"He has been working for somebody who wants you to be hurt."

Mitch spoke from where he stood behind Beau. "Did Wyatt say who he worked for?"

Haley thought. "No, but he said his job was finished. It was something about making you care about me. Now that you do, he doesn't think his boss will protect him. He's afraid of a man . . . " She searched her memory for Wyatt's exact words. "He called him the Janitor. He said he doesn't know who sent him, but I think he may suspect his boss did." She remembered. "He said the Janitor was going to kill him like he killed the other guys."

Beau sat back on his haunches, a stunned look on his face. "You're sure that's what Millan said? He said the Janitor was going to kill him?"

"Yes." Then she remembered more. "What time is it?" She looked past Beau to the wall clock. "It's been over a half hour! He said he'd tell you everything if you helped him. You're supposed to meet him at the old warehouse on Willow Street. He said in an hour, and it's already been nearly forty-five minutes."

Haley watched as Beau looked up over his shoulder at Mitch. "We can't leave her here like this. She needs to go to the hospital and be checked out."

"I'm okay." Even as she said it, she knew she wasn't. Besides the aches from being manhandled by Wyatt Millan, her head was throbbing.

Beau turned back to face her. "You hit your head on the table when you passed out. I'm afraid you might have a concussion."

"The ambulance should be here any moment." Mitch had barely finished speaking when Haley heard the siren.

"Blondie!" Wayne rushed through the door, which Haley now saw lay in splinters, a few moments before two EMTs walked in.

"Wayne, will you stay with Haley while Hardy and I take care of something?" There was urgency in Mitch's voice.

Confusion reigned on the deputy's face as he nodded. "I won't leave her side."

Beau stood and looked longingly at Haley's face. Then he leaned over and gently kissed her cheek. "I'll be back as soon as I can."

Tears came unbidden to her eyes. "Be careful, Beau."

"I will," he promised before turning and following Mitch out of the room.

Haley watched the empty doorway until Barney Nettles stepped into her line of vision. What if that man—a janitor?—somehow found Wyatt while Beau was with him? Would they kill him too? Or what if Wyatt were lying? Would he exchange Beau's life for his own? She didn't doubt for an instant he would.

Even as the EMT examined her injuries, Haley did the one thing she knew would help. She prayed.

Wayne stayed with her, even following the ambulance in his squad car. He must have made a phone call while she was being X-rayed because Nancy Shepard arrived before they had Haley settled back in her bed.

"What happened?" Nancy asked. "Wayne just called and told me you'd been hurt."

Nancy was Mavis's aunt and had no children of her own. That was the only explanation Haley could come up with as to why the waitress was always so motherly toward her. Not that Haley was complaining. She needed a mother right now.

"I don't know exactly what happened, myself." Wayne defended himself to the older woman. "I just knew you'd want to be here with her."

Nancy straightened the sheet covering Haley's hospital gown clad shoulders. "Of course I want to be here with her." Her expression softened as she looked at Haley's face. "You have a bruise on your forehead. Can you tell me what happened, honey?"

"I passed out and hit my head when I fell." That was the simple explanation.

Nancy wasn't going to let her get away with it, though. "And why did you pass out? Wayne wouldn't be here if it wasn't something serious."

Haley still hadn't come to grips with what had happened. "Wyatt . . . Wyatt Millan showed up at my apartment and scared me. I can't say more because it's police business."

Understanding dawned in the kind woman's eyes. "Well, you don't have to be afraid now. You're safe."

"And she has a concussion," Dr. Potter cheerfully announced as he entered the room. He walked over to the bed and smiled down at his patient. "You are very fortunate, young lady, for you came awfully close to fracturing your skull. I'm going to admit you just so we can keep an eye on you."

"But work—"

"Will wait." Wayne spoke firmly. "You know Mitch would throw a fit if you tried to work when the doctor says you need to stay here. Now, just be quiet and listen to Dr. Potter."

Haley bit her tongue and listened to the doctor's instructions. He was barely out of the room before she turned to Wayne.

"Please, can you make sure Beau is okay? I have to know he's okay." She felt herself growing frantic.

Nancy placed a soothing hand on her shoulder as Wayne spoke.

"I'll go see if I can raise him or Mitch on the radio. Just don't try to get up or anything while I'm gone. Promise?"

"I promise." She would have promised him just about anything if she could find out Beau hadn't been hurt.

A tear trickled down her cheek as she looked at Nancy. "He has to be okay. I don't know what I'll do if he isn't."

"Let's pray, honey," Nancy suggested, before closing her eyes and bowing her head. Haley listened as Nancy asked God to place a protective hand over Beau. She prayed Haley would have the assurance in the midst of her fear, of remembering God was with them through all things.

Although she was still troubled, Haley felt better after the prayer was finished.

It seemed like forever before Wayne walked back in.

"He's fine," he assured Haley. "He'll be here as soon as he can. Mitch couldn't tell me what happened, but he said it might be a few hours before Hardy gets here."

A deep breath of relief left her. "I can wait. I just needed to know he hadn't been hurt."

I can wait. Haley found herself regretting those words over the next twelve and a half hours as they passed with no sign of Beau. Wayne and Nancy had both left, but a state police officer was sitting right outside her door. Mitch sent him over so Wayne could leave, saying only Haley wasn't to be left unprotected under any circumstances.

She could only imagine what had taken place at that warehouse.

It was nearly nine o'clock when she heard Beau's voice outside her door. He was freshly showered, in jeans and a sweatshirt when he walked in a few seconds later.

"Beau." It was the first real smile she'd had all day.

"Hey." He walked straight to the bed and leaned down to gently kiss her lips. His hand found hers as he straightened up. His eyes anxiously searched hers. "How are you?"

"I have a concussion," Haley impatiently answered. "What happened, Beau? Did Wyatt tell you who's after you?"

His reluctance to tell her was evident in his face, but finally, he softly spoke. "I'm sorry, Haley. We found Millan in the alley behind the building. He was gone before we got there."

"Gone? You mean he's . . . Somebody killed him?" Even though the man had terrified her, she would never wish him dead. "Do you have any idea of who he was working for, Beau?"

Resolve was in his eyes as he spoke. "I'm fairly sure it's not Dohner, but other than that I don't know. The important thing right now is to keep you safe."

"What do you mean?" she asked. "Why are you so concerned about me being in danger?" Was it even worse than they'd originally warned her about?

His eyes clouded. "Millan told you his job was to make me care about you. His boss wants to hurt me, and the best way to hurt me right now is to hurt the woman I love. Mitch is arranging for around the clock protection for you."

Haley fought her fears away as she considered his words. "Did he make you care about me, Beau? Was it because of the way he acted toward me that you responded—"

"I promise you, that man had nothing whatsoever to do with my feelings for you." There was steel in his voice. "I responded to him the way I did because I already cared for you. I won't have you thinking he had *anything* to do with us."

She breathed a pent up sigh of relief as she saw the truth in his eyes. "What's going to happen now? What are you going to do?"

"I have a meeting with Mitch and some other officers in the morning. There's some information I can gain access to that might help us." His hand tightened on hers. "But tonight, I'm going to go home and try to forget what I've seen today. I've never liked this aspect of my job."

"Is there anything I can do?" she softly asked, wanting only to ease his pain.

He looked deeply into her eyes. "You've done it just by being here. I'll think about you and our future together tonight. That's how I'll cope."

There was only one thing she could say. "I love you, Beau."

"I love you, too."

And that was enough for both of them.

Chapter 47

"So, tell us what you know about the Janitor," Mitch instructed Hardy.

Hardy stood and walked to stand beside the sheriff. He looked around the room at his fellow deputies and half a dozen state police officers. He had just gotten off the phone after an hour-long conference call with his brother-in-law, Tom Fowler, and Rich Stephens, and now had solid information to share.

"The Janitor is a very expensive hit man with a reputation for finishing the job." Those had been Elliott's exact words. "He always works alone and cares about only one thing—money."

"Has Ted Dohner hired him?" Mitch steadily asked.

"The Chicago undercover unit doesn't think so, and neither do I." He could see the skepticism on his boss's face. "As I said, the Janitor is a paid hit man. Dohner has his own men, who would be effective enough on their own. He would view it as a sign of weakness in his organization to hire from outside it" Mitch had explained Hardy's knowledge of the situation to the state police by introducing him as a former organized crime expert, not revealing who he really was.

Jeff Fielding lifted the sketch he was holding. "Do you think this is him?"

Hardy and the other three men had discussed that very possibility during their phone conversation. "I don't know. This guy is smaller than the agency always assumed the Janitor was, but he can't be ruled out."

Of course, that meant it may have been the Janitor who tried to kill H.B. Davis, a fact Hardy would have to process later.

"How come this janitor guy isn't in the system?" one of the state police officers asked.

"He has never been caught," Hardy replied. "There is no description of him in the system because he's never left anybody who could identify him alive. He is suspected in paid hits all over the country, too. Over the course of the last thirty-five years, he's killed, disappeared, and then shown up somewhere else. An FSA agent just told me it has been so long without any known activity from him, they thought he'd either died or retired."

A seasoned state trooper leaned forward in his chair. "Then how are we supposed to be on the lookout for him? I mean, if it's this guy," He held up the sketch, "at least we have some kind of picture, but you're telling us he could be any stranger we see."

"He may have left the area." Even as Hardy said it he knew the likelihood was small. "But the only suggestion I have is to look for a stranger—somebody new to town or passing through. He's been doing this for three decades, so we know he's not a young man."

"We have reason to believe the Janitor has been hired to hurt Hardy." Mitch spoke firmly. "And we believe he may intend to do that by harming his girlfriend, Haley Johnson. You all know her; she's my chief dispatcher. We plan to provide her with around the clock protection. She'll be fine when she's here on duty, but she's going to need one of us with her the rest of the time."

The older trooper who had spoken before cleared his throat. "I can speak for all of us. We'll pitch in and give Haley protection, even if we do it on our own time, won't we, men?"

When the men unreservedly agreed, Hardy was once more moved by how much people in this community cared about Haley. She really did have a family of sorts in these folks.

"I know you've been given part of this information, but I want to make sure we're all on the same page here," Mitch told the men.

Hardy took a few steps back and let the sheriff have the floor.

Mitch kept his gaze steady as he looked around the room. "We believe there is an individual intent on harming Beau Harding. I can't tell you why, so don't ask. You'll just have to trust me." He waited for a few minutes, as if giving the men a chance to voice their objections to being kept partially out of the loop. None came, so he went on. "William Baxter, Roscoe Callen, and an as yet unidentified man were hired by this individual to vandalize businesses here in Shadow. The goal was to capture Hardy's attention. Something happened, and one of them shot and killed Callen." Mitch looked at Hardy. "Will you explain what we and your friends at the agency have come up with?"

Hardy once more stepped forward. "Callen's murder wasn't planned and probably angered the person who hired them. He then sent out the Janitor to take care of them."

"But where does Wyatt Millan come into this?" Wayne asked.

"We feel certain Millan was hired by the same man who hired the first three men. They may have even worked together. But he had a more precise assignment, and once it was believed to be accomplished, the Janitor was sent after him, as well."

"Millan was hired by the bank using extremely well-produced fraudulent credentials," Mitch spoke up. "Wyatt Millan didn't exist until approximately three months ago. His prints didn't show up in the system, so we don't have an ID either. We believe he's been using different aliases for a long time."

Hardy told them what Stephens had shared. "They think the individual behind this whole scheme most likely helped Millan relocate. He probably helped him set up his new identity and paid for the forged documents he needed."

"What makes you so sure this Janitor won't come straight after you, Harding?" one of the state troopers asked.

"I hope he does." Hardy didn't blink. "I'd much rather be the target than think Haley or anybody else is in danger because of me."

"You'll have to be careful, too," Jeff warned him.

"I can take care of myself." Hardy wanted their focus to remain on keeping Haley safe, not worrying about him. "Let's just figure out how to make sure he can't get to Haley."

After nearly an hour, they had come up with a solid schedule insuring Haley would never be unprotected. When Hardy suggested nobody else would be needed when he was with her, he was met with vehement objections. The general consensus was it would be too tempting for the Janitor to take Haley out right in front of Hardy and then finish him off, too. Hardy hated to admit they had a point.

"A lot of people care about Haley," Hardy quietly observed after all of the men besides him and Mitch had left. "But then she's easy to care about."

The sheriff leveled his gaze at him. "You're really serious about her, aren't you?"

"I've never been more serious in my life." Hardy was happy to tell the truth.

"I owe you an apology." Mitch spoke solemnly. "I wasn't sure you'd stick with Haley. I figured you'd run off and leave her, first chance you got. I'm glad I was wrong about you."

"I could never leave her now." And he knew he couldn't. "She means too much to me."

"Good." The sheriff nodded. "Good."

And Hardy found himself in complete agreement.

Chapter 48

He sank to his chair, full of disbelief. Both the missing men and James were dead. A pure and blinding rage took hold of him as he dialed the phone.

"Yes." Weiss's curt greeting angered him even more.

"You'd better tell me why Samuels has killed my men." He was past caring whether he upset Weiss or not. "We had a deal."

"Samuels hasn't killed anybody." Weiss sounded genuinely confused. "He's still embarrassed about the old lady getting the best of him."

"I know he was in Shadow."

"Okay." The man sounded sure of himself. "I sent him to town just to check on your men. With the lowlifes you had to hire and that loon of a son you have, you can't blame me for wanting to have the situation checked for myself. I have as much as you do riding on this plan."

The man was about as trustworthy as a rattlesnake, but he didn't think Weiss was lying now. "Then, who do you think killed Harve and Brockman? And now James?"

"Samuels said Harve and Brockman were nowhere to be found when he was in town, but he saw Jim skulking about at the campsite. I don't know anything about them being killed." Weiss cleared his throat. "But I'm sorry. I know it must be hard for—"

"The only thing hard about it is how it affects our plan! I'll have to rely on my son now, and we both know his limitations."

A low whistle came out of the phone. "Do you want me to send Samuels to town to help out?"

He considered the idea for a few moments. "No. I think we're close enough to the end my son will be able to handle what he has to. If not, I'll go there myself. Just be sure the records stay lost. And keep your ear to the ground. We need to find out who's killing our men."

"You're the boss." Weiss's skepticism was apparent.

Without another word, he disconnected the call. Perhaps he should feel something for the men who had died, but he didn't. Not even for James. All he felt was concern that whoever was ridding the world of his men might damage his plan. He would do whatever he had to in order to keep that from happening.

Chapter 49

"I'm so happy to be free, I don't even care that I'm stuck in this horrible wig again!" Haley declared, leaning against Beau.

You do realize you're sitting in the backseat of an FSA vehicle with two agents in the front seat and a police officer beside you. Are you sure you're free?" Beau's eyes were sparkling with laughter as he looked at her.

"We've all been in this car for almost two hours. Charlie and Fred are our friends now, aren't you?" She addressed the other two men, who were studiously looking straight ahead.

Fred Warburton finally turned in the passenger seat to look at Haley. "I feel like we're practically family."

Haley laughed. "You made a joke! Did you hear that, Beau? Fred made a joke!"

All three men chuckled before Fred spoke again. "Actually, it kind of feels like we're free, too. As much as we like H.B. and Sharon, it was nice to let Dickens and Scott take over for a couple of days."

"I wish H.B. were well enough to be with us this weekend." Haley felt her smile falter as she spoke to Beau. "It's going to be great to spend the weekend with your sister and her family, but it would be even more special to have your entire family there."

"Soon," Beau assured her. "We'll all be together soon."

Haley felt content with his answer as she turned to look at the passing scenery. After nearly three solid weeks of constant police protection, she was suffering from some convoluted sort of cabin fever. When Mitch let both Beau and her off for the entire weekend, and Elliott offered to arrange their transport to his house, Haley jumped at the chance. She hadn't even protested her awful getup, especially when she was told they wouldn't have to leave until eight o'clock in the morning.

"I could get used to you in that wig," Beau's voice was for her ears alone. "You may have to take it along on our honeymoon."

"Our honey—?" She turned to him incredulously. "Beau Davis!"

He shrugged. "I just thought you should get used to the idea."

Okay. He hadn't actually proposed. It was more like he announced that he was going to at some point in the future. Her heart took wing and soared. "I think I could get used to that pretty quickly."

The teasing light was back in his eyes. "We'd better hope Dohner gets put away soon. Haley Davis still sounds much better than Haley Harding."

Now he sounded like his mom. "I don't care what your name is," she told him. "I love you."

"I love you, too," he calmly said. "Now, do you think what I bought for the kids is okay?"

They spent the remainder of the trip talking about his sister and her family. Haley felt like she already knew the woman before she had even met her.

"You told me your brother-in-law was rich." Haley's voice was full of awe as she looked at the house they pulled up to. "But you didn't tell me they live in a mansion!"

Beau's brow went up. "You didn't get suspicious when we had to stop at the gate back there? It might look open and inviting back here, but Elliott has top of the line security in place. That's why we don't have to keep anybody with us this weekend."

Haley hadn't known what to think when they pulled into a driveway and stopped at a fancy iron filigree gate. One of the two men in uniform had come out and spoken to Charlie, but Haley hadn't been able to understand what they'd said. Then she'd been too awestruck by the landscaping to ask Beau.

But now this house . . . "I can't stay in a house like this," she told him. "I won't know how to act."

Beau laughed. "My sister was raised by the same two people I was, Haley. Don't let this fool you. Callie and Elliott are just ordinary people. You'll feel so welcome you won't have time to worry about how to act."

Her knees started shaking as she waited for Beau to retrieve their overnight cases from the trunk of the car.

"We'll see you Sunday night," Beau told Charlie and Fred before the car continued around the circle drive and back down the long lane.

Haley wanted to hold Beau's hand, but he had a suitcase in each one. She settled for walking as closely to him as she could.

The door opened before they had quite reached it, and a very lovely brunette woman with porcelain-like skin and deep brown eyes stood there with a smile on her face.

"Beau. You really came." A mixture of surprise and pleasure was in her voice.

"Hi, Callie." Beau sat the bags down on the porch and hugged his sister. They embraced like two people making up for lost time. There were tears in Callie's eyes when Beau released her.

"Callie, this is Haley." Beau put his hand on Haley's back.

"I'm so glad you came," Callie welcomed her. "Come on in, and let's get you settled. The kids have been up since six, waiting on Uncle Beau to get here, so you'd better watch out when they see you."

Before Haley quite realized what was happening, she found herself and her suitcase left in a beautiful, comfortably furnished bedroom. She set a personal speed record getting out of her disguise. Unsure of what to do next, she looked the room over. The shades of blue it was decorated in gave her a sense of peace. And while the room surpassed any she'd stayed in before, it wasn't so fancy she felt out of place in it. Maybe Beau had been right, and she'd feel comfortable here after all.

"You okay?" Beau spoke from the open doorway, a sack in his hand.

She looked at him and nodded. "Let's go meet your niece and nephew."

He took her hand as they walked back into what Callie had called the family room, where two children were bouncing on their feet.

"Are you our Uncle Beau?" The little brown-eyed boy that could have been a miniature Beau Davis addressed his uncle.

Beau dropped Haley's hand and knelt in front of the child. "I'm your Uncle Beau, but you're too big to be Blake. He's just a little boy."

Blake puffed his chest out and stood to his full height. "I'm six years old."

"I'm four." The little blonde angel standing next to him carefully raised four fingers on her right hand.

"You're big, too, Tabitha," Beau told her. He pulled the sack around in front of him. "Are you too big for this?" He pulled out a brightly colored doll with a pink dress and long yellow pigtails.

"Thank you." The little girl accepted the doll and grinned at her uncle, her top two middle teeth missing. Haley wanted to scoop her up and hug her, she was so precious.

"And how about this, buddy?" Beau asked Blake, offering him the box of plastic logs he'd brought. "I hear you like to build things."

"Thank you, Uncle Beau!" Blake grabbed the toy and held it up for his mom to see. "Look, Mom! Now I'll have enough for my whole farm!"

"You sure will." Callie smiled warmly at her son.

"Hey, Blake." Beau waited until his nephew was looking back at him. "This is Haley. Will you tell her hi?"

Blake giggled. "Is she your girlfriend?"

Beau looked at Haley and winked. "She sure is."

"I don't have a girlfriend," Blake solemnly informed Haley. "Dad says I'm not old enough."

"I'm his girlfriend!" his little sister declared.

Blake rolled his eyes and confided in Haley. "She's just my sister, but she's little. She doesn't know any better."

"Well, I'm happy to meet both of you." Haley didn't think she'd ever seen kids as cute as the two she was looking at. Beau would never have a son who favored him any more than his nephew did. And Tabitha . . .

"She looks like her dad." Callie's smile told Haley she knew what Haley was wondering. "Elliott should be home any moment."

"He's home right now." The man who was speaking stood inside the door while two little children left their uncle to run over to him.

"Daddy!" Tabitha raised her arms to be picked up, her new doll's dress tightly clenched in her fist.

Elliott leaned over and scooped the toddler into his arms. "What do you have there, Tabby?"

"Look, Dad!" Blake wanted his dad's attention. "Uncle Beau gave me some new logs. Now we can build a whole farm."

"Uncle Beau gave me a doll," Tabitha informed her dad, nearly hitting him in the eye with her new toy.

"That was nice of Uncle Beau." Elliott obviously loved his children. Still carrying his daughter and with Blake right beside him, he walked on into the room.

"You must be Haley." His smile reached his eyes.

Haley was immediately aware of two things. The man she was looking at could be Brad Pitt's twin brother, and both the other adults in the room were watching her closely for her reaction.

She decided not to disappoint them.

"You look exactly like Brad Pitt." She grinned at the surprised expressions on all three adults' faces. "But you're still not as handsome as Beau."

Astonishment shone in Elliott's eyes for a brief instant before he burst into laughter. "I like you." He turned to his brother-in-law. "You'd better keep her, Beau."

Beau walked over and curved his arm around Haley's shoulders. "I plan to, Elliott."

"Come on, you two," Callie instructed her children. "Let's go see what the new puppies are doing so Daddy can talk to Uncle Beau and Haley."

"Oscar had puppies," Blake informed them. "I told Tabby he was a girl, but she didn't believe me, and now we have four puppies out there."

Haley bit her lip to keep from smiling. She was certain there was a story to be told concerning a female dog named Oscar. Beau was right. She liked this family.

"So, any news?" Beau asked his brother-in-law as soon as Callie and the kids were out of the room.

Elliott smiled grimly. "Don't get your hopes up, but I may have good news about at least one of our problems."

Beau pulled Haley tighter against his side. "We'll take any good news we can get."

"Somebody high up in Dohner's organization is talking. She contacted the office in Chicago and told them she was ready to make a deal. They're in the process of working things out right now, and if this woman talks, Dohner will be done for good."

Beau suddenly dropped his arm from around Haley and stepped a few feet away from her. "Who's turning, Elliott? What's her name?"

Elliott frowned. "It's Ted Dohner's niece. Her name is Audrey. Why?"

Audrey. Haley immediately recognized the name, and her heart sank. She was the woman Beau had dated for four years, and even though their relationship hadn't been what it seemed, it was there.

"I'll leave you two alone." She spoke softly, but Beau didn't even acknowledge her words before she turned and left the room.

Not knowing where to go and feeling completely lost, Haley found herself back in her bedroom. The way he stepped away from Haley at the mention of her name--it couldn't have been more apparent Beau was worried about Audrey Dohner. Beau must have feelings for her. Maybe he hadn't realized how deep they were until he found out she was in danger. Haley felt an emptiness settle in her heart, for she knew she was going to lose the man she loved back to the world he'd left. And there was nothing she could do about it.

She gave in to the tears and sank onto the bed, her heart breaking into a million pieces. After giving her heart, completely with no reservations, to Beau, he would no longer want it. The stress and fear she'd dealt with nonstop for the past several weeks contributed to the tears that were falling, and she gave in to them. She had never felt more alone.

Chapter 50

Hardy's heart pounded. Audrey Dohner was turning against her uncle. She could shut the entire organization down. The concept of freedom from the danger associated with the man was unbelievable. It meant a whole new life with Haley, able to openly give her his real name. It was too much.

"What is the matter with you?" his brother-in-law demanded, sounding angry.

Hardy looked up, his mind whirling. "I just can't believe Audrey is doing this."

"Who is she to you?" Elliott seemed a little calmer, but still unhappy.

What did who Audrey was to Hardy matter now? He waved his hand. "She was just part of my cover. We pretended to be a couple so she could be with her real boyfriend, and I didn't have to play the field. We weren't even really friends; we just used each other for what we needed."

"Well, then, you just did the most stupid thing I've ever seen you do," Elliott flatly informed him.

"What do you mean?" Beau looked around, wondering why Haley was suddenly so quiet. "Where's Haley?"

"I'm going to tell you what I mean, and then you'll be able to figure out where she is." Elliott crossed his arms in front of him. "When I mentioned Audrey's name, you went all mushy-eyed, brother. I had the distinct impression this Audrey was somebody who meant an awful lot to you."

"But Haley knows the truth about Audrey."

"Since Haley looked like she wouldn't have minded if the earth opened up and swallowed her whole right before she excused herself and fled the room, I'd say she thought the same thing I did."

"She knows the truth—about everything."

"I don't think what you've told Haley matters right now. If you don't want to lose her, you'd better find her and straighten this out. Now."

What had he done? After Haley's initial knee-jerk reaction to his pseudo-relationship with Audrey, she'd gotten past it. And now, Hardy had unintentionally given her reason to believe it meant more to him than it did.

"Which way did she go?" His voice was hoarse.

"Toward the back hall. Probably her bedroom." Elliott sadly shook his head. "I hope you can fix this, Beau. That woman is the best thing that's ever happened to you."

"Don't you think I know that?" Beau asked before he turned and headed toward Haley's room.

What was he going to say to fix this? He was still trying to figure it out when he reached her room. Her door was closed, so he softly knocked. When there was no answer, he knocked again and then waited a few moments before quietly opening the door.

The room was empty. "Haley?" Maybe she was in the adjoining bathroom. When she didn't answer, he walked in, only to see the bathroom door standing open and unoccupied.

Where was she? Hardy fought back his initial panic with the knowledge they were on Elliott's estate, surrounded by security that allowed his niece and nephew to freely play outside. No matter where Haley had gone, she was safe.

But he still needed to find her—to explain his reaction to Elliott's news. Why hadn't he held onto Haley more tightly?

Thinking maybe she'd gone outside to find Callie and the kids, he stopped at his room long enough to pick up his jacket. Elliott was no longer in the family room when Hardy walked through on his way to the back door.

Callie and the children were just coming in when Hardy reached the door.

"Have you seen Haley?" he quietly asked his sister.

Her accusing eyes met his. "She's out at the barn. I thought it might help her to visit Dipper."

Dipper was the horse Callie had gotten for her sixteenth birthday. He had lived at their grandparents' and then been stabled nearby until she married Elliott and moved to the estate.

Callie waited until Blake and Tabitha had headed to the bathroom to wash their hands before she turned on her brother. "I don't know what you did, but she's been crying. Hard. Like her heart is broken. Now, if you're just going out there to upset her more, leave her alone with Dipper."

"I made a foolish mistake, and I need to set things right." Hardy just had to figure out how to accomplish that. "I won't upset her anymore."

Callie gave him a measuring look before she stepped aside to let him walk out the door. Hardy had only been out to the barn a couple of times, but didn't recall it being this long of a walk.

His own heart broke when he saw Haley with her head against the old horse's shoulder, her hand rhythmically petting the roan. He could see her red, swollen eyes from there.

"Haley." He softly spoke her name.

She didn't look at him. "Will you please call Charlie or Fred to come get me? I don't have their numbers, and I want to go home."

Hardy opened the gate and walked closer to her. "Please, Haley, listen to me. Give me a chance to explain. Things aren't like you think they are."

His heart caught in his throat when her bloodshot eyes met his. "You had a life before we met. I know that. I just fooled myself into believing a four-year-long relationship didn't really mean anything to you. I know better now. It still matters to you. She still matters."

"No." He shook his head and walked toward her. "Audrey doesn't mean what you think she does. I love you, Haley, only you."

"I saw how you reacted when you realized she's in danger." Haley's voice was full of defeat. "You couldn't get away from me fast enough. It's okay. I understand. I just need to go home now."

Hardy had finally reached her, but it was clear she wouldn't let him touch her. "I'm sorry for how I reacted, but I'm telling you the truth. All I was thinking about was if Audrey follows through with this, I will finally be free from Dohner. I could be Beau Davis again, to everybody. I could give you my real name. That's what I was thinking."

Haley shook her head and slid back along the horse's side, farther away from Hardy. "If I were who you were thinking about, you wouldn't have let go of me. If you won't call one of the men, I'll just ask Elliott to."

There was only one thing left to say, and then he was going to tell her everything. "Haley, I used Audrey. It's awful, and I'm ashamed of myself, but she and I weren't even friends. We used each other to meet our needs. That's all it ever was. And the truth is, I'm looking at her as a tool now, too. She's a human being, putting herself in danger, and all I'm thinking about is what it will mean to me if she goes through with it."

"I don't believe you." Tears were once more welling in her eyes. "You kissed her and held her, like you do me. It meant something to you, Beau, and you're lying to yourself if you say it didn't."

"It didn't." Why wouldn't she believe him? "Nothing has ever meant what you do, Haley. Nothing has even come close. I've never felt this strongly about another human being." It was time to share everything. "You asked me to explain why I was mad at God." He drew a deep breath and prayed for her to understand. "Her name was Kari Jeffries."

She looked sharply at him. "You had another girlfriend?"

"No." No more holding anything back from the woman he loved. "I watched Kari Jeffries die. She was only twenty years old, and I watched her die." He could feel the pain deep in his soul, finding its way to his heart. "If you look my real name up on the internet, you'll see that Harding Davis died a hero." He laughed derisively. "It's all a lie, though. It was at a convenience store. A man pulled a gun. I was able to get behind the counter with the cashier—Kari Jeffries. She gave me the owner's gun, and the man and I ended up in a standoff. I still don't know why, but she stood up. She just stood up. I shot him, but not before he shot both of us. She was killed instantly."

"And that's why you've been mad at God?" Haley quietly asked.

"Yes." He finally touched her, his hand on her shoulder. "But you've changed that. You've changed everything. I see my undercover life as a big lie I lived for five years, with nothing to show for it except bad memories and regret. And I see it wasn't God's fault Kari stood up and was shot."

"It wasn't yours, either." Haley's beautiful eyes were open wide. "You didn't have any control over that other man or that girl. You tried to help and could have died yourself."

"I know." And he finally did. "Thanks to you, I know."

"You're not mad at God anymore?" Her lips were trembling.

He looked into her eyes, willing her to see the truth. "I'm not mad at him anymore. I want to make things right with him and live the way I'm supposed to. With you. Only you." Hardy could feel long held back tears fill his eyes. "Please, Haley. I don't want to lose you. I love you."

"I love you too." The words gushed out of her mouth as she moved willingly into his arms.

Hardy felt tears flowing down his face, and for the first time in his adult life, he let them. It was time to cry. It was time to heal. It was time to love. He buried his face in Haley's hair and held her as tightly as he could without hurting her.

He had no idea how long they stood, both mourning his past mistakes, but he felt like a burden had been lifted from his chest when he finally looked in her eyes.

"Thank you."

She linked her hands behind his head and pulled his mouth to hers. It was the first time Haley had initiated a kiss, and it was the sweetest thing he'd ever experienced.

He brushed her hair back from her face and smiled gently. "My timing stinks again, but will you marry me?"

Her dimples grew deeper as her smile widened. "Yes." She reached around his neck and hugged him, laughing the entire time. "We're standing beside a horse in a smelly paddock, and I've never been happier in my life."

He smiled and tightened his arms for a moment before releasing her. "I promise I'll wait for a very romantic moment to give you a ring."

"Okay."

He had to make sure everything was truly okay between them. "And you understand about my past? You accept I made mistakes and love me anyway?"

Her brows came down in a frown. "I still think you have some feelings for Audrey, Beau. You wouldn't be human if you didn't." She placed her finger over his lips when he started to protest. "But I believe you didn't love her. Okay?"

There wasn't any use in arguing with her. "Okay."

He kept a tight hold of her hand as they walked back to the house. "So, if you think I'm more handsome than Elliott, you must think I'm more handsome than Brad Pitt."

She reached over and batted his shoulder. "You know you're good-looking. Don't go getting a swelled head."

They were still laughing when they walked into the family room, where Callie and Elliott sat.

Callie's eyes searched her brother's for a moment before she slowly smiled. "I take it you fixed things."

Hardy looked at Haley and smiled. "If asking her to marry me and hearing her say yes qualifies, then yes, I fixed things."

Callie and Elliott both came to their feet, Hardy's sister clapping her hands. "Wait until Mom and Dad hear. The last time I was there, Dad kept talking about Dimples!"

She pulled Haley away from Hardy and hugged her tightly. "Welcome to the family. I've always wanted a sister."

Elliott shook Hardy's hand. "Hopefully, everything will go smoothly, and you can have a regular family wedding. Your mom will want everybody there."

"I know." Hardy looked over to see Callie leading Haley out of the room, talking about wedding dresses and flowers. Maybe the two women would have the whole thing planned before he and Haley had to leave tomorrow evening. He liked the idea of being married to Haley; he just wasn't sure about all of the necessary preparations.

"Have there been any more signs of the man who's after you?" Elliott was once more back to business, which shouldn't have surprised Hardy.

"No, and I'm not sure there will be." Hardy thought about what he knew. "He has to know by now we're on to him. I don't think he'll take any more chances of being recognized." He remembered the last meeting he had with Mitch. "We're not easing up on Haley's protection, though. Just in case he's waiting for that. I'm not taking any unnecessary chances with her life."

Elliott's cell phone rang before he could respond to Hardy. He checked caller ID and frowned before he answered.

"Lawrence here."

His frown deepened as he listened. "Say that again."

Hardy saw skepticism on his brother-in-law's face as he listened for several minutes. "And you're absolutely sure about this?"

Elliott's eyes found Hardy's as his caller spoke. "He's right here. I'll let him know."

"Okay. Thank you, Stephens."

What had Rich Stephens told Elliott?

The FSA agent appeared to be stunned as he spoke. "It looks like we may not have to worry about the Janitor anymore."

"Why not?" What had changed?

"A body was found. They believe it's the Janitor."

Hardy shook his head. "That's impossible. There's no way he can be identified."

"He had several photographs of you and Haley, as well as a torn up picture of Wyatt Millan. They're running ballistics on the forty-five they found on him." Elliott shook his head as if he had trouble believing it himself. "They were even able to locate the motel room he was staying in. He was registered as Vincent

Samuels. Stephens said there were more pictures hidden in the lining of a suitcase. Pictures of the three men who were killed."

Hardy tried to process the news. "Okay. But who took him out? He's supposed to be the best."

Elliott looked gravely at his brother-in-law. "There's no way to know yet, but we have to consider the chance Ted Dohner had it done. We have to move you, Beau. If he knows the Janitor was after you, then he knows you're alive."

"But he may not know where I'm at." Hardy's mind raced. "I can't just disappear now. I can't ask Haley to do that, and I'm not leaving her behind."

"Okay." Elliott held his hand up in a stop gesture. "You're both safe here. Stephens said Fowler has his undercover cops looking into it. We should know one way or the other what the facts are before it's time for you to leave tomorrow. If not, we may extend your visit here a few days."

Hardy needed to tamp down his emotions, to keep a level head. He wouldn't do Haley or himself any good by jumping the gun and panicking. "Let's not tell Haley right now, Elliott," he decided. "She's been through enough, and she's finally happy. Let's not take that away from her unless we have to."

"I can live with that," Elliott agreed. "Now, what do you say we go see what mischief my children have gotten into? They've been too quiet for the past half hour."

Hardy followed the other man out of the room, his thoughts focused on Haley. She was his primary concern—her safety. And he would do whatever it took to keep her safe. No matter what it cost.

Chapter 51

He quickly packed the last shirt in his bag before zipping it shut. Things had gotten out of hand and snowballed. As much as he disliked it, he was going to have to get his hands dirty.

He hadn't believed it when the newscaster announced the body of a man thought to be a notorious hit man known as the Janitor had been found. And then Vince Samuels' picture was shown. The implications of his identity were astounding.

It meant Weiss had his own agenda and had been one step ahead of him all throughout this process. And if Weiss had hired somebody as well-known and expensive as the Janitor, he was receiving funds from another source. Another source with more power and money than he had. And even though he had no idea what Weiss hoped to gain, he felt confident he was next on Weiss's hit list.

His only hope now was to take care of Harding Davis Jr quickly, before Weiss or his unknown benefactor hired somebody else. He didn't know who had done him the favor of killing the Janitor, but as a result, he would have a small window of opportunity to complete his plan.

Now, there was no question whether or not to leave his son alone in Shadow. He would have to go and make sure Harding Davis was taken care of himself. He needed to finish this and disappear. Alone. His son would be another casualty, but that couldn't be helped. It would be impossible to disappear with him along.

He just needed to get to Shadow. Then he'd slip away after he finished with Davis. He had a whole new identity waiting, and was totally prepared to vanish. Starting over wouldn't be all that bad. Especially with the large payouts from the Kelley girl's insurance.

But first, he had to finish with Davis. His plan was still going to work.

Chapter 52

Haley smiled as she hung up the phone. It was the second time today her future mother-in-law had called to discuss the wedding. If H.B. were still in the hospital when they got married, the wedding would take place in their church. Although Haley would miss having her friends there, it gave her a sense of contentment to know she'd be marrying Beau in the church he grew up attending.

Of course, they still hadn't set a date. While the Janitor was dead, the person who hired him and those other men was still out there, and now it appeared Dohner had his suspicions Beau was alive. So far, he was fishing, keeping his ear to the ground and eyes open. Beau wouldn't be able to visit his parents again until they arrested Dohner.

Her heart lifted. Thanks to Audrey Dohner, things might be taken care of soon. Elliott had described it as a race—Audrey reaching an agreement with the FSA and turning the evidence over before her uncle confirmed Beau was alive and located him. Haley often prayed for it to happen that way. The last time Beau had spoken to Elliott, Rich Stephens reported Audrey was coming in with evidence in hand, this coming Monday. That was two days away. Surely, Ted Dohner wouldn't be able to confirm his suspicions and locate Beau before then.

The thought of the criminal locating Beau scared Haley more than anything. Primarily because the reason he refused to leave was her. Even though she told him she'd go with him, he wouldn't uproot her from Shadow and make her live on the run. He stated that Shadow was his home now, and it was as good of a place as any to make a stand. Dohner might come after him, but Beau had his plans. And support from an entire community.

Her doorbell rang, jolting her out of her thoughts. Even though she no longer needed protection from the hired hit man, Haley still automatically checked through the peephole. She was surprised when she saw who her visitor was.

"Matt!" She smiled as she opened the door. "What are you doing here?"

He walked into the living room and dropped onto the sofa. "I haven't had any tickets or fines to pay lately, so I haven't seen you around. I just wanted to make sure my favorite girl is doing okay."

She knew she was blushing. "I'm doing wonderfully."

His brows rose. "That wouldn't have anything to do with a particular man and a rumor I've heard, would it?"

Her face grew warmer as she smiled. "Beau and I are getting married."

"I knew it!" He slapped his knee. "I knew the first time I saw the two of you together; this would happen. You were made for each other."

"I think so, too," she admitted. "I can't imagine my life without him."

Matt's smile faded. "I've heard something else, too, Haley. That the two of you might be in danger."

Now Haley frowned. "Where did you hear that?"

He shrugged. "Hardy told me. Have the two of you thought about moving away and starting over somewhere else? Where you'll be safe?"

Beau and Matt were friends. Haley just hadn't realized Beau confided in him. "This is home . . . for both of us. Beau doesn't want to leave. Besides, there's a chance this whole problem will end very soon."

"What about the person who hired those men?" Matt asked, his gaze penetrating.

Haley was once more surprised by the depth of information Beau had shared with the other man. "The FSA has some leads on him. For now, they're sure he'll stay out of the picture. He's too much of a coward to come after Beau himself. He'd have to find somebody else like those men to hire, and the FSA is ready for something like that."

Matt's expression was unreadable. "Sometimes, a person gets desperate enough to do something he'd never do otherwise, Haley. It might be best if you and Hardy just left town and disappeared."

"We're not going to do that." Haley didn't understand his insistence that they leave. She decided to change the subject. "Can I get you something to drink? I keep my refrigerator stocked with cola since Beau likes it so much."

"No thanks." He stood up. "I'd better be going. I just wanted to stop in and say hi."

At first, Haley couldn't identify the expression on his face, but then she realized what it was. "Are you sad about something, Matt?"

He forced a smile. "No. I guess I'm just tired. Maybe I'm getting too old for this route. I think I should do something else for a while."

"You should be happy," she told him as she touched his arm. "You're too special not to be happy."

His eyes lingered on her face as he touched her cheek. "You're the one who's special, Haley. I wish . . ." He stepped away from her and shook his head. "I have to go. My truck is parked across four spaces, and any moment one of those deputies is liable to show up with a ticket pad."

Haley stared at the closed door after he'd left, and thought what a strange visit that had been. Matt seemed intent on convincing her that she and Beau should run, and then he'd started to say he wished something and stopped. Since she had known Matt for over six months and he'd never shown the slightest romantic interest in her, she knew he hadn't been about to say something untoward. No. Something was going on with him. She just couldn't figure out what it was.

She had just finished putting a load of towels away when her doorbell rang again. This time, a huge smile came to her face when she saw who it was.

"Aren't you supposed to be on duty?" she asked her uniform-clad fiancé.

He grinned as he backed her into the apartment. "I'm checking out a disturbance."

"And what would that be?"

Beau leaned down and softly kissed her lips. "I'm disturbed we can't make any definite wedding plans yet." His strong arms wrapped around her made her feel safe.

"I see." She loved it when he held her like this. She felt safe and loved . . . cherished. "Maybe after Monday, we'll be able to."

She could feel his sigh through his shirt. "I'm praying for that, Haley."

He seemed reluctant when he finally released her and stepped back. "I don't like working on Saturday when you're free. We could be doing something fun together."

"But then I wouldn't be able to wrestle my vacuum around and dig a sock out of the dryer vent," she teased.

He shook his head and chuckled. "The first thing I'm buying after we're married is a new vacuum. That thing you have is an antique that would probably suck up small animals if they were close enough."

"Did you drive by the Pickler house?" She hoped he had.

"I like the looks of the place." He smiled warmly at her. "And if Luke wants to lease the farmland, we can keep the goats and chickens if you want."

"Really?" Haley bounced on her toes. "I'm sorry Mrs. Pickler has decided to move to the nursing home, but I really would like to live out there. We'd only be a few miles from Luke and Holly."

His eyes sparkled with laughter as he frowned. "But you have to promise not to walk in the woods without me. At least not until you've passed a test on identifying the leaves of poison ivy, oak, and sumac."

She raised two fingers. "I promise. You have to promise me you'll teach me to take care of the goats and chickens. And I want a garden, Beau. A real one like Holly's. Mrs. Pickler has always had the best garden."

He pulled her back into his arms. "You can have whatever you want. As long as the house is structurally sound and you like it, we'll buy the place."

Haley snuggled against his chest again. "Thank you."

"Haley?" Beau sounded uncertain.

She drew back and looked into his face.

"Is this romantic?" he asked.

"Anytime I'm in your arms, it's romantic." She answered him, confused by the question.

"Good." Haley felt him take her hand in his and slide something on her finger. Tears of joy came to her eyes when she raised her left hand to see the diamond engagement ring resting there.

"I just wanted to make sure everybody in town knows you're taken." He kissed her, the most tender kiss she'd ever experienced.

"I love the ring," she told him, "but I'm pretty sure everybody in town already knows I'm taken."

"Just in case." He hugged her tightly.

"I'm sure all my friends know." Then she remembered her visitor. "Beau, do you know if something's bothering Matt?"

He drew back and looked quizzically at her. "No. I haven't seen Matt in a couple of weeks. Why do you ask?"

"He was here a while ago. He acted . . . different." That was the best way she could think to describe it. "He was worried about whoever hired those men and the whole situation. He insists we would be better off leaving town and disappearing. Then he seemed sad. He just wasn't himself."

Beau backed up, his hands on her shoulders. "Wait a minute. What do you mean, he was upset about those men and whoever hired them? How does he even know about them?"

She frowned at him. "Didn't you tell him? He said you did."

"Haley, I told you I haven't seen him for at least two weeks." Beau shook his head. "And even though I consider Matt a friend, I wouldn't have told him about those things. He has to have gotten his information from somebody else."

Haley was puzzled. "But who? I can't believe Mitch told him." Then she had a thought. "Do you think Crystal has overheard enough at the station to pass it on to Matt? I don't want to think bad things about her, but she's done it before."

"I don't see how." Beau's frown deepened. "Mitch and I have been very careful to keep her out of the loop. He saw her coming out of Biggs Bar and Grill on Karl King's arm just the other night, and we definitely don't need any of this information in the newspaper."

"Karl King is married!" Haley firmly pushed her engagement ring on her finger. "Please tell me he wouldn't sink low enough to have an affair to get news."

Beau placed his hand under her chin and tilted her face up so she was looking into his eyes. "I know you want to see the good in people, and that's one of the things I love about you. But sometimes, we have to open our eyes to see what's really there. I'm going to have to tell Mitch about what Matt knows. If he decides Crystal has anything to do with it, I imagine he'll fire her."

"But Matt's not having an affair with her." Haley was horrified by the idea. "He wouldn't do that."

"I'm not saying he is," Beau said calmly. "But that doesn't mean she wouldn't tell him things."

"I know." She was saddened by the thought.

"Don't worry, Haley," he implored her. "How about if we ask Pastor Rollins to have lunch with us after church tomorrow?"

When Beau made his peace with God, he'd jumped back into his faith with both feet. Not only was he in church with Haley every Sunday, but he also attended the adult Sunday school class. Since Pastor Rollins taught it, the two of them had become good friends.

"I'd really like that."

Haley silently thanked God for answering another prayer. The man she loved and intended to spend the rest of her life with felt the same way about God as she did. And their marriage would include God as well.

Beau looked at his watch and grimaced. "I better get back to the car. I'm liable to end up back over at Hubert Belton's again. He told me he might need to rinse off better when I left him a while ago."

"Isn't it too nippy for outdoor sponge baths?" Haley smiled at the image of Beau instructing the old man to go inside or put some clothes on.

"You'd think so." Beau sighed. "He just said his skin dries quicker in the cold air. I wish Betty Livingston would decide it's too cold to go outside and peek around the bushes. That's the only way she sees him."

"I think I'm glad I'm just the dispatcher." Haley didn't think she'd like to deal with either Mrs. Livingston or Mr. Belton very much.

"I'm glad you are, too." He leaned down and gently kissed her. "I have to go. I'll see you around six. You're still fixing fried chicken, aren't you?"

They had both been pleased to discover she liked to cook for him. And Beau was enjoying the home cooking so much it had become nearly a daily ritual, interrupted only when their work schedules precluded it, or he simply wanted to take her out. Married life was going to suit them very well.

"I'll have it ready," she promised him.

"Okay." He gave her another quick kiss. "I love you."

"I love you, too."

Her apartment immediately felt empty after he left. How quickly Beau Davis had filled her life! And soon—hopefully very soon, he would fill it even more. Haley had much to be thankful for.

Chapter 53

Walking into the station on Monday morning, Hardy realized how easily he'd fit in at the Shadow County Sheriff's office. And even though he was the new guy, Mitch hadn't given him a lousy schedule. Of course, it helped that Hank and Wayne took turns working evenings with Jeff Fielding; and Tom Winkler and Jerry Young were night owls. Mitch had been able to let Hardy work days.

Hardy still laughed about the odd-duck pairing of "Tom and Jerry." He'd finally figured out they favored Jerry Lewis and Dean Martin and were almost as comical. Hardy liked them, even though he'd found it necessary to inform the unmarried Jerry, who hadn't lived in Shadow very long, that the "hot, blonde chief dispatcher" was very much spoken for. He'd gone out and bought Haley's ring not two hours after that conversation.

As if the thought of Haley had produced her, she walked into her dispatch area from the back of the building just as Hardy reached it.

"Good morning, beautiful." He wanted to pull her into his arms and kiss her, but he wouldn't disrespect her job.

She turned, her dimples firmly in place, and took a step toward him. "Good morning."

"Did you just get here?" She usually parked in back and came in that way.

"Good morning, Ray. How are you this morning? Did you have a nice night?" Ray Fine's dry voice captured both of their attention.

Haley's cheeks were pink when she spoke to the night dispatcher, who still sat at the computer. "I'm sorry, Ray. How was your night?"

Ray's eyes sparkled with laughter as they briefly met Hardy's before he answered. "Pretty routine. I had to send Tom and Jerry to the Thompsons."

Haley's smile broadened. "What happened?"

Ray grinned. "Reuben said Alice was trying to kill him."

"She poured his alcohol down the drain again?"

Hardy hadn't heard of this couple. "Domestic disputes over that?"

Ray pinched his lips closed as he seemed about to burst into laughter. He finally pulled his fingers away. "This time, instead of Alice dumping his bottle, she took a bath in it."

Haley's ponytail swung as she laughed.

Hardy was quickly becoming accustomed to small town life, but this was unbelievable. "She did not."

Ray shrugged. "Ask Jerry or Tom. She dumped two bottles of whiskey in the water like she would bubbles."

"It has to be true, Beau." Haley's smile tempted him to get a quick fix. Just one little kiss. "They do something this every so often." Her gaze slid to Ray. "How would that be killing Reuben?"

"When he called, he told me it was cruel and unusual punishment to be thirsting for a drink while his wife was—and these are his words—prancing around, smelling like a brewery."

"Hardy finally chuckled. "And, here I thought outdoor baths were funny."

"Good morning, Haley, Ray." Mitch's deep voice interrupted them. "Hardy, you have a minute?"

"Sure." Hardy winked at Haley before following Mitch into his office.

"Please close the door," Mitch instructed him.

Hardy hoped nothing was wrong. So far, evidence the state crime lab was turning up supported their theory about the four dead men and the Janitor, who it turned out, bore a striking resemblance to the sketch they had. They'd even identified the fourth man as Joe Brockman, a local man with a slightly tamer record than Callen's. Nobody could explain it, but both Callen's' and Brockman's prints had magically appeared in CODIS after weeks of not showing up in the system.

"I'm going to fire Crystal Stanley." Mitch was blunt.

Hardy wasn't surprised. After his unsettling conversation with Haley, he'd called the sheriff and shared his concerns. The information Matt Ashford knew wouldn't just provide sensational news; it would endanger him, and consequently Haley. "Are you sure she's the one talking, then?"

Mitch shook his head. "I don't care. I've let her get away with too many things, and now since I know she's seeing Karl King, I have no faith in her at all. I had a conference call with the majority of the county board members bright and early this morning, and they agree with me. We just can't have a person we don't trust working here."

"So, I assume the other three dispatchers will have to take up the slack until you replace her." Hardy knew he was selfish, but he didn't want Haley tied up more than she already was.

"I'll hire a replacement right away. One applicant has dispatched for nine years and has moved here to take care of her father. She has a great record in Philly," Mitch replied. "I hope you and Holly won't need time off for a honeymoon in the near future, though, because she's going to have to train whoever I hire."

"I'd like to be able to publicly give her my real name." With those words, the apprehension he'd been fighting since he awakened came back in full force. "Elliott will call me as soon as Audrey comes in." The sheriff knew about Audrey Dohner's planned defection. "Then it will take a few days for the agents to get their ducks in a row so they can arrest Dohner."

"Do you believe when it comes right down to it, Audrey Dohner will actually turn on her uncle?" Mitch asked. "I've seen pictures of you two together. You were pretty close to her, weren't you?"

Hardy didn't like what the sheriff was implying. "Not like you're suggesting." He tried to hold onto his temper. "I've already explained it to Haley, and she understands. That's going to have to satisfy you."

The other man gave him a measuring look. "I won't pretend to know what your life was like back then, so I can't judge you."

Hardy's ringing cell phone kept him from replying. He stood up and answered his phone, his heart in his throat. It was too early for Elliott to be calling.

"Beau." It was his sister.

"Is Dad okay?" He couldn't imagine what else would prompt a seven-fifteen a.m. call, even though she hadn't used the emergency signal.

"He is now, but I have to tell you something." There was urgency in her voice. "Dad gave me a message for you, and he wants you to know right away."

That surprised him. "What did he say?"

"He got upset right after his friend left, and started saying Tell Beau cheese is water and Carries is water. I honestly thought that's what he said, Beau. I was afraid Dad was having another stroke or something."

"You didn't call to tell me that." At least she better not have.

"Of course not." She was offended by the suggestion. "Mom came back from breakfast when Dad was really starting to get upset. She understood what he was saying. He was saying, 'Tell Beau, she's his daughter.' Do you know what that means, Beau?" Trepidation was in her voice. "You don't have a child, do you?"

"That would be impossible." Seeing as how he'd never partaken of the activity that produced children.

Callie sounded relieved. "Mom and I didn't think so. So, do you know who he's talking about? Who 'she' is, or whose daughter she is?"

Probably because he was waiting for Audrey to turn herself in, hers was the first name to pop into his mind. But that didn't make any sense. "Tell Beau she's his daughter. What did Mom think the rest of what Dad said meant? Carries is water."

"She said he's still saying his daughter, but we can't make heads nor tails out of the rest." She seemed deeply regretful. "I asked Mom if Dad was upset because he'd found out you had a daughter. I'm sorry, Beau."

Hardy fought back the frustration brought on by her words. After all, the lifestyle his family must have assumed he lived while undercover would lend credence to the possibility of him fathering a child. He'd never explained the exact nature of his relationship with Audrey to any of them—not even Elliott. They would have seen pictures of the two of them together and assumed the worst. What had he expected? "I understand." He couldn't help but think of how his sister and mother's misassumption would hurt Haley if she knew. "If Dad says anything else or you figure out what he's saying, please call me again. I don't want to tie up my phone too long now in case Elliott tries to call." Maybe Audrey would show up early just to get it over with.

"Okay. I'll talk to you later." The line went silent for a moment before his sister's soft voice came back. "I hope that woman shows up at the office right away, Beau. I really do."

"Thank you, Callie. So do I."

They said their goodbyes and hung up.

"I didn't mean to eavesdrop, but I couldn't help but overhear part of what you were saying," Mitch hesitantly offered. "I think I might know what your dad is saying."

The sheriff had Hardy's undivided attention. "What?"

Mitch appeared uncomfortable. "It sounded to me like he's saying 'Tell Beau she's his daughter. Carrie's his daughter.'" He leaned forward in his chair. "Do you know anybody by that name?"

Carrie—no, Kari's his daughter. He will hurt you. She's his daughter. Be careful. Kari's father wanted revenge. It made perfect sense . . . except Hardy had no idea who the "his" H.B. was referring to. "You're right. He's probably referring to Kari Jeffries, the . . . young lady in the . . ." He couldn't finish. "But as far as I know, she lived with her mom. Her dad wasn't in the picture. He wasn't even mentioned in her obituary." It made him feel even more guilty to know a mother had lost her only child and didn't have a husband to comfort her. "I need to call my sister back, Mitch."

The sheriff nodded and stood up. "I'll just go out here and speak to Haley. She needs to know about Crystal, and since it was my decision I'd like to be the one to tell her."

Hardy barely heard him, already intent on dialing his sister's number. The rest of her words had sunk in. One of his dad's friends had just left when H.B. became agitated and told Callie to tell Beau about Kari. And his mom had chalked his father's last bad spell following the visit of his friends to a flashback. But what if it were something else?

His heart sped up as he waited for his sister to answer. Could it possibly be that one of his dad's friends was Kari Jeffries' father? And what if H.B. had somehow found out? Hardy wasn't a doctor. Nonetheless, he couldn't help but wonder if discovering that might have brought on the stroke in the first place. And the attempt on his dad's life could have been to silence him. Things were starting to make sense.

"Hello?" Callie answered.

"Callie, I just need to know one thing." His mind was racing. "Which one of Dad's friends visited him this morning? It's important that I know."

"I'm not sure." His sister sounded confused. "It was one of those guys he spends time with, but I don't know which one." Her voice cleared. "But it wasn't Dr. Tarp! I know him."

"Can you ask Dad?" At that moment, Hardy couldn't even remember the other two men's names.

"No. The doctor gave him something to help him sleep," Callie replied. "He was afraid Dad might have another stroke because he was so agitated."

"Then, please ask Mom."

He could hear Callie speak to their mother before she came back on the line. "She didn't see who was here, but she said if it wasn't John, it either had to be Rob Weston or Phil Welsh. Why, Hardy?"

"It may be nothing." Hardy didn't have time to explain. "I'll call you back pretty soon."

"Is something wrong?" Mitch stood inside the door, concern on his face.

Hardy needed another opinion on his theory. Maybe he wanted to find an answer too badly.

"My dad has become very upset two times, both following the visit of at least one of the men he fishes and golfs with. Today, he told Callie about Kari Jeffries's father right after one of his friends left. I believe that man is the one Dad's talking about."

Mitch appeared interested. "Is his name Jeffries?"

Hardy shook his head. "But there could be lots of reasons for her having a different last name."

"So, who is your dad's friend?"

"There are three of them, but Callie only knows one—John Tarp. She said he wasn't the one visiting my dad. That leaves two possibilities: Rob Weston and Phil Welsh. I've only just met Weston once, and I don't really know Welsh very well." Hardy searched his mind, trying to remember his impression of the men. "Can I stay at the station for a while, Mitch? I'd like to use a computer to do some research on these guys."

Mitch's gaze remained level. "If you find Kari Jeffries' father, you most likely will have found the person responsible for all that's gone on in Shadow. You realize that, don't you?"

He did, but hadn't really processed it yet. "I just hope I'm not going on a wild goose chase."

"I don't think you are," Mitch said assuredly. "Go on out to the dispatch station, and give Haley one of the names. Tell her what you need. Then you can come back in here and use my computer to research the other one. You'll find what you need in half the time that way."

It felt good to know his boss believed in him. "Thank you."

It took Hardy a few minutes to explain the situation to Haley. Like him, she didn't remember the men very well. Only that his mom had disagreed with them. It encouraged him to hear his mother had referred to them as not being able to settle down with one woman. It was much easier to imagine one of them fathering a child without taking responsibility. In fact, Haley had given him another idea.

"I'm going to ask my mom." Why hadn't he thought of it before? She would be able to tell him which one of the two would have more likely fathered Kari.

Haley's eyes lit up. "That's a good idea. I'll go ahead and get started on Rob Weston, though." She made good on her word and sat down at the computer and started typing.

His mom answered on the second ring.

"Oh, Beau, I'm so sorry for thinking even for one moment you could have fathered a child," was the first thing his mother said.

"Mom, it's okay." He didn't have time for this. "I just need to ask you a question."

Sharon sounded puzzled. "Okay."

"Which one of Dad's friends would be more likely to father a child and not give her his name?"

"I don't understand."

Hardy drew a deep breath and counted to ten. "I think one of Dad's friends is Kari Jeffries's dad, and he's out for revenge. That's what Dad's been trying to tell me. And I think it's whoever visited him this morning. Now, which one do you think it would most likely be?"

He was met with a couple of minutes of silence before he heard his mother's fear-filled voice. "But that means one of your father's friends is responsible for those men down there robbing and killing and—"

"I know, Mom." Hardy saw the sympathetic look Haley threw over her shoulder and immediately calmed. "Please tell me who you think it is. Rob Weston or Phil Welsh?"

"Well, I've never allowed myself to think of such a thing happening." It sounded like Sharon was starting to cry. "But the way they've both always been with women, I can see either one of them fathering a child."

"Would one of them be more likely to want revenge for his daughter's death? Even though he never gave her his name?"

"Oh, Beau, I just don't...I don't like their lifestyles, but these are your father's friends." Her voice became steadier. "Your dad is stirring. I'll see if I can rouse him enough to find out who he's talking about."

"Please do." Hardy's heart was pounding so hard Haley must be able to hear it. He felt like he was on the edge of something crucial.

"She's asking Dad," he told Haley as he listened to his mom speak to her husband. "I hope he can wake up enough to answer her."

Haley immediately stood up and placed her arms around his waist, laying her head against his chest. "Your dad will answer her. I just know he will."

Forget proper office decorum. His free arm went around her and pulled her snugly against him. "I'm so glad I have you."

She pulled back from him far enough to look in his eyes. "I love you."

"I love you, too." What would his life be like had God not brought this woman to h

"Beau?" His mom was back.

"Yes."

"He's talking about Rob Weston. Rob Weston is Kari Jeffries's father." A sob broke through. "Rob was here this morning, Beau. The man who tried to have H.B. killed was right here in this room this morning."

"Mom, call the city police. Elliott and Stephens are both tied up with the Audrey Dohner case so they won't be able to help. But you know Dad's co-workers will take care of you."

A muffled noise made him realize how tightly he had pulled Haley to his chest. He relaxed his hold to let her step back.

"I'll call as soon as we hang up," Sharon promised him. "You have enough to worry about today without your father and me being among them."

"Is Callie still there?"

"No. She went home about twenty minutes ago."

"After you call the police, please call her and tell her to stay home. She and the kids will be safest there. I'm going to make some calls, and we're going to catch him, Mom. I promise." Since Hardy could put a face and name to the man who'd been doing his best to make Hardy's life miserable, he felt better equipped to fight. "Now, go ahead and call. I love you."

"I love you, too, Beau."

He shoved the phone in his pocket and looked at his curious fiancée. "It's Rob Weston, Haley. He is Kari Jeffries' father, and he's been doing all this to get even with me."

"Get even for what?" She was incredulous. "You got shot trying to protect that girl!"

"I guess he doesn't see it that way." He reached over and gently touched her cheek. "He sees it the way I did before you came into my life."

"Well, he's wrong," she declared. "And I'd just like to sit him down and tell him."

Hardy chuckled, in spite of what he'd found out. "Somehow, I don't think a lecture from a beautiful woman will do much for rehabilitating the man, sweetheart."

"Maybe not." She crossed her arms. "But praying will."

He nodded. "Prayer always helps." He brought his mind back to what he'd learned. "I need to talk to Mitch. We need to have the state put out a BOLO for Rob Weston. I want this guy in jail before he hurts anybody else."

"I'll call state dispatch right now. It'll be on the radio before you even finish telling Mitch about it."

He left her on the phone, telling the state dispatcher what was needed. Rob Weston didn't know it yet, but he was finished with his scheme of supposed vengeance. For Hardy had one paramount factor on his side. God was with him.

Chapter 54

Thank you, Hank." Haley spoke to the young deputy who had followed her home and walked her to the door of her apartment. He even waited while she opened the brand new solid steel door and left her standing just outside as he walked through to make sure there weren't any uninvited guests.

"Remember, you promised you'd stay here," Hank sternly reminded her. "Hardy will have my head on a platter if anything happens to you."

"I won't leave," she promised. "Now, you'd better get back out there and help look for that man. The sooner he's off the street, the sooner our lives can return to normal."

He gestured for her to go inside, and she knew he was still right outside the door when she fastened the deadbolt and chain locks. As the doorknob twisted and she realized Hank was testing it, she said a silent thank you to the Lord for the friends he'd brought into her life. If she hadn't insisted Hank was needed in the massive state-wide hunt going on, Mitch would have assigned him as her personal bodyguard. It was only after Haley assured him and Beau she would remain safely locked in her apartment all evening they had relented.

"It's been a long day, Harriett." It looked like the angelfish could care less, but Haley wanted to talk. "Beau is still waiting to hear from Elliott or Rich Stephens. I don't know why that woman is taking so long to do this. All she has to do is walk into the office. They'll take care of her just like they have other people. Beau says they're even letting her boyfriend go into witness protection with her." Maybe Ozzie would pay more attention. "And it's not even like she'll have to be in it for that long. It won't take more than a couple of years for everything to be over. What's two years in the grand scheme of things, Ozzie?"

Since it didn't look like either fish was interested in her, Haley decided to feed them and leave them alone. It wasn't until she picked up the empty container she remembered the new can she'd left in her car.

"Now what are we going to do?" The fish hadn't been fed since yesterday morning. She didn't know how long a fish could go between feedings, but she didn't want her kissing fish to go the way of the septic system.

"I'll be right back." She turned and walked to her front door. If Beau or Mitch ever found out what she was about to do, they would put her through the grinder. But she would be careful, and she'd only be outside for a couple of minutes—just long enough to run to her car and get the fish food out of the front seat.

The only thing visible through the peephole was a distorted image of an empty sidewalk and her car parked in its space. Since she lived on the end of the building, Haley only had one next door neighbor, and he worked second shift at the tool factory. So there wouldn't be anybody close enough to bother her.

Even though she'd told herself it was perfectly safe, she was so flustered that she dropped the fish food on the ground. Then she had surely set a speed record for herself when she hunkered down and grabbed the small gold can before it rolled completely under the car. Her heart was pounding in her ears when she shut the door and locked it a few minutes later. It was okay, though. Mrs. Vickers, who lived three apartments down, had been carrying her groceries in, but Haley hadn't seen anybody else.

"I guess I'm not as courageous as I thought," Haley told the fish as she fed them. "Don't look at me like that, Ozzie. You just try running outside like I did. It's not as easy as you think."

It had been a long day, and she needed a shower. Since Mitch was keeping his men on the roads looking for Rob Weston, she didn't expect to see Beau this evening. She decided to have dinner and make an early night of it. A good night's sleep would be wonderful.

Haley felt very relaxed when she got out of the shower and dressed in her comfortable pajamas. She looked skeptically at her nightwear. Once she and Beau were married, she'd need to start wearing something more feminine than cotton pants and T-shirts. And the bunny slippers would definitely have to go. She could only imagine what he'd say about the large ears sticking straight up from her feet.

After realizing if she went to bed this early she was liable to wake up in the middle of the night, she decided to watch television. After lying down and making herself comfortable, she picked up the remote control and turned the TV on.

Something was wrong with her set, though. It appeared she had left the DVD player on. Now she'd have to wait for the disk to load before she could push stop and eject it. Otherwise, her ancient player would freeze up.

Only instead of the menu appearing, the movie itself began playing.

It was a little grainy, and it took a couple of minutes for Haley to realize what she was looking at. She swung her feet around and sat up.

It was a split screen with two opposing angles of the interior of some kind of store. Since gas pumps were visible through the window behind the young woman at the counter, Haley surmised it was a convenience store.

Suddenly the shape of a man's head went across the edge of the picture, so quickly it was impossible to tell anything about it. A second man—one she easily recognized—walked up to the counter and set a small jar of coffee on it. Then her heart began to pound harder when a third man appeared, this one brandishing a pistol.

Everything happened so fast. Beau somehow scrambled around behind the counter, and the young woman had disappeared behind it as well. Then, suddenly, there Beau stood, seemingly vulnerable to the man with the gun.

The scary man was yelling something at Beau, and it appeared Beau calmly answered him. Then, both of their attention seemed focused on the back of the store for just an instant before the criminal began yelling again.

Beau was speaking, but he was clearly talking to the woman on the floor beside him. Haley's heart stuttered when the woman suddenly stood up. She just stood up. Beau spoke to the man again, and the crying woman said something, too. More words were exchanged between the two men. Then it happened.

Tears came to Haley's eyes as she saw her fiancé be shot. Even wounded, Beau managed to pull the trigger, and the other man dropped to his knees. The criminal managed to fire one more time before he fell prone on the floor. This one hit the woman's head, and she dropped down behind the counter. The screen went black.

How had this movie been on her TV? Had Beau somehow left it so she would see what happened to Kari Jeffries? As soon as the thought occurred to her, she knew he wouldn't have. Beau would never want Haley to see such violence.

"I'm sorry I didn't fix popcorn." Haley nearly jumped out of her skin as she whirled to see who was speaking. "I don't know where you keep it."

"What?" Haley had to be having an award-winning hallucination. That was the only explanation for how Wyatt Millan was standing in her living room, a nasty looking gun aimed at her. "You're dead."

"No, I'm not, you silly girl." Wyatt grinned cheerfully for a moment before sadness washed over his face. "Harding Davis killed my brother. He didn't kill me."

Haley started to stand up but halted when he gestured with his free hand that she was expected to remain seated. "I don't understand any of this." She fought back rising panic and took a deep breath. "Why are you here? Why did you want me to see that movie? And what are you saying about a brother?"

Wyatt responded by covering his ears with both hands, the pistol awkwardly clutched in one. "Don't ask me that many questions. I can only hear one at a time."

For just a second, Haley considered trying to make a run for it. But he would be able to aim the gun and shoot at her in seconds. She'd just try to deal with the strange man. "Okay." Why are you here?"

His answer was quick. "Father told me you don't understand about my sister. If you understand, maybe he'll let me keep you." A look of satisfaction appeared on his face. "You saw it, so now you know."

Father? His sister? What was he talking about? "What do I know?"

He suddenly pointed at her feet and giggled like a little boy. "Your feet look funny in those shoes." Then just as suddenly, his frown returned. "Harding Davis told my sister to stand up. He got her shot." His eyes pled. "You have to know, or I can't keep you."

Wyatt's mannerisms and speech finally sank in. Haley realized she was dealing with a deeply disturbed individual. She kept her voice calm and firm.

"You need to leave now, Wyatt." She felt a little encouraged when he broke eye contact for a minute, but when he looked back up, there was a new look of determination on his face.

"I'm keeping you." He pulled something out of his jacket's pocket. "I won't mind Father this time. You're smart. You'll learn about Harding Davis." He was impossible to deal with.

"Just leave, Wyatt. Right now."

But Wyatt wasn't listening. Instead, he walked toward her, and she now saw he held a syringe. "I'm keeping you. You can come with Father and me."

Gun or no gun, Haley wasn't going to sit there and let him inject who knew what. She jumped to her feet and smacked his arm as hard as she could. When the gun fell to the floor, she thought she had a chance. He had too tight of a hold, though. Even as she scratched and clawed at his hands and anywhere else she could reach, she knew he was too strong.

"I'm a doctor like the ones on TV." He wasn't even breathing hard, and before she could take a breath, a sharp needle entered her arm.

Even knowing nobody could hear her, she screamed. "No!" She felt herself weakening and knew she was in trouble. "No." Once more, she tried to convince him to stop. "Please, Wyatt. You can . . ." What could he do? Her head was spinning, and his arms felt too tight wrapped around her. 'N--" As her world disappeared, she wondered if this was what death felt like.

Chapter 55

Hardy had never felt such conflicting emotions in his life. He had just gotten off the phone with Elliott, and Audrey Dohner had turned herself in. She and her boyfriend would both present evidence and testify against Ted Dohner, with a small concession. Somehow, she discovered Hardy was alive, and Audrey would not follow through with her promises until she met with him. He didn't know how Haley would handle that.

And there had been no sighting of Rob Weston. A car registered to him was discovered in the parking lot of a large mall in a Chicago suburb, but a close investigation showed no sign of the man. If Mitch hadn't insisted Hardy take a few hours off to spend with Haley, he'd still be out on the streets looking for his dad's supposed friend.

Hank had radioed in from his car just two hours earlier that Haley was safe and sound at home, and had promised to stay there. He called the diner, where Nancy had been happy to fix up a nice take-home dinner for them. He didn't want to share his fiancée with the world tonight; he was determined to enjoy dinner with her before he had to get back on the road. It was going to be a long night.

Hardy moved the cardboard soda holder into his left hand, catching it with his fingers under the foam trays so he'd have a hand free to knock on the door.

His smile faded when he didn't hear her footsteps approaching the door from the other side. He knocked as hard as he could. Blood pounded in his head as he tried the doorknob, and he was literally blinded for a moment when it easily turned and the door swung open.

Instinct took over. Hardy dropped the food and pulled his pistol.

"Haley, answer me please!" he called out as he stepped into the room. He was met with dead silence.

A quick sweep of the apartment told him what he already knew. Haley wasn't there. His blood ran cold when he saw her purse on the floor by the fish tank. She often dropped it there while she talked to her fish.

He spun around, searching the living room for any signs of what had happened. His gaze froze on the television. There, on the screen, was an image he immediately recognized. It was the split-screen view of the convenience store. And it was paused on the still image of Kari Jeffries and himself just seconds before she was shot. A small piece of paper was stuck to the corner of the screen.

Hardy strode over and pulled the paper off. His blood ran cold as he read it.

You took something from me. If you don't come alone, I'm going to take Haley away from you.

An address Hardy didn't recognize was written on the bottom of the paper. What was he going to do? Of course, he would go. And he would go alone. But he hadn't been a cop for over ten years without learning a thing or two.

"Hardy?"

Hardy spun around, his pistol aimed, to see Matt standing just inside the door.

"He took Haley." Hardy let his hand drop to his side. "Rob Weston has Haley."

"No!" Matt's voice was full of agonizing disbelief. He evidently cared more about Haley than Hardy realized. "Where is she? We have to get her back."

Hardy knew he wasn't thinking straight. He should call Mitch and wait for backup. But this was Haley who was in danger. Maybe already . . . No. He wouldn't allow himself to go there.

"I have to go alone."

"Let me go with you." There was a tone in Matt's voice Hardy had never heard his friend use before. "I can help. I know what to do."

Hardy looked on in disbelief as Matt reached behind him and produced a pistol. "What are you doing?"

"I have to get Haley away from that man." Matt leveled his gaze at Hardy. "Now, you can either waste valuable time arresting me, or let me leave with you right now. What's it going to be?"

There wasn't time for Hardy to deal with legalities. "You'll call Mitch Landon while I drive us there." He was at least going to get reinforcements. Legal reinforcements.

"Okay."

Hardy led Matt out of the apartment, knowing fully well he was breaking the law by taking an armed citizen with him. But he didn't care. Haley was in danger, and he had to get to her fast.

Because Rob Weston wanted to hurt Hardy, and what better way to do so than to make him watch Haley be hurt or killed.

He could care less about the legalities; he'd gladly take any kind of repercussions as long as Haley was okay.

Father, protect Haley. It was all he was able to pray, but he knew, with God, all things were possible.

Chapter 56

Haley's eyes snapped open. Something smelled awful. Then she realized Wyatt was waving a small bottle under her nose. Whatever it was had at least revived her.

She tried to hide her alarm when she was unable to move. It was only when she started to speak she realized with horror she was gagged.

"I'm sorry." The disturbed man set the bottle of stinking ingredients, which smelled like a mix of vinegar and who knew what else, on the floor. She tried to pull her tightly bound hands away when he knelt and placed his over them. and "I just need you to listen to me. People don't listen to me very well if they can talk."

What was the matter with this man? Haley pulled at her wrists and ankles, but the man who somehow had to be Wyatt had bound them too tightly to the uncomfortable chair. And it was a good thing Haley hadn't eaten her dinner because if she were to throw up with this gag in her mouth, she could very well choke to death.

She had to remain calm. Panicking wouldn't do her any good. If she could figure out why Wyatt brought her . . . Where was she? She looked around the room, and her heart went to double-time as she recognized the location. Wyatt had brought her to the laundry on the south edge of town. It had gone out of business after only six months of operation simply because of its poor location. People chose to visit the facility closer to the mall.

Surrounded by three noisy factories, she doubted if more than a few people remembered it was here. Wyatt had chosen well; nobody would see or hear anything that happened.

If she hadn't already had her suspicions about Wyatt's sanity, the wire laundry cart with carefully folded shirts and towels in it would have shown her. It appeared the owners hadn't gotten around to having their appliances unhooked, so Wyatt had decided to multi-task. He'd just do his laundry while holding Haley hostage. The thought brought on a fit of hysterical laughter, which wasn't easy with a gag in her mouth.

Wyatt responded immediately, his brows furrowed with worry. "Are you laughing at me? Please don't laugh. I'm not like Jim. I sit quietly at church, and I mind my manners. I even use please and thank you. Did you hear me use them?"

His words coupled with a childlike look of earnestness only added to Haley's hysteria. She knew she should feel sorry for him, but it was difficult. He appeared to be an expert turkey trusser and didn't seem to have any intentions of letting her go.

It didn't help at all when he stomped his foot. "Stop that right now, or I'm going to tell! You'll be in just as much trouble as Harding Davis if I tell on you for laughing at me. And he's in a lot of trouble for telling my sister to die and killing my brother."

What had he said? A sister? Haley was finally able to get her laughter under control. "Please take this gag off." Of course, her spoken words sounded more like gargling than speech.

"So, I see you managed to get her here." Haley's eyes quickly swept left and focused on the man standing there. She had no trouble recognizing Rob Weston. None of this was making any sense, and she was tired of it.

Since she knew her words would be unintelligible, she contented herself with a hostile glare aimed directly at him. Logic was soon replaced by pure outrage when the older man laughed at her.

"You're both crazy!" She didn't care if they couldn't understand her words. She at least had the pleasure of saying them.

"My son told me you're a spitfire," Weston calmly observed.

"Jim called her a spitfire." Wyatt's slightly defiant voice reached her ears. "I said she's special, Father."

· Son. Father. Sister. Things started to click into place, but Haley still couldn't believe it was true. But from what Wyatt had said . . . "Beau tried to **help** Kari Jeffries!"

"I think your special girl has something to say." The cold gray eyes looked disinterestedly at her. "Why don't you take that gag off? It might be amusing to pass the time listening to her blather."

"I'll blather you!" She nearly bit Wyatt's hand as he pulled the now untied cloth out of her mouth. "You're a coward, Mr. Weston, hiring men to do all of those evil things. And somehow you've convinced this sick man your lies are true!" She turned her attention to Wyatt. "You have eyes, Wyatt. You can see for yourself in that film Beau tried to keep her hidden. I don't know why she stood up, but she did it despite Beau, not because of him!"

"It's okay." Wyatt crooned like he was speaking to a baby. "Father says after Davis is dead, I can keep you. You'll like living in the islands. And you'll get used to being with me. I'm a lot nicer than my brother."

"That's enough, Tim." Weston's voice sounded anything but paternal. "We still have to take care of Davis."

Haley was all too aware of what "taking care" of Beau would entail. "What do you hope to accomplish?" she demanded of Rob Weston. "None of this will get your daughter back!"

"But you can be my new sister," Wyatt announced as though he'd just given her the title of Miss America. "So Father will have a daughter again."

"Wyatt, listen to me." She ignored Weston. "You're sick. Let me help you."

The immediate rage on the disturbed man's face told Haley she had made a critical error. "I am not sick! Not anymore! Father let me quit taking my medicine when Jimmy died!"

"Okay. I'm sorry." Haley tried to soothe him.

"She's upsetting you, Tim." Rob Weston's fake consoling voice made Haley want to gag. "She won't make a good sister. Go ahead and put her in the special room."

"But, I wanted to watch— "

"You can join her later." The true feelings of the monster toward his son had shown up. Only, Wyatt would never realize a pack of gum probably meant more to Rob Weston than his son.

Haley had no idea what the special room was, but she was certain she didn't want to find out. "You don't have to do that, Wyatt."

"Good boys always mind their fathers," he blandly announced before walking over and grasping her shoulders from behind. "Always."

Despite Haley's protests and pleas, Wyatt somehow managed to scoot and tug her across the room, knocking her over several times along the way. She amped up her efforts when she saw the barely visible door in the darkness of the corner.

Haley felt like a ship that had been bandied about in a storm-ridden sea. "I don't need to go into the special room, Wyatt."

"Didn't you hear Father? I can come back with you to see the fireworks. You'll like it."

After some more awkward maneuvering and near topples, Haley found herself in some kind of utility room. She could barely see from the dim light cast through the door.

The lights came on, blinding her for a minute.

"I don't like the dark," Wyatt announced in his childish voice. "But when I come back, I promise to shut the lights off before the fireworks start."

"Wait." Her eyes traveled frantically around the room and froze in disbelief on an item sitting beside a large water heater. "Is that a bomb?"

Wyatt giggled. "That's the fireworks maker, silly."

Haley wasn't an expert, but she was pretty sure the "candles" she was looking at were sticks of dynamite. And what appeared to be a telephone cord was somehow fastened to them. The other end of the line was connected to an alarm clock. A Mickey Mouse alarm clock.

"I don't need fireworks. You can take them with you." She'd try anything at this point.

Wyatt's response was more laughter. "You have to be quiet now."

Once more, Haley struggled to the best of her abilities, but from his pocket he pulled a cloth and . . . Was that the Lone Ranger mask? As he manhandled her, getting the gag back in her mouth, she said a quick prayer of thanks for not getting another injection. It was probably good that he gagged her first. Otherwise, the bright yellow smiley faces over the eye holes of the mask would have set her off, and she wasn't sure it was a good idea to laugh at him again. That didn't stop her from fighting, though.

He none too gently got her in a headlock so he could put the mask on her. The last thing she saw before her world went dark was the maniacally gleeful eyes of the man in front of her. The sound of the door locking made her want to scream. Not to mention the mask was evidently a child's size and her head probably resembled the number eight.

"Where's Tonto when you need him?" Only her heart cried out for Beau.

Chapter 57

Hardy was still trying to process the information Mitch had been able to give him. As soon as Matt finished telling him about Haley, he'd handed the phone to Hardy. Then, Hardy listened to Mitch while driving. He hoped what he'd learned would save Haley. That's all he cared about at this point.

"Let me out here." Matt pointed to the gates of the tool factory. "I'll come on foot the rest of the way. Weston won't be expecting me, so he'll think you're alone."

Hardy was well aware he was the police officer and should be planning Haley's rescue. His emotions were too deeply involved this time, though, and Matt's idea made sense. He pulled over and waited until Matt was out of the car before driving away.

The address Weston led him to was that of an out-of-business laundry. There were no vehicles or people in sight when Hardy pulled into the parking lot. Since there was no way of knowing what the risk was to Haley, he decided to simply walk into the building.

I need some help here, Father. Lots of it. If it's my time to go, then take me. But please don't take Haley. She deserves to have a full life. Please show me how to save her. Please don't make me watch the woman you gave me to love die. Please.

Hardy took a deep breath and walked into the building.

"Give me your gun." After what Mitch had told him, Hardy wasn't at all surprised to see Wyatt Millan standing there.

It did disturb him to see the gun in his hand. Tim Miller was twelve eggs shy of a dozen, and there was one thing more dangerous than a man holding a gun. A man who didn't know how to use it holding one. He silently pulled the nine-millimeter out of his shoulder holster and leaned over to drop it on the floor.

"Put your hands up," Wyatt ordered him.

"That's not necessary, Timothy." The smooth voice drew Hardy's attention to the other side of the room. He recognized the man immediately.

"Where's Haley?" he asked Rob Weston. "I'm here, so you can let her go."

Wyatt shook the gun at him. "You can't have her. She's my new sister." Suddenly, his anger was replaced by childish joy, and he giggled like a child. "She's my new sister, and we're going to see the fireworks pretty soon. Wanna come?"

If it would get Beau to Hardy, he'd go see whatever the disturbed man wanted to show him.

"No." Rob Weston "Those are only for you and your new sister. Remember?"

A blank look slowly disappeared as Wyatt looked at his father. "Should I shoot him now?"

Again, if Hardy thought it would help Haley, he'd take a bullet. But Weston was making it pretty obvious that his son mattered very little, if at all. Hardy had too much experience with men like his dad's supposed friend; if the old man had his way, not a one of them would walk out the door alive. He would even sacrifice his son.

"He can— "

"Why are you doing this?" Hardy interrupted what was more than likely permission for Tim Miller to pull the trigger. Besides, Matt wasn't there yet; Hardy needed to stall. "You were my dad's friend." He ignored the younger man and spoke to Weston.

"You let my sister die, and you killed my brother." Although he sounded like an adolescent, it seemed Wyatt didn't want to be left out.

Hardy gave the disturbed man his attention. "I tried to stop your sister from dying, but it was too late before I even got there. She was already as good as dead."

Wyatt's jaw moved soundlessly up and down as he must have been weighing Hardy's truth against his father's lies. Hardy wasn't very surprised when Weston's influence won. "That doesn't make sense. I saw it. You were with her when she died."

"Why don't you tell your son the truth, Weston?" Hardy had to keep them talking. It was his only hope. He could only imagine what Wyatt's "fireworks" might be.

Rob Weston smirked as he sat on a chair. "You go ahead. It will be interesting to hear your version, and he won't understand it, anyway."

Wyatt—Timothy, listen to me." This was the way Hardy had approached the juveniles hoping to get in on the Dohner action. He had saved several boys and girls by talking them into walking away. He had to be calm and forceful. "Your sister stood up because she wanted to die. Your father helped her hire those men to shoot her. She *wanted* to die."

Wyatt wildly shook his head. "Father loved her. Like he loves me, and like he loved Jimmy."

"Do you know how insurance works, Wyatt?" Hardy calmly asked.

Weston's exaggerated eye roll told Hardy the older man thought he was wasting his time.

But Wyatt had heard him. "Insurance is when you pay some people to give you money. Jimmy and I used to get lots of money from insurance before we found Father."

"But you found me, and you didn't have to do that anymore. Remember?" Was Weston starting to worry?

Harding still had Wyatt's attention. "Your father paid money to a bunch of companies, for your sister. If she died, they would give him a lot of money. He found out she wanted to die. But if she did something to herself, the company wouldn't give your father any money. So he helped her hire two men to come into the store and shoot her."

"Forget about your sister." Weston saw the same thing Harding did. He was getting through to Wyatt/Tim. Weston snarled. "He killed Jimmy. You can go ahead and kill him now."

"Your father had Jim shot. Or he may have tried to kill your brother, himself." Hardy spoke quickly, seeing confusion come to Wyatt's face.

"I did no such thing." Weston actually sounded affronted. "It was another man who killed my team and James. Somebody else hired him; I didn't."

The con man had evidently forgotten his son was listening. "Another man . . ." Wyatt covered his ears with his hands and shook his head. "You can't say that! You said Davis did!"

"Shoot him!" Spittle sprayed from his father's mouth as he yelled.

"I think he'd be better off dropping that gun." Matt's calm voice came from directly behind Wyatt right before he stepped into the light. Hardy immediately saw that his friend was holding his pistol steadily aimed at Rob Weston. "I'm pretty sure you wouldn't bat an eyelash if I shot your boy, Weston, but I know you're mighty fond of yourself. Now, tell him to put the gun down."

Wyatt looked helplessly from Hardy to his father as he dangled the weapon in the air, precariously aimed at Hardy. "What do you want me to do, Father? I'll mind you. I'm a good boy."

For what seemed like forever, Hardy actually believed Weston was going to instruct his son to shoot him. But, instead, a grim smile came to the older man's face.

"Put the gun down, Tim." Something was wrong. Weston was too pleased by the situation. "We'll just all stay and see the fireworks with Miss Johnson."

Wyatt immediately dropped the gun and clapped his hands. "I like fireworks, Father!"

Hardy had his gun aimed directly at Weston's heart before Wyatt's had barely hit the floor.

"Where is Haley?" He had a feeling time was of the essence. "Tell me right now."

"Or you'll what?" Weston smiled smugly at him. "You're just like your old man, you know. Too good at your job for your own good. The minute my name and the insurance payouts hit the paper, you'd have figured it out. And if H.B. wasn't so good, he might not have noticed when I found your address on his computer."

"My father is a thousand times more of a man than you will ever be." Hardy wasn't going to quietly stand there and listen to the criminal put down H.B.

"He's a snoop." Weston's eyes went back and forth between Hardy and Matt, once again showing his lack of paternal feelings.

"You're a murderer." Hardy was about three seconds from handing his gun to Matt so he'd have both hands free to pulverize Rob Weston.

Apparently, Weston wasn't good at reading people. "H.B. wouldn't have learned about Kari and the insurance, or my plans, if he hadn't snooped in my desk." Hardy tightened his grip on the pistol.

Still, Weston smirked as he continued. "Did you know some prescribed drugs are known to cause strokes, Davis? In fact, my son over there was on pretty powerful medication with a common side effect of causing a stroke. Your father shouldn't have finished his coffee after he decided it tasted funny."

If he'd been angry before, Beau Davis was now full of rage. He took a step, intent on making the criminal pay for what he'd done to H.B.

"We have to find Haley." Haley's name and Matt's calm voice broke through the fog of fury threatening to engulf him. "She's what's important right now, Hardy."

Haley. His heartbeat slowed down, and he took a deep breath. Then he managed a small smile. "It's too bad my mom took out the man Sam Weiss hired for you."

It was evident Hardy had finally hit a nerve. "How do you know about Weiss?"

"He confessed." Hardy took a step closer to him. "He figured out you hired the Janitor, and he decided not to wait until you put him on the list for your next hit man."

"I did not hire the Janitor!"

"Where's Haley?" Hardy was finished with the chitchat. "Tell me right now."

"She's with the fireworks!" Wyatt seemed blissfully unaware that Matt stood beside him with a gun aimed directly at his head. "We'll all see the fireworks when Mickey is ten."

Hardy realized what Tim Miller was talking about at the same time Matt spoke. "There's a bomb with Haley. Wherever she is."

Suddenly, a loud and erratic thumping came from a dark corner of the room.

"Go check it out," Matt told Hardy. "These guys aren't going anywhere."

Hardy wasted no time in walking to the source of the noise. Barely visible was a locked door he assumed opened into a utility room, and someone was definitely causing a ruckus on the other side of it. With Weiss's surrender, all the people involved in this mess were accounted for. So, it could only be one person in that room.

It took every bit of his strength as he pulled at the door, but it finally flew open. Hardy was totally unprepared for what met him. A fireball of hitting, kicking, biting woman pounced on him.

"Tie me up with shoelaces, you . . . you . . .!" She yelled as she went after him. "You didn't even double knot them!"

"Haley!" Hardy wasn't defending himself because he didn't want to take the chance of hurting her, but she was going to do some real damage. "Haley, it's me! Stop!"

"Beau?" Her arms and legs went still, and Hardy barely had time to get his arms under her before she went down like a lead weight.

"She passed out." He held her tightly against his chest.

"Get her out of here," Matt instructed. "It's nearly ten o'clock, and if there's a bomb in here . . ."

Hardy didn't need to be told twice. He rushed out of the building with Haley safely in his arms. He had just reached the edge of the parking lot when what sounded like gunshots rang out. Then Matt appeared, running full speed toward them.

The explosion knocked Hardy off his feet. He was barely able to protect Haley's head when they fell. His ears were ringing so loudly he didn't even hear the sirens before he saw Mitch leaning over him.

Then it seemed like scenes from a movie he'd never want to see again. It ended with the ambulance pulling away to take Haley to the hospital. Neither he nor Matt had suffered more than scratches and bruises. Mitch told them to let Wayne drive them in to be checked, just in case, but Matt refused.

Since Hardy wanted to be where Haley was anyway, he followed Wayne. He heard Matt's words as he walked by him and the sheriff.

"I was distracted by the bomb, I guess. Wyatt got his gun and shot the old man. Then he shot himself before I could stop him. I had to get out of there before the bomb blew."

So, that's what he heard—a murder-suicide. Even with everything Tim Miller had done, Hardy felt sorry for him. If his father hadn't convinced him to go off his medication and hadn't blatantly used him, the mentally ill man might have stood a chance.

Hardy pushed it out of his mind for now. Right now his focus was on Haley. She was more important than anything else.

Chapter 58

The first thing Haley saw when she opened her eyes was Beau, his head resting on the hospital bed beside her stomach and his hand gripping hers. He was asleep.

"Beau?" She only knew she was in the hospital. What had happened?

"How are you feeling?" His voice was hoarse. "You've been asleep for hours. Dr. Potter said your body needed time to recover from the stress you were under, so he sedated you."

"I'm all right." She reached over and touched his cheek. "What about Weston? Is it over?"

Beau's eyes were troubled as he answered her. "Matt said Miller—Wyatt—somehow got the gun and shot his father, and then himself. They were both dead before the explosion."

Wyatt had probably snapped.

She smiled as her fingers brushed his jaw. "You need to shave."

"I know." His eyes met hers, and the small smile on his mouth faded. "I've never been so scared in my life, Haley. I mean when I didn't know where you were. I don't think I've ever prayed so hard before."

"You found me." She was amazed by the man she was going to marry. "I'm sorry I attacked you. I thought you were Wyatt coming back in."

"You and my mom." Beau smiled wryly. "You didn't even need a bedpan. You just used bunny slippers."

"Did I hurt you?" She tried to sit up so she could see more of him.

His hands firmly pushed her shoulders against the pillow. "Nothing a couple of Band-Aids and iodine didn't take care of." He frowned in puzzlement. "Did you say something about being tied up with shoelaces?"

Haley still couldn't believe it herself. "I practically bent in two, but I managed to get the stupid mask off. Thanks to Wyatt's fear of the dark, I could see that he used regular shoelaces to tie me up. And he tied them just like you'd tie a shoe. All I had to do was get my leg up high enough to catch the loop, and then my right hand was free to untie the rest."

Beau shook his head. "He had a problem, didn't he?"

"You think?" Haley knew she should, but she couldn't quite bring herself to feel sorry for him yet. "Beau, he had his laundry there. He was washing his clothes while he kept me there." Then she remembered more of the experience. "He spoke about having a brother and sister, Beau. I think Kari Jeffries was his sister."

"Are you up to hearing everything? Mitch has found out a lot." His eyes were full of concern. "And my dad was able to help, too."

No. She'd rather bury her head under the covers and try to pretend that none of this happened. But that was exactly why she needed to know. "Tell me."

"Wyatt Millan never existed. He was a character James and Timothy Miller took turns playing. From what I understand,

Tim was stuck at home most of the time. Even before he went off the medication, his problem was hard to hide."

She thought of what Melissa called his bipolar behavior; two Wyatt's made sense.

"They've been con artists since they were in their teens," continued Beau. "Somehow, James found out Rob Weston was their biological father. He and Tim planned to con him, too. Only Weston turned the tables on them."

"What do you mean?" Haley reached over and laced their fingers together.

His grip tightened reassuringly. "Weston presented them with a sister. The twins saw her from very different perspectives. To Tim, she was his little sister. He was supposed to be her big brother and take care of her. Jim saw her the same way their father did. As a moneymaker. Kari Jeffries had attempted suicide at least four times. Weston offered her the perfect solution. He helped her hire two men to kill her. It was guaranteed to be successful." Beau turned his head and kissed her fingers. He evidently needed physical contact with her as badly as she did.

"Weston had over a million dollars of insurance policies out on her. Jim and the other guys Weston hired thought they were going to get a share of them once he collected. But I messed everything up."

"I don't understand." Maybe she had hit her head too hard again. "I know your mom said he was aware that you were alive, but how did Weston know where you were?"

Beau smiled sadly. "At some point, my dad let something slip. Then I guess Weston waited until they had a get-together at my parents' house and somehow, he was able to get on Dad's computer and find my address. Dad's more tech savvy than you'd think, though. He knew right away somebody had been in the files, and it didn't take him long to suspect Weston." He couldn't quite hide the anger in his eyes. "Dad repaid the favor. Weston saw him digging in his files the night Dad had his stroke."

"But if your dad knew the kind of man Rob Weston really was, why did he stick around? If Weston caught him, I mean, why . . ."

"Dad didn't know Weston saw him." Anger flashed in his eyes. "Weston gave Dad coffee laced with medication that most likely caused his stroke. Weston wanted him out of the way."

"Why did he want you dead so badly? His daughter was gone, and he didn't have to worry about suicide nullifying the insurance. Not when everybody thought it was murder."

"Weston didn't stop to wonder if his daughter's suicide attempts were reported, and when most of the insurance companies wouldn't pay until it was proven to be a murder."

"How can a man use his children . . . So, he was afraid you'd see it?" She still wasn't getting a clear picture.

"It's no secret that I have a gift of excellent memory. Weston feared me seeing him named as Kari's father. I'm pretty sure I'd have figured out enough to turn him in. With the insurance companies already investigating, my reporting it would have been enough at least to tie the money up, or maybe completely void the policies. He needed to get rid of me once and for all."

Haley shuddered at the thought of losing the man she loved. She bit back a sob. "I love you so much, if . . . if . . ."

As though he'd read her mind, he leaned over and softly kissed her. "I'm right here, and I'm staying. God gave us this love, so he's for us. Isn't there something about if God is with us, we have nothing to fear?"

"You know there is." The past Sunday, the Delgado family set up their instruments and sang a song with a catchy chorus about God being with them so who should they fear. Beau hummed it off and on all day.

He winked right before he hummed a few bars of the song.

As he sat back up, a frightening idea struck her. "What about your mom? She's already up in arms about his gambling. She would have figured it out, too."

"I've been trying to figure that one out, myself. Maybe Weston didn't have the heart to have my mother hurt." He shook his head. "It's a mess, Haley."

"A convoluted mess," she agreed. "Has everything been explained? Because I feel like I'm listening to those two old comedians with that "Who's on first" routine."

"We know what happened." He leaned over and kissed her cheek.

"Please tell me."

Beau sat straight. "It might be the craziest scheme I've ever seen, but we have it straightened out." His chest rose as he took a deep breath. "Weston hooked up with a crooked cop named Sam Weiss. Weiss says he hired a couple of guys who regularly did his dirty work, but it looks like Vince Samuels was the Janitor."

That made no sense. "I thought he was supposed to be big, and that guy your mom fought off wasn't as tall as you."

"It's downright bizarre to discover he was the other man at the convenience store. Especially with Weiss's budget, that certainly doesn't seem like a job the Janitor would have taken."

"How did their prints leave the system?" She hadn't spoken with the state police lately, and they were running them through again and the last time she checked, still had no responses.

Beau shook his head as if to clear it. "We can thank our crooked cop for that. He somehow managed to get fingerprints out of CODIS temporarily and make Kari's records disappear. When he saw the bodies piling up, he figured Weston wasn't going to cut him in on the insurance any more than he planned to with the others."

"That man had no thoughts of anybody but himself."

"Weiss figured he'd probably end up as the fall guy if things went south. So, last night he turned himself in to try and make a deal. That's how we know everything." He reached with his free hand and swept hair off her forehead.

"These men gave money the top position in their lives, and would do whatever it took, even murder, to get it."

"Money bugs you?" He had a strange look on his face.

"I don't like the handling of it, but it's useful if stewardship is used." She knew lots of wealthy people who used money as a tool, not as the center of their lives. There was one last question to ask. "Who killed the Janitor?"

"I don't know." Beau didn't appear too happy about his answer. "There's still a chance Dohner was somehow involved, but unless our undercover guys find something out, we may never know."

"At least we only have Dohner to worry about now." Haley never thought she'd be thankful only one hoodlum was after Beau.

"I have more news, too, sweetheart."

Haley didn't like the troubled expression that had come to his eyes. "What? Does Ted Dohner know where you are?"

He caressed her cheek. "The undercover guys say he still doesn't know I'm alive for sure, but just in case he figures it out, one of them has a story ready for him. He'll be looking for me in Idaho."

Her heart resumed a normal rhythm. "Then what do you need to tell me?"

"First, remember you know the truth about my undercover life." His eyes searched hers.

"I remember." Why did she think she wasn't going to like his news? "Please, Beau, just tell me."

He took a deep breath. "Audrey Dohner showed up at the FSA office late yesterday afternoon. She brought a bunch of paperwork with her and has a lot more hidden in a safe place."

"But that's good news, isn't it?" Haley was confused.

His expression pled with her for understanding. "The thing is, she found out I'm alive. She won't give up any more information or testify until she sees me. I have to go talk to her, Haley."

"She loves you." Tears came to Haley's eyes. "Of course, she does. How could she have spent that much time with you and not fallen in love? And she thought you were dead. Now that she knows you're alive—" Her heart nearly stopped. "What if she won't go through with a deal unless you're back together with her?"

"Haley." His voice was tender as he reached up and wiped a tear from her face. "Audrey doesn't love me. She wouldn't even consider going into witness protection unless they promised her boyfriend could go with her. I don't know why she wants to see me, but it isn't to try and rekindle a relationship that never existed in the first place."

"How do you know she's not with her boyfriend as a second choice? She thought you were dead, and now she knows—"

Her words were interrupted by Beau's mouth pressed firmly against hers. Then he softened the kiss and made it so gentle it brought even more tears to her eyes.

"I love you." His words were certain when he finally pulled away from her. "I don't believe she sees me like that, but even if she does, there is no way I'll ever do anything to jeopardize what you and I have. I won't go if it's going to hurt you."

She shook her head. "You have to go. The FSA needs her too much." She took a deep breath and fought back the tears. "I love you, Beau, and I trust you. You go do whatever you need to do to make things safe for you."

Beau kissed her again before speaking in a husky voice. "I'd like to go in the morning and be done with it. Would it help if you went with me?"

It was tempting. Haley would see Beau with Audrey Dohner, and know once and for all. But she'd told him she trusted him. "You'll have to be careful the way it is. You don't need to worry about taking me with you."

His eyes searched hers. "Are you sure?"

Haley made up her mind. She either trusted him unconditionally or not at all. "Yes. You go do what you have to." She reached up and ran her finger across his lips. "Just promise to come back home to me."

A light shone deep in his eyes, and she knew he spoke the truth. "Nothing could keep me away from you. I promise."

She managed to sit up far enough for him to wrap his arms around her. Neither of them said a word; he just held her. And she knew everything was going to be okay.

Chapter 59

The years hadn't been kind to the woman sitting across the table from Hardy. Her once long, healthy, black hair looked dry and brittle. And eyes that once sparkled with victory at having fooled her uncle were now dull and lifeless. Audrey looked ten years older than the thirty-two Hardy knew her to be.

"I thought he killed you." Those were the first words she'd spoken since he walked into the room and sat down. "I thought Ted found out where you were and killed you."

"I'm sorry." Those two words had been a long time coming. "I'm sorry I had to lie to you all those years, and I'm sorry for using you like I did."

Her smile looked as though it might be painful. "We used each other, Joe. Remember?"

Hardy slowly nodded. "But you didn't know exactly to what extent I was using you. I could have been leaving you in a lot of danger when my cover was blown. Did your uncle think you knew I was a cop?"

She looked past him for a moment before focusing on his face. "What he did to me wasn't your fault. He knew I was keeping a secret from him, but he believed me that it wasn't your real identity. He's been trying for months to catch me with Cass. We haven't been able to spend more than a few minutes together. That's one of the reasons I'm ready to see my uncle go to jail."

"So, you're still with Cass." Hardy had assumed she and Cassidy Rhine were still together.

Her eyes wavered for a moment before fixing on his again. "We're married. Not even the FSA knows it, but we're married."

Audrey had just surprised Hardy. "You should tell Stephens. They'll be sure to give you an identity of a married couple."

"Okay." She frowned. "How about you? Have you found a woman who knows the real Joe Ryman? Or should I say, Harding Davis?"

Now he could tell her the truth. "I'm engaged to an amazing woman. She knows everything about me, and we're very much in love."

"Did our fake relationship cause any trouble?" she asked hesitantly. She produced a small smile. "You and I were masters at poses, weren't we?"

Hardy had forgotten how they'd back into corners, or turn his back to the room so nobody could see that his passionate kisses were them whispering to each other. "I still think I can name all the presidents."

"Silly word games saved us."

He nodded. "The best part it, I explained this—what we had to do."

"If you need me to talk to her—tell her what it was like, just say the word."

While he forever be grateful for her bringing her uncle down, he couldn't forget she wasn't a law abiding citizen. There were many times she shared with him what her uncle did—the kinds of crimes. She didn't even seem aware that she could and should do something to stop him then.

"I was scared." It was as though she'd read his mind. "I knew that stepping back and letting . . .atrocious actions occur without stopping them was wrong. But, I was afraid he'd hurt me like he did my…"

"It's okay." And finally Hardy realized the truth. "We were players in a game of lies and pretenses. I'm finished letting my doubts control me, and I hope you are, too."

"I'm trying." Her small smile looked more like a grimace. "I can start by telling your girlfriend everything we did and didn't do."

He was truly glad it seemed like Audrey was on a better path, but he didn't want Haley around any of this. Besides, he'd already told her the truth, all of it. "My word is enough. She trusts me."

"Good." Audrey suddenly seemed like a stranger. They had never truly known each other. Her voice was a monotone when she spoke again. "Go get your agent friends. I'm ready to tell them where the rest of my paperwork is hidden."

Hardy had to ask a question first. "Why did you want to see me, Audrey?"

She shrugged. "I've always wondered if somehow, my uncle found you and killed you. I guess I just needed to see you with my own eyes and know you're alive and well."

So, he wasn't the only person who'd been struggling with guilt. "Okay." He stood up. "Have a good life, Audrey."

"You too, Joe."

He turned and walked out of the room, the knowledge he would most likely never see the woman again giving him peace of mind. This was one chapter of his life he could close.

After telling Rich Stephens and Tom Fowler that Audrey was ready to talk to them, Hardy walked into Elliott's office.

"So, how'd the visit with your old flame go?" Elliott asked, his brow lifted.

Hardy gave his brother-in-law a level look. "First of all, she's not, and never was my flame. But she's talking to Stephens and Fowler right now." He sat on one of the chairs across the desk from Elliott. "So, tell me what you found out. What happened in that laundromat, and where is Matt?"

Elliott slid a folder across his desk. "You can see for yourself. It gives me a headache if you want to know the truth."

Hardy felt a profound sense of disbelief as he read the papers he pulled out.

Matthew Ashford had been born in Rochester, New York—in nineteen-two. The social security number he had given to Sky Trucking was bogus, as were his past residences and places of employment. The prints they had been able to obtain from his abandoned semi came up empty. Matthew Ashford didn't exist.

While it was still too soon for definitive findings, the coroner's initial report said both Timothy Miller and Robert Weston died from a single gunshot wound to the front of the head. Unless Tim Miller's arms were significantly longer than they had appeared, suicide was impossible.

"We have a BOLO out for Ashford," Elliott spoke quietly. "I'm sorry, Beau. I know he was your friend."

"Haley thought the world of him." Hardy tried to imagine how painful it would be for Haley if she discovered the man she thought of as an uncle was most likely an assassin.

"We're handling this all under the FSA umbrella. I give you my word if we find out what I'm thinking is the truth, it won't go public."

"I don't want to know anything else." Hardy breathed a sigh of relief. "I'd have to lie to Haley, and I just can't do that." He would tell her the basics and wouldn't lie if she questioned him. But, if he stayed out of this, there would be nothing else for him to tell her.

Hardy closed the file and pushed it away, along with the possible implications it provided.

"Do you have any idea how long it's going to take for Dohner and his gang to be out of business? How long will it take before I can be Beau Davis again?"

"In a hurry to give Haley your name?" Elliott asked.

Hardy remembered the joy Haley expressed about buying the surprisingly well maintained house. "Yes. We have a farmhouse picked out. She thinks we're going to have to go into debt to buy it, though."

"You haven't told her about your money?" The FSA agent's face was a mask of astonishment. "Don't you think that's something your fiancée should know?"

"It's not like I have as much as you do," Hardy felt the need to remind his brother-in-law. "It's just I made some good investments with what I had. We can live comfortably on our incomes. Or mine, if she decides she'd rather stay at home."

"I still think you'd better tell her right away." Elliott's expression was grave. "Callie would have killed me if she hadn't found out about my money until after we were married."

Hardy shrugged. "Haley isn't Callie." The image of her beautiful face filled his mind. "In fact, she isn't like anybody else, Elliott. She's the woman God put on this earth for me."

And he was going to thank his Lord for her every day for the rest of his life.

Chapter 60

The convoluted nightmare was over. Haley had told herself that every day for the past two months. And soon even the possibility of some of Dohner's people coming after Beau out of revenge would disappear. She had a lot to be thankful for.

Haley stood back and frowned at her reflection. Why she'd let Missy talk her into a purple dress was beyond her. It seemed like a good idea at the time, given that Mitch and Tessa's wedding was going to be in shades of lavender. But now she felt like a . . . Grape! Maybe she had something else suitable to wear.

She had taken a few steps toward her bedroom when her doorbell rang. Wonderful. Beau was right on time. Whether she liked it or not, her fiancé was going to see his future wife resembling a fruit.

"Be quiet, Ozzie. You're no beauty yourself," she instructed her fish. She walked over and opened the door. Her breath immediately caught in her throat.

"Wow." Her man cleaned up nice, but what a tux did for him went beyond words. "You look . . . Wow."

He smiled lovingly at her. "You look beautiful." His eyes swept her length. "Is that the dress you and Missy found?"

Haley rolled her eyes. "You don't have to be polite. I'd fit right in on a cornucopia."

Surprise shone on his face. "I'm not just being nice, Haley. You do not look like a grape. You are the most beautiful woman I've ever seen."

Impishness took hold of her as she grinned. "Good. I'll just have my wedding dress made with the same pattern."

"You can wear one of my shirts as far as I'm concerned." Her face grew warm at the image. "I don't care what you wear as long as you're ready to say 'I do' in four weeks."

"Four weeks?" Her heart soared. "Do you mean . . ."

"You are now engaged to Harding Beauregard Davis Junior." It gave him a deep sense of satisfaction to tell her that. "The Dohner organization is all but finished. The few members who didn't turn on Ted or get caught themselves, have fled the area. They're going to be too busy watching their own shadows to worry about Harding Davis."

She wrinkled her nose. "Does that mean you'll have to do a press conference, like Rich said you might? I'm still worried too many people will see you that way."

"I'm afraid so." His gaze held hers. "But it will be a blip on the radar because I'll be gone. Newshounds aren't going to care what a small-town deputy is doing, believe me."

Her frown grew. "A wealthy, small-town deputy." Haley shook her head. "I still can't believe you didn't tell me about that sooner, Beau."

He suddenly grew serious. "Does it change the way you feel about me?"

That got her dander up. "You know it doesn't. I'd love you if you were living out of a shoebox!"

Beau's smile returned. "Then, you can love me even though I'm not. We're not. Because what's mine is yours. Remember?"

"Are you sure the farm is a nice enough place to live? You can build a dream house or—"

"Haley." His lips silenced her. A few minutes later, his voice was unsteady when he spoke. "I like the farm very much, and any house you live in is a dream house. Okay?"

She had barely caught her breath. "Okay."

"Now, are you ready to go see our friends get married?" His smile warmed her heart.

"I'm ready to go anywhere with you, Beau." And she found she honestly was. God had given her a wonderful man, and she was very thankful for him.

"Let's go."

Epilogue

Three shots and it would be over. He carefully lined the sight of his rifle on the heavy-set man walking up the courthouse stairs. The other two targets were on either side of his primary one.

Shoot. Aim. Shoot again. Aim. Shoot again. All in rapid succession. Three men lay on the courthouse steps with pandemonium erupting around them. Each of them would be found to have died from a single shot to the head.

He broke his favorite two-twenty-three rifle apart and returned it to the duffel bag. Nobody paid the slightest bit of attention to the middle-aged, black-haired man leaving the three-story sports gym, dressed in his workout clothes and carrying a bag.

For the first time in his life, he felt a sense of satisfaction that had nothing to do with money. He'd already taken care of Robert Weston and the "gang" he put together, and now Ted Dohner and his two top henchmen were dead. The organization, already sinking due to the FSA and Chicago PD's efforts, would now go completely under. If another one arose to replace it, the people in it would have no interest in a former undercover policeman and the woman he loved. The woman both of them loved.

It was time for the Janitor to retire for good. He wished he could have spent more time with her. With his daughter. She would never know how much her parents loved her. That the mother who had given her those bright blue eyes and beautiful dimples died giving her life. Or that he had loved her enough to keep her away from his ungodly, unsavory existence — to give her to his sister and her husband to raise as their own. Haley would forever think she belonged to the Johnsons. He had hurt a lot of people with his sinful life, but his daughter would not be one of them.

He looked at his watch. He'd have to hurry if he were going to be on board the private jet leaving O'Hare. He would soon be headed for New York, where he would transfer flights. Bryan Grimes had a whole new life waiting for him overseas. And he was leaving his daughter happily and safely ensconced in hers. The Janitor was finished.

Beau and Haley Davis were sitting in the living room of their farmhouse watching the evening news when a special report came on. They were shocked to hear that Ted Dohner and two others believed to be his top men had been gunned down on the steps of the courthouse as they entered for the fifth day in appellate court.

In fact, they were so shocked neither of them paid any attention to the report of an airplane crash. A small private jet leaving O'Hare and bound for New York had crashed just outside the Chicago area. There were no survivors.

BONUS STORY

Read about Callie and Elliott's first meeting in this award-winning short story.

"Gotcha!"

by Georgia Florey-Evans

Elliott Lawrence shook his head in disbelief. The most beautiful woman to grace the earth was standing a few yards away from him . . . and he had to arrest her.

Maybe a seasoned FSA agent would take this in stride. As a rookie, he found it difficult to believe he was looking at "Sally." How could the fresh-faced woman with shades of brunette locks cascading over her shoulders and big brown eyes be a major drug trafficker?

That had to be her, though. "Kirby Tyson" was supposed to meet her on the veranda in precisely three minutes. Since the party was in full swing, and she was the only other person out there, he was certain she was Sally.

He softly closed the door and approached her.

"Do you have what I need?" It was a line he'd rehearsed repeatedly, to sound natural.

The woman swung around to face him, her eyes wide with disbelief. "What did you say?"

Elliott turned on his most charming smile. "Come on, honey. You know what I'm here for."

He barely saw her arm move before her hand connected soundly with the side of his face.

"Listen here, you Brad Pitt wannabe." Sally stood facing him, her eyes blazing with fury. "If you think that just because I'm standing out here by myself, I'm fair game, you'd better think again. You may bat those baby blues at other women and have your way, but it's not going to work this time."

"I'm here to meet you." He'd try again.

A very unladylike snort erupted from her lovely face. "Sure, you are! How many women have you used that pathetic pick-up line on?"

Something wasn't right. "That wasn't a p—"

"I wouldn't even be at this stupid party if my mom hadn't forced me to come!" Her voice rose as she spoke. "It's not that I don't think it's for a worthy charity; it's just that I hate getting dressed up and hobnobbing with idiots like you!"

Oh, no. "Sally?"

Her eyes widened. "How do you know my name?"

Elliott was growing more confused. "I'm Kirby Tyson. I'm supposed to meet you."

Sally's face was covered with dawning horror. "Oh, my gosh, you're one of those stalkers, aren't you? Did you see me in the parade last week and decide we were meant to be together? I saw that in a movie just the other day, and it didn't end so well for the woman."

"I'm not a st—"

"If you don't leave right now, I'm going to scream!" She took several steps backward.

Elliott glanced through the French doors, where it appeared that his companion's rantings were starting to draw attention.

"Listen, Sally, if you just give me what I need, I'll be on my way." His first undercover mission was not going as planned.

"My father is a cop, and he's right inside that door. If he comes out here, you'll be sorry."

It seemed that she wasn't finished threatening him. Wait a minute.

"Is that why you're not cooperating? Your dad will see?" His mind raced. "We can take a walk. Nobody will see us in the rose garden!"

If anything, her eyes widened. "You are . . . ,I can't believe you suggested that! Do I look like the kind of woman to take out into a flower garden and get busy with? I didn't want to do this, but you've left me no choice."

Elliott watched in disbelief as she kicked off her high-heeled shoes and assumed a classic martial arts pose. He supposed she looked about as ferocious as possible for a barefooted woman in a formal dress.

He bit back laughter. "Just show me what you have, and I'll give you the money. There's no need for this drama."

"Now you want to *pay* me?" Her left hand lowered a few inches before she resolutely brought it up and motioned in a "come and get it" signal.

"You've seen too many movies, honey." Elliott looked at the doors once more, and was horrified to discover they had acquired an audience. He couldn't make a drug bust now. He raised his hands in surrender. "Okay. I'll just leave."

As he turned away, Sally emitted a squealing sound and bounded over to stand in front of him once more.

"So you can go after another unsuspecting woman?" she demanded. "One who can't defend herself? I don't think so!"

"Look, Sally, I don't know what your problem is, but if you step aside I'll be on my way." And his associates would never let him forget this fiasco.

Before he could take a step, she attacked. Or he guessed that's what she was doing. She looked more like a tightrope walker trying to maintain her balance.

Hearing laughter from the onlookers and realizing his undercover mission had flopped, Elliott decided to salvage as much from the situation as he could. At least, maybe he'd be able to keep the persona of Kirby Tyson intact.

After effortlessly dodging several kicks and punches, he decided to take matters into his own hands and end this once and for all. Since Sally seemed incapable of logical thought processes, and he wasn't about to fight a woman, there was only one option left. He endured her blows long enough to lock his arms around her waist, and then he kissed her.

Sally's lips were like velvet-encased steel as her hands went to his chest and began to push. Elliott tightened his grip around her waist and increased his efforts. Just when he was about to release her, a tiny sound emitted from her throat. Before he could do anything else, her hands slid up over his shoulders and locked around his neck. Now she was the aggressor.

Elliott was no longer aware of anything other than the woman in his arms. He was twenty-six years old; this wasn't his first kiss. Yet none other had ever affected him like this. Their lips were meant to be together. Her mouth was designed for his.

A sound gradually appeared in his consciousness, and suddenly, reality hit him square in the solar plexus. People were applauding. An FSA agent was locked in a passionate embrace with the very person he was there to arrest. His career was over before it had barely begun.

Sally was persistent as he pulled his mouth away, moving with him to keep her lips on his. Just as he finally managed to grasp her head and hold it in one place, a deep voice boomed through the night.

"Callandra Lynn Davis, what is the meaning of this?"

Obviously startled, the woman dropped her arms and stepped away from Elliott. Her voice was breathless when she spoke. "I don't know, Daddy. This guy just kissed me."

The older man, apparently Sally's father, turned an accusatory glare toward Elliott. "What do you have to say for yourself?"

"Now, H.B., calm down." The firm voice came from a lady with a remarkable resemblance to Sally. "I'm sure he has a very good reason for kissing Callie."

Did he? Elliott couldn't very well explain to Sally's—Wait a minute. "Callie? Did you say *Callie*?"

"Do you mean to tell me that you kissed my daughter, and you don't even know her name?" The older man was understandably irate. "You'd better explain yourself, or I'm going to arrest you for assault."

Arrest him? That's right. Sally—Callie had mentioned that her father was a police officer. Maybe Elliott could straighten this out and salvage his mission yet. "If I can speak to you in private, I'm sure you'll understand."

The other man frowned deeply as he looked from his daughter to Elliott. Then he turned to the crowd of onlookers. "Okay, folks, show's over. Go on back inside."

Elliott couldn't help but notice the grin on Agent Nick Mahaffey's face before he winked and turned away. Wonderful. He would never be given an undercover assignment again.

"Okay." The deep voice of Callie's father brought Elliott's attention back to him. "We're alone out here. You have sixty seconds to explain to me why I shouldn't haul you in."

"I thought your daughter was somebody else." Stick to the truth, as much as possible. "It's simply a misunderstanding."

"What do you mean, you thought I was somebody else?" The beautiful woman—Callie—demanded. "You called me by name."

Elliott sighed. "I thought your name was Sally, not Callie."

Callie looked at the other woman, puzzlement in her eyes. "I don't understand, Mom. Why is he saying he thought my name was Callie, but not Callie?"

Her father answered in a loud voice. "He's saying *Sally*, not Callie." He grimaced at the young woman. "That swimmer's ear is worse than we thought, isn't it?"

"Will somebody tell me what's going on?" Callie was irate. "He saw me in the parade last week, Dad. He's been following me ever since."

"That's not true," Elliott quickly assured the older man. "I've never seen your daughter before this evening."

"I don't like this, H.B.," his wife proclaimed. "Something isn't right."

H.B. nodded. "I agree." His gaze didn't waver as he looked at Elliott. "You and I are going to the station and get this sorted out. Do I have to cuff you, or are you coming peacefully?"

"I can't go to the station with you." The words popped out before Elliott could stop them. "I mean; I haven't done anything wrong. There's no reason for you to take me in."

"Have it your way." The officer reached under the back of his suit jacket and produced a pair of handcuffs. "Hold your arms out here."

Elliott looked at the determination on the other man's face. "I can't go with you."

"You know what else, Daddy?" Callie questioned her father. "He offered to pay me to visit the flower garden with him."

If the man hadn't already been aggravated, he was now. "Sharon, go get Phil. It looks like I'm going to need some help."

"Wait." Elliott couldn't let this continue any further. He'd try Callie's mother. "Let me show you something."

"I beg your pardon!" Sharon's face was bright red.

"Did you just hit on my mother?" Callie demanded. "What kind of pervert are you, anyway?"

Elliott felt like he'd stepped into a horrible sitcom. "I'm not a pervert. Look, I'm with the FSA." He reached into the pocket of his dress pants and pulled out—a handkerchief.

A disbelieving laugh came from Callie. "What? Are you going to perform a trick and turn that into a badge?"

"No. I don't have my badge on me." Elliott rushed to explain. "I'm here undercover."

"Well, son, no undercover agent I know would go around kissing strange women." H.B. held the cuffs higher. "Sharon, go ahead and find Phil."

Okay. Elliott was breaking every rule in the book, but he had to put a stop to this fiasco. "I'm here undercover to buy drugs. I was supposed to meet a woman named Sally—right here. When I saw your daughter, I assumed she was Sally. She said that was her name."

"She can't hear very well right now," Sharon told him. "She probably thought you were saying Callie."

"You kissed me!" Callie seemed to have conveniently forgotten that she had been a willing participant. "Just because you look like Brad Pitt doesn't give you the right to up and kiss a woman like that."

Elliott had been hearing about his resemblance to the famous actor since he was in high school. It was, in fact, the reason he had been chosen for this operation. Special Agent Harold Binkley had decided that Elliott's looks would be beneficial in dealing with a young woman. Well, they weren't helping him very much with this one.

"I'm sorry." But, somehow, he wasn't. That had been the most incredible kiss he'd ever experienced. "She kind of got phys—wild, and too many people were paying attention. I couldn't think of anything else to quiet her down."

"Wait a minute." Callie's father dropped his hand to his side. "Don't tell me she went all martial arts on you."

"Callandra." Her mother was obviously dismayed. "I've told you a million times how unladylike that is."

"Beau taught me to take care of myself," the younger woman proclaimed.

"Your brother said it wouldn't matter how long he instructed you; you'd never have the strength to kick a fly off your horse." Her dad spoke bluntly.

Elliott couldn't keep the smile from his face as he pictured Callie's futile efforts. He sobered as he once more addressed her father. "Listen, I'm sorry about this whole mess, but I promise,

I'm an undercover agent. Your daughter misunderstood me, and she took offense. When she went cr—reacted, I had to stop her. All I could think to do was kiss her. That's the truth."

H.B. gave Elliott an assessing look before he spoke. "That story's too crazy not to be true. I believe you."

"Well, I don't!" Callie marched over and stood toe to toe with Elliott. "I think you're some sicko who wanted to get it on with the Pickle Queen. And, now that you've been caught, you've come up with this ridiculous story."

Elliott didn't flinch. "I didn't even know you were the Pickle Queen. For the last time, I'm an undercover agent."

Callie stood on her tiptoes and stuck her face as close to Elliott's as she could get. "I don't believe you!"

Without another thought, Elliott closed the short distance between them and sought her lips with his. This time, she didn't struggle; her arms wrapped snugly around his neck and she moved with him to deepen the kiss.

A throat loudly clearing brought Elliott back to his senses. Callie calmly slid down to rest the side of her face against his chest. Elliott's arms didn't seem inclined to relax their hold on her.

"I see." H.B.'s voice was dry.

Elliott was surprised by the smile on the other man's face. "What's that?"

He noticed Callie's parents exchange an amused look. Her father answered. "Nobody has ever calmed our daughter that quickly. What did you say your name is?"

"Is everything okay out here, Lawrence?" Nick Mahaffey had appeared.

Callie slid out of Elliott's arms but didn't move far from his side.

"This is Callie . . ." He didn't know her last name. "And her parents. She's not the woman I was supposed to meet."

"Are you sure about that?" Nick's dimples deepened as he smiled. "Looks like she's exactly the woman you were supposed to meet."

"I'm Officer H.B. Davis and this is my wife, Sharon." Callie's father introduced himself. "The woman attached to your friend's side is our daughter, Callie."

Nick flipped out his badge. "Nick Mahaffey—and my friend is Agent Elliott Lawrence, if he hasn't already introduced himself."

"You're really an FSA agent?" Callie's eyes widened with despair as she stepped away from him. "You only kissed me to shut me up."

"Yes . . . No . . ." Elliott was at a loss for words. "I mean, yes, I'm an FSA agent, and the first time I kissed you was to calm you down, but that wasn't why I kissed you just now."

"Why did you kiss me, then?" She was back in front of him.

"Yes, Lawrence." Laughter was evident in Nick's voice. "Please, tell us all. Why did you kiss her?"

"I wanted to." The words were spoken before he thought twice. Now her parents were practically beaming, and a becoming shade of pink covered Callie's face. He turned to his colleague. "What about the operation? I blew it big time."

"Oh, that." Nick waved him away. "Sally was pulled over for a routine traffic stop, and she hadn't hidden her stash very carefully. They caught her with enough merchandise to put her away for a long time."

To say Elliott was shocked would be putting it mildly. "When did that happen?"

"I just received the call a short while ago." The seasoned agent's smile grew. "I was actually on my way out here to tell you when I found myself stuck in your audience."

"So, the FSA is active." H.B. Davis had turned to ask Nick. "The department usually gives us a heads-up when you guys are around."

"Oh, let me tell you—" Nick's voice faded as he led Callie's parents through the door.

There was a moment of awkward silence before Callie spoke. "How long have you been an agent?"

Elliott smiled grimly. "This was my first assignment. It's liable to be my last."

Callie appeared uncertain. "I'm sorry if I caused you any problems."

His eyes met hers. "I'm the one who should apologize. I said some pretty inappropriate things to you."

"How old are you?" The question came out of the blue, but Callie's eyes lit up with curiosity.

"Twenty-six." Elliott thought he knew where this was going. "How old are you?" Please don't tell him he had just kissed an older looking sixteen-year-old.

Her smile brightened. "I just turned twenty."

That wasn't too young. "Are you in college?"

"Nope." She looked pretty pleased to provide that answer. "I was sick and missed an entire year of elementary school, so I just graduated high school last month."

Her life was only beginning. "What are your plans now?"

"I want to get married and have a family." Callie announced her wishes as calmly as she might have discussed the weather. "My mom and dad married young, and my mom has made a full-time job out of being a wife and mother."

He had to ask. "Any candidates for a husband?"

"Maybe." Her blush was back. "One might have just appeared."

"Oh, really?" Elliott's heart sped up. "And what makes you think the guy would be interested in the position?"

Callie didn't hesitate. "Because he kissed the stuffing out of me."

"Yeah, well, he's about to do it again." Elliott smiled as he pulled her back into his arms. Nick was right. It seemed Elliott had found the right woman, after all.

Would you like to know how Luke and Holly ended up together? Or the heroics of Clarence the dog? Catch up on the *In Shadow* trilogy by reading book number one

A reunion, a stalker, and a vengeful man—what's a woman to do? If that woman is Holly Morris, she relies on her faith, friends, and a dog named Clarence.

After six years of peace, Holly's college stalker has returned with a vengeance. If she doesn't remember she belongs to him, somebody is going to be hurt. To add to her fun life, the man she helps turn in for child abuse blames her for everything, and he's going to get even–threatening to "finish her off." With a reunion of students who barely looked at the chubby girl, Holly Morris, coming up, she's about at the end of her rope. It's a good thing the Lord has provided a support system to keep her from falling.

Luke Walker has loved Holly as long as he can remember. He protected her from bullies in school, and he'll protect her from the monsters after her now–even while dealing with threats and vandalism on his farm. Nobody is going to scare him away from Holly. When he lets his beloved Heinz 57 dog, Clarence, spend nights as her watchdog, everybody feels better. The amiable giant has always gone into killer mode when he thought anyone was too close to Holly.

Join Holly and Luke as they discover the depth of friendship and love...and that God's love is stronger than any evil.

COMING SOON

A woman with no memory of the past five years and a man who loves her too much to let her go

Ellie Walker doesn't remember the past five years—not after driving off a bridge. She's come to Shadow and made a new home near her cousin and his wife. She even has a steady boyfriend who seems to mean more to her than he should. Sometimes, Ellie is so content she's not sure she wants to remember.

Brady Donovan was ordered by the doctors to let Ellie remember on her own, but he's not about to let her forget him. He's banking on her falling in love with him all over again.

Although Brady is the head of the AMAR, he has passed himself off as an author who has found a quiet place to write his great novel.

When it appears the organization they're trying to stop has set up shop in Shadow. Brady and his team know this isn't a coincidence. Nobody knows how Ellie ended up nearly dying in that wreck, and the AMAR team realizes Ellie knows something important. She just can't remember.

Secrets and suspicions may be too much for Ellie and Brady to survive. When she remembers everything, will she love Brady? Or is there something in her past to keep them apart? The criminal they've been looking for may turn out to be much closer than any of them anticipated.

Lives are in danger, and hearts break as Brady and Ellie search for the truth.

SPOILER ALERT:
DO NOT READ THIS UNTIL YOU'VE READ THE BOOK

A Note from the Author

A few of my beta readers weren't very happy with me for killing off Matt. Believe it or not, I hadn't planned to. I tried too many times to count, but I couldn't redeem him. It helped a little to find out about his daughter and how much he loved her, but had the Janitor turned himself in, he would have gone to the electric chair, or at the very least, spent his life in prison. And I liked him too much to do that.

As for whether his new location is in heaven or far south of it, who knows? When the plane was going down, maybe he had an epiphany and asked forgiveness before it hit ground. That's what I'd like to think.

On a lighter note, probably three-fourths of the readers I've spoken with or received messages from wanted Clarence, Luke and Holly Walker's dog, to be in this story. If you've read it, you know he's in this book. He is also in *Staying in Shadow*, book three, which has a planned release in August.

I'd enjoy hearing your opinions. You can read my blog and contact me at www.georgiaevansauthor.com

Blessings,

Georgia florey-Evans

www.ingramcontent.com/pod-product-compliance
Lightning Source LLC
Chambersburg PA
CBHW030238030726
47493CB00023B/109